THE GIRL ON THE CARPATHIA

Eileen Enwright Hodgetts

The Girl on the Carpathia is a work of fiction. All characters, with the exception of well-known historical characters, are products of the author's imagination and are not to be construed as real.

ISBN: 978-0-578-90320-0

www.eileenenwrighthodgetts.com

Published by Emerge Publishing

PART ONE
RMS CARPATHIA
NORTH ATLANTIC

CQD CQD SOS TITANIC TO ALL SHIPS.
POSITION 41.44 N 50.24 W. WE HAVE
COLLISION WITH ICEBERG. SINKING. COME
AT ONCE. WE STRUCK AN ICEBERG. SINKING.

CARPATHIA TO TITANIC. PUTTING ABOUT AND
HEADING FOR YOU.

OLYMPIC TO TITANIC. CAPTAIN SAYS GET
YOUR BOATS READY. WHAT IS YOUR
POSITION?

TITANIC TO ALL SHIPS. SINKING HEAD DOWN
41.46 N 50.14 W. COME AS SOON AS
POSSIBLE.

BALTIC TO CARONIA. PLEASE TELL TITANIC
WE ARE MAKING TOWARDS HER.

TITANIC TO ALL SHIPS. WE ARE PUTTING
PASSENGERS OFF IN SMALL BOATS.

OLYMPIC TO TITANIC. AM LIGHTING UP ALL
POSSIBLE BOILERS AS FAST AS CAN.

TITANIC TO ALL SHIPS. ENGINE ROOM
GETTING FLOODED.

VIRGINIAN TO CAPE RACE. PLEASE INFORM
TITANIC THAT WE ARE GOING TO HIS
ASSISTANCE. OUR POSITION IS 170 MILES
NORTH.

TITANIC TO ALL SHIPS. SOS TITANIC
SINKING BY THE HEAD. WE ARE ABOUT ALL
DOWN. SINKING.

CHAPTER ONE

April 15, 1912
Cunard Liner RMS *Carpathia*
North Atlantic

Kate Royston stood by the rail and felt the wind tugging her hair free of its heavy dark braids. The night was calm, but the *Carpathia*'s steady eastward progress created its own breeze. Behind her she could see smoke from the *Carpathia*'s funnel creating a gray smudge across the starry night sky. Light from the stars glimmered on the ice flows surrounding the ship, and dark water marked the ship's careful progress through the scattered drifting floes.

Kate looked at her watch. The hands had inched past midnight, bringing her into April 15, 1912, her twenty-first birthday, but instead of dancing at her birthday ball, she was fleeing across the cold, dark ocean without a penny to her name.

As she stepped away from the rail, she narrowly avoided colliding with a man who slithered heedlessly down the ladder from the bridge deck. The light spilling from above showed that he was wearing an officer's uniform. She took another step away from the rail, hoping that her presence would not bring a reprimand. She shouldn't be here on the first-class promenade deck. She should be in the stuffy, overheated cabin that she shared with the two children of Daan and

Magda van Buren, where she was an employee and, therefore, not a first-class passenger.

The man acknowledged her with a slight nod of his head as he fumbled in his pocket and produced a crumpled cigarette packet. She watched a brief blossoming of light as a match flared in his cupped hands.

"All those people," he said as he dragged on the cigarette and the tip glowed red.

"What people?" Kate asked.

The officer turned to face her. The light from the bridge deck showed her his young, agitated face. She had a moment of self-consciousness, knowing that her hair was unbraided and that, beneath her heavy coat, she wore only her nightdress.

"They're sinking, but he won't believe me."

"Sinking?" Kate asked in a small voice. "Are we sinking?"

"No, not us. The *Titanic*."

"*Titanic*?" she repeated. "Are you saying that the *Titanic* is sinking?"

"Yes."

"But I read the posters. She's unsinkable." She patted his arm consolingly. "I think you're having a bad dream."

The officer dragged on his cigarette again and gestured with the glowing tip. "Over there, about fifty miles away, the *Titanic* is going down."

"You can't know that."

"Yes, I can. I'm Harold Cottam. I'm the radio officer, and I took the Marconi message."

Cottam suddenly tossed his cigarette into the water and began to pace an agitated path along the rail, speaking frantically, as if he had a need to convince Kate that what he was saying was true.

"I should have been in bed, but I'd taken Marconi messages to forward to the *Titanic*. She had so much traffic through her radio, she couldn't take them all, so I was working a relay. I tried earlier in the evening, but their operator said for me to shut up because he was working Cape Race. He'd just come in reach of the relay station, so he was sending outgoing messages for the passengers. I decided to let it go for a while and try again later, when things had quieted down, and so that's what I did."

Cottam stopped pacing and snatched off his cap. "I shouldn't even have been on duty. I was going to send the messages on and then sign off for the night." He ran an agitated hand through his hair. "I should already have been off duty, but I wasn't. That means something, doesn't it? It's not a coincidence. God wanted me to hear them, didn't he?"

"I don't know," Kate said helplessly.

"You don't believe me," Cottam declared.

"No," Kate snapped. "I don't understand you." She spoke in the same tone she had used on her father on the night his drunkenness had given way to babbling self-pity. "Pull yourself together, Mr. Cottam, and tell me what has happened. I don't understand all this talk about Marconi and Cape Race, but I think I understand that you passed some messages to the *Titanic*."

Cottam shook his head vigorously. "No, I didn't have a chance. I had them lined up, ready to transmit, but as soon as I turned on the Marconi and tried to transmit, *Titanic*'s operator flashed in. 'CQD. CQD.'"

"CQD? What does that mean?"

"It's a distress signal. It means for me to stop transmitting and listen. I asked if it was serious. I thought maybe their operator was just joking with me or wanted me to stop because he was so busy, so I flashed back and asked if it was serious. He said yes. 'Come at once. We've struck a berg.'"

Kate stared around at the vast, dark ocean and up at the trail of smoke from the funnel. The *Carpathia* showed no signs of slowing down or turning. If the officer's story was true, and the *Titanic* was in trouble, surely the *Carpathia* would go to her aid, and yet nothing was happening.

"Where is the *Titanic*?" she asked. "In what direction?"

Cottam gestured with his thumb. "Back that way."

"Why haven't we stopped?"

"Because the officers on the bridge don't believe me. I told the officer of the watch. I told the whole bridge crew, and none of them will believe me."

"Did you tell the captain?"

"He's asleep."

Kate felt the flaring of temper that had so often been her downfall, and possibly accounted for the fact that she was now very far from home.

"So what are you going to do? Are you just going to stand there smoking and allow the *Titanic* to sink because you're too frightened to tell the captain?"

Cottam straightened his shoulders. "No, of course not. I'm going to wake him. I just needed a moment alone to convince myself."

"Of what?"

"Our Marconi messages don't come in words. They come in Morse code, just little clicks of sound, dots and dashes, and we have to translate them. This message seems so unbelievable that I have to make sure I have it right before I go to the captain and put the whole ship on alert."

"And are you sure now?"

Cottam nodded. "Yes, I am."

"Well, then," said Kate, "let's go. Where is the captain's cabin? I'll come with you."

Cottam shook his head. "There's no need."

"I want to."

"Why?"

A sudden gust of icy wind swirled out of the west and for one brief moment, Kate thought she heard the sound of a thousand screams. Cottam stood still. Their eyes met. Had the wind brought him the same certainty?

"Because I believe you," Kate said. "Lead the way."

Cottam indicated a short metal ladder reaching straight up to the forbidden world of the bridge. He waved an urgent hand. "After you, miss."

The wind swirled again, as if inviting her to stop and listen once more to the echo it carried, but Cottam was close behind her. The time for doubt was long past. The metal of the ladder bit icily into her hands and her feet in satin slippers were insecure on the rungs, but she climbed to the top and waited for Cottam as he completed the climb.

He jammed his hat on his head and pointed the way along a narrow corridor lined with metal doors. At the end of the corridor the glow of night-vision lights revealed the bridge with shadowy figures moving back and forth. Up here on the bridge deck, the wind of their passage was bitterly cold and Kate stepped gratefully into the warmth of the corridor.

"All right," she said, pushing Cottam ahead of her. "You know you're right. Go and tell him."

Cottam straightened his shoulders and moved along the corridor, stopping halfway down to knock on an anonymous door and announce himself in a shaky voice. "Wireless message, Captain."

Something akin to a questioning bear growl rumbled from the other side of the door, and Cottam replied. "Captain Rostron, sir, we've a message from the *Titanic*. Urgent."

The door opened, revealing a shadowy form in a dressing gown.

"What message? Why are you here? Take it to the bridge."

"Begging your pardon, sir, but the bridge doesn't believe me."

Captain Rostron stepped out into the corridor in a state of undress. Kate pressed her back against the wall. Now was not the time to be seen.

"What's the message?" Rostron asked.

"She's sinking, sir. The *Titanic*'s going down."

"*Titanic*?" Rostron queried. "Are you sure it's her?"

Cottam's voice was steady now. "Quite sure, sir. She's close by, sir."

"I'll be the judge of that," Rostron barked. "Give me the message. Word for word."

Cottam's words came in a breathless rush. "'Forty-one degrees forty-six minutes north, fifty degrees fourteen minutes west. Come at once. We have struck a berg.'"

Rostron nodded. "She's close. We may be the only ones. Tell me your name again."

"Harold Cottam, sir."

"Well, Harold Cottam, do you have any reason to doubt what you heard?"

"No, sir."

"Very well. I will choose to believe you and act accordingly."

Rostron untied the belt of his dressing gown, revealing a white undershirt and black pants. He stepped back into the cabin and emerged a moment later buttoning his jacket.

Kate remained pressed against the wall. She should leave. She had done all she could do, and she didn't belong on the bridge or anywhere in the officers' quarters. Unfortunately, she could not make her mind tell her feet to move. She had no wish to creep back to the outer deck and slither back down the ladder. She told herself that she would wait until the captain was on the bridge with all of his attention on making the *Carpathia* change course, and then she would leave.

Rostron stood in the center of the corridor with his back to her, bellowing orders. Officers in dark jackets with gold-braided sleeves swarmed from the bridge into the corridor.

Kate remained rooted to the spot as Rostron issued a flood of orders.

"Turn us around … Get me the chief engineer … Turn out all hands … Divert all steam to engines. Yes, the cabins will be cold, but not as cold as on the *Titanic*. Get me the purser. We need blankets, warm food. Clear every inside space you can. *Titanic* has two thousand passengers, and for all I know, we'll have to take all of them."

Rostron turned to Cottam who was almost lost from sight in the press of officers. "Mr. Cottam, tell her we're coming. Four hours at the most, sooner if we can. Stay by the radio. I want to hear every message from every ship. I hope to God someone is closer than we are."

Cottam saluted and pressed past Kate without even looking at her.

Rostron continued his instructions. "Break out the lifeboats and ladders. We'll need lights. Rig something. Don't ask; just do it. Wake the medical staff and all the doctors on board, even passengers."

A voice from the back raised a question. "Shall we fire rockets?"

"Not yet. She's over the horizon. If we can't see her rockets, she can't see ours. Give it another hour, and then fire green rockets every fifteen minutes. Those poor devils need every hope we can give them."

Kate was still listening in awe to the captain's rapid-fire instructions when she felt a hand descend onto her shoulder. She gave a guilty start and turned to face a tall, rawboned woman. Her hair was neatly coiled into a bun and her dark dress was ornamented only with starched white collar and cuffs and a metal pin bearing the emblem of the Cunard Line.

"What are you doing here, girl?"

Captain Rostron quite unintentionally came to Kate's rescue. He looked over the heads of his officers and acknowledged the woman in the dark dress.

"Glad to see our chief stewardess is here," he declared. "I was going to send someone to wake you, Mrs. Broomer, but I see that there is no need. We are going to need every stewardess we have. I am sure that Captain Smith on the *Titanic* has followed the rule of the sea, and we will have very many women and children. They will need a woman's touch. I leave that up to you."

Mrs. Broomer nodded and squeezed Kate's shoulder with sharp, painful fingers. "You're not one of mine," she hissed.

Kate shook herself free. "Of course I'm not. I'm from first class."

I'm not lying, she thought. *I've been traveling in a first-class cabin even if I haven't been eating in the first-class dining room or dancing in the first-class ballroom.*

Mrs. Broomer took a step back and surveyed her with distrustful dark eyes. "What cabin?"

Kate resurrected the confident, polished voice of her youth—a voice unsuited to a penniless governess—and held up a stern finger. "We have no time to waste, Mrs. Broomer. I am sure that you will need a great deal of assistance tonight, and I intend to assist you. I will go and change my clothes. Shall we meet in the Grand Salon? That would be best, wouldn't it, for the ladies?"

Mrs. Broomer continued to eye her suspiciously, but Kate had learned how to deal with suspicion. Boldness was the key. If she hesitated now she would be sent back to her cabin and no doubt Magda van Buren would be informed of her behavior. On the other hand, if the *Titanic* really was sinking, and if hundreds or even thousands of terrified passengers would be coming aboard, Mrs. Broomer would soon be too busy to be suspicious.

As Kate made her way toward the Grand Salon, she steadied herself by clinging to the rails set along the walls of the corridors. The ship, whose motion had been slow and steady since leaving New York, began to pitch and roll as the engineers raised steam and the helmsman sent the *Carpathia* into a sweeping turn to the west, heading back toward New York.

Kate knew she should change her clothes. According to Captain Rostron's estimate, she would have four hours to prepare, but would a change of clothes be the best idea? Of course, a lady, or someone who would wish to be thought of as a lady, should not be out in public in her nightclothes, but surely the women from the *Titanic* would be in their nightclothes. If Kate went down to the cabin now, she would probably find the children awake. The motion of the ship had become quite violent and the crew was making no attempt at silence. Doors were banging; voices were raised; and late-drinking gentlemen were emerging drunkenly from the smoking room.

She tried to find sympathy for the children of her employer, awake and wondering at the commotion. Their mother, Magda van Buren, was a light sleeper, and perhaps she was already in the children's cabin and wondering what had happened to their new governess. If Kate ventured into the room, she would not be allowed out again—best to button her coat, rebraid her hair, and stay well away.

She prowled through the unfamiliar first-class hallways. Although she slept with her charges in a first-class cabin, she had taken her meals in the dining room reserved for lady's maids, valets, and unfortunate young women forced to become governesses to the wealthy. Now she roamed freely amid the ordered chaos of preparation until she noticed the door to the ladies' reading room. Finding the room unoccupied, she slipped inside and took up a position in a quiet reading nook where she could see without being seen.

An hour passed, and then another. The room, which had been comfortably warm, grew chilly and then downright cold. She remembered the captain's words. *Divert all steam to the engines.* The cabins would be cold now. No doubt someone in first class was already complaining, probably Mr. van Buren, who expected to get value for his money. From what she had seen of her employer, she doubted that he had enough sympathy in his whole body to spare a thought for the passengers on the *Titanic*.

She could not stop thinking of her conversation with Harold Cottam. She had not seen him again but she assumed he was still working, still sending and receiving messages from the *Titanic*. She remembered reading articles about the great ship which had attracted the cream of society into her first-class cabins. Not only did the *Titanic* have first-class accommodations that would rival the facilities of even the grandest hotels, but even the third-class passengers could enjoy running water and electricity, and sleep only four to a cabin. And the greatest boast of all: *Titanic* was unsinkable.

Kate felt a change in the rhythm of the engines. The *Carpathia* was slowing. They must have received another message to say that the *Titanic* was still afloat and on her way to New York and a rousing welcome. Very soon the *Carpathia* would turn around and resume her course toward Gibraltar where Kate had every intention of going ashore and leaving the Van Buren children to their own devices.

She spared a sympathetic thought for Harold Cottam. He was the one who had raised the alarm, and it had all been a mistake. She peered at her watch in the dim light of the night lights. Only two hours had passed. She crossed her fingers and hoped against hope that the children had stayed asleep and that Mrs. van Buren would not know that they had been left alone.

As Kate rose from her secluded seat, the door of the reading room banged open admitting bright light from the corridor. She shrank back against the wall as a half-dozen crewmen invaded the room carrying armloads of blankets and pillows. An officer—very junior judging by the dearth of gold braid on his jacket—issued directions.

"Push chairs together to make beds. It won't be enough. We'll have to put people on the deck. The doctors can use this room. There'll be some injuries, but it will mainly be cold and exposure, poor devils."

Kate gasped. So it hadn't been a mistake. They were still heading toward the *Titanic*. She stepped out into the light. She shouldn't be here, but he was a junior officer and he was not to know that.

"You there," she said. "What's happening? Why have we stopped?"

The officer gave her a brief startled glance and turned to help the crew members who were rearranging the chairs and sofas. "We're in the ice, ma'am," he said over his shoulder. "We have to pick our way through or we'll end up like the *Titanic*. We'll have her in sight in another hour, if there's anything to see."

"What do you mean? Why would there be nothing to see?"

The officer straightened from his task and looked at her. His young face was a mask of worry. "Her radio's gone," he said. "No more messages."

Kate found herself fighting against the truth. "Perhaps something's happened to the equipment," she suggested.

A gray-haired crewman shook out a blanket and spread it across a chair as he spoke. "Too right something's happened to it. It's gone down along with the ship."

"Are you sure?" Kate asked. "Has she really gone down?"

"Her last message was an hour ago," the officer said. "'Sinking head down, come at once.' And after that, nothing, but I won't believe it until I see it. She's unsinkable—that's what they said. It's all a mistake. We have to go, of course. It's the first rule of the sea, but she won't be gone. She can't be."

Kate shivered and thought of Captain Rostron's volley of instructions. Maybe this young officer was not expecting the ship to sink, but Captain Rostron seemed to be in no doubt. She listened to the muted sound of the engines. They were creeping along now, fearful of the ice. Just one day before she had stood on the deck with the children and seen the massive icebergs drifting across the horizon. The captain had steered them safely through that ice field in the daylight and promised plain sailing to Gibraltar. Now they had turned and were heading back into the ice, with only the stars to light their way.

The Home of Senator William Alden Smith
Washington, DC
12:20 a.m. (Eastern Standard Time)
Senator William Alden Smith

The Senator was awake, although he could not say why. Moonlight filtered in through a gap in the heavy brocade curtains and illuminated the face of the clock on the nightstand. Twenty minutes past midnight—the beginning of a new day. He stared up at the ceiling thinking idly of how far he had come in life, from selling popcorn on the streets of Grand Rapids to lying in bed wondering whether or not to help William Taft in his next run for president.

He turned onto his side and tried to settle his head on the pillow. If he helped Taft now, would Taft help him in four years' time when he made his own run for the presidency?

"Bill?"

Bill turned and looked at his wife. The moon spread a flattering light across her face and she met his appreciative look with a smile.

"Sorry to wake you," he said, leaning up on one elbow.

She smiled again. "It's all right. I don't mind. Why are you awake? Are you worried about Taft?"

"No, I'm not," Bill lied. "The president and I have an understanding."

"What if he loses the election?"

"Then I'll have to deal with Roosevelt," Bill said, "but it won't affect my plans." He settled his head back on the pillow and stared up at the ceiling. "The White House, Nana. Just think of it."

A frown creased Nana's face. "If Taft loses you're going to need to find some new supporters to back your bid," she said. "You should be rubbing shoulders with the rich and famous and gathering political support just in case. Why don't we take a transatlantic voyage on one of the new ocean liners? If we travel first-class we could meet all kinds of people. I hear that the new *Titanic* is a real marvel. She's on her maiden voyage now and everyone who is anyone is on her. She'll be in regular service soon and it would be a good career move for you." She smiled hopefully. "Should we do it?"

"Not while ..." Bill hesitated. He had been about to explain that sailing to Europe while the Senate was in session would be political suicide, but he felt a shiver pass down his spine. It wasn't the thought of the Senate that disturbed him, or even the idea of making a run for the presidency—it was the *Titanic*. He found himself grasping at the wisps of a troubling dream that he could not fully recall. The *Titanic*. Something about the *Titanic*.

"Jacob Astor and his new wife are sailing on her," Nana continued, unaware that Bill's attention was wandering. "The Guggenheims, the Thayers, the Ryersons, and Major Butt's coming back from seeing the Pope."

"He didn't go to see the Pope," Bill said abruptly trying to turn his thoughts away from the tingling in his spine and the feeling of foreboding. "The president sent him to try to steer the Germans away from starting a war. He's very impatient for a report."

"War?" Nana said. "Surely not."

"Nothing to worry about," Bill said. "It won't concern us. America will never be involved."

Nana frowned again. "Don't forget we have a son who is old enough to be a soldier."

"We won't be involved," Bill insisted. "It's Europe's war. Now tell me who else is on this great ship. I know you've memorized the passenger list."

"Well, the Countess of Rothes, she's very rich, but not J.P. Morgan, even though he practically owns the White Star Line. Apparently he decided to stay in France. Some think there could be a woman involved."

"And who else?" Bill asked.

"Mr. Straus, who owns that department store, and one other person, one of your favorite people."

"Really? Who would that be?"

"Eva Trentham."

Nana laughed as Bill sat up and groaned. "Now I'll never get back to sleep," he complained. "Why did you have to mention her?"

"She's your most ardent supporter," Nana said.

"She's an evil-tempered old harridan," Bill replied.

"But a very wealthy one," Nana said, "and very influential. If you want the White House, Bill, you have to keep her on your side. Now, try to go back to sleep. You have an appointment with the president in just a few hours, and you'll need your wits about you."

Bill thought of the day ahead—an early appointment with Taft, a meeting with the chairman of the Committee on Commerce, and then lunch with a deputation from his home state. He wondered what they would ask of him and whether he could give them what they would ask for. He could not afford to lose his seat in the Senate, not now. He comforted himself with the fact that the deputation was led by Joe Bayliss, sheriff of Chippewa County. Joe was a reasonable man. He would not ask for anything that Bill couldn't deliver.

Somewhat comforted by that thought, Bill turned to look at the clock. He read the time. One o'clock. The moon went behind a cloud and the room was wrapped in darkness. He closed his eyes and tried to recapture the shreds of his dream.

CHAPTER TWO

On Board the *Carpathia*
4:30 a.m. (Ship's Time).
Kate Royston

Kate pushed her way through a throng of passengers and crewmen. After a long night of preparation, the *Carpathia* was almost at her destination. The first rays of dawn were filtering above the horizon and glinting blue white on the surrounding icebergs. Now Kate understood why the *Carpathia* had made such slow progress. Surely the captain, the crew, and every person on board wanted to speed to the rescue of the *Titanic*'s passengers, but in the predawn dark, surrounded by ice, all they could do was creep toward the stricken ship.

At night the icebergs had been invisible, but Kate had felt their lurking presence, darker than the dark of the ocean, searching hungrily for another ship to sink. A light breeze arrived with the dawn, doing little more than ruffling the surface of the ocean into a short chop, and the icebergs seemed to spread themselves like the sails of a great ship, drifting across the horizon. At another time, she may have thought them beautiful, but not today.

With a sudden hiss and a flare of green light, a rocket shot up from the bow of the *Carpathia*. *We are coming*, it seemed to say. *We are almost there.*

Kate had worked alongside the crew all night, preparing blankets and beds, and moving passengers from their cabins. She had even moved the Van Buren children from their beds. She had stood to one side under the protection of Mrs. Broomer, the chief stewardess, as Magda van Buren complained bitterly at having her children moved to sleep on blankets on the floor of their parents' cabin.

Mrs. Broomer barely listened to Mrs. van Buren's unhappy whining. "We know that the *Titanic* has gone down," Mrs. Broomer said, "and we do not know how many people are in the lifeboats. We do know that they will be suffering from shock and severe cold. Your children will come to no harm and the Cunard Line is grateful for your cooperation."

"But what about Miss Royston?" Mrs. van Buren asked, eyeing Kate with malevolent intent. "We are entitled to her services. She is governess to our children."

Mrs. Broomer managed to hide her surprise. Of course she had not known that Kate was a governess.

Although the chief stewardess raised a curious eyebrow, she did not give an inch. "Miss Royston is assisting the crew," she said. "We cannot spare her at this time."

Now the preparations were complete. The *Carpathia* was nosing past the icebergs to the last known position of the *Titanic*. Kate wondered what they would find. Some of the crew speculated that they would find the great liner listing heavily, maybe with water washing over her decks, but she wouldn't go down, not so quickly. She had waterproof compartments. She could not sink. They crossed their fingers as they spoke. That young radio operator had it wrong. The Marconi device was not to be trusted. The words of that infernal Morse code were a mistake. Of course they would do as the captain ordered, but they would not believe a word of it. The *Titanic* could not sink.

Kate saw Harold Cottam at the rail and pushed her way toward him. His face was haggard in the morning light with no hint of triumph at being proved correct. He had said the *Titanic* was going down, and it seemed that he'd been right, for she was nowhere in sight. Kate wished that he'd been wrong.

As she pushed toward him, he turned and looked at her. "Have you been up all night?" he asked.

"Of course I have. Have you?" she responded.

He nodded. "I've just come off duty. Captain sent me to get some rest. He said we'd be busy once we bring the survivors on board." He waved dispiritedly at the empty ocean. "If there are any survivors," he said softly. "I don't see anyone, not a thing, not even any wreckage. This is where they should be, and—"

"There! Over there!"

The hoarse cry drowned out Cottam's whispered words as the crew lined up along the rail began to shout and point. Kate clung to the rail, refusing to be jostled from her vantage point, and found herself looking down at a body floating facedown as if staring into the inky Atlantic deep. The body, held on the surface by a beige life jacket, was that of a woman. Her drab brown dress billowed as the waves passed beneath her. Her hair was loose, rising and falling on the waves.

"Irish," Cottam muttered.

Kate turned to look at him. "How can you know?"

"By her dress. The *Titanic* was packed full of Irish immigrants. Her last port was Queenstown."

Far below them, the woman's body drifted gently alongside for a long, painful moment before the *Carpathia*, adjusting her course, dragged it down beneath her hull. If only they could have pulled her aboard, Kate thought, perhaps she could have been revived. She knew the thought was pointless. The woman was frozen in death, her hands white and stiff, with chunks of ice clinging to her hair, and even if she were still alive, how would they bring her aboard? The hull of the *Carpathia* was as high and smooth as any mountain cliff. If the poor woman raised a hand, no one could lean down and grasp it.

"We're setting out rope ladders for those who can climb, and canvas slings for those who are too weak, and cargo nets for whatever else we find," Cottam said, as if reading her thoughts.

Although Kate had spent the last few hours assisting Mrs. Broomer and the stewards in preparing for survivors, she had not given a thought as to how the survivors would be brought aboard. Obviously, Captain Rostron had everything planned. When Kate had boarded the *Carpathia* in New York, the ship had been alongside a pier, and a gangplank had allowed the passengers to walk easily onto the promenade deck and proceed to their cabins. Impatient to leave New York behind and be safely on her way to Europe, Kate had been only vaguely aware then of the size of the liner or how high she stood above the water.

Now she startled as the *Carpathia* blew a long blast of her horn. Another green rocket shot into the air, and an amplified voice echoed across all decks. "Stand by to pick up survivors."

Cottam pointed. "Over there."

Kate looked out toward the horizon. The dawn light, which had first revealed the icebergs, now revealed a small cluster of lifeboats rising and falling on the short, choppy waves.

"God help us," Cottam whispered. "Is that all of them?"

As Kate watched, a red flare rose upward from the huddle of boats, and a plaintive cry reached them across the water. Kate searched in vain for another flare from another direction. Surely there were more lifeboats.

She looked down as something splashed into the water far below. Leaning out over the rail, she saw that the crew was on the boat deck, placing ropes and ladders and cargo nets.

Cottam stepped back. "I'll have work to do," he said. "We'll be taking names as they come aboard and sending messages back to Cape Race. People will be waiting to hear. The *New York Times* is holding the front page."

Kate looked at him in astonishment. "They know about this?" she asked.

He nodded. "Oh, yes, they know. This will be a feather in his cap for Marconi, I suppose, and maybe it'll be a good word for us radio operators. Now people will realize we can do more than just send messages to other ships. Cape Race picked up the *Titanic*'s distress signal and passed it on to New York. Already the newspapers know that the unsinkable ship is sinking and we are racing to her rescue. We're the first ones here, so whatever signal we send next will tell the world what we found and who we found. Fortunes will be made and lost today if the richest men in the world are not in those lifeboats alongside their wives."

"It's hard to believe," Kate whispered.

Cottam stepped back and looked at her. "You should get dressed," he said, "while you can."

Kate brushed away a long strand of dark hair and realized that, despite the horror ahead, she was blushing. In spite of everything that had happened in the last year, the terrible accusations against her father and the loss of her family's fortune, she was still the victim of her mother's rigorous, unswerving etiquette. Young ladies did not appear in public with their hair loose and without a corset.

She looked back at the cluster of lifeboats. She imagined that Captain Rostron wanted to reach the survivors as soon as he possibly could, but he had chosen caution over speed. Although the ladders were deployed and the crew was standing by, the *Carpathia* had not raised extra steam. Her approach was still painfully slow and steady. Kate would have time to dress properly before reporting to the Grand Salon to help Mrs. Broomer.

She took one last look down at the water. The *Carpathia* had gained an escort of floating debris, deck chairs, crates, furniture, and human bodies, some in life jackets, some tangled in the flotsam. She saw men and women, many in immigrant clothing, others in nightclothes, a few in crew uniforms. When the first child floated by, little more than a baby held in the frozen arms of its mother, she turned away. She could do nothing about the horror that had already taken place, but she would do what she could for those who still lived.

The Home of Senator William Alden Smith
Washington, DC
6:45 a.m. (Eastern Standard Time)
Senator William Alden Smith

The senator stared down at his empty coffee cup. He looked across at the sideboard, where he would expect to find the silver coffeepot, a selection of chafing dishes, a rack of toast, and a maid waiting to serve his breakfast. When he found none of these things, he called out for his wife.

"Nana, where's my breakfast?"

Nana did not answer. He knew she was up and about. Just a few minutes before, she had been laying out his clothes while he had shaved, and she had commented on his choice of vest "Wear the green one, dear. Taft will see it as support for the Irish."

"Do I support the Irish?" Bill asked mildly.

"You support Henry Cabot Lodge, and he represents Massachusetts, and therefore Boston, and what could be more Irish than Boston?"

"And Lodge supports Taft," Bill agreed as he finished shaving and opened his closet to take out a dark green vest. "I am lucky to have you, Nana."

"Of course you are," she agreed. "I'll go and see about breakfast. You'd better hurry or you're going to be late."

Bill, now alone and abandoned in the breakfast room, called out again. "Nana, where's my breakfast?"

Once again his wife failed to reply, but he thought he heard the sound of sobbing coming from the kitchen. He stood and pushed his chair back. Obviously Nana was dealing with some kind of servant problem. Well, he was not above serving his own breakfast. He did not really need a silver coffeepot or a selection of chafing dishes. His youthful poverty had made him self-sufficient.

He pushed through the door into the kitchen and found Nana consoling Molly, their Irish kitchen maid. The coffeepot and breakfast tray had been pushed aside, and Molly was slumped across the table with her head on her arms.

"What is it?" Bill asked. "Has someone died?"

Nana placed a comforting hand on Molly's head and looked up at Bill. He saw that her face was white and her eyes brimmed with tears. His thoughts turned to his son. Had something happened to young Bill? He was their only child and Nana hated that he had been sent away to college in Michigan. Bill dismissed the idea of bad news involving his son. If anything had happened to the boy, Nana would have been the one weeping, but it was Molly who was sobbing and Nana who was offering comfort.

"It's terrible news," Nana said, "but it can't be true."

"It is. It is," Molly sobbed. "I feel it in my bones. I know it's the truth."

"I'll get the newspaper boy," Nana said. "We'll get to the bottom of this."

Bill stood in the kitchen, watching the weeping maid as Nana opened the back door and admitted a small, ragged boy—a boy who reminded Bill of himself as a child.

"Well, Timothy," Nana said, bending down and looking the boy in the eye. "What's this all about? Why are you spreading rumors?"

"Not rumors," Timothy said. "It's God's honest truth. She's sunk. She's gone down."

The maid burst into renewed sobs, and Bill decided that he would have to pour his own coffee. His hand was on the coffeepot when the boy spoke again.

"Sunk with all hands, that's what they say. That's why the newspaper's late. *Washington Post* is holding the front page. *New York Times* has the scoop, you see."

Bill released the coffeepot and crossed the room to take hold of the boy's collar. "Speak up. What are you talking about? What's sunk?"

"The *Titanic*, sir."

Bill fought against the tightening of his throat. "Impossible," he barked. "Stop spreading rumors and upsetting my staff." He released the boy and looked down at Molly, who lifted her head to meet his eyes. "Stop crying, Molly. The boy's making it up."

Molly contradicted him in a shaky voice. "I had cousins on that ship," she said, "and I know it's the truth. I felt it, sir, in the night. I woke up and I felt them go."

Bill tried to stop himself from speaking. Surely he had nothing in common with a superstitious girl like Molly, fresh off the boat from Ireland and raised on stories of fairies and leprechauns and Catholic flummery, and yet he had to ask the question. "What time, Molly? What time did you wake?"

"It was after midnight, sir," Molly said. "I don't have my own clock, sir, but I can hear the clock in the hall. I woke suddenly all of a shiver, and then I heard the clock strike the half hour. I lay awake then, not knowing what was wrong, and I was still awake when the clock struck one."

"So you woke at twenty minutes past twelve," Bill said.

"Could be, sir," Molly agreed.

"That's the same time you woke," Nana said, looking at Bill with a trace of fear on her face.

Bill nodded and turned his attention back to Timothy. "What have you heard? Tell me everything." He looked up at Nana. "The boys on the streets of Grand Rapids always knew the truth long before their masters were told anything."

"Well, sir," Timothy said, "they say the *Titanic* hit an iceberg and she sent out a message on that new Marconi invention, the one that lets ships talk to each other. Sent out a distress signal and said she was sinking."

"Is that possible?" Nana asked.

"Could be," Bill said. "She was due in New York today, so she was somewhere off Cape Race. The relay station there could have picked up her signal. What else do you know, boy?"

"All sorts of ships are trying to reach her," Timothy said. "*Carpathia* says she's picked up passengers from lifeboats."

Nana leaned over and patted Molly's shoulders. "There you are, Molly. Everything's all right. The passengers were put in lifeboats, and they've all been picked up. Now, dry your tears and get the senator his breakfast. Your cousins will arrive safely and with a grand story to tell."

Molly stumbled to her feet and swiped the back of her hand across her eyes. "I had the shivers," she said. "If they are all safe, why did I have the shivers?"

"I can't answer that," Nana said firmly as she ushered Bill out of the kitchen and into the breakfast room. "Hurry up with the breakfast."

Bill stood unhappily beside the breakfast table. He reached out for Nana's hand. "You're wrong, dear. You shouldn't have told her they would be all right."

"Of course they will be," Nana said. "The *Carpathia* has them. You heard what the boy said, and you seemed to believe him."

Bill shook his head. "If the White Star Line had to choose who to save," he said, "do you think they would save the immigrants or would they save the rich and famous? It may be Irish nonsense, and I'm no Irishman, but I know that I awoke in the night and I felt it."

"Felt what?"

"A terrible sadness. I think I felt them dying."

On Board the *Carpathia*
7:45 a.m. (Ship's Time)
Kate Royston

It seemed to Kate that Captain Rostron needed to be in three places at once, and somehow he was succeeding. He was making sure that the helmsman kept the *Carpathia* on station and did not allow her to drift away from the sea of flotsam that marked the grave of the *Titanic*. He was also supervising the long process of bringing the survivors safely aboard, with many of them too weak to climb the rope ladders and having to be pulled up in a canvas sling. In addition, he had given priority to ensuring that the name of each shocked and frozen passenger was correctly given and passed to the Marconi operator.

For hours now, ever since the first survivors had stumbled half-frozen onto the *Carpathia's* deck, Kate had been standing beside Dr. Lengyel, the ship's Hungarian doctor, as he made rapid assessments of each survivor. She could only guess that the doctor had once served as an army medic—nothing else could explain his ability to make rapid decisions. He knew when to offer brandy and blankets, when to send an injury to be bandaged by one of the other doctors, and when to demand urgent treatment of frostbite. He made no distinction between rich and poor, steerage class and first class. He treated each frozen, semiparalyzed scrap of humanity in the same brusque but compassionate manner.

Kate, in a starched apron handed to her by Mrs. Broomer, worked as best she could trying to understand and record names forced out between chattering teeth while somehow avoiding answering the inevitable, stuttering questions: "Where is my husband? Where is my child?" Once or twice she had been able to give a positive response. She had been able to assure Mrs. Thayer, one of the richest women in America, that her son Jack was safely on board; she had seen him herself. Mrs. Thayer had not asked after her husband. Neither had Mrs. Astor, pale, delicate, and pregnant, or Mrs. Ryerson, clutching the hand of her daughter.

Women such as Mrs. Ryerson and Mrs. Astor were wrapped in furs. Even their maids, who had managed to accompany them, were dressed in warm coats, but the few immigrants who had made their way up from the bowels of the *Titanic* and onto a lifeboat had only shawls and scraps of blanket; some wore only nightclothes.

Kate saw Dr. Lengyel's impatience with those members of the *Titanic's* crew who had managed to secure themselves a place as an oarsman in a lifeboat. These men were warm and dry, and yet they grumbled when they were set to work assisting in bringing the survivors aboard.

Most of the other men, those who had been dragged from the water and into the lifeboats after the *Titanic* had gone down beneath them, were in the worst shape and took much of Dr. Lengyel's attention. Some had severe cuts and head injuries where they had dropped from the sinking ship as she had plunged beneath the waves.

All of them had spent the long night in salt-soaked, frozen clothing. Some of these men were officers who refused medical treatment, insisting instead that they should speak to Captain Rostron, that they should assist with bringing the other lifeboats on board, that they should know how many people had been saved. Not one of them, not even the most senior officers, asked after their own captain. It had not been said, and Kate knew that it did not need to be said—Captain Smith was not in a lifeboat. He had gone down with his ship.

With the sun now well above the horizon and the crew preparing to haul another boatload of survivors up the steep ladder, Kate paused to take a breath. Dr. Lengyel flashed her a weary smile. "You have done well, young lady." His accent bore traces of his Hungarian nationality but his English was excellent. "You have not told me your name. I must know your name so that I will remember."

Kate considered for a moment. Yes, she had done well. Why should she give this doctor a false name? If he planned to remember her, let him remember who she truly was. All other considerations aside, he was Hungarian, and he had told her that he was not interested in immigrating to America. Her father's name and her family's disgrace would mean nothing to him. If an old Hungarian doctor wanted to remember her, he would remember her for her work here tonight and not for her father's sins.

"I'm Kate," she said. "Kate Royston."

His pale, tired eyes gave no flicker of recognition.

"From Royston, Pennsylvania," Kate continued. She had done it. She had attached her name to the town that her father had founded in his own name and to the dam her father had built to bring water to his pulp mill.

Dr. Lengyel nodded. "I am grateful for your help, Miss Royston."

"I wish I could do more," Kate said as she took up her pencil and prepared to receive the next influx of passengers. Lifeboat number eight.

She had become accustomed to hearing crying, weeping, and cursing as the survivors stumbled onto the safety of the *Carparhia's* deck, but the first passenger to come aboard from lifeboat eight was neither crying nor weeping. She was a tall blonde woman wrapped in a fox-fur coat. Her cheeks were flushed red by cold but her nose and her fingers showed no hint of blue. She seemed to have survived her ordeal very well.

"Countess of Rothes," she declared in answer to Kate's question. "I'm fine. I don't need a doctor. I've spent countless hours on the Scottish moors. I know how to look after myself.

I am also quite warm, as I have been rowing all night, as have the other ladies in my boat. If I had not taken charge, I cannot imagine what would have happened. After you haul up the crew that was sent to row us you can set them to work. They've done nothing all night. None of them even knew how to hold an oar. It's a disgrace and I will make my feelings known in due course. So many fine men who could have taken charge and saved lives were left behind simply because of some ridiculous rule of the sea. Women and children first. How is that to work if you put only women, children, and incompetent stewards and cooks into the lifeboats and leave behind athletic men who would do their duty?"

Kate stared up at the tall, beautiful countess. How could she say such a thing? Surely the tradition of saving women and children from war and shipwreck and all manner of disasters was the mark of a civilized nation.

The countess was speaking again. "Where is the other ship?"

"What other ship?"

"There was another ship. We saw a light and we were told to row towards it."

"There is no other ship," Kate said. "No one has said anything about another ship. We were fifty miles away. You could not have seen our lights."

"We saw someone's lights," the countess insisted. "Ask any of the passengers, and they'll tell you the same thing. First we were told that we would be put into the lifeboats while the crew fixed the problem with our ship and we would be back very shortly, and then we were told that a light had been seen, a ship was coming for us, and we were to row towards it."

Kate looked down at the paper in her hand and saw that she had been so distracted by this new information that she had not even recorded a name.

"I'm sorry," she said. "Could you repeat your name?"

"Lucy Noël Martha Leslie, Countess of Rothes."

Kate decided she would wait until another time to check the spelling of the name. The countess was looking flushed and was swaying on her feet. "This is quite a shock," she whispered. "Are you sure there has not been another ship? Are we really all that have been rescued?"

"I'm afraid so."

The countess seemed to be blinking back tears. She was not asking for pity, but Kate felt pity for her. This woman had rowed for hours, thinking all the time that she was making for a nearby ship. She had spent the long night under the impression that their little flotilla of lifeboats was just one part of a greater rescue, and now she knew differently. Now she knew the full horror of what had occurred, and it seemed that she knew who to blame.

"Do you have brandy?" the countess asked.

Before Kate could reply, she was interrupted by Dr. Lengyel. "The last boat is coming up now, Miss Kate. Come along. We have work to do. There is an old lady coming up, and she is going to give us trouble."

"Is she injured?" Kate asked.

"I don't know if she is injured, but she is very angry, and so, I think, is everyone with her."

As Kate stepped out from the shelter of the doorway, she realized that the countess was behind her. Together they peered down to look at the crammed lifeboat that was now secured to the foot of the ladder. Up on deck, a group of seamen hauled wearily on the ropes attached to a canvas sling containing an elderly lady swathed in what appeared to be a very damp fur coat. The sling swung in an uncontrolled arc and her complaining voice carried above the instructions of the crew and the warnings from the shivering passengers still in the lifeboat.

"I'm not letting him go."

"Just drop him."

"I will not."

"If you fall, you'll have us all in the water."

"I'm not letting him go."

"It's just a dog."

"And you're just a sailor," the old lady responded.

Kate leaned over the railing to study the speaker. She was wrong about the fur coat. The old lady was not wearing a fur coat; the fur coat was wearing her. Against all probability, the sailors were hauling up a sparrowlike woman wearing a bright red hat and holding a large and very wet dog. The dog was not taking kindly to riding with the old lady. Apparently they were strangers to each other, and the dog was not comforted by the old lady's pleas for him to "sit still and be a good dog."

Kate could fully understand the reason for anxiety. If the dog—, he appeared to be some kind of large hunting dog—fell into the tightly packed boat below, there was every possibility that it would tip or maybe even sink.

The sling inched its way up the side of the *Carpathia* until at long last it was level with the boat deck. The dog, seeing its way to freedom, leaped from the woman's arms. The sling tipped, with the old lady clutching frantically for the hands outstretched to help her. Kate held her breath. Although there was no longer any danger of the dog landing in the lifeboat, there was every possibility that the dog's rescuer could still fall headfirst onto the people below.

With a shout of triumph, one of the *Carpathia's* deckhands finally managed to grasp the sling and bring it within reach. The old lady fell onto the deck with a cry of pain, and Kate heard the sharp crack of a snapping bone as the woman's legs crumpled beneath her.

As Dr. Lengyel stepped wearily forward to assess the damage, Kate was surprised to hear a burst of laughter from the countess, who was holding the bedraggled dog by the scruff of its neck and smiling triumphantly.

"Well done," she called. "He's a purebred. Well worth saving. Good job."

Kate turned to look at the countess in amazement. "She nearly killed herself."

"And that," said the countess, "would have made a lot of people very happy."

"Who is she?"

"She's Eva Trentham, possibly the richest woman in America, and quite definitely the most unpopular."

Kate watched as the unpopular Mrs. Trentham was carried away by two sailors while the countess shook her head in wry amusement.

Dr. Lengyel peered over the side and then turned to Kate. "That was the last boat. That is everyone."

Kate sensed movement behind her and turned to see a stocky middle-aged man who wore a heavy overcoat over his pajamas. He kept his hands in the pockets of his overcoat as he strode to the rail and looked down.

"That is everyone," Dr. Lengyel repeated.

The stranger nodded, turned abruptly, and walked away. Kate saw him speaking to one of the *Carpathia's* deck officers. He pulled his hands from his pockets and began to gesture angrily. A slip of paper fluttered to the deck as he argued with the officer. Eventually, they seemed to reach some kind of agreement, and they walked away together. Kate darted forward and picked up the paper. Perhaps it was important. For people who were coming aboard with nothing, everything was important.

She tried to catch his attention. "Mr. … uh … sir …"

He ignored her and disappeared into the interior of the ship.

Kate picked up the paper and put it into the pocket of her apron. She turned to the countess. "Who was he?" she asked. "I don't recall recording his name."

"Well, make sure you record it now," the countess replied. "Make sure you get it right. That's Sir Bruce Ismay, chairman of the White Star Line, the man who saved himself while his passengers drowned."

CHAPTER THREE

The White House
Washington, DC
9:00 a.m. (Eastern Standard Time)
Senator William Alden Smith

The senator waited outside the door of the president's office. He held a handkerchief to his nose and hoped he would not have to wait for very long. Sawdust and paint fumes still lingered in the air as a reminder of the construction of the new West Wing of the White House and Taft's new and unusual oval office. The president often worked with his office door open, but today it was closed, with Charles Hilles, Taft's personal secretary, hovering protectively outside.

"He won't see you, Senator."

Bill removed the handkerchief from his nose and spoke quietly but firmly. "I have an appointment."

Hilles shook his head. "Unless you have news of Major Butt, he will not see anyone."

Bill pursed his lips impatiently. "The *Carpathia* has been transmitting names as the survivors come aboard. Major Butt was not on the list."

Hilles sighed. "I know. The president is apprised of every name on the list, but he finds the situation unacceptable."

"We all find it unacceptable," Bill said irritably.

Hilles smiled sadly. "The president continues to hope that some of the rumors we hear are true and perhaps another ship has arrived on the scene and taken in the remaining passengers. We have a list of only seven hundred names, and it's impossible to think that there are no other survivors. Half of New York society was on that ship, and so far we have only been given the names of the women, such as Mrs. Astor, Mrs. Ryerson, and Mrs. Thayer."

"The rule of the sea," Bill said impatiently. "Women and children first."

Even as he spoke, Bill wondered if that rule had really held true out there on the deep Atlantic with no one to see what was happening. Had forceful men like Jacob Astor, Arthur Ryerson, John Thayer, Benjamin Guggenheim, and Martin Rothschild really followed such an archaic, unwritten law and allowed poor immigrant women to board the lifeboats first? Had Major Archibald Butt, confidant of the president and bearer of secret messages from the German kaiser, given up his seat in favor of a lady's maid or a half-starved Irish child?

Before Bill could give in to temptation and voice his doubts, the door of the president's office opened and Taft himself stood framed in the doorway. The president's considerable bulk obstructed Bill's view of the new office. He caught only a glimpse of deep-green walls and a massive desk littered with papers, but Taft showed no sign of inviting him inside to sit down and talk about the reelection campaign. Perhaps it had been unreasonable of Bill to think that on this spring morning, with the *Titanic* disaster headlining every newspaper, William Taft would want to talk about an election that would not happen until November.

Taft acknowledged Bill with a brief nod before turning to Hilles. "Any word?"

"No, Mr. President. We are told that the list is complete. The *Carpathia* has wired the names of every survivor they have taken on board."

"But what about the other ships?" Taft asked in a pleading tone. "There are other ships. The *Virginian*, the *Parisian*. What about this rumor that the ship is under tow and headed to Halifax? Don't you know what the newspapers are saying?"

When Hilles hesitated, Bill spoke up. "Mr. President, I know what the newspapers are saying, but they are publishing wild rumors. The Marconi operator on the *Carpathia* is transmitting the truth. I'm sorry to say it, sir; there are no other survivors. The *Titanic* has gone to the bottom of the Atlantic. The only survivors are on the *Carpathia*, and they are mainly women and children."

"But the men must be somewhere," Taft argued. "Is it possible that they are on an iceberg, waiting for rescue?"

Hilles shook his head. "I don't believe they could climb onto an iceberg."

"Well, floating ice," Taft snapped. "They could be on an ice floe. Even now a ship could be coming for them. I've ordered ships to be dispatched to continue the search."

Hilles nodded. "We're sending the *Mackay-Bennett* as soon as she's provisioned and ready. She's in Halifax and she's the closest ship we have."

Taft frowned, with his eyes turning to mere slits above his puffy cheeks. "From what I hear, there were any number of ships close by, and surely they have arrived on the scene by now."

Bill looked at Hilles. Official news from the *Carpathia* had been passed on to the offices of senators and congressmen, and Bill was confident that his information was up to date, but no one had mentioned another ship. Was it possible that some of the rumors were true? Had another ship been close by?

Hilles shook his head. "Another British ship, the *Californian*, arrived on the scene this morning, sir, but the *Carpathia* was already preparing to depart. She had picked up every survivor. She could do no more. The *Californian* has returned to her original course, and the *Carpathia* has broadcast a message to all shipping that the rescue operation is complete. When the *MacKay-Bennett* arrives, it will be to pick up bodies, not to search for survivors."

"No!" The president's voice was firm and commanding. "This is not the end of the matter. I'm told that the *Titanic* had waterproof compartments. Is it possible that some of the passengers are even now sheltering in those compartments, maybe even below the surface? Could we send down divers? If Butt is alive, I want him found."

Taft's eyes turned toward Bill. "Senator Smith, I cannot see you today. I will see no one."

"Yes, Mr. President."

Taft turned to Hilles. "I want him found."

Hilles spoke as a man would humor a child. "Yes, Mr. President, of course."

Taft, his shoulders drooping, lumbered back into his office and closed the door, not with a bang but with a quiet click. Bill thought it was the sound of despair.

On Board the *Carpathia*
10:00 a.m. (Ship's Time)
Kate Royston

Kate stood on the deck watching as the *Californian* made a belated search of the floating wreckage. The cargo ship had arrived too late to be of assistance and soon she would resume her course toward Boston. There was nothing she could do, no one left to rescue. The *Carpathia* had already done all that could be done. Every survivor was on board. Even the lifeboats had been taken up and stowed on the foredeck. The grave of the *Titanic* was marked by nothing but a sea of debris and a ghastly procession of floating bodies—too many for the *Carpathia* to bring aboard.

What was the point? Kate thought. Those bodies that could be snagged and brought onto the deck would only be returned to the sea as soon as they had been identified. Only the rich and famous were sewn into canvas shrouds and laid alongside the lifeboats on the foredeck. The poor, who had risked everything for a chance to make good in a new land, were stripped of their life vests so that their bodies would not float into the shipping lanes, and then they were returned to the ocean with prayers from the ship's chaplain. Perhaps the chaplain prayed his Protestant prayers over unknowing Catholics, Jews, and atheists, but the dead could not know, and Kate chose to believe it would not matter. The bodies were mere remnants, and their souls had already been returned to their maker.

Listening to the prayers had brought memories of another mass burial where bodies had lain side by side, not on the deck of a ship but on the green grass of Pennsylvania. Choking back sobs, Kate turned away from the deck and the sight of the *Californian* making her fruitless search. Blinded by tears, she pulled open the closest door and stepped inside, trying to find a corner of the ship where she could weep in peace.

As soon as she was inside, she was greeted by a blast of warm air and a wash of sound from hundreds of voices. How absurd to think that she could find a private corner or that she could weep alone. Seven hundred survivors of the night's tragedy were crammed in among the *Carpathia*'s existing passengers. Distinctions between classes barely existed. Women in shawls and ragged, hollow-eyed children filled the passageways and crammed into the first-class smoking room.

Kate, exhausted from the night's activities and completely overtaken by her own memories, sat down among them. Finally she had found a place where she could weep unnoticed. No one here would be aware that she was weeping for her own reasons and for her own losses.

For the first time in a year, Kate allowed herself to remember the mangled and drowned bodies that had been collected and committed to the rich earth of Royston, Pennsylvania. She remembered her father standing expressionless as vile words were flung at him. She wished that she had done something, anything, to help him stand beneath the weight of those words. Instead, she had turned her back on the place where she had been born and started on the journey that had brought her here on board the *Carpathia*, masquerading as a governess and sitting among widows and orphans.

Finally her choking sobs turned to quiet tears, and she experienced a feeling of relief that she had been seeking for almost an entire year. She took a deep breath. She had faced her past, faced her father's guilt, even faced her own part in his final tragedy, so what was she to do now? Her conscience prodded at her. *Do something for them. You did nothing for your father's victims; do something for these people.*

She looked at the people surrounding her, mostly women but a few men and a few children. The tall, angular figure of Mrs. Broomer, the chief stewardess, was moving among them, apparently searching for someone. As Kate rose to her feet, she caught Mrs. Broomer's eye and realized that she need look no farther. Mrs. Broomer would find her something to do.

The stewardess beckoned her forward, and they left the smoking room together for the relative peace of the ladies' reading room which was occupied only by Dr. Lengyel and the most severely injured survivors.

"I want to help," Kate said.

Mrs. Broomer nodded. "And so you shall, Miss Royston."

"You know my name?"

"I learned it from Dr. Lengyel. He was most impressed with all that you did during the night. However ..." Mrs. Broomer paused and looked at Kate with an expression worthy of the sternest schoolmarm. "However," she repeated, "I find that you are not a first-class passenger and you are, in fact, a governess."

"Well ..."

"No doubt you are penniless, like most of your breed—we see them all the time on a ship such as this—but you are not without education. I imagine that you have somehow fallen on hard times, but I will not ask for details. Your past is none of my business and I feel that you are a young woman who will rise to a challenge."

"I just want to help," Kate said.

"And so you shall," said Mrs. Broomer. "First, of course, I will expect you to get dressed. It's all very well for these wretched women to be in their nightclothes and rags, but I imagine you have a dress somewhere in your cabin."

"Of course I do, but I am not sure if I still have a cabin. I was told that the survivors were to occupy some of the cabins."

Mrs. Broomer nodded. "Yes, your cabin is indeed occupied, somewhat unsuitably, in my opinion, but I can assure you that the occupant, or I should say occupants, have no interest in your belongings. Go and get dressed and then report back here. I have a task for you."

Kate thought there was an element of veiled menace in Mrs. Broomer's words. "What task?"

"You will see. Better wash your face too. It's obvious you've been crying. Pull yourself together. The survivors we have on board have every reason to cry, but you do not."

"If only you knew," Kate muttered to herself as she left Mrs. Broomer behind and made her way to the cabin she had shared with the Van Buren children.

She paused outside the door. Mrs. Broomer had said the cabin was occupied. In fact, she had hinted it was occupied by more than one person. What if one of the gentlemen had taken up residence? How was she to go in there and change her clothes? Would he leave if she asked? It was all very well to have spent the night with nothing but a coat over her nightgown and with her hair unbraided, but this was different. Now it was daylight. Now the terrible urgency of the night before was behind them, and she was suddenly self-conscious. She remembered how she had flung herself at Harold Cottam, how she had climbed the crew ladder in her slippers and spent hours helping the doctor without even a passing thought of her disheveled appearance. She shrugged. Her family's reputation was already in tatters. What difference would it make for a gentleman to see her in her nightclothes?

Her gentle tapping on the cabin door was answered by a growl and then a deep bark. She took a step back. What on earth was in her cabin?

The door opened a crack, and the blonde head of the Countess of Rothes peered out. "Oh, it's you, the recorder of names. Come on in. Wolfie won't hurt you."

"Wolfie?" Kate queried.

"A dog should have a strong name," the countess replied. "Come in and meet him."

Kate stepped inside the cabin that had once been hers and inhaled an overpowering smell of wet dog. Wolfie, the dog who had almost drowned Mrs. Eva Trentham, was stretched out on one of the beds. His fur, still stiff and spiky with salt water, was drying to a shaggy brown-and-black pelt. Despite his name, he bore no resemblance to a wolf. His eyes were wide and brown, and his ears long and drooping.

Kate, remembering her father's insistence that dogs, even small ones, belonged outside, eyed Wolfie suspiciously. "Shouldn't he be in the ship's kennel?"

The countess extended her hand and patted Wolfie's head. "After everything he's been through, he deserves a nice warm bed. In fact, we all deserve a nice warm bed. I don't think the kennel would be at all suitable. I thought it would be best to get him off the floor and give him a chance to dry. We don't want a sick dog on our hands."

"Are you going to keep him?" Kate asked.

"Heavens, no. As soon as I get him dry, I'll take him to Mrs. Trentham. There'll be hell to pay if we lose the creature now after she practically drowned a boatload of very important people in order to save him."

The countess reached under the pillow on Wolfie's bunk and produced a whiskey bottle. "Drink, Miss Royston? You are Miss Royston, aren't you?"

"Yes, I am, and no, thank you. I came to change my clothes. The chief stewardess has work for me to do."

The countess looked her up and down and then nodded. "I agree, you should change. You look quite fetching in that outfit, my dear, but this is hardly the time for it, is it? We all need to roll up our sleeves, tie up our hair, and get down to business."

"Well, you seem to ..." Kate bit her tongue. What was the point of complaining? The countess was firmly ensconced in the cabin. Wolfie was no doubt soaking the blankets on one of the bunks, and goodness knew what else he would do if he wasn't taken outside soon. The whiskey that the countess poured for herself brought back sharp, angry memories of Kate's father. Best to say nothing, change her dress, and get out of there and never come back.

Kate opened the closet and took out a modest gray woolen dress. She removed her nightgown and slipped the dress over her head; now was not the time to truss herself up in a corset. She rebraided her hair and pinned the braids to the top of her head. The countess had ceased to pay attention to her and was reclining on the bunk beside Wolfie and sipping lazily on the whiskey. She looked up as Kate was about to leave.

"Well done," she said. "You look quite smart."

Kate closed the door behind her with a resentful bang. *Quite smart!* There had been a time when people had called her a beauty and prophesied that she would marry well, that her father's money might even attract the attention of an impoverished noble family. The Royston dollars and Kate's looks could reel in an English earl or a German count. The possibilities were endless so long as Kate was willing to pay with her body for her father's ambition for his grandchildren.

Mrs. Broomer waylaid her in the corridor and nodded approvingly. "You look the part. Now, remember, whatever happens, keep a cool head. The old lady has a reputation for making trouble, and I'm afraid she's in a good deal of pain, so that will make her even worse. I'm searching among the immigrants for a woman with nursing experience. You are not required to nurse her. To be honest, I don't know what will be required of you. All she will tell me is that she requires someone who can read and write and comport herself well in polite company. She will no doubt try your patience but not for long. It has been decided that the *Carpathia* will return to New

York, so you will only be needed for two or three days."

Kate's heart sank. "We're returning to New York?"

Mrs. Broomer raised her eyebrows. "Where did you think we would go? Did you think we would take all of these people on a Mediterranean cruise?"

"Well, no, but—"

"They were all bound for New York, so the least we can do is deliver them to their destination. We heard talk of Halifax, but who is to say that Canada will give them entry? No, we're bound for New York. It will be up to each of our own cruise passengers to make a decision when we reach there. Perhaps some of them will not wish to take to sea again after what they have witnessed. You, of course, will have to speak to your employers about your commitment to them."

"Oh yes," Kate muttered, "my employers."

She shuddered at the thought of returning to the country she had so recently fled. "Will we be required to leave the ship in New York?" she asked.

Mrs. Broomer narrowed her eyes. "Do you have any objection to leaving?"

"I would prefer to stay."

"That will be up to Mrs. van Buren. If she and her children decide not to continue with their cruise and prefer to leave the ship, then so must you. Now, please stop asking questions. I am very busy, and Mrs. Trentham is very demanding."

"Mrs. Trentham," Kate repeated unhappily. "The woman who brought that dog on board?"

"Try to please her," Mrs. Broomer said. "She's in a lot of pain. Her leg is broken and her wrist is sprained, so she cannot move and she cannot write. She tells me that she has Marconi messages to send, so it will be up to you to make sure that Mr. Cottam sends them. Try not to fail her. She has a way of making life very unpleasant for people who displease her."

The Russell Senate Office Building
Washington, DC
10:30 a.m. (Eastern Standard Time)
Senator William Alden Smith

Bill stared down at the printed paper laid neatly on his desk and then looked up at the worried face of Richard LaSalle, his new, young clerk.

"So this is it, LaSalle?"

"Yes, Senator. They say this is the final list from the *Carpathia*. Here are the names of everyone brought on board. Seven hundred and six people and four dogs."

"Dogs?"

"Yes, Senator. Two Pomeranians, one Pekinese, and one large hound of unknown origin. The small dogs were carried on board by their owners, and the large dog was rescued from the water by Mrs. Eva Trentham. The owner is unknown, presumed drowned."

Bill scrutinized the list. "How is this divided?"

"Third class, second class, first class, crew, and officers."

Bill nodded and continued to read. "Third class did not do well," he commented.

"No, sir."

"Why is that?"

"We don't know, Senator. We cannot know anything until the *Carpathia* docks."

"Oh, we'll know before that," Bill commented. "I hear the president has sent two military cruisers to intercept the *Carpathia*. He's desperate for information on Major Butt."

"Major Butt is not on the list of survivors."

"I know that, LaSalle, and so does the president, but he is not willing to believe it."

LaSalle frowned. "I know that Major Butt was a great help to the president, but if he is not on board, I don't see what can be gained by dispatching military vessels to ask questions."

Bill continued to study the list, but his clerk was not prepared to let the question rest. "Senator, I've heard that Major Butt was on a mission. Some say to the Pope; others say that he did in fact go to Germany."

"You should not listen to what other people say."

"But—"

"We will not discuss Major Butt. Do you understand?"

"Yes, sir."

"Very well. Now, take another look at this list. What do you see?"

"I see that the captain and the first officer were not saved."

Bill nodded. "I sailed with Captain Smith several times. He was a good man, and a good commander. I cannot imagine how he could put his ship in collision with an iceberg."

"It was dark, sir."

"That's no excuse. I just don't understand it. Now, look at these other names. Four deck officers were saved, but no engineering officers. One assumes they were trapped below in the engine room. One Marconi operator lost, one saved, along with another operator, who was traveling as a passenger. Only one senior fireman saved, but a great number of stewards and cooks. It's hard to imagine what was happening here or how priorities were established. Thomas Andrews, the man who designed the ship, went down with her, but Sir Bruce Ismay, chairman of the White Star Line, owner of the *Titanic*, did not. Apparently, he is safe on board the *Carpathia*. I don't know what to make of that, LaSalle, but I don't like it."

CHAPTER FOUR

On Board the *Carpathia*
12:00 p.m. (Ship's Time)
Kate Royston

Kate had met women who aged gracefully—her own grandmother had still been a beauty at seventy-five—but Eva Trentham was not such a woman. However, according to Mrs. Broomer, Eva had once been a great beauty.

"The toast of Paris, Rome, and London," Mrs. Broomer said as she ushered Kate toward Eva's first-class suite. "Men fought duels for her favors. Try to remember that. Flatter her whenever you can."

Kate stopped outside the wide walnut doors of the suite, the finest accommodation on the *Carpathia*. "How did you persuade the people in here to move out?" she asked. "They paid for the best. Why would they move?"

"Because they want Mrs. Trentham to be in their debt, that's why. There is no end to the favors that can be obtained if you have the Widow Trentham on your side. She has senators and presidents in her pocket."

"How?"

"She buys them. She has had three husbands, each one richer than the last, and each one now dead. Rumor has it that she was born poor and her first marriage was for love, and maybe that's the truth, but her next two marriages were strictly for the money, old men who would soon be dead. And now she's the richest woman in the United States, maybe even in Europe. Any man who wants to win a seat in the Senate, or a seat in the British parliament, or perhaps even a seat in the White House, needs her on his side."

Mrs. Broomer paused to pull a key from her pocket. "We have found a wheelchair for her, but she will not permit herself to be pushed out among the other survivors, and so she sits and fumes. I will unlock this door and give you the key. She will be in your care, and if you play your cards right, perhaps it will no longer matter if you have to leave the ship in New York. Maybe you will not need to flee to Europe."

"I'm not fleeing."

"I think you are."

"No."

"Well, let it be. You were helpful to the doctor last night, and so now I am helpful to you."

Mrs. Broomer pressed the key into Kate's hand. "By the way, she wants to take possession of the dog she rescued. I have sent a steward to fetch it."

"Wolfie," Kate said. "The countess has named him Wolfie."

Mrs. Broomer shook her head. "Oh dear, I hope he doesn't live up to his name." She gave Kate a gentle shove. "In you go. Do your best."

Kate knocked, received an unintelligible response from within, and unlocked the door. Eva Trentham was in the center of the parlor, seated in a wicker wheelchair with red upholstery. She was swathed in blankets, and the red hat she had worn on arrival was still perched on her head atop wisps of white hair. Her eyes swept over Kate from head to foot once and then concentrated themselves on the folds of Kate's dress.

"Come here, girl."

"My name is Kate."

"Come here, Kate."

Kate approached tentatively, and Eva's clawlike hand shot out from beneath her blanket cocoon and fingered the fabric of Kate's skirt.

"Ha!" she said triumphantly. "You are not what you appear to be.

I thought as much. They tell me you're a governess, but you don't have the air of a servant. Where's my dog?"

"He's coming."

"So he's a male dog?"

"Yes, ma'am."

"Don't call me 'ma'am.' I think you are unaccustomed to calling anyone 'ma'am,' so don't begin to do it now. This disaster may be the very thing to change your apparently failing fortunes."

"I don't understand, ma'am … Mrs. Trentham."

"Mrs. Trentham. Yes, I was Henry Trentham's wife. He left me a great deal of money, but I never liked the name. Trentham, so very ordinary. I was once a contessa, but that is behind me now. I think you shall call me Miss Eva. No, no, that won't do. That sounds too much like a piano teacher, and I despise piano teachers. Call me Eva, and I will call you Kate. You see, we shall get along fine so long as you are honest with me."

Kate attempted to take a step back, but Eva still held her skirt in a firm grasp. "Is this your own dress, Kate?"

"Yes, it is."

Eva fingered the fabric. "A very fine wool," she said, looking up at Kate with shrewd blue eyes far too lively for her wrinkled and folded face. "And look at the way it fits. This is no hand-me-down. This was made for you by a very good dressmaker. You have attempted to make it plain, but there is nothing plain about the drape of this fabric. I can see where you have unpicked a lace collar rather clumsily, and once there was beading at the shoulder. A dress for half mourning, I think. Who did you mourn?"

Kate answered without thinking. "My mother."

"And your mother was a wealthy woman who dressed you in finery. Oh, Kate, what are you doing on board this old tub?"

"I'm working my way to Europe. I had planned to leave the ship in Gibraltar."

Eva released Kate's dress and held up a horrified hand. "Oh no, not Gibraltar. It's a naval base, and if there's one thing more dangerous than being a penniless virgin at an army base, it's being a penniless virgin at a naval base. You will not find your fortune in Gibraltar, and you will be lucky if you manage to escape *virgo intacta* into Spain."

The old lady laughed mirthlessly. "Don't look so shocked.

46

Someone has to tell you the truth. Be glad I'm the one, because I don't mince my words. You're a pretty little thing, and maybe you will find a protector in Spain if you succeed in crossing the border, but—"

"It doesn't matter," Kate interrupted, certain that she was blushing to the roots of her hair. "We're not going to Europe. We're going back to New York."

"That is what I also hear," Eva said. "In fact, that is what I told the captain to do."

Kate remembered Captain Rostron thundering from his cabin at the first word of the *Titanic*'s plight. She remembered his string of orders delivered almost without pausing for breath. She could not imagine Eva Trentham, wealthy, influential, or otherwise, telling the *Carpathia*'s captain what he should do. She wondered if Eva was not quite as influential as she made herself out to be.

"Do you have paper and pencil?"

Kate nodded. "I do."

"Very well, then. You will send a message to Senator William Alden Smith on my behalf."

"How will I do that?"

"On the Marconi wireless, of course. I am sure that every wealthy man and bereaved socialite on this ship is attempting to send wires to New York, but I will expect you to prevail and insist that this message is sent immediately. Please me in this, Kate, and I may find ways to help you."

"I don't need your help."

"I think you do. Any woman who is desperate enough to leave the ship in Gibraltar or throw herself at some Spanish conquistador is greatly in need of help. Don't look so sullen. I've told you that we will get along fine if you do what I ask. I am in the unusual position of being unable to do anything for myself, and so you will have to do things for me."

"I'm not here to nurse you."

"Of course you're not. I require a skilled nurse, and one will be found for me among the immigrants. A good Irish girl will suit me fine. I need you for something else, and I am very pleased with what I see in you. You try to hide from sight in your dull dress, but you are not that kind of woman. You and I are very much alike, and I think we will get along just fine, and you will have no need to run away to

Spain."

"I'm not running away."

Eva waved her hand dismissively. "Forget about Spain, and remember why we are here together. I sailed on the greatest ship ever built, an unsinkable floating palace, or so we were told, and yet here I am, on an old tub of a boat, filled with weeping women. I can hear them weeping. Even here I can hear the echoes of the weeping and the screaming, and the terrible cries."

"Perhaps you should not speak of it," Kate said. "It's best not to remember."

"Perhaps so," Eva said. "I think you speak from experience, but whatever it is you remember, it will not be as dreadful as that night on the ocean. Let me speak. I have to speak."

Kate watched the sudden change in Eva's expression. Her eyes had been alive and sparkling, but now they became clouded and unfocused, and her voice fell to a whisper. "I thought it was all foolishness. We were put into a lifeboat and sent away from the ship, but none of us thought she would go down. Her lights were still blazing, and yet we were forced to take to the lifeboats and row far away. It seemed to be an absurd idea—a ridiculous inconvenience."

Eva reached out a hand, and Kate took it instinctively into her grasp. The old lady's hand was cold, as though the hand itself held the memory of ice and the deep, cold ocean.

"Our oarsmen said they were told to row toward a light somewhere in the distance, and we should all search the horizon for this light. There was no moon, but the sky was clear, and it was hard to distinguish just one light from the thousands of stars. I looked—everyone looked—and then we heard an explosion behind us. When we turned, we saw sparks shooting up from the ship, and we heard terrible cries. The lights were still blazing, and we could see people clinging to the railings, slipping and falling, and then the lights went out, and there was nothing but darkness and crying."

Eva suddenly released Kate's hand and shook her head. Her eyes regained focus, and her expression was grim and determined.

"It was the most terrible thing, but sitting here talking will serve no purpose. We must act. We shall bring down powerful men, Kate. Someone must pay for the lives that were lost."

Eva's words echoed in Kate's ears, and a terrifying memory forced itself to the surface. She looked from the window of her house and saw the people climbing the hill and breaking down the gates. *Someone must pay. Someone must pay.*

"Kate!" Eva's voice broke through the memory. "Are you listening to me, Kate?"

Kate pulled herself back to the present and to the disaster that was so much greater than the one she had witnessed.

"But it was an accident," she said, just as her father had said a year ago. "An act of God."

"The iceberg was an act of God," Eva agreed, "but colliding with it was an act of man, and trying to fit two thousand people into thirteen small lifeboats was an act of man. There is human fault here, Kate, that is nothing to do with God."

"Then we must blame the captain," Kate said. "And he is not here. He has gone down with his ship."

"I agree that the captain is beyond our reach, but there are men still alive who can be reached and ruined, and I intend to ruin them."

"Why?" Kate asked. "It will not bring the dead to life."

"I have my reasons," Eva said. "I intend to reach very high, very much higher than anyone will expect. If you will help me, we can bring down the most powerful man in America."

"The president?" Kate asked.

Eva shook her head impatiently. "No, not the president. He's not the most powerful man in America. He's a political pawn. He's bought and paid for, just like any other politician. Money, Kate. Money is power, and don't you forget it. When I speak of power, I speak of the king of greed himself, James Pierpont Morgan. I intend to knock him from his throne."

"Why?"

"Why?" Eva repeated. "Because the *Titanic* was his ship. He hides himself behind a financial wall, but he is the man pulling the strings. Ismay is just his puppet, but we'll begin with Ismay, because there is a very good case to be made against that man, and when we've knocked Ismay down, we'll go after Morgan. You saw Ismay, didn't you? You saw him standing there bold as brass and dry as a bone. He was safe and smug while hundreds of the wretches he tried to drown were pulled aboard the *Carpathia* and a thousand more went down to the bottom of the Atlantic."

"Are you saying that the tragedy was his fault?"

Eva nodded, her red hat bobbing in agreement. "I am saying it is quite possible. Ismay was in such a hurry to reach New York and claim the Blue Riband crossing speed record that he drove us into the ice. It's an open-and-shut case."

"But how will we prove it? Will you take him to court?"

"Not yet," Eva said. "First we will convene a Senate inquiry."

Kate looked at the old woman in amazement. "Can you do that?"

Eva nodded. "I cannot personally do that, but I know who can. We will send a Marconi message to Senator Smith of Michigan. He is the man who can make this happen, and I believe he will do it because he is a good and honest man and not just because he needs my backing if he is to take a run at the presidency. All it will take is a slight nudge. Take up your pencil and paper, Kate, and let's get started. Let's give Senator Smith a nudge."

A few minutes later, Kate was making her way toward the radio room with Eva's message clasped in her hand. Passing along the carpeted corridors of the first-class deck, she encountered a group of women standing outside a closed door. Although they were disheveled, the clothes they wore gave clear evidence of their wealth. Some wore evening dress; some wore nightclothes; but they all wore warm coats and even fashionable hats. Obviously, these were the first-class passengers from the *Titanic*.

Although they had escaped and were warm and dry, Kate could only imagine the tragedy that lay behind their angry faces. These women had been forced to leave their husbands and sons behind on the sinking ship with the promise that the separation was temporary. They would all be saved—rescue was on its way. Rescue had not come. The night had been filled with the cries of the dying, and the rising sun had shown them only the floating dead. Now the search was at an end, and the *Carpathia* was steaming at all possible speed toward New York, leaving the scene of the tragedy behind.

As she attempted to push her way through the throng, Kate saw that the women were gathered outside Dr. Lengyel's quarters. She tapped one of the ladies on the shoulder. The woman turned toward her. She was young, fine featured, but very pale. No doubt she bore a famous name, and now she bore it as a widow.

"The doctor is not there," Kate said. "He's tending to the sick in the smoking room."

"We're not looking for the doctor," the woman replied. She pointed at the door. "Ismay is in there. He's been in there ever since

50

he arrived on the ship, and see what's written on the door."

Kate peered over the shoulders of the other ladies and saw that a handwritten sign had been pinned to the door. *Please do not knock.*

A hand pushed Kate aside, and a woman spoke loudly above the murmuring of the ladies. "We'll see about that," she said as she rapped loudly on the door.

"He won't come out, Mrs. Ryerson," said the woman beside Kate.

Mrs. Ryerson continued to knock and call out in a loud voice. "Open up in there, Ismay. We know you're there."

A man's voice intruded on the protests. "Ladies, ladies, please return to your quarters."

Kate turned to see one of the ship's officers approaching rapidly along the corridor.

"Quarters," sniffed Mrs. Ryerson. "I do not call them quarters when we are sleeping on the floor. Poor Mrs. Astor is covered in bruises."

Apparently, Mrs. Astor was the pale lady who had been speaking to Kate. She pulled on the officer's arm. "We shouldn't complain. We know the captain is doing his best, but how is it that Sir Bruce Ismay is occupying this cabin? My husband is dead. All of our husbands are dead, and yet he does not have the decency to come out and speak to us."

"He is very disturbed by the loss of his ship," the officer said, "and of course, he has urgent business. He has a constant flow of Marconigrams."

Kate knew at once that the poor man had given the wrong reply, and Mrs. Ryerson proved her right.

"Marconigrams," she said. "I'd like to send a Marconigram, but Sir Bruce is monopolizing the radio operator."

As a babble of outraged voices sprang up around her, Kate remembered the paper she was carrying. If the radio operator was too busy to send Marconigrams for anyone other than Ismay, would he send one for Eva Trentham?

She smiled to herself, realizing that she had a card that no one else could play. Harold Cottam owed her a favor. She was sure that even without her prompting, he would have roused Captain Rostron and delivered the *Titanic*'s message, but nonetheless, she had helped. She had been a voice of encouragement in his time of doubt. He could hardly forget her.

She moved on toward the bridge and the radio room, making her way determinedly past officers and crewmen, who raised their eyebrows in surprise but were too busy to do anything about her. Perhaps it was the plain gray dress she wore. Eva had noted its fine quality, but to anyone else, it was the plain dress of a woman who was going about her business. Maybe they mistook her for a stewardess. A number of first-class stewardesses had been rescued from the *Titanic*; maybe that was how she was perceived.

Whatever the reason, she was allowed to go on her way unimpeded until she reached the radio room. Here she found a closed door and a notice forbidding entry. Well, even though Harold Cottam would surely remember her, it didn't seem right just to open the door and force her way in.

She knocked, politely but firmly.

No response.

She knocked again, harder and with authority.

The door opened, and a face peered out. It was not the face of Harold Cottam. How could that be? He was the only Marconi operator on the *Carpathia*, and he was inundated with messages. How could someone else be in the radio room? She knew this was not an operator from the *Titanic*. One operator had died at his post, and the other one had been recovered close to death and was under the care of Dr. Lengyel.

The face at the door was, she noticed, quite a handsome one, topped with blond curls and framed by a neat blond beard. The eyes, bright blue and set far apart, regarded her with interest, but the lips failed to smile.

"Sorry, miss, we're not able to take any more Marconigrams."

Kate kept her grip on the paper and remembered the importance of her mission. If anything she did today would harm the reputation of Sir Bruce Ismay, then that would make today a good day. How dare he—

"Miss, I'm sorry."

The door was still partially open, and the blue eyes were still looking at her with interest.

"I want to speak to Mr. Cottam," Kate said. "In fact, I insist on speaking to him. Tell him it's Kate."

The face at the door turned away and spoke to someone in the room. "There's a girl out here. Says her name is Kate and she wants to speak to you."

Cottam's voice spoke from inside. "Is she a pretty girl with black hair?"

The face turned toward Kate again, and the lips formed a smile. "Yes, I would say she is. Very pretty."

"Let her in."

"Really?"

"Oh, yes. I owe her a favor."

The door opened, and Kate stepped inside a cramped room filled with unfamiliar equipment and tangled wires. Harold Cottam rose from a crouching position at the single desk and greeted her with a smile.

"We're really busy," he said, "but if you want to send a message, I can do it for you anytime, and if I'm not here, Danny will do it."

Danny, who gave the impression of having Viking forebears and who was rather too large for the room, nodded enthusiastically. "I'll do it. Anytime. I'm Danny McSorley."

Kate studied Danny, wondering why he was not in uniform and why Cottam had not mentioned that the *Carpathia* had another Marconi operator. It took a moment for her to understand. "You came from the *Titanic*?"

"I did."

"But I thought there were only two operators."

"There were. I'm a passenger ... I was a passenger. Second class."

Kate listened to his softly accented voice. Scottish, maybe, or some part of northern England.

"I'm on my way to Newfoundland," he said. "I was to take up a post at the Cape Race relay station, and I thought to see something of New York before I went up there to the middle of nowhere."

"I've never been so glad to see anyone," Cottam said. "I can't do this on my own. I was sending lists and Marconigrams hour after hour and fending off newspapers all the time. I couldn't keep it up, but Danny volunteered. He's good. Better than I am." He looked at the paper in Kate's hand. "Do you want to send a Marconigram?"

"It's not for me. It's Mrs. Trentham. She wants me to send it to Senator Smith."

She passed the message to Cottam, and he whistled softly as he read the words. "A Senate hearing," he said. "She wants a Senate hearing?"

"Yes, she does."

"Do you think this senator will do it for her?"

Kate nodded. "I think he will."

Cottam passed the paper to Danny, who stared at it for a moment and then handed it back. "I don't know anything about American politics. I suppose there'll be an inquiry, but the *Titanic* is a British ship, so it will be a British inquiry."

"But American people died," Kate said. "Mrs. Trentham thinks the American public should know what happened."

"I'd like to know that myself," Danny agreed. "It was like being in a nightmare. People screaming and shouting, the steam whistle shrieking, ropes tangled, immigrants locked down belowdecks, lifeboats launched sideways and upside down, and some of them half-empty, and all those people left behind." He paused and closed his eyes. Kate could only imagine the horrors playing out behind his eyelids. "Someone should find out what happened, but we won't find out from the captain. He never even tried to save himself."

"But Sir Bruce Ismay saved himself," Kate said.

Cottam nodded. "Yes, I know, and for that reason, I'll send your message, Miss Kate. If I get an answer, I'll let you know. Where will I find you?"

"I suppose I'll be with Mrs. Trentham," Kate replied. "I think she's not going to let me go until we reach New York."

"We'll find you," Danny said.

Cottam had already turned away as the Marconi equipment stuttered into life with a new message. Kate left the radio room and closed the door behind her.

As she went back through the maze of corridors, she carried the memory of a blond beard, a warm smile, and a man who had not tried to save himself, and yet he had been saved.

Danny McSorley

He wondered when the shock would wear off and when his hands would stop trembling. Cottam moved aside, and Danny sat down in front of the Morse key that lay at the heart of a great agglomeration of wires, coils, and condensers. He took a deep breath to steady himself. He had to stop thinking about the blood-soaked envelope he carried in his pocket and start thinking of ways to help Harold

Cottam, who was worn out from hours spent hunched over the Morse key. He thought about the girl who had just departed. If he concentrated on her, perhaps he could forget about everything else that had happened.

"She your girl?" he asked, as casually as he could.

Cottam shook his head. "No. That could never happen. She's a first-class passenger."

"Oh, I thought her dress looked kind of plain. Not as flashy as first class."

"She was on the first-class deck when I met her, and wearing a coat over her nightgown," Cottam said. "It was just after I received the SOS from the *Titanic*. I'd been up to the bridge to tell them, and no one up there believed me."

"You're joking."

"No, really. They said the *Titanic* couldn't be sinking and I should go away and stop being stupid. So I went down the ladder to the deck. I was going to have a quick cigarette and then go back and recheck the message, and if I had to, I was going to wake the captain. Honestly, old man, when that SOS came through, I had trouble believing it myself."

Danny nodded, remembering the disbelief he had witnessed for himself on board the *Titanic*. He could still hear the chorus of scornful voices.

"She's unsinkable."

"Bloody nonsense if you ask me. I'm going to the bar."

"I don't see why I should put my wife in a lifeboat. It's just some ice, nothing to worry about."

"No, no, I'm not going without my jewels. You'll have to fetch them from the purser's safe."

He had listened to those voices for some time before he had ventured out from second class and pushed his way through a melee of increasingly agitated officers and crew until he could see into the radio room.

"Poor old Phillips," Danny said. "I saw him signaling, and Bride was running messages to the bridge. They say Phillips stayed at his post until the end."

"You knew him?" Cottam asked.

"I'd met him before," Danny said. "You know how it is. If we happened to be in port at the same time, we'd meet up. He was a good sort." He shook his head. "I'm sorry he didn't make it. Without him, no one would have known what was happening."

"The *Titanic*'s other operator is here on board," Cottam said.

"Bride, yes. I don't really know him, but I'm glad he got picked up," Danny said. "I hear he's in a bad way. Frostbite." He shivered, realizing that his thoughts had taken him to a place he did not want to be. "What about this girl, then? What was she doing on deck in her nightgown?"

"I don't know," Cottam said. "I didn't have a chance to ask her. I'd come down off the bridge deck, and I was out on the deck lighting a cigarette and talking myself into waking up the captain, and suddenly she was there. I'd been leaning over the rail, and I think she thought I was going to … well, you know …"

"Jump?" Danny queried.

"Oh, yes, I really think she thought I was just some desperate crewman who wanted to end it all. So anyway, I told her about the message, and you should have seen her. She's not just a pretty face— she was practically on fire. I thought she'd go and wake the captain herself. We went up the ladder together, and she waited while I woke the captain. I was going to do it anyway, but having her behind me set me moving."

He leaned over Danny's shoulder. "Are you going to send the message or just sit here all day thinking about that girl?"

"I'm going to do both," Danny said. His hand hovering above the Morse key had stopped trembling. "Go and take your break. I'll take care of this."

CHAPTER FIVE

April 16, 1912
The White House
Washington, DC
Senator William Alden Smith

Hilles was once again blocking the door to the Oval Office. "You can't go in there, Senator Smith. The president will not see anyone."

Bill eyed the closed door and then looked back at Hilles. "You know this isn't right. Whatever his personal tragedy, this can't continue. The nation is in mourning, and still the president, the man who should lead our national mourning, sits behind his desk and grieves for one man—one man out of hundreds. It's not right."

"What do you expect me to do?" Hilles asked. "I follow orders."

"Then follow my orders. Follow the orders of the people I'm elected to represent. I'm going to talk to him, and you are not going to stop me. If you can't agree with me, at least look the other way for a moment."

Hilles gave the briefest of nods and stepped away from the door. "Good luck, Senator."

Afternoon light was filtering through the tall windows, making patterns on the cork floor. The small lamp on the president's desk cast a pool of light over Taft's slumped head and shoulders. Bill could feel the pall of gloom and self-pity that spread throughout the room. He spoke with loud impatience.

"Mr. President."

Taft raised his head to look at his visitor.

"I respect your grief, Mr. President, but we have an urgent situation that must be settled."

Taft shook his head. "Not now. I am waiting for a reply to my telegram."

"Did you send another Marconigram to the *Carpathia*?" Bill asked. "They have told you already that he is not on board."

"No, no, I have sent a telegram to the White Star office in New York. Here it is."

Taft pushed a paper across the desk, and Bill picked it up and read aloud. "'Have you any information concerning Major Butt? If you will communicate with us at once, would greatly appreciate.'"

He set the paper down in disgust. The pleading tone astonished him. "Have they replied?"

Taft shook his head. "No, they do not answer."

"Do they know that this comes from you?" Bill asked. "Perhaps they think it is from some underling." He refrained from adding any comment on the pleading tone of the message.

"They know who it's from."

Bill leaned forward and placed his hands on the president's desk. "Are you telling me, sir, that the White Star Line is refusing to respond to an official request from the president of the United States?"

"They are apparently too busy."

Smith shook his head. "No, that is not the issue. What we are looking at here is a diplomatic crisis precipitated by the arrogance of the British. They do not wish to answer you, because they do not wish to take responsibility for the death of American citizens. This cannot be permitted. We have to act now, before it's too late."

Taft lowered his head again, and Bill stepped back in disgust. It was apparent that Taft was incapable of taking action with his mind still fixated on the death of Archibald Butt. *Well, so be it.* At least Taft would not stand in his way, and he could turn that to his own advantage and also keep Eva Trentham on his side for the future.

"Mr. President," Bill said with as much respect as he could

muster, "I have brought an emergency resolution before the House, establishing a Senate hearing with my own name suggested as chairman. Do I have your permission to say that you will support my appointment? Speed is of the essence."

Taft shook his head. "I don't see why. Speed won't bring back the dead, Senator. I'm sure the British will hold their own inquiry. The *Titanic* was a British ship."

"I respectfully disagree," Bill said, in a tone that carried very little respect. His patience was wearing thin, and he could picture in his own mind the impatience of the American people. The story had caught the national imagination, and the president should be at the center of it, not sending pleading telegrams to the White Star Line like the grieving relative of an unimportant immigrant.

"American citizens died," Bill said, "and American fortunes will be lost. Our people will demand an explanation, and they'll get nothing from the British. There is a lot at stake here, sir. We have to consider the question of compensation for the victims."

"Let the British pay."

"That may not be possible without a full inquiry and the fixing of blame. Under the terms of the Harter Act, we will have to prove negligence by the White Star Line. The British will not do that for us. We will have to do it for ourselves."

"She hit an iceberg," Taft said impatiently. "That is not really anyone's fault. From what I hear, the crew behaved well; the captain went down with his ship; women and children were saved. I believe that the British behaved in an appropriately British fashion according to their own laws, and it is their ship sailing under their flag."

"Once again, I beg to differ," Bill said. "We must ask ourselves what the ship was doing in the midst of an ice field."

"It's the North Atlantic," Taft said, arguing with a little more of his usual energy. "This time of year, there is always the danger of ice."

"But not the danger of hitting an iceberg, not with a good lookout and a careful captain. I believe that the White Star Line brought undue pressure to bear on Captain Smith and insisted on proceeding at an unsafe speed."

"Can you prove it?"

"I can certainly try. The chairman of the line was on board, and I intend to prove that he was responsible for the speed of the ship."

"Well, you can hardly ask him," Taft said, "now that he's at the bottom of the Atlantic."

"But he's not. Sir Bruce Ismay saved himself. He is on the *Carpathia* and heading for New York."

A spark of light came into Taft's eyes. "I wonder if he knows anything about poor dear Archie."

"Sir, really, I must ask you to concentrate on the question at hand. I believe we should proceed with our own inquiry. Do you agree?"

Taft leaned back, and his chair groaned as he shifted his considerable weight. For a moment, he was himself again, shrewd and questioning. "This is an ambitious move," he said. "Do you think it will bring you enough votes to sit in this chair?"

"I'm not concerned with votes. I am doing this for the survivors, the immigrants and widows."

Taft waved a hand. "Get on with it, Smith. I can see right through you, but you're not wrong. It needs to be done, so just do it."

On Board the *Carpathia*
10:00 p.m. (Ship's Time)
Kate Royston

Kate stepped aside as Bridie Conley wheeled Eva out of the bedroom and into the parlor. The Irishwoman had bathed the old lady, combed her wispy hair, and prepared her for bed, and although Kate had heard a great deal of loud complaining coming from the bedroom, both Eva and Bridie seemed to have survived the ordeal. Very soon Bridie would help Eva into bed, and then, if Bridie followed the routine of the night before, she would help herself to a glass of rye from the cabinet in the parlor and sit down to relax. Kate would sit with her—maybe she would pour herself a drink—and they would wait together for the steward to return Wolfie from his evening exercise.

Now that Wolfie was dry and smelling a good deal sweeter, Kate had to admit that he was a handsome dog. Eva declared that he was a valuable specimen of his breed, although she could not actually say what breed. They still did not know who had brought him on board the *Titanic* or what had been his final destination. The White Star would no doubt have a record of his owner, but even Eva would not take up valuable Marconi time in making inquiries.

Kate smoothed the second dress she had managed to retrieve from her former cabin. This one was navy blue, and Eva declared it just as fine as the gray dress. The two dresses were currently all that Kate possessed. Like many other of the women on the *Carpathia*, Kate had donated her spare clothing to the hundreds of women who had still been wearing their nightclothes and their salt-stained dresses. She was not sure how she would replenish her wardrobe, but at this time and in this place, it did not seem important.

Kate knew very little about Bridie Conley, but she knew enough to admire her. Although she was a widow, it was not the *Titanic* that had robbed her of her husband.

"Gone many years," Bridie said the first time they had met. "And me with three small children to raise any way I could. So I found myself work with the Sisters of Charity, not nursing—that was for the nuns—but a woman like me was good enough for skivvying and bedpans and the like. Sure, Mrs. Trentham is no problem. She doesn't weigh more than a small sack of potatoes, and me used to heaving around great fat, lazy men. I'll give you a hand, and all I ask is to lie on a bed and not the floor."

"What will you do when you get to America?" Kate asked.

"I have a fine son in Chicago," Bridie said, "and I'll make my way to him, just like I make my way everywhere, with the help of the Blessed Virgin. Isn't it her who put me in a lifeboat?"

"The Virgin Mary put you in a lifeboat?"

"Well, it wasn't the crew did it," Bridie said. "The crew would have left all of us Irish folk down there in the bottom of the ship without a second thought. No one came to us and said the ship's sinking and we should get ourselves up on deck. 'Tis a miracle that any of us were saved. There was a gate, you see, so that we folk down in steerage couldn't go up on the other decks. That gate had been locked since Queenstown. The folks up above didn't want germs, you see, from us Irish.

"Well, this gate was still locked when we heard these great doings up above and running and shouting, and we wanted to know what it was. One of our fellows tried to break the lock so we could go up, but a sailor came by and threw him down the stairs. I don't know what happened to him after that, because there were so many of us, but then a whole gang of sailors comes back and says that the women and children can go up and unlocks the gate just for us. So up I went.

And just in time."

"Was the ship sinking?" Kate asked.

"Leaning," said Bridie. "Listing, they called it—tipping over to one side—but we didn't know why. There was a great coming and going, and we saw lifeboats being lowered down from up above with ladies in them, and some gentlemen. And then this one boat came down and stopped right in front of us. I don't think it meant to stop. They say its ropes were tangled. All I know is, it was right there in front of us and not more than a handful of people in it, and I said to myself that I was going to give it a try. I wanted to see my son in Chicago, and I thought that if I didn't go then, maybe I would never go. And just as I'm thinking this, a woman comes by with a baby in her arms and throws the baby into the lifeboat. Then she tried to jump, but she couldn't do it, because her shawl caught on something, and she fell down between the boat and the lifeboat—down into the dark. So then I says to myself, 'Who's going to look after that baby?' I crossed myself and I prayed to the Virgin and I jumped, and here I am, safe and sound and drinking that rich lady's rye."

"What about the baby?"

"She's here. There was a woman who lost a young'un, and she still has her milk, so now she has that baby."

Kate stared at Bridie's unconcerned face. "But that's awful."

Eva, who had been listening quietly, leaned forward in her chair. "That's how life is for poor folk," she said. "Bridie will do better in America."

Bridie looked at her with a hint of a smile. "You know, don't you?"

Eva shook her head. "No, I do not, and if you want to stay on the right side of me, you will never make that suggestion again."

A tap on the door heralded the arrival of the steward who had been walking Wolfie. Kate still could not imagine why Eva wanted to keep the dog, but she had to admit his behavior was improving. He did not sleep on the beds, and he no longer growled at Kate, but he still growled at strangers. She supposed that was not really an undesirable trait in a dog. She just wished that he would not leave a trail of loose hair wherever he went. At least, thanks to Bridie's administrations, he no longer smelled of wet wool and seawater.

The steward was departing, having handed Wolfie's leash to Bridie, when another figure appeared in the doorway. Kate felt a sudden flush rising in her cheeks at the sight of Danny McSorley's tall figure and blond beard.

He approached hesitantly. "Miss Kate, Mr. Cottam thinks you should see these telegrams."

"Are they for me?"

"No. They've been sent by Sir Bruce Ismay to the New York office of the White Star Line, and, well, Mr. Cottam thinks they're important."

Eva turned a questioning face to Kate. "Who is this young man?"

"He's one of the *Titanic* survivors."

Eva scowled at Danny. "Are they allowing everyone into the radio room?"

"No, ma'am," Danny said firmly. "I'm a qualified senior radio officer. I was traveling as a passenger on the *Titanic* on my way to my next posting."

"Mr. McSorley is assisting Mr. Cottam with the Marconi messages," Kate said. She was still blushing. How absurd.

Eva extended an imperious hand. "Give them to me."

Danny stepped forward, and Wolfie offered a warning growl. Danny looked down at him. "Oh, shush," he said firmly. "I'm not going to hurt anyone."

Wolfie looked up with sad, intelligent eyes, and Kate wondered what story the dog could tell. How had he managed to stay afloat while so many had drowned?

Danny ruffled the shaggy hair on Wolfie's head and grinned. "I saw him in the water," he said. "I'm glad he's safe. He's an otterhound; you don't see many of them. Someone must have paid a good price for him."

Eva regarded her rescued canine with renewed interest. "Someone with money," she said. "Probably wanted to beat Morgan."

Kate looked from the dog to Eva and back again. "What does this have to do with J. P. Morgan? I know your plans, but how can Mr. Morgan be involved with this dog?"

Eva gave an impatient wave of her hand. "He breeds collies. Wins the Westminster Dog Show every year. Someone with money and a grudge was obviously bringing a rare dog over to give Morgan a run for his money. Wolfie there probably had a mate for breeding."

Danny ruffled Wolfie's hair again, and Kate tried to read tragedy in Wolfie's drooping eyes. Was the poor creature mourning the loss of a mate?

"They have webbed paws," Danny said. "That's probably how he managed to swim for so long, and all that hair keeps the cold out. He's a true survivor."

"So are you," Eva replied, "and so am I, so stop talking about the dog, and tell me what's in these messages that you are about to show me. I'm sure it's something the White Star Line doesn't want the public to know."

"Well," said Danny, "you see—"

Eva interrupted him immediately. "Sit down. Just sit down over there on the chair next to Wolfie. You are entirely too tall, young man, and I can't abide having to look up at you. Sit down and get on with it."

Danny perched himself on the edge of a striped satin Hepplewhite chair and separated the first sheet of paper. "These are messages from Sir Bruce to the White Star office in New York. Mr. Cottam and I believe that Sir Bruce is making arrangements for the *Titanic* crew, what's left of them, to sail immediately back to England without setting foot in the United States."

Eva leaned forward in her wheelchair. "Just read it. I'll tell you what it means."

Danny began to read. "'Most desirable *Titanic* crew aboard *Carpathia* should be returned home earliest moment possible. Suggest you hold *Cedric*, sailing her daylight Friday. Returning in her myself.'"

Eva nodded. "Read the next one."

"'Very important you should hold *Cedric* daylight Friday for *Titanic* crew. Answer.'"

Eva nodded again. "And you say that he has sent these messages to his New York office?"

"Yes, he has. There's one more." Danny resumed his reading. "'Think most unwise to keep *Titanic* crew until Saturday. Strongly urge detaining *Cedric*, sailing her midnight if desirable.'"

Eva sat back and gave Danny an approving nod. "You and Mr. Cottam are quite correct. He's going to get his crew onto the White Star's own ship, the *Cedric*, and be halfway across the Atlantic before anyone can stop him. He has no intention of answering to an American inquiry."

Kate thought about the man she'd glimpsed standing against the rail and watching the bedraggled survivors climbing painfully on board the *Carpathia*. She thought about the throng of angry women and the sign on the cabin door. *Please do not knock.* So that was what he was doing inside there. He was working out how to escape the wrath of the American survivors.

So far as Kate knew, Eva had not yet received a reply to her Marconigram to Senator Smith and her suggestion—well, more than a suggestion—that he should convene an inquiry. She put her thoughts into words. "He'll be long gone before your friend the senator can convene an inquiry, won't he?"

"He would like to be long gone," Eva agreed, "but we have to stop that from happening."

"The British will hold an inquiry," Danny said. "He won't be able to escape that."

"A British inquiry won't get us what we want," Eva declared. "They'll do everything they can to wriggle out of any blame. They don't want to see their Atlantic trade ruined because people don't trust British ships. Any British inquiry would be a farce. It has to happen here, and it has to happen now, while the memory is fresh."

Eva leaned forward and looked Danny in the eye. "You need to pass these messages on to Senator Smith. Can you do that?"

Danny shook his head and let his hand rest on Wolfie's head. "I don't know. As Marconi operators, we have a code of honor, and we maintain the privacy of the people who send messages through us. The newspapers are already trying to find out what we know. They're even offering money. Mr. Cottam and I have been ignoring them, but I can tell you it's going to be a madhouse when we get within reach of New York. After that, nothing will be secret."

"And every survivor will have a different story," Eva said. "Their memories will be confused. I'm confused myself, Mr. McSorley, aren't you?"

"It's beginning to feel unreal," Danny admitted.

"So the story has to be told before it's changed by time and memory and wishful thinking," Eva said. "It has to be told now. By the time Ismay has sailed across the Atlantic with the *Titanic* crew, who knows what they will have dreamed up? But it won't be the truth."

"She's right," Kate said fiercely. "I wasn't on board the *Titanic*, and I don't know what you all went through, but I have some experience of being terribly shocked and very afraid. It was a year ago now, and I know my memory is changing. I probably don't remember everything correctly. If I had to give evidence now, I would ..." She stopped speaking. This was not the time to speak about what had happened to her or confess to the fact that she had run away. She wondered if things would have been different if she had stayed and spoken up, or if someone had insisted on an inquiry.

"I should have said something," she whispered. "People should be given a chance to speak."

Kate met Danny McSorley's inquiring gaze. A shadow lingered in his blue eyes—the memory of cold and shock and utter despair.

"You think I should send the messages," he said.

"I do."

"Then I will," Danny said. "I'll do it now."

April 18, 1912
The Home of Senator William Alden Smith
Washington, DC
5:30 a.m. (Eastern Standard Time)
Senator William Alden Smith

Once again the senator sat in a breakfast room that was totally devoid of breakfast. He was up early, and he would have to wait a full hour before the kitchen maid started to prepare breakfast. He supposed he had the right to wake her, but all things considered, he preferred to leave her to sleep. The last time he had seen her, she had still been red-eyed from weeping for her cousins lost on the *Titanic*.

If they are really lost, Smith thought. Of course, he had the list compiled by the Marconi operator on the *Carpathia*, but who could attest to its accuracy? If the president himself was unwilling to admit that the absence of Archibald Butt's name meant the absence of Butt himself, why shouldn't little Molly want to believe the same? *Maybe because a young Irish maid has more sense than the president of the United States*, Smith thought angrily.

Molly at least believed what Bill had told her. There were no other rescue ships, no groups of gentlemen marooned on an ice floe, no survivors in waterproof compartments. The *Titanic* was gone, and with it had gone some of the richest men of New York society and some of the poorest people of Europe.

Nana, with a shawl thrown around her shoulders, bustled in with a tray of tea. "I don't know why you're up so early. A few hours of sleep won't make any difference to those poor people," she said.

"I have to set the hearing in motion," Bill said, "and give formal notice of the Senate's intention to hold an inquiry, and then I'm going to New York to meet the survivors. The *Carpathia* is due in at about nine thirty tonight, and I think I should be there to represent the people of the United States. Goodness knows, the president isn't going to do anything about it. He just can't get his chin off his desk. I liked Major Butt as much as anyone—he was a good sort—but this grieving has to stop."

Nana lifted the teapot and began to pour. "You can't put a time limit on grieving."

"You can when you have to," Bill said firmly. "His presidency is at stake. We haven't even talked about the fact that he lost the Pennsylvania primary last week. A sitting president asking for another term, and he's beaten in a primary election. If he doesn't wake up and get himself out among the people, he'll lose the presidency to Roosevelt."

"And what will happen to us?" Nana asked.

"I still have my plans," Bill said, "and this Senate inquiry will put me in the public eye. It's important." He stirred sugar into his tea. "That's why I have to be in New York. I can go up on the afternoon train." He glanced at the rain streaming down the tall windows of the breakfast room. "I should take an umbrella."

"Will you stay the night?"

"I suppose so. By the time the people have disembarked, it will be far too late for the midnight train. I'll stay and have a word with some of the survivors. I want to talk to Ismay. I want to know what his story is."

Nana passed him a slip of paper. "These are the names of Molly's relatives. If you have the opportunity, would you …?"

"I'll try, but I doubt I'll succeed. Immigration will be a bureaucratic nightmare. I don't suppose any of the immigrants have their papers."

Nana poured her own tea and sat down across the table. "Those poor people. They were coming here for a new life, and now what will they do?"

Bill shrugged. "I don't know. Perhaps one of the New York charities will help them. It's a manageable number. Seventy-five third-class men, seventy-six women and seven children out of eight hundred eighty-five who boarded in third class." He slipped the paper into his pocket. "There is very little probability that Molly's family were saved."

"But there's a chance. Just see what you can do."

Bill sipped the tea and was silent for a moment. Finally he set down his teacup. "I'm puzzled," he said. "All the first-class children were saved, and all the second-class children, but fifty-two third-class children drowned. There's something there that we're not being told. I choose to believe that if the children were on deck, they would have been saved."

Nana set down the teapot with an angry thump. "No one cared about a gaggle of immigrant children," she said. "They didn't even try."

Bill shook his head. "I don't think so. We don't have the whole story yet, but I hope to find out that we are better than we appear. The *Titanic* had three hundred twenty-five first-class passengers, and from that number, one hundred forty women were saved, and all the children, but only fifty-seven men. That means that one hundred eighty first-class men were not saved, and I can think of only one explanation. I believe that those men obeyed the first rule of the sea. They put the women and children in the lifeboats and sent them on their way. They were the cream of society, millionaires, industrialists, military men, true gentlemen, and they did not try to save themselves. Mistakes were made, and I'm sure that some people put their own lives above the lives of others, but I think that there were heroes, and they need to be honored. If I ask the right questions, perhaps I'll find out who they were, and their names will live on."

Nana's attempt to reply was interrupted by the jangling of the telephone in the study. Bill glanced up at the carriage clock on the mantelpiece. "Who would call me at this ungodly hour?"

He set down his teacup and went across the hall to answer and to give someone a piece of his mind.

The telephone line crackled as it always did on rainy days, but Bill could make out the voice of his clerk, Richard LaSalle.

"I'm sorry to wake you, Senator."

"You didn't wake me. What is it?"

"I'm in the office, sir. We've received a Marconigram from the *Carpathia*, and I think you should come at once."

"Why are you in the office? Do you know what time it is?"

"I came in to prepare the papers for the Senate committee, sir."

"Well," Bill said, "I congratulate you on your enthusiasm, young man, but surely you can do that without phoning me so early in the morning. If you need help, you can wait until Mr. McKinstry comes in."

"Mr. McKinstry does not have a telephone, sir, or I would have called him and not you. We—or I should say, you—have a Marconigram, and I think it is something you should know at once."

LaSalle's voice crackled with urgency, but Bill could not tell from his tone whether the Marconigram was good news or bad news. "What does it say?" he asked impatiently.

"It says that the White Star Line is trying to get the crew of the *Titanic* out of New York without them ever setting foot on American soil. They don't intend to answer questions, sir. If we don't move fast, they'll be beyond our reach."

"Why should I believe this? Who sent the Marconigram?"

"Your friend Eva Trentham, on board the *Carpathia*."

Bill nodded. Now he didn't need to be convinced. Eva never did anything without a very good reason.

"What should I do, sir?"

Bill hesitated for a moment while he gathered his thoughts. LaSalle was an intelligent young man, but he didn't have the age or experience to deal with what would happen next. On the other hand, Will McKinstry, Bill's aide, would know what to do.

"Sir?"

"Get a cab and go to McKinstry's house, and wake him up if he's not already awake. He'll know what to do. We'll have to serve a subpoena on Ismay and the remaining *Titanic* crew to get them off the *Carpathia* and keep them in New York. I'm on my way to the office now."

Bill set down the telephone receiver and hurried up the stairs to his bedroom, with Nana following close behind.

"Bill, what's happened?"

"Bruce Ismay is trying to get the advantage. If he succeeds in getting the *Titanic* crew out of New York before we can question them, we'll never get a true reckoning of what happened. Five of his officers survived, and they're the ones I want to speak to."

He turned to look at Nana, who had pulled a small suitcase from the closet and was carefully folding clean white shirts. He imagined that the angry expression on her face was a good reflection of what he would see in the faces of his own constituents when they found out what had happened on board the *Titanic*. Perhaps the *Titanic* officers who had survived the sinking were true heroes who had gone down with their ship and somehow managed to surface and reach a lifeboat. He didn't know. No one knew. No one would know anything until the *Carpathia* arrived in New York, and then the stories would be told. Some people would speak the truth; some would lie deliberately; and some would simply have no idea what had taken place as they had scrambled to leave the sinking ship. Eva Trentham's idea of pinning the blame for the disaster on the British chairman of the White Star Line and his British crew would be a diplomatic risk, but one worth taking.

Let the British bluster, he thought as he snapped the lid of his suitcase and hurried outside to find a cab. With the possibility of war brewing in Europe, Britain would expect, maybe even demand, the support of the United States. Yes, they would be offended at the detention of their citizens, but they would not risk their unspoken partnership with the United States. He only hoped that Taft would not suddenly shake himself from his grief and realize what the senator from Michigan was up to. He would need to present Taft with a fait accompli—an investigation already underway and witnesses already facing the Senate committee. There would be no time to move the witnesses to Washington. He would have to make a start in New York, maybe a room at the Waldorf Astoria. Well, one thing at a time, and the first step would be to issue a subpoena to Bruce Ismay before he could sneak himself off the *Carpathia*.

Bill arrived at the Russell Senate Office Building just as the junior staff members were making their appearance for the day. The senators would arrive later. Bill would have to ask McKinstry to make certain that Senator Newlands was advised of the situation, because Newlands would also have to go to New York. Bill could not do this alone.

Bill glanced in at the door of his own office and found it unoccupied. Well, Bill thought, he didn't need either one of his aides to tell him what to do next. He had his own law degree; he knew what was required, and he had no time to waste. He imagined the *Carpathia* steaming steadily toward New York. She would be well south of Halifax by now. Although Captain Rostron was no doubt anxious to land his seven hundred unexpected passengers, he wouldn't be racing for New York. Icebergs were still drifting close to the shipping lanes, and the overloaded *Carpathia* could not afford a collision. She would not have sufficient lifeboats for another seven hundred people.

Bill paused outside the door of the sergeant at arms. No, the *Carpathia* would not have lifeboats for another seven hundred people, but what about the *Titanic?* The *Carpathia* had only picked up thirteen lifeboats. Where were the other lifeboats? Had they failed to launch? Had they been lost, or had they never existed?

Bill opened the door without knocking and found Daniel Ransdell at his desk. Ransdell rose respectfully.

"Senator Smith."

Bill could not waste words on polite niceties, not with the image of the *Carpathia* steaming past Nantucket and only hours from New York. "Sergeant at Arms, I need you to come to New York and serve a subpoena on the owner and crew of the *Titanic* before they are landed."

Ransdell set his lips in a straight line. "I'm sorry, Senator, but I can't do that."

"Why not?"

"It's beyond my authority, Senator. I can't be arresting foreign citizens on a foreign-registered ship. If you wait until they come ashore—"

"They're not coming ashore."

Ransdell shook his head. "Then I can't help you."

Bill looked at the set of Ransdell's face and knew that nothing he could say would move the sergeant at arms to travel to New York with him.

He walked slowly back toward his office, wondering where he would find a law officer willing to risk his career by playing a game of diplomatic brinkmanship with the British. With only a few hours before the *Carpathia* docked in New York, Bill could think of no one.

CHAPTER SIX

On Board the *Carpathia*
Kate Royston

Danny McSorley was once again perched on the striped satin chair in Eva Trentham's suite. His shock of blond hair was standing on end, and his jacket was spattered with rainwater. Wolfie, equally as wet and ungroomed, lay at Danny's feet, wreathed in an odor of wet wool but gazing at Danny with adoring eyes.

Bridie bustled in from the bedroom with a towel for Danny's hair. "Wipe your head," she said, "but don't be wiping that dog."

Eva Trentham, ensconced in her wheelchair, shook her head at Bridie. "It's not our towel, Bridie. We don't have to do the laundry. Let him do what he likes with the towel." She gave Danny one of her rare smiles. "I'm just glad you took Wolfie for an airing. I don't understand why the steward refused to walk him."

"Because it's pouring with rain and the steward is very busy," Kate said.

"I think I should register a complaint," Eva sniffed. "We're in a first-class suite, and I expect first-class service."

"Well," said Bridie, leaning on the back of the wheelchair, "you didn't pay for the cabin, did you, missus? None of us paid to be on this ship."

Eva shook her head. "Don't be snippy with me, Bridie, not if you expect me to employ you in New York."

Bridie took a step back. "Well, I wasn't expecting you to—"

"So you would rather be cast up on the shore, penniless with no papers, would you?"

"Well, no, of course not, but I have my son in Chicago."

"And how are you to get to Chicago? Stay with me while my leg heals, and I'll see you get there."

Kate registered the note of pleading in Eva's voice. The old woman would never say please or make a humble request, but it was obvious that she needed Bridie, and equally obvious that Bridie needed her.

And what about me? Kate thought. She had carefully avoided contact with her employers since she had been hijacked by Eva Trentham. With *Titanic* survivors crammed into every corner of the ship, avoiding Mrs. van Buren had been easy, but soon they would land in New York, and then what would happen? Would they want to reemploy the governess who had abandoned them? Would they even pay her wages for the few days they had been at sea and she had cared for the children?

She realized with a sinking heart that there was a very real possibility that she would have nowhere to go when she landed. She looked at Eva and wondered if she could continue as her helper. It was not that she liked the comfort of Eva's suite—she had willingly abandoned that kind of comfort months ago. And it was not that she liked the old lady—well, not really. If she stayed with Eva, it would be out of sheer desperation, and she suspected that where Eva was concerned, a direct request would be rebuffed, not because Eva did not want her but because Eva could never be anything but contrary.

Wolfie gave a low growl, and a moment later, Kate heard a light tapping on the door. As Bridie had returned to the bedroom and Danny was busy drying Wolfie's wet fur, she crossed to the door herself and pulled it open.

"If it's the steward, tell him he's too late," Eva said, "and I will not be giving him a tip when we reach New York."

"It's not the steward," Kate said, looking at the middle-aged man waiting in the doorway. His tweed suit and vest were a perfect fit, and he did not have the stunned look of a man who had been in a shipwreck. Kate assumed, therefore, that he was one of the *Carpathia*'s original passengers and not a survivor of the *Titanic*.

"Mrs. Eva Trentham?" he asked, smiling ingratiatingly from behind a small black mustache.

"No," said Kate.

The stranger nodded. "Very well. If you are not Mrs. Trentham, are you another survivor of the wreck?"

"No, I'm not."

The stranger took a step forward. Kate put her shoulder against the door and tried to push him back. "You can't come in. What do you want?"

"Carlos Hurd of the *St. Louis Post-Dispatch*. My wife and I were on the *Carpathia* on our way to Naples. Now I am interviewing survivors. I would like to get the full story behind the sinking. The world is waiting for news. Newspaper publishers have already hired boats to carry their reporters out to meet us."

"Surely not," Kate said.

Danny looked up from his dog grooming. "It's true. They have. But I don't think you should speak to that man. We know all about him in the Marconi room. He's been trying to send messages to his newspaper and arrange for what he calls a scoop. We don't let him in anymore."

Hurd peered past Kate and saw Danny kneeling on the floor beside Wolfie. "Oh, it's you."

"Yes, it's me," Danny said, rising to his feet, "and we are not sending any more messages for you or your wife. You'll have to wait like everyone else. This lady asked you to leave, so I suggest you leave before I throw you out."

Kate felt a sudden surge of elation realizing that she had a protector.

Hurd rummaged in his pocket and produced a small scrap of paper—Kate thought it looked very much like toilet paper—and a stub of pencil. "I'd like to interview Mrs. Trentham," he said.

Kate stared at the scrap of paper. "If you're a real newspaperman, why don't you have a notebook?"

"He doesn't have any paper," Danny said. "The captain has made sure that no one will give him paper. He can't buy it at the gift shop, and we've taken the paper out of the writing room. He has nothing

74

left to write on." He took a step toward Hurd. "Go away. Mrs. Trentham won't tell you anything."

Eva's voice rose angrily from the interior of the suite. "Stop that. Don't let him leave. Bridie, push me forward. Hurry up. I want to speak to this man. Don't stand there, Kate. Let him in and find him a real piece of paper. I have a lot to tell him."

Bridie appeared from the bedroom and began to push Eva toward the door. Hurd pushed past Danny triumphantly. "So, Mrs. Trentham, what can you tell me about the sinking?"

"I can tell you who caused it," Eva said. "Danny, get out of the way and move that smelly dog. Let Mr. Hurd sit down while I tell him all about Bruce Ismay."

Hurd took the paper and pencil Kate was holding out to him and sat down, resting the paper on his knee and writing in a form of shorthand Kate had never seen before. She assumed it was the only way a reporter could make a verbatim record of an interview.

"I have been unable to interview Sir Bruce," Hurd said. "I don't believe he's come out of the doctor's cabin."

"Of course not," Eva hissed. "He's hiding. Wouldn't you hide if you knew you had been responsible for killing all those people?"

"Responsible?" Hurd queried, lifting his pencil from the page. "I have heard from a number of people that he should not have had a seat in a lifeboat. His behavior was not that of a gentleman, but he only took up one seat, and that does not make him responsible for all those deaths. I have even heard that he sent lifeboats away before they were full, but still—"

"Stuff and nonsense," Eva snapped. "I'm not talking about seats in lifeboats. I'm talking about driving his ship at full speed into an iceberg."

"But that was the captain's responsibility."

"No, it wasn't. I heard you say that you are going to scoop all the other papers. If you can tell me how you plan to do that, I will tell you what I know, and I will give you a real scoop."

Kate dropped to her knees beside Eva's wheelchair. "Are you sure you should do this? What do you really know that no one else knows?"

"Don't tell me what to do," Eva responded under her breath. "I told you that I'm going to bring down Ismay, and now I know how to do it. If this newspaper fellow knows how to get his scoop ahead of everyone else, it won't matter what comes out later. The first story people read will be the story they believe."

"But you can't lie," Kate whispered.

"I can if I want, but it just so happens that I don't need to. I know how to prove that he was the one behind the ship's speed. I have witnesses. Now, get out of my way and let me talk to him."

Kate moved aside reluctantly, and Eva faced the newspaperman. "What's your plan? How do you intend to be first with the news if the radio operators will not allow you to send messages?"

"We won't," Danny confirmed.

Hurd's mustache lifted as he sneered. "I sent the only message I need to send long before you and your colleagues decided to deny me access and play your silly games with stopping me from having paper to write on. Now I have paper, and now you'll see what I can do. The *New York World* is sending out a fast boat, and they'll be looking for my dispatches, which I intend to throw overboard in a watertight container when I catch sight of them." He looked at Danny. "We'll have our scoop with interviews with the survivors, and you can't stop us."

"Eva," Kate said, "please don't do this. Do you know what it means to ruin a man's reputation?"

"It won't be the first time," Eva replied. "Let me tell Mr. Hurd what I know, and you can listen if you wish. I think you'll be very interested in what I have to say. You may even change your mind about Sir Bruce Ismay and where the blame lies for all these deaths."

She turned to Hurd, and Kate watched in fascination as his pencil flew across the paper, making squiggles that could only be read by another newspaperman.

"It was Sunday," Eva said, "about three thirty, and I was taking my tea on the first-class promenade." She paused for a moment. "It seems like a lifetime ago," she said softly.

She shivered and abruptly returned to her normal sharp tone. "It was very cold on the deck, and I sent the steward for blankets. I must say that the crew was not very efficient. They seemed to be only partially trained. I know it was a maiden voyage, but one does expect better. Perhaps that's why they didn't ..."

"Didn't what?" Hurd asked.

"Didn't know how to launch the lifeboats," Eva snapped. "Didn't know how to row. Didn't know the damned ship was sinking. Didn't know anything."

Hurd's writing flowed across the paper, taking down Eva's complaints. As he wrote, he licked his lips. *He's enjoying this*, Kate thought. *He's getting his scoop.*

"I saw some passengers walking toward me," Eva said. "I knew at once that the ladies were Mrs. Arthur Ryerson and Mrs. John Thayer, and of course, the Thayer boy was with them. I think his name is Jack. I've seen him since we came on board the *Carpathia*, so I know that he was rescued along with his mother. His father, of course, was not rescued."

She paused again. Kate thought that Eva was not finding it easy to tell this story. For all her irritable sharpness, she was not without emotion.

"They were not alone," she continued. "They had Sir Bruce Ismay with them. I wouldn't normally give that man the time of day, but I thought I should say something to Mrs. Ryerson. It was the first time I had seen her outside her cabin. She had been shut away ever since we left Cherbourg. The family suffered a loss, you know. A son killed in an automobile accident. I thought I should offer sympathy.

"They reached me before I could even get myself out of the deck chair, and Mrs. Ryerson was just chattering away. She's like that. She's a chatterer. I can't stand women who chatter. She started to tell me that we were in the vicinity of icebergs. Well, I could have told her that myself. Why else would it be so cold?

"Before I could stop him, Ismay started waving papers in my face and telling me what a wonderful thing the Marconi was and how the captain had personally shown him these ice warnings and how there was no danger of us being in the ice, because he now knew where the ice was. You would think he was personally steering the ship. He said they were going to fire up a couple more boilers, and they would have us in New York in record time. When Mrs. Ryerson continued to fuss about the ice, Ismay pointed up at the crow's nest and said they had doubled the lookout and there was absolutely no danger."

Eva was silent for a moment, and her sharp, bright eyes were suddenly shadowed. "The captain wasn't in charge of the ship," she said. "Ismay was."

Hurd made a final notation on the paper. "May I keep the pencil?" he asked. "I'm afraid we only have one other, and my wife is using it."

Eva nodded enthusiastically. "Certainly you may if it will help you speed your message to your editor. Are you sure your container will float?"

Hurd grinned triumphantly. "Champagne corks," he said. "No one has stopped me from collecting champagne corks. I'll attach them to the box, and it will float. I believe we are already in sight of land. It won't be long now, and even with this rain and wind, I have no doubt my editor will secure a boat to meet us."

"It's going to be chaos," Danny said.

When Kate looked at him quizzically, he gave her a disbelieving smile. "You don't know, do you?"

"Know what?"

"Thousands and thousands of people are waiting for us. We are the biggest story since the assassination of President McKinley, or maybe even the assassination of Lincoln."

"Well, it's a tragedy," Kate said, "but it's not like a presidential assassination."

Eva leaned forward in her chair. "You're wrong, Kate. Some of the men who died had more money and more power than any president." She made a shooing gesture with her hand to send Hurd on his way. "Write it up, Mr. Hurd, and make sure you have enough champagne corks."

When the door closed behind Hurd, Kate saw a change of expression on Eva's face: triumph replaced for just a moment by a look of utter despair.

Bridie leaned down from her position behind the wheelchair and rested a hand on Eva's shoulder. "There, there," she said soothingly. "Don't fret yourself. Just do what you can for those who can't do for themselves. It's the only way through grief."

Anger flickered across Eva's face. She pulled away from Bridie's comforting hand and gave Kate a self-satisfied smile. "Ismay is going to regret the day he told the captain to light up another boiler."

☐

CHAPTER SEVEN

The Russell Senate Office Building
Washington, DC
Senator William Alden Smith

Bill paced back and forth in front of Will McKinstry's desk. "He should be here by now," he declared. "You should have gone yourself instead of sending LaSalle."

McKinstry shook his head. "I thought it best to send LaSalle while I prepared the paperwork. He'll find him, Senator. Of course, if you knew where he was staying, it would be easier."

"Of course it would," Bill snapped, "but I don't know. I doubt it's the Willard—Joe doesn't have that kind of money—but it will be somewhere close. Maybe a boarding house."

McKinstry nodded and returned to shuffling papers. "I think this is all we'll need. I have a subpoena for Sir Bruce Ismay, another for the officers of the *Titanic* by name, Charles Lightoller, Herbert Pitman, Joseph Boxhall, and Harold Lowe. I have one for Frederick Fleet, the man who was on lookout and did not, apparently, see the iceberg, and another that allows you to detain all or any of the remaining White Star employees at your discretion. I have added a subpoena for the remaining Marconi operator, Harold Bride. They are all British citizens, and this will create a diplomatic problem, but these documents are fully legal under the law of the United States, and if your friend Sheriff Bayliss is duly sworn, we should be able to achieve our objective."

"If we can find Bayliss," Bill added as he resumed his pacing.

"We'll find him," McKinstry said firmly. "We still have several hours before we need to board the train. The *Carpathia* is not due in until this evening, and Senator Newlands has gone home to pack his suitcase."

"And you've reserved a meeting room at the Waldorf Astoria? We can't bring them all back to Washington. We'll have to make a start in New York."

"I have the meeting room," McKinstry said, "and I have also reserved accommodation for our entire party. When the *Carpathia* docks, I think that a number of passengers will come ashore looking for a place to stay, and we need to get ahead of them, or we'll have nowhere to lay our heads tonight."

"Well done," Bill said as he continued pacing.

"And one more thing," McKinstry said.

"What?"

"I think we should also subpoena the *Titanic*'s logbook."

Bill stood still and looked at his secretary with sudden admiration. "I didn't think of that. Would the logbook have survived? It could have gone down with the ship."

"No, that should not be the case. When the order is given to take to the lifeboats, the captain is required to give the logbook into the care of the first officer to enter a lifeboat. Of course, we don't know yet who that is, but I think we can be certain that Captain Smith would have followed tradition, and one of those surviving officers has the logbook. We just have to find which one."

"I knew him," Bill said. "I knew Captain Smith. My wife and I sailed with him on several occasions. He was a good man. I can't imagine what happened. He was very experienced, and he'd sailed that route dozens of times, maybe even hundreds. He would know to look for icebergs."

Bill shook his head, remembering Edward Smith, with his neatly trimmed white beard, his immaculate uniform, and his air of command. He sighed, suddenly overcome with grief as he put a face to the disaster. Hundreds had died, but at that moment, Edward Smith was the man he chose to remember. He fought against a prickling at the back of his eyes. There would be much crying in the days ahead, but he would not cry.

As he fought back the tears, he was relieved to hear footsteps on the marble floor outside his office. He turned to see LaSalle accompanying a tall, lanky man in an unfashionable suit. Sheriff Joe Bayliss of Chippewa County, Michigan, the man who had the courage to do what needed to be done.

Bayliss greeted Bill with a wolfish grin and a firm handshake. His voice was the low growl of a man who had seen many cold Michigan winters, smoked too much rough tobacco, and drunk too much rough whiskey. It was a voice to be reckoned with.

"Are you willing to do this?" Bill asked. "It may have consequences for all of us."

The grin faded as Joe, towering over Bill, set his face into a mask of grim determination. "Hang the consequences," he said. "Take me to your sergeant at arms. If he doesn't have the guts for the job, well, I do. Let him swear me in, and I'll serve the subpoenas."

On Board the *Carpathia*
Outside New York Harbor
Kate Royston

Danny stood in the doorway of Eva Trentham's suite. Once again his hair was standing on end. Kate wondered what he would look like with his hair and beard groomed, and wearing a suit instead of a borrowed fisherman-knit sweater. She wondered what he was going to do now that he was arriving at the end of his dreadful journey. Would he still continue on to Cape Race? Did he have money for his passage north into Canada? Would he even want to get on board another ship?

Eva, her hair combed, and wearing a borrowed coat and hat, sat in the wheelchair that had become her throne, with Bridie attending her. Bridie had managed to cut and shape a blanket into a traveling cape for herself, and her expression was relaxed. She and Eva had reached a compromise. Bridie would stay with Eva until her leg healed, and then Eva would pay for her to join her family in Chicago.

As Eva insisted on saying repeatedly, Bridie had luck on her side, but Bridie did not believe in luck. So far as she was concerned, it was the Virgin Mary who had found her a place in a lifeboat, kept her alive through the long, cold night, and finally brought her here to attend to Eva.

"Sure, Mrs. Trentham is a nasty old soul," Bridie had whispered to Kate, "but she's doing the Holy Mother's work in finding me a place. What in the world will happen to all those poor immigrant folk when they're cast ashore?" She shook her head. "The grieving has not even begun. When the shock wears off, and those poor folk stand in their new land with nothing but the clothes they're wearing, women without a husband, children without a father or a mother, then you'll hear the keening and the crying, and not a soul to help them."

"Are any of you coming up on deck?" Danny asked from the doorway. "It's raining and blowing, but it's a sight to see."

"Why would I go out in the rain and cold?" Eva asked. "After the night we spent in that lifeboat, I don't intend to be cold ever again. I don't understand you, young man. You are far too cheerful."

Danny stepped into the room. "Well, I've good news. I have a message from Cape Race to say that money has been wired for my journey north, and some extra to replace my clothes. I'm one of the lucky ones. I know where I'm going. I don't know where I'll lay my head tonight, but it can't be in a worse place than I've been in the last few nights."

Kate looked at him thoughtfully. She had not thought to ask where he was sleeping. Even in the isolation of Eva Trentham's suite, she had heard about conditions on board, people sleeping on the open deck, even a man who had tried to sleep in a bathtub and had to be removed by the crew.

"I've been sleeping on the floor in the radio room," Danny said. "It's better than some people have." He gave Kate an encouraging smile. "Come up on deck, Miss Kate, and see what's happening. The harbor is full of boats all racing out to meet us. Please come and look. You won't see the like of this again."

Kate hesitated. The luxury of Eva Trentham's suite reminded her of the comfortable life she had once lived. She would never find such comfort as governess to the Van Buren children, whose parents were comfortably well off but definitely not rich. She wanted to go up on deck, but she didn't want to spend time away from Eva Trentham and the possibility that Eva might offer her employment as a traveling companion. Paid traveling companion was definitely one step up from governess, and as long as Kate stayed by the old lady's side, she could still hope that Eva would make her a last-minute offer.

On the other hand, if the old lady had no intention of offering her employment, she really should find the Van Burens and discover whether she still had a position with them. If they told her they were not continuing their voyage, or if they told her that she had let them down and they no longer wanted to employ her, she would be no better off than the poorest immigrant from the *Titanic*.

Eva dismissed Kate with a wave of her hand. "Go with him, and take Wolfie with you."

Danny McSorley

Danny watched as Kate clipped an improvised leash on the collar he had fashioned for Wolfie using an old leather belt. When he had first met her in the radio room, Kate had seemed full of fire and determination, but today she looked pale and worried. He wondered what position she held with Mrs. Trentham. Cottam had said that Kate was a first-class passenger, but in Eva's suite, she seemed to be more like a servant, or a secretary, and she was still very plainly dressed. He told himself that he only concerned himself with who or what she was in order to take his mind off other things. The memories still rushed at him, and the blood-soaked envelope was still in his pocket. It was far easier to think about Kate than to think about what was behind and what lay ahead.

He led Kate out onto the first-class promenade deck. In the confusion and crowding on the *Carpathia*, class distinctions had become irrelevant, and the railing along the first-class promenade deck was lined with passengers standing in the gusty wind and blowing rain to see the lights of New York. Looking ahead, Danny could see a US Navy cruiser clearing a path for them through the myriad of private boats swarming from the shore to meet them. He saw fishing boats, private yachts, and even ferryboats bearing down on the *Carpathia*. Around them, the night was made bright by the lights of a thousand camera flashes, revealing flickering glimpses of the Statue of Liberty on her windblown island. He had been at sea since he was eighteen and had arrived at harbors all over the world, but he had never seen an arrival like this.

He reached out impulsively and took Kate's hand to pull her toward the rail. Wolfie resisted the pull on the leash but finally gave in and followed them. Danny was thrilled that he now had a clear view of the Statue of Liberty, and he turned to Kate, hoping she would join in his excitement. "So that's her," he said. "That's the Statue of Liberty. There were moments when I thought I would never live to see her."

Kate looked up at the towering statue. For some reason, she seemed unhappy to be seeing it. Her mood puzzled him. Surely she was glad to be returning to New York. The journey on the *Carpathia* had been a nightmare for everyone, not only the survivors from the *Titanic* but also the passengers on the *Carpathia*.

"We talked about this in the lifeboat," Danny said. "We promised each other that we would survive and we would live to see the Statue of Liberty." He squeezed her hand. "There she is, and I'm alive to see her and standing next to a pretty girl."

Despite the cold rain, Danny thought he saw a flush on Kate's pale cheeks. He wished he could read her expression. Either she was flattered by his attention, or she was embarrassed to be holding hands with a mere radio operator. Something about her somber mood washed off on him. He was elated to see New York, but this was not the end of the road. Eventually, he would go on to Cape Race, but before he did that, he had a pledge to fulfill, and he had no idea what would be involved.

It was her turn to stare at him. She squeezed his hand and then released it. "Are you all right?" she asked.

He looked down at her. "How do I get to Washington, Miss Kate?"

"I've never been there myself," Kate said, "but I suppose you would take a train. I thought you wanted to see New York."

He shook his head. "I have to go to Washington."

Wolfie growled a warning as someone pushed him aside and took a position beside the rail. Carlos Hurd, the newspaperman, gave them a triumphant smile and showed them the package he held in his hands. So this was his scoop, Danny thought, a bulky package wrapped in waterproof yellow fabric torn from a raincoat or a sou'wester, and dozens of champagne corks trailing from strings.

The *Carpathia* nosed its way forward with the *Chester* clearing a path. A brightly lit tugboat approached at speed and dodged past the US Navy cruiser. A light on the tugboat flashed on and off in rapid sequence.

"There you are," Hurd said. "That's my signal."

He hurled the package from the rail, and Danny found that he was holding his breath to see if it would float. He knew what the package contained. Despite the captain's orders to the contrary, and despite a concerted effort by the crew to deprive Hurd of writing paper, he had managed to obtain interviews with almost every survivor on board. His newspaper would have its front-page headlines before any of the other papers had even been allowed a single interview. No doubt the papers would feature Eva Trentham's damning indictment of Sir Bruce Ismay, accusing him of being personally responsible for the loss of the *Titanic*. Danny thought about the messages that Cottam had intercepted. Ismay would try to keep the *Titanic*'s crew from setting foot ashore. If he succeeded in returning to Britain, it would not matter what the American newspapers said about him, but if he stayed in America, it would be quite a different story.

The package fell toward the water but quickly became entangled in rigging on the deck below. Hurd cursed under his breath, and just as he was turning away, no doubt to run down to the lower deck, an arm reached out from the deck below, untangled the package, and helped it on its way. The tugboat sent out a searchlight beam that knifed through the rain and settled on Hurd's floating package. The *Carpathia* plowed on relentlessly, but Danny looked back into the ship's wake and saw a crew member from the tugboat leaning out across the water with a long-handled boat hook.

Carl Hurd crowed triumphantly and rubbed his hands together. "Well, that's my work done." He nodded to Kate. "Tell Mrs. Trentham I'm really grateful."

Before Kate could respond, she was startled by a short, sharp blast from the *Carpathia*'s horn. Danny saw her step back at the sudden shock, and her hands flew up in surprise, releasing her hold on Wolfie's leash. Wolfie barked excitedly and hurtled toward the rail. He rose onto his hind legs. He was going to jump. Danny shouted an angry command at the heedless dog. After all that Wolfie had been through, surely he wasn't going to drown right here and right now, just yards from safety.

Kate pulled her hand from Danny's grasp and flung herself toward the rail. She grasped a handful of Wolfie's hair, and the dog, deprived of an opportunity to hurl himself into the water, fell backward and landed on top of Kate. The ship began to turn, and the deck tilted. Kate and Wolfie were sliding toward the edge.

For Danny, time seemed to stand still. He was no longer on the *Carpathia*. He was one of the hundreds of helpless people sliding across the deck of the *Titanic* as the ship buried her bow into the icy water. The rain gusting around the *Carpathia* became the icy water of the deep Atlantic swirling around his feet. He relived the moment of the gunshot and the blood and the letter thrust into his hands.

He fought off the paralysis of memory and lunged forward. He grasped Wolfie's collar with one hand and Kate's collar with the other hand. He was not willing to let either one of them fall into the churning waters of the Hudson River. Before he could pull Kate to her feet, he was surrounded by helping hands and raised voices, and he was left to hold Wolfie's collar while other hands set Kate on her feet. He realized that she would never even know what he had done to save her or how hard it had been to overcome that momentary paralysis.

Kate cast off the helping hands and smoothed her coat with shaking hands. "Is Wolfie all right?"

"Sure," said Danny. "Wolfie's fine." He was suddenly angry with her. She had come close to drowning herself, and him along with her, because if she had gone over, he would have gone after her. "You didn't need to try to drown yourself," he said.

"He was going to jump."

"He can swim," Danny said. He took a deep breath and made an effort to overcome his anger. She would never understand, so why try? He forced a smile. "You should have seen him out there, swimming between the lifeboats and looking for a hand to pull him out. He's a survivor."

"So are you," Kate said a little breathlessly, still smoothing her clothes. "How did you manage to survive?"

Danny shook his head. "I don't want to talk about it. It's over, and we're here—that's all that matters."

"We're still turning," Kate said. "Why are we doing that? I thought we'd arrived."

Danny wiped the rain from his face and leaned out over the rail, grimacing as he saw the water far below. Perhaps it was a good thing that his posting to Cape Race would keep him on land for a while.

He looked across at the crowded shore and a mass of people standing silently in the rain alongside Pier 54, the Cunard dock. The men removed their hats and the women bowed their heads as the *Carpathia* passed them by.

He felt Kate's presence beside him. "We're not stopping," she said. "What's happening?"

Danny leaned farther out and looked forward. "The crew is doing something with our lifeboats."

"What do you mean?"

"Our lifeboats," he repeated with a lump in his throat, realizing that the *Titanic* and her lifeboats would be forever his to remember. "They're lowering the *Titanic*'s lifeboats."

The *Carpathia* had slowed almost to a standstill. Danny leaned over the rail again. He shook his head as he felt tears prickling at the back of his eyes. "They shouldn't do this," he whispered. "It's too much. Too much."

Kate threaded her hand through his arm, but he could not speak. He could only watch as the *Carpathia* ghosted toward the White Star dock. Without any orders given aloud, or words spoken from the shore, the *Carpathia* lowered the *Titanic*'s lifeboats into the water, and a remnant of the *Titanic*'s crew took to the oars and rowed them into the gaping mouth of Pier 59 to return all that remained of the *Titanic*.

Kate Royston

The grim silence lingered as the helmsman backed the *Carpathia* away from Pier 59, leaving the lifeboats as a ghastly reminder of the *Titanic*'s fate. Time seemed to crawl as the *Carpathia* drifted almost silently into her berth on Pier 54. It was not until the great mooring ropes had been fed to the waiting longshoremen that the *Carpathia*'s steam horn blew one long, mournful whistle. *Arrived in port.* Now people on the shore began to call out, and the passengers and survivors on the *Carpathia* turned away from the rail and hurriedly prepared to disembark.

Looking down, Kate could see the gangplank being extended from several decks below. Uniformed officials waited at the foot of the gangplank, and police held back an eager crowd. The flotilla of boats that had rushed down the Hudson to meet them in the harbor now tried to squeeze into the berth alongside the *Carpathia* while cameras flashed and reporters used megaphones to shout questions and even offer money.

The *Carpathia*'s stewards passed among the throng of passengers, some with luggage, some with nothing but the clothes they stood up in.

"*Carpathia*'s passengers will be first ashore. *Carpathia* passengers to the Grand Salon. All *Carpathia* passengers must go ashore. If you still intend to sail with *Carpathia*, you will be issued a ticket. We will sail again in three days. *Carpathia* passengers to go ashore. All *Titanic* passengers wait on the stern deck. *Carpathia* passengers only."

Kate stood still for a moment. Should she go back to Eva, or should she find the Van Burens?

"Shouldn't you be leaving?" Danny said. "You were a *Carpathia* passenger, weren't you?"

"Yes, I was, but …"

Kate waited, not at all sure what she wanted Danny to say. He thrust out a hand. "It's been a pleasure to know you, Miss Kate. Good luck."

Kate returned his handshake, considered kissing him on the cheek just to make him feel uncomfortable, then thought better of it. She rested a hand on Wolfie's head. "Good luck, Wolfie. Stay dry."

As Kate left the promenade, she discovered Mrs. Broomer waiting for her. "Ah, Miss Royston, I've been looking for you. I want to tell you how grateful we are for your assistance with Mrs. Trentham."

"Is she …?"

"What?"

"Is she asking for me?"

"No, I don't think so. I believe she's employed one of the immigrant women to take care of her needs, and of course, her own household servants will be here to meet her. You're free to go now, Miss Royston, with the thanks of the Cunard Line. Your portmanteau is in your cabin."

So that was it. Eva Trentham had her own servants. She had no need of Kate. So now all that was left for Kate to do was find the Van Burens before they disembarked.

Kate entered her cabin for the first time in two days and found the Countess of Rothes lounging on one of the beds. "I've packed your bag," she said. "I folded your apron and put it in there. I assume it is actually the property of the *Carpathia*, but I thought you should have a souvenir of what you did for the survivors." She gave Kate a genuine smile. "You did well. I hope the White Star Line will find a way to express its appreciation."

Kate shook her head. "I doubt that anyone even noticed me, with so many important people coming aboard."

"I noticed you," the countess said.

Kate lowered her eyes and stared at the floor.

"I see," said the countess. "You don't want to be noticed, do you? Are you running away?"

"Of course not," Kate said brusquely. She looked around the cabin. "What have you done with my identity papers?"

"I placed them on top of your clothes, where they will be easy to reach when you leave the ship. I put them together with your ticket. You'll need them both when you leave the ship. If you plan to do a lot of traveling, you should get one of the new passports. So much easier."

Kate remained silent, and the countess laughed gently. "You don't know what you plan to do, do you? Well, if it's any comfort, I have also included my calling card. If you find yourself short of employment, you may present it to my housekeeper, and she will find a way to assist you."

Kate stared at the countess in disbelief. Domestic work! Did the countess really think that Kate was desperate enough to take work as a parlor maid?

The countess continued to prattle on, apparently oblivious to the effect of her words. "You're better off than the rest of us who have no papers," she said. "You should be careful not to let yours be stolen."

Kate tried to avoid scowling. She didn't need the countess to tell her how to handle her papers.

"Of course," the countess continued, "I won't have a problem. I have a very recognizable face and, shall we say, persona."

Kate bit her tongue. She could see no point in arguing or defending herself, and in fact, the countess could be correct in her assessment. Perhaps all that was left for Kate was to become a parlor maid.

"By the way," the countess asked, "how is Wolfie?"

"He's fine. He'll go with Mrs. Trentham."

The countess raised her eyebrows. "Oh dear. Poor dog. That woman is truly dreadful, but no one else will say it, because she can ruin anyone just like that." The countess snapped her fingers. "Not me, of course. I do nothing to protect my reputation, and so she can do nothing to ruin it. I'm told she has her knife in Sir Bruce Ismay."

"With good reason," Kate declared as she picked up her bag. "He saved himself."

"So did I."

"But you're a woman."

"Yes, seems a bit unfair, doesn't it? I save myself, just like Molly Brown, and we're both heroines. Sir Bruce saves himself and he's a villain, a blaggard." The countess shrugged her shoulders. "Run along, Miss Royston. Run as fast as you can, before you lose your firm grasp on right and wrong."

Kate turned sharply and hurried out of the cabin, struggling with the weight of her bag. She had so few earthly possessions—how could it be so heavy? As she entered the Grand Salon, now only a very untidy shadow of its former grandeur, she saw the Van Buren family waiting with their hand luggage resting at their feet. Mr. van Buren, a tall, balding man with a mustache worthy of a walrus, peered over the heads of the crowd, searching for someone. His eyes lit up when he saw her, and he waved her toward him.

Kate took a deep breath—time to find out what the future held in store. She was not sure what outcome she could expect, but she knew the possibilities. The Van Burens would refuse to pay her for her time with them, because she had, in fact, deserted them, or they would pay her for her time but would not want to employ her again, or they would rebook their Mediterranean cruise and ask Kate to continue with them.

As she made her way through the milling passengers, Kate tried to face up to each possibility. What would she do if she was summarily dismissed, thrown off the ship without a penny? Even if she could raise the money for a third-class ticket, she was no longer confident about her original plan to jump ship in Gibraltar and make her way through Spain and eventually to England to her mother's family. Eva Trentham had been shockingly candid about what awaited Kate if she arrived alone and penniless at the British naval base in Gibraltar. Kate stiffened her spine. No point in standing here and wondering when Mr. van Buren was beckoning her to his side.

Two men in rough clothes, apparently very eager to depart, jostled Kate, and she found herself pressed against Mr. van Buren's chest while he enclosed her with a protective arm. Well, maybe not entirely protective. He was holding her very close, very close indeed. She pulled away and turned to face Mrs. van Buren, whose face was sour and pale as she studied Kate.

"Where have you been, Miss Royston? I have searched for you for three days. You have obviously not been in your cabin, which was instead occupied by that very obnoxious countess."

"I was helping with the sick," Kate said. "I have some small experience with nursing, as I told you in my résumé."

Mrs. van Buren's lips twitched with disapproval. "You abandoned the children."

"There were other children," Kate snapped, "without mothers or fathers."

Mr. van Buren loomed over his wife's shoulder. "She's right, Magda. We can't fault her for being helpful."

Mrs. van Buren shrugged. "I suppose not, but it doesn't matter now. We have decided not to proceed with our journey. The children are very upset. This has been quite terrifying for them. We shall be returning home, and the children will return to school. We'll have no need of your services."

For a sickening moment, the deck seemed to drop away beneath Kate's feet. She had known this was a possibility, but now that the possibility had become a fact, she felt a wave of panic. Where would she go? What would she do? She would have to find another ship, another employer, another way to reach Europe.

"Miss Royston!" Mr. van Buren's arm was suddenly around her waist. Had she been about to faint? Mr. van Buren's arm remained firmly in place as he turned to his wife. "I think we must take Miss Royston home with us tonight," he said. "We can hardly cast her adrift on a night like this. She can stay tonight and leave in the morning." His face was now very close to Kate's. "That would be best, wouldn't it, Miss Royston?" His tongue flickered out and licked his lower lip.

She wanted to push him away and tell him never to touch her again, but she couldn't form the words. He was right. She had nowhere else to go, not tonight. She would have to go with them. Suddenly all her girlish ideas of charming her way across Europe on the strengths of her good looks and innocence were revealed as nothing but naive fantasies. Eva had been right. Kate had no idea how to behave around men. Flirting was beyond her. The very idea of Mr. van Buren's arm around her waist horrified her.

At another sour look from his wife, Mr. van Buren removed his arm from Kate's waist. "I'm going to find a cab. Magda, you and Miss Royston can bring the children."

Mrs. van Buren looked at seven-year-old Brigitta, who was tugging at her mother's coat. "Not now, Brigitta. Hold Miss Royston's hand." She tipped her head at Kate. "Bring both of them."

Kate shook her head, appalled at the idea of holding Brigitta's hand, and likewise the hand of her twin brother, Herbert. She knew how those hands would feel: sticky, and demanding, and ready to pinch when she was not expecting it, the pinching accompanied by a whining refusal to do what she asked. She realized that a secret place deep in her heart was relieved not to be continuing the journey with the Van Burens.

"I have to carry my bag," Kate protested. "I'll follow you, but I don't have a free hand for the children. They'll have to walk by themselves."

Mr. van Buren spoke sharply to his offspring and equally sharply to Kate. "Follow me, all of you. Now!"

Kate trailed behind her former employers, watching Mr. van Buren's tall figure as they descended the grand staircase. She was hemmed in by the *Carpathia*'s passengers, all shuffling toward the gangplank and the waiting crowd. Of course, the crowd was not waiting to greet the *Carpathia*'s passengers; they were waiting for the tragic procession yet to come—the survivors of the *Titanic*. Nonetheless, cameras flashed. Reporters wasting film, Kate thought.

Mr. and Mrs. van Buren and the children were well ahead of Kate as she reached the top of the gangplank. She stepped from the warmth of the interior into the gusty rain and saw Mr. van Buren ushering his family past a phalanx of police officers, who were not only keeping the crowds at bay but very obviously making sure that no one from the *Titanic* was able to sneak ashore. Of course, she thought, that made perfect sense. The *Carpathia*'s passengers were people on their way to Europe; the *Carpathia* was not carrying immigrants trying to find a new life in the United States, but the *Titanic* had carried immigrants from all over Europe, and now those immigrants had no papers or possessions, and some were children without parents, and some wives without husbands. Processing them as they came ashore on this cold, wet, windy night was just another part of the nightmare.

As she stood, looking and thinking and arguing with herself, she glanced sideways and saw that the two rough men who had jostled her were now on the deck below the gangplank. While she watched, she saw them lean over the railing and call to one of the boats that hovered and buzzed like aggressive insects along the hull of the *Carpathia*. What were they doing? Soon both men had climbed over the railing, and they stood poised as if ready to jump into the dark, churning water. A small boat, jostling the other boats, made toward them. A camera flashed.

A raised voice carried above the sound of the crowd. She made out the shouted question. "*Titanic* survivor? I'll give you a hundred bucks for your story. Jump."

The first man jumped, missed his target, and plunged into the dark confusion of waves and current far below. The men in the boat turned their heads for only a moment and then turned back to the other man. "Two hundred. Jump."

This man was now hesitating, but other men were crowding the rail. The offer was repeated, raised this time to three hundred.

Kate was pushed from behind, and an impatient voice grumbled in her ear. "Move along, miss."

As she took another step down the gangplank toward her unknown destiny, she saw that the police were parting the crowd and escorting a group of men up the gangplank, like fish swimming against the current.

She had time for only a very quick impression of the men in civilian clothes, a dapper gray-mustached gentleman in an elegant homburg hat, a young man in a high-collared suit, and a tall, lanky man with cold gray eyes who cleared a path for himself and his companions just by being.

She turned her eyes away from him and focused on the leading police officer. "A man jumped," she gasped. "He's in the water and no one's looking. They're offering money."

"Who is offering money, miss?"

"The reporters in the boats. They're offering money to men from the *Titanic* and telling the men to jump, but one of them jumped already, and he missed the boat, and no one seems to care."

"All right, miss. Where did you see this?"

"I was coming down the gangplank and looked over to my left, and I saw it."

The policeman tipped his hat. "Thank you, miss. We'll take care of it. You be on your way, and be careful." He turned to the man in the homburg hat. "Sorry, Senator. I'll have to take care of this myself. You go on ahead. He's in the doctor's cabin, or so they say."

Doctor's cabin! Senator! Kate's brain made an instinctive leap. This must be Senator Smith, the man Eva had summoned, and she knew of only one man who was in the doctor's office, and it wasn't the doctor. Dr. Lengyel was supervising the care of injured survivors. He had hardly left the smoking room since the survivors had been picked up. He would not now be in his cabin.

The policeman blew his whistle and gesticulated at other officers, waiting on the shore. Kate thought it very unlikely that the man who had jumped would be saved, but perhaps someone else could be stopped from jumping. How desperate would a man have to be to think of jumping from the deck of the *Carpathia* onto a tiny boat darting back and forth on the dark, choppy water?

The senator hurried forward, nodding to her as he passed and addressing his younger companion in an irritated voice. "Where the devil is the doctor's cabin? We have to get to him before he has a chance to slink off. We have to get to all of them before White Star Line sends a launch to get them away without setting foot ashore."

She spoke without pausing to think of the consequences of delay and the possibility that the Van Burens would leave without her. "I can show you. I'm the person who sent you the messages from Mrs. Trentham."

☐

CHAPTER EIGHT

Senator William Alden Smith

Bill followed the pretty dark-haired girl, who was attempting to lead the way while struggling with the weight of a clumsy portmanteau. So this was Eva's new protégée, heaven help her. She was very young, with large, innocent brown eyes that were at odds with the determined set of her chin.

Joe Bayliss leaned down and plucked the bag from her hand, and she turned on him, a nervous Daphne to Joe's looming Apollo.

"We'll move faster if I carry this," Joe said as the girl stared up at him, frankly fearful.

"The sheriff will take good care of your bag," Bill said.

Joe's title seemed to mollify her as Bill had hoped. Joe was a sheriff. He could be trusted. Bill wondered who the girl was. She was simply dressed in a dark woolen coat over a gray dress, and she wore no hat. Perhaps her bag represented everything she had been able to save from the shipwreck. On the other hand, she had been on her way down the gangplank when she had spoken to the police escort. The *Titanic*'s passengers were supposedly being kept on board, so she must be a passenger from the *Carpathia*, yet she said she had been working for Eva Trentham. Well, she was a mystery, but she knew her way around the ship, and Bill could not afford to waste time or thought wondering about her.

"This door," the girl said. "This is Dr. Lengyel's cabin. He's in there."

Joe shook his head. "We're not looking for the doctor."

"I know. You're looking for Sir Bruce Ismay, aren't you?"

"Yes, we are," Bill said.

The girl spoke with a slight edge to her voice. "Well, he's in there. He's been in there ever since they brought him aboard, and he's had that sign on the door the whole time."

"'Please do not knock,'" Joe said with amusement in his gravelly voice. "All right, then, we won't knock."

He dropped the girl's bag at her feet and gave her an encouraging smile. "You wait here, miss, and when I'm done, I'll come and carry that for you. Little thing like you shouldn't be lugging around a heavy bag." He leaned toward her, and she took a nervous step backward. "Are there no gentlemen on this ship?"

"I think that most of the gentlemen are at the bottom of the Atlantic," the girl said quietly.

Joe nodded gravely. "You're probably right. Sorry—I should have thought. Well, never mind that. I'm here now. Do you mind telling me your name, miss?"

"It's Kate," she said. "Kate ... just Kate."

"All right, Miss Kate. Wait for me here. This won't take long. The senator has business with Mr. Ismay, and that may take a little longer, but all I have to do is serve him a subpoena. When I've done that, you can show me where I can find the *Titanic*'s officers. You seem to know your way around."

"And after that," Bill said, "ask the young lady to conduct you to Mrs. Trentham. I want Eva to know that we have this matter in hand."

Joe turned to Will McKinstry. "All right, Mr. McKinstry, give me the paper, and let's get on with it."

McKinstry opened his briefcase and produced a single sheet of paper. So few words, Bill thought, but enough to light an international fire.

Joe took the paper and looked at the handwritten sign on the door. "'Please do not knock,'" he said under his breath. "Well, see what you think about this."

True to his word, Joe did not knock. He did not even turn the handle. He simply set his shoulder to the door and shoved. The door burst open, revealing a man in shirtsleeves and waistcoat, standing in the center of the doctor's small cabin. His wavy black hair was slicked back from his face, and dark, startled eyes stared at Joe from above a luxurious mustache. "What the devil?"

Joe looked over his shoulder at the girl who had accompanied him. She returned his look with an admiring stare.

"Well done," she whispered. "That's what I wanted to do."

Joe winked at her. "Wait there, Miss Kate. No need to come in."

Ismay was beginning to splutter. "Who said you could come in here? I'm not to be disturbed. Who the devil do you think you are?"

"Now, now," Joe said. "Let's watch our language in front of the young lady. We're just going to come in and close the door, and then we'll have some quiet words with you."

"I don't want to—"

"It's not about what you want," Joe said. "It's about what the United States wants. You are Mr. Bruce Ismay, aren't you?"

"I am Sir Bruce Ismay."

Joe cocked his head to one side. "We don't go in for titles on this side of the Atlantic, Mr. Ismay. But just so we can be certain, I'll ask you again. Are you Joseph Bruce Ismay?"

"I am."

Joe tucked a sheet of paper into the front of Ismay's waistcoat. "You've been served, and these two gentlemen are my witnesses."

"Served? What do you mean by 'served'?"

"The senator will explain. I'll leave you now and take Mr. McKinstry with me. We have other work to do."

Joe turned away and, with some effort, closed the door that he had all but pulled from its hinges. Bill was now alone with Ismay, who stared in disbelief at the paper in his hand.

"What is this?"

"It is a subpoena, sir, requiring you to give an account of your actions on board the *Titanic* on the night of April fourteenth and fifteenth."

Ismay shook his head. "I am not required to do any such thing."

Bill realized that he had already acquired an instinctive dislike of Bruce Ismay. He suspected that even if he had met him under entirely different circumstances, he would not have liked him. He thought of the sign on the door and the fact that Ismay was smartly dressed in a laundered and starched shirt. He reflected on how he had stood on the pier and watched the *Carpathia* drifting toward her berth in the driving rain while, all along the waterfront, men stood bareheaded and women cried, and all craned their necks searching for a familiar face among the bedraggled survivors. He was no longer worried about Taft or anyone else. What he wanted now was justice. It was for this moment that he had worked his way up from the streets of Grand Rapids to a seat in the Senate.

He made no attempt to keep pride of position from his voice. "I am Senator William Alden Smith of Michigan, and I have been appointed chairman of the Senate investigative committee on the sinking of the White Star liner *Titanic*."

Ismay shook his head. "There is no need for your Senate to conduct an inquiry. The British Wreck Commissioner will look into the whole matter."

"I'm afraid that's not good enough, Mr. Ismay. The American people require a reckoning for the death of so many American citizens."

Ismay lifted a hand as if to fend off Bill's words. "Senator, really, must you do this now? I am sure that in the fullness of time, we will—"

Bill tamped down the heat of his anger. This moment called for cool determination. Let Ismay splutter—Bill would remain in control.

"I don't think you are interested in the fullness of time," Bill said. "In fact, I believe that you intend to leave this country immediately and that you will not return to answer for your actions."

"No, no, Senator. I will, of course, be very willing to speak to your committee or whatever it is. Now, if you'll excuse me ..."

"No, I won't excuse you. I know full well that if I turn my back on you, you and your crew will leave this ship without ever setting foot on American soil."

"I don't know where you get that idea."

Bill reached into his pocket and pulled out a handful of papers. "Marconigrams," he said, "messages sent by you from the *Carpathia* to your office in New York."

"You have no right to read my messages," Ismay complained.

Bill continued as though Ismay had not even spoken, separating the papers one at a time and setting them on the bunk as he finished.

"'Most desirable *Titanic* crew aboard *Carpathia* should be returned home earliest moment possible. Suggest you hold *Cedric*, sailing her daylight Friday. Returning in her myself.' ... 'Very important you should hold *Cedric* daylight Friday for *Titanic* crew. Answer.' ... 'Think most unwise to keep *Titanic* crew until Saturday. Strongly urge detaining *Cedric*, sailing her midnight if desirable.'"

Ismay shook his head. "You don't understand. I am concerned for the welfare of my crew. They have wives and children in England, and they should be allowed to go home."

"I know that the list of survivors has been published in Britain," Bill said. "The wives and children know what they need to know. Let me make myself clear, Mr. Ismay: you and your crew will be detained until our Senate committee arrives in New York to speak with you."

Bill was suddenly aware that Ismay was looking past him, and his expression had become hopeful. "Here's Mr. Franklin from our New York office," Ismay said. "He'll take care of this."

Bill looked at the man who was standing in the passageway outside, eyeing the damaged door that now hung partially open. Franklin was a bald-headed, broad-shouldered man. His round face was pale and shocked, and his eyes were red rimmed. Bill knew that the White Star offices had been surrounded by reporters and relatives of the missing ever since the first report had come over the wires. No doubt the man was exhausted. Nonetheless, Franklin's voice was firm. "What's going on? Are you all right, Ismay?"

"No, I am not." Ismay waved the subpoena angrily at Bill. "This man—he says he's a senator—tells me that I cannot leave the ship."

Bill shook his head. "No, I told you that you must leave the ship. You must come ashore, you and your crew, and appear before my Senate committee."

Ismay looked past Bill and spoke angrily to Franklin. "Do something. I'm a British citizen. He has no right to detain me."

Franklin took the subpoena from Ismay's trembling hand. He was silent for a moment as he read, and then he sighed wearily. "Legally served," he said, "by Joseph Bayliss, sheriff of Chippewa County."

"Where the devil is Chippewa County?" Ismay asked. "And what gives him the right to detain a British citizen?"

Franklin returned the paper to Ismay. "It doesn't matter where he comes from. He has been sworn in by the sergeant at arms of the US Senate. This is a valid subpoena. Granted, you are a British citizen, and it may raise some questions, but—"

"So call the British ambassador," Ismay said. "See what he has to say about this."

"The British ambassador has already called me. He will not interfere, or at least not yet," Franklin replied. "Frankly, old man, this is a public-relations nightmare. Heaven knows I've done my best. I've been fending off a pack of reporters for the past three days, not to mention dealing with some of the richest and most powerful families in New York society, who want to know what happened to their fathers and sons. I've had the Guggenheims in my office, and Mrs. Astor's father. I can't help you, Ismay. If the US Senate wants to know what happened, you will have to tell them."

"I don't know what happened," Ismay said. He ran a hand through his hair, disturbing the carefully arranged waves. "I'm as ignorant as any other passenger."

"But you are not just any other passenger," Franklin said. "You are chairman of the White Star Line." He turned to Bill. "With your permission, Senator, I'll escort Sir Bruce ashore. I can assure you, on behalf of the White Star Line and on my word as a gentleman, that Sir Bruce will appear before your committee and tell you what he knows. I trust that is sufficient for you."

Bill took a moment to consider. He recognized that Phillip Franklin was not just a fellow American but also a possible ally. New York traffic in Lower Broadway had been brought to a halt by the throngs of people, both rich and poor, who had laid siege to the White Star offices, asking Franklin questions he could not possibly answer. He must have been thinking that the situation would be much easier if Ismay had perished with the ship. But he hadn't perished. He was here, and the public knew he was here.

Bill nodded. "Very well. I will see you tomorrow, both of you, at the Waldorf Astoria. Ten o'clock."

"No, no," Ismay stuttered. "It's too soon. I have urgent matters to attend to."

"Tomorrow, ten o'clock," Bill repeated as he pushed open the broken door and stepped out into the passageway.

Kate Royston

Kate had no choice but to lead the way for Joe Bayliss through the ever-moving throng of passengers. She should really try to find the Van Burens before they changed their minds about allowing her to stay the night, but the sheriff had taken possession of her bag, and she could not imagine trying to wrest it from his grip. She was also very curious to see what he would do next.

"I think the officers from the *Titanic* have been staying together in the officers' mess," she said. "They were standing watch with the *Carpathia*'s officers on the voyage, but—"

Joe leaned down and spoke in a low voice. "A young lady like you should not know where the officers are sleeping," he said.

Kate shook her head. "Oh, I don't. I mean, I've only spoken to one of them. Harold Bride was the radio operator, and he's been helping on the *Carpathia*, so I spoke to him. He's had an awful time with frostbite on his feet."

"So you've been doing your own interviewing," Joe said. "Maybe I should serve you with a subpoena."

"But I don't know anything." A sudden thought brought Kate to a complete standstill, which caused the senator's aide, Mr. McKinstry, to bump into her. Fortunately, Joe's presence stood between her and the press of people, and gave them a moment to untangle themselves.

"I have to tell you something," Kate said. "There's a radio operator; his name is Harold Cottam. You should talk to him."

"Was he on the *Titanic*?"

"No, no. He was here on the *Carpathia*. He took the first message, and he took it to the bridge, but they didn't believe him."

Joe raised his scraggly eyebrows. "Is that so?"

"Yes. He had to wake the captain himself and tell him. After that the crew were wonderful, but I think that Harold, Mr. Cottam, should have some kind of recognition for persevering and not giving up when the bridge officers wouldn't believe him."

"Ah," said Joe. "Now, you and this Mr. Cottam, are you …?"

"No, of course not. I just wanted to tell you."

"And now you have," Joe agreed. He winked at her again, and she wondered why she was suddenly blushing. Was it because he thought that she and Harold Cottam were having some kind of shipboard romance, or was it because he had winked at her?

Joe gestured with a large hand. "Lead on, Miss Kate. Let's find these officers."

Kate brought her companions to the door of the officers' mess and waited for Joe to hand over her bag. He set the bag on the deck, but as she reached down for it, he shook his head. "I told you, I will carry it and I will escort you from the ship. There's a rough crowd out there tonight. You may not be safe." He pulled a slip of paper from his pocket and handed it to McKinstry. "Go down among the immigrant survivors, and see if you can find this family."

"The senator asked me to be your witness when you serve the subpoenas."

"And the senator also asked us to find this family, who are relatives of his kitchen maid. I can't send Miss Kate in among those people, so I'm sending you. Miss Kate will make a perfectly fine witness to me serving the subpoenas."

McKinstry pocketed the paper but still hesitated. "Get a move on," Joe said. "God only knows what will happen to them once they leave the ship. Go and see what you can do."

McKinstry turned, obviously reluctant, and pushed his way back into the stream of passengers moving along the corridor.

Kate eyed the closed door of the officers' mess. "Are you going to break this one?"

"Would you like me to?"

"No, of course not." *But it would be exciting!*

Joe grinned. "We are going to enter politely. I imagine these officers are good fellows who've had a rough time. There'll be no trouble unless they make it themselves, and the presence of a young lady like you might make them think twice about what they say."

Kate closed her eyes, remembering the words that had been said about her father. The presence of Kate had made no difference on that occasion. Vile words had come from men she'd known all her life, men who had always called her Miss Kate and addressed her mother as "ma'am." Nothing the officers could say would surprise her.

She followed Joe into the officers' mess, where five men sat around the mess table. In the days since they had come on board the *Carpathia*, their clothes had been dried, but their dark sweaters and watch coats were streaked with salt. Although they had shaved and combed their hair, their faces were haggard, and their eyes were still shadowed by all they had seen. From what Kate had been able to hear of shipboard gossip, some of these men had not taken to the lifeboats. They had gone down with their ship and been plucked half-frozen from the water.

The only man she recognized was Harold Bride, the Marconi

operator, whose bandaged frostbitten feet were resting on one of the chairs. While the other men sprang to their feet, Bride remained seated and looked at her curiously. "Who is this, Miss Kate?"

Joe took over the conversation before Kate could reply. With some instinct that Kate could not fathom, he picked on only one man. "Mr. Lightoller, I believe."

Lightoller, a sturdily built man with a wide, honest face, eyed Joe. His blue eyes measured Joe's inscrutable gray eyes and seemed to find something to respect.

"Charles Lightoller, second officer."

"You are now in command?"

"I am the most senior officer to survive."

Lightoller spoke with a light burr to his voice. Not Irish, Kate thought, not Scottish, not Welsh, and definitely not London. It was a voice that spoke of a rural upbringing well away from the big cities. It was the voice of a man who was now very far from home, but it was not lacking in confidence. Lightoller stood straight-backed and gazed at Joe as one equal to another. "What can I do for you, Sheriff?"

"You and your men are expecting to leave this ship," Joe said, "and take passage on the *Cedric* to Southampton."

"We are."

"And I'm here to stop you."

A low protesting murmur rose from the officers around the table. Lightoller waved them into silence.

"Well, Sheriff, that is something you will have to take up with Sir Bruce Ismay. He has made the arrangements."

"But you are the senior officer," Joe said, and Kate detected a note of cunning in his voice. "I'm not a naval man myself, but I've done my time in the service of my country. Are you saying that you are answerable to Mr. Ismay?"

Lightoller hesitated before replying, and Kate realized that something very significant was taking place. This was the moment Eva had predicted. Lightoller need only say that he and his officers took commands from Ismay, and the question of blame would rest firmly on Ismay's shoulders.

Lightoller shook his head. "To tell you the truth, Sheriff, we are no longer employees of the White Star Line. Things in the merchant navy are very different from things in the Royal Navy or even in your navy. When the ship stops moving, whether it be in port or in the middle of the ocean, our employment comes to an end. All of us at this table, and all of our surviving crew, have been cast adrift, so to speak, without employment. The White Star Line has no obligation to return us to England, but they are willing to do so, and we are willing to take up the offer."

"Well," said Joe, "you are no longer adrift. The US government will take responsibility for you from now on. You will be our guests."

The men murmured again, and Lightoller silenced them with a look. "And if we choose not to be?"

Joe produced his sheaf of subpoenas from his pocket. "I have already issued Ismay a subpoena to appear before a Senate inquiry, and I am about to do the same to you, with this young lady as my witness. Introduce me to you officers, Mr. Lightoller, and let's get on with it."

Lightoller paused for a moment and then seemed to accept the inevitable. "We might as well get this over and done with, I suppose. There'll be another inquiry when we get to England, but if you want to have one, we're in no position to stop you. We have nothing to hide. We'll tell you what we know, not that any of us will enjoy remembering."

Kate thought that the sturdy Englishman shivered as he spoke, and the haunted expression in his eyes grew darker and deeper. He pointed to each of the men at the table. "Herbert Pitman, third officer; Joseph Boxhall, fourth officer; Harold Lowe, fifth officer; Harold Bride, radio operator."

Joe thumbed through the papers and handed one to each man. "That's done," he said, "and witnessed. I need one more thing. I need your logbook."

The five men looked at each other, and the man Lightoller had introduced as Harold Lowe, fifth officer, finally spoke. He sounded surprised. "The logbook?" he queried. "What makes you think we have the logbook?"

Kate saw Joe tensing his shoulders, and for a moment, she feared he would become violent. He had already broken down the door of the doctor's cabin without any provocation. Joe's words came out in quiet, measured tones that carried their own threat just by being spoken. "When the captain gives the order to abandon ship, maritime law requires that the captain gives the logbook to a responsible officer in the first boat away."

"Well," said Lowe, "I'm not sure if that is law or just custom, but it doesn't matter, as I don't recall the captain giving any order to abandon ship." He looked around at his fellow officers. "Did any of you hear the order?"

"Couldn't hear anything," Boxhall said. "When we found water coming in on the lower decks, the captain gave the order to stop engines while the carpenters went below to sound the ship. The chief engineer had to vent steam, you see, and that makes a terrible noise. We could hardly hear a word. I certainly didn't hear any order to abandon ship."

"And yet you abandoned her," Joe said.

Boxhall shook his head. "No, I would not say that. I took command of the second lifeboat to leave, but it wasn't a case of abandoning ship. It was just a precaution, and we had no intention of abandoning our command. We could see the lights of another ship close by. We were firing rockets to signal her. I was not given the logbook. It was not considered necessary."

Lightoller tapped Boxhall's shoulder. "Sit down, Mr. Boxhall. We have no need to explain ourselves to this man. We'll say what we have to say when we are called before the committee, but we'll say nothing now." He looked up at Joe, not at all intimidated by the fact that Joe towered over him. "You've done what you came to do. Now please leave us in peace. We do not have the logbook, and I have nothing more to say about it. I bid you good day." He nodded at Kate. "And you too, miss."

Kate caught her breath as she met his brief glance. He was not as tall and weathered as Joe, not as charming as Danny McSorley, or as painfully determined as Harold Cottam, but he radiated strength and honesty. She knew that whatever testimony he gave would be the truth. This was a man who could not lie.

She felt a sudden overwhelming shame. If she had not told Eva about Ismay's telegrams, none of this would be happening. Because of Eva's determination to bring down Sir Bruce Ismay, and through him J. P. Morgan, these men could not return home. Because Eva had harassed Senator Smith into holding an immediate inquiry, wives and children far away in England would have to endure a long, painful wait until they were reunited with their husbands and fathers. She lowered her eyes. She could not look at Lightoller. She could not look at any of them, knowing that they would be forced to face false accusers. She could not endure that again. She could not watch the ruin of innocent men.

She picked up her portmanteau, darted out of the door, and forced a place for herself in the steadily moving stream of people, then followed the flow until she found a side corridor. Of course, there was no reason for Joe Bayliss to follow her, but she moved as fast as she could, dodging and darting through a maze of corridors and dragging the bag down a flight of stairs until she felt the wind and rain on her face as she stood at the top of the gangplank.

Senator William Alden Smith

Bill entered the suite occupied by Eva Trentham. He was not at all surprised to see that she had found a comfortable place for herself, or that she had a sturdy Irishwoman standing by to fetch and carry for her. He was, however, somewhat surprised by the size and shagginess of the dog that Eva had managed to rescue and by the tall young Viking who held the dog on a tight leash as Bill entered the suite.

Eva sat in her wheelchair like a queen on a throne and waved a beringed hand at him as he entered. "Ah, Senator, at long last. I informed the officials that I would not leave the ship until I had spoken to you."

"No one from the *Titanic* has left the ship yet, so it was not an issue," Bill said, glad to have the chance to take some of the air out of Eva's bubble of importance. He didn't dislike the old lady, and he certainly liked the fact that she so frequently used her influence to assist his career, but he liked to place limits on her self-aggrandizement. She was an important member of New York society, one of the last of the grande dames, but even she would not be going ashore until it was her turn and until the crowds outside were brought under control.

"Well," Eva asked, "did you see Ismay?"

"I did, and I served a subpoena."

"And how did he take it?"

"Not well."

Eva smiled. "Good."

"He will be appearing in front of the Senate subcommittee tomorrow morning at ten," Bill said.

Eva clapped her hands. "I can't wait to see it."

Bill moved to pull up a chair, and the dog growled.

"This is Wolfie," Eva said. "We don't think he bites."

"You don't think …?"

"Well, we really don't know anything about him. We found him swimming, and I insisted he be put in my lifeboat. He's rather handsome, isn't he?"

Bill eyed the scruffy animal, taking in his long, drooping ears and sad bloodhound eyes, partially hidden by a fringe of untamed brown hair. "What is it?"

The young man with the leash leaned down and smoothed the dog's head. "Wolfie is an otterhound, sir. We don't know how he managed to reach the water or make his escape."

Bill nodded. "I'm sure that's a puzzle," he said. "If a dog like this could save himself, how could so many people die?"

"That's something for you to ask Ismay," Eva said. "I can't wait to hear the answer."

Bill sighed. This was the second time that Eva had mentioned attending the hearings, and now was the time to put an end to her expectations.

"The hearings will be closed," he said. "I'm sorry, Mrs. Trentham, but it will not be possible for you to attend."

"Stuff and nonsense, Senator. Stuff and pure nonsense. Do you think you'll be able to keep people out? We want to know what happened. We're entitled to know what happened."

"We will allow a small number of reporters."

"Ha!" said Eva. "A small number indeed. You had better make arrangements for a large number of reporters and a large number of interested parties. I will be there." She indicated the blanket-wrapped woman standing behind her chair. "Bridie will be there. She's entitled to know what happened to her fellow Irishmen, and Mr. McSorley will be there, won't you, Mr. McSorley?"

"Well, I—"

"Of course you will. Where else would you go?"

McSorley spread his hands. "I'm going to Cape Race, ma'am."

"Not yet. You have plenty of time before you have to go up there into the wilds." Eva looked at Bill. "This is Danny McSorley, and he is a radio operator for the Marconi company. He was traveling second-class on the *Titanic*. You may need his testimony. He'll be staying with me at my Park Avenue house tonight. And of course, there's young Kate." Eva looked up at Danny. "Do you know where she is?"

"I assume she's gone, ma'am, along with the other passengers from the *Carpathia*."

"Why would she do that?" Eva asked.

"Those were the instructions, ma'am," Danny said. "*Carpathia* passengers were to go ashore first."

Eva shook her head vigorously. "That doesn't mean she should go ashore. I need her here with me. So, she's gone off and left me to fend for myself after everything I've done for her. What an ungrateful little madam."

Bridie leaned forward. "Begging your pardon, missus, but did you tell her you wanted her to stay?"

"Why would I need to tell her?" Eva snapped. "Surely she could see for herself. If she's gone, it's because she didn't want to stay." She shrugged. "Oh well. Easy come, easy go."

"I could go ashore and look for her," Danny offered with a hint of desperation in his voice.

"No, I'm afraid you couldn't," Bill said. "All *Titanic* passengers are to remain on board and await immigration authorities, and we will be keeping them here until we know who we will want to interview. We've placed a tight guard on the gangplank to make sure that no one sneaks away, and we have police watching the pier. I'm sorry, young man, but you'll have to wait."

"Stupid, ungrateful girl," Eva muttered. She glared at Danny. "Don't look so crestfallen. There are plenty of other single girls in New York."

Danny tugged on Wolfie's leash. "I'll take him out for some fresh air," he said. "I suppose I'm allowed to do that."

Bill saw the way that Danny was looking at Eva: the look of a Viking about to wreak some terrible vengeance. He felt nothing but sympathy for the young man as he slammed out of the suite with the shaggy hound at his heels.

Kate Royston

Kate pulled her identity papers from her bag, along with her stamped passenger ticket proving that she, Katherine Elizabeth Royston, had been a passenger on the *Carpathia*.

An immigration official ushered her through the police cordon. "You're one of the last ones, miss," he said. "We'll be dealing with the *Titanic* passengers next. Do you know where you're going?"

Kate nodded. "Yes, I'm fine. My employers are waiting for me."

The official touched his cap. "All right, miss. Good night."

Rain battered Kate as she followed the narrow path created by the police cordon. Arms reached out toward her, and she caught snatches of questions.

"Have you seen ...?"

"Do you know ...?"

"My mother was ..."

"How about an interview, miss?"

She waved the questions away. She had no answers for these people. She hesitated. Someone should answer them, and if not Senator Smith, then who would it be? Who would find the truth?

She walked until she was clear of the crowd and the voices, and finally stopped on a deserted street. She set down her bag and tucked her passport and ticket safely into the interior, among her few items of clothing. How much time had she wasted helping Joe Bayliss? How long had she been walking since she had left the *Carpathia*? Where were the cabs? Where were the Van Burens? She turned around and watched the distant camera flashes and the lights of the *Carpathia*, now some distance away. She couldn't go forward without any idea of where to go. She would have to turn around and make her way back on board the *Carpathia*, where she could find the purser and explain her problem, or maybe she could find Mrs. Broomer; she would surely be able to help her. They would know how to reach the Van Burens, and then Kate could explain what had happened. She had been helping the senator; surely they would understand and not refuse her a bed for the night.

She shook her head, disgusted at her own stupidity. At this moment, the Van Burens, however unpleasant, were her only security, and all she'd had to do was follow them to a cab. If she had held Brigitta's hand, they would have waited for her, but instead, she'd gone running off trying to interfere in Eva Trentham's affairs. And it was not as though the old lady cared anything for Kate, dismissing her without a second thought.

Well, none of that mattered now. The *Carpathia* was still at the pier. Someone on board would surely recognize her, and if they could not tell her how to reach the Van Burens, maybe they would allow her to stay on board for the night. Tomorrow she would make a new plan—hopefully, a better one.

As she turned to pick up her bag, someone or something slammed into her from behind, shoving her face downward onto the cobbled street. She screamed in pain as her face collided with the stones, and she tasted blood in her mouth. She heard the sound of running footsteps and rolled over onto her hands and knees just in time to see a figure retreating into the curtain of rain. She sat up and blinked at the rain and blood streaming down her face. She reached for her bag, for a handkerchief, but she knew already that the bag would not be there.

She could not even feel surprise. It was all gone—her papers, her ticket, her clothes. She was no one now, just another fatherless girl alone on the streets of New York.

She used the sleeve of her coat to wipe the blood from her eyes. If only she could have put her papers in her pocket, she would not feel so helpless. Unfortunately, her coat, made by her mother's dressmaker, was designed for a young lady to wear—a young lady who would carry an elegant purse and would not spoil the lines of her coat by having a pocket large enough to jam full with important items.

She trudged back toward the flicker of flashbulbs and the glow of lights from the pier. The crowd that had been so silent was loud now and seemingly out of control. Above the wailing of women and the shouting of men, she heard the shrills of police whistles.

Soon she was at the back of the crowd, and she could hear the reporters calling out.

"That's Mrs. Astor. Over here, Mrs. Astor!"

"Mrs. Guggenheim!"

"Lady Rothes!"

That's it, Kate thought, hearing the name of the countess. *I don't have to get back on board. I'll tell the countess what happened. She knows me. She'll know what to do. She'll think I'm a complete ninny—not five minutes off the boat, and I've already been robbed—but there's a kind heart somewhere under that cool exterior.*

Kate swiped the blood from her eyes again and pushed forward, determined to speak to the countess. She caught a glimpse of her standing hatless in the rain, with her blonde hair disheveled and her eyes searching the crowd. Kate pressed against the police cordon separating the first-class passengers from the crowd. She called out, but the countess did not even turn her head as she moved forward, gliding swanlike toward two impeccably dressed gentlemen who had obviously come to meet her. She was gone in moments, and Kate was, once again, in the midst of the surging crowd.

"Here they come. Here they come. Here's third class."

A group of uniformed officers stood at the foot of the gangplank. Kate heard the murmur of voices in the crowd. "Immigration. They won't let them in without papers."

"How can they have papers? They have nothing."

"Will they take them to Ellis Island?"

"Not tonight."

Kate wriggled through the crowd and ducked beneath the linked arms of the policemen. For a moment, she was in the open, looking up at the *Carpathia*'s gangplank and seeing the first of the Irishwomen descending the gangplank with shaky steps. When the woman's knees buckled beneath her, one of the policemen stepped forward to catch her, and Kate managed to dart past him and gain a place on the gangplank, but not for long. The immigrants tottered down the gangplank, unsteady after so long at sea, ragged, terrified, some crying, some crossing themselves, some grasping the hands of the few, very few, children who had been saved.

Their surge toward land was irresistible, and Kate was caught up and carried back toward the dock. Hands reached for her. She tried to force them away.

A woman's voice spoke softly in her ear while someone else held on to her arms. "It's all right, dear. We're here to take care of you. You come with us. You'll be all right. Do you speak English? Do you understand me?"

Kate squinted through the film of blood that had once again gathered before her eyes. She thought she must have a head wound. She knew head wounds could bleed without being serious. No, she wasn't severely injured. She could walk. She could manage. She could get back on board the *Carpathia*.

The woman's voice came again. "I don't think she speaks English, but look at her, poor soul. She's bleeding."

Kate managed to free one of her arms and wipe the blood from her eyes. She found herself surrounded by young men and women in Salvation Army uniforms.

Kate tried to pull away, but the young woman who held her was apparently as strong in her body as she was in her faith, because her grip was unrelenting.

"I have to go back," Kate said. "I have to go on board."

"Oh, you do speak English. That's good. Now try to understand—"

"I have to go back," Kate insisted. "I'm not an immigrant."

Another, older woman with rain dripping from her bonnet joined Kate's captor. "Some of them are very confused," she said, "but we can't stand out here in the rain arguing with them. The police say we're to take them to our hostel tonight, and they'll come in the morning to inspect them."

"I don't need to be inspected," Kate insisted. "I'm not an immigrant."

"Well, then," the older woman said acerbically, "if you're not an immigrant, where are your papers? Do you have anything to say who you are?"

"Of course I do," Kate said. "I was a passenger on the *Carpathia.*"

"Do you have anything to prove that?"

"No. I was robbed. I had my passport and my—"

"You're confused, dear, and you've had a bang on the head. The *Carpathia* passengers are all long gone. You and your fellows are the only ones left. Now, you come with me before I have to fetch the immigration officers to arrest you. It's best not to begin your life in a new country by being arrested."

"But—"

"But nothing. It's me or the police. Now, you look over there and see what's happening to those that won't behave themselves."

Kate looked up in time to see three police officers take down a strongly built immigrant man who had evidently tried to make a run for it.

"He'll be on his way to jail," said Kate's captor. "You don't want that to happen to you. You can sleep in our hostel tonight, and the health inspectors will come in the morning. You speak very good English, and I know you understand me. You'll be held in quarantine while we find out who you are and where you're going, and then, if you're free of diseases, you'll be released."

Kate could not find the will to resist as the two women dragged her toward the ominous black shape of a police wagon. She could not go back aboard the *Carpathia*. She could not walk through the night to the Van Burens' house. She certainly could not expect any help from Eva Trentham. *Tomorrow*, she said to herself. *I will sort this out tomorrow*.

She stepped up into the closed back of the wagon and took her seat among the immigrant women. She closed her eyes. Words danced in her mind: *jail, quarantine, health inspectors, police*. Someone slammed the van doors, shutting out the rain. A key rattled in the lock. *Jail, quarantine, health inspectors, police*.

New York Times
April 19, 1912

When the ship finally pulled into dock near Fourteenth Street, two thousand people were on the pier and waiting in almost complete silence. Near the pier another 30,000 had gathered and 10,000 more lined the Battery. In addition to friends and relatives, medical personnel and government officials were on the scene. The Carpathia *passengers disembarked first, because the ship's captain realized that the scene would become tumultuous as soon as the* Titanic *survivors first appeared. That moment came when a woman passenger with teary eyes and makeshift clothes descended the gangplank and stumbled away from the boat on the arms of an officer and the crowd started to wail with sounds of shrieks and sobs.*

☐

PART TWO
NEW YORK

Simple Resolution 283 in the Senate of the United States
April 17, 1912

Resolved, That the Committee of Commerce, or a subcommittee thereof, is hereby authorized and directed to investigate the causes leading to the wreck of the White Star liner Titanic, *with attendant loss of life, so shocking to the civilized world.*

NEW YORK HERALD
APRIL 19, 1912

This country intends to find out why so many American lives were wasted by the incompetency of British seamen, and why women and children were sent to their deaths while so many British crew have been saved.

CHAPTER NINE

April 19, 1912
Salvation Army Hostel
New York
Kate Royston

"That's another door locked against us."

Kate looked up from her breakfast as an angry young Irish girl pushed her way onto the bench beside her.

The newcomer eyed the food on the table suspiciously. "What are they giving us to eat?"

A middle-aged woman responded from the other side of the long table. "Eggs and bread. Good food." The woman's accent was heavy with echoes of her Swedish origins. She smiled at the angry girl. "You eat. You feel better."

The Irish girl ignored her and frowned at Kate. "I don't know you. Where did you come from?"

After a night spent tossing and turning on a lumpy mattress, Kate was in no mood to explain how she had come to be scooped up by the Salvation Army. What could she say to these women who had lost everything, including their husbands and maybe even their children? All Kate had lost was her luggage and her identity papers. The women—German, Scandinavian, Irish, Jewish—had cried and lamented through the dark hours of the night in a cacophony of their own native tongues. Kate was certain that no one in the dormitory had managed to sleep for more than a few minutes.

Now the women seemed to be without words. They had arrived at their destination with no idea of what future would await them. They sat at long tables in the hall of the Salvation Army hostel in a kind of stunned silence. The Irish girl was the first one who had actually spoken.

"What do you mean by 'locked against us'?" Kate asked, deliberately avoiding the initial question.

"I've tried all the outside doors, and they're locked up tight," the girl said. "They've locked us up just like they did on the *Titanic*. If my da had not broken down that gate, I wouldn't be sitting here now. None of us would." She looked at Kate suspiciously. "I didn't see you in a lifeboat."

The Scandinavian woman pushed a bowl of scrambled eggs toward the girl. "You eat, you not be so angry. I not see you in lifeboat, but you here now."

"Well, I was in one," the girl said, "with my sister. It was the last one to leave, and my da had to fight to get us a seat."

The Scandinavian woman spooned eggs onto the girl's plate. "What your name?"

"I'm Kitty." She looked up at another girl, who was squeezing onto the bench beside her. "This is my sister, Maeve."

Kate studied the girls. Kitty was still scowling, but Maeve was red-eyed, as though she had cried all night. They were pretty girls, with black hair and blue eyes, and seemed very close in age, maybe even twins.

The Scandinavian woman waited to speak until Maeve had settled herself into a seat. "Well, Kitty," she said, "I am Freya. Now, you tell again. What you mean when you say 'locked up'?"

"The gate from third class was locked," Kitty said as she reached for a thick slice of toast.

Freya shook her head. "Not then, now. The past is over. We go on. I go to Minnesota. I go without my husband and my son, but I go."

"But aren't you angry?" Kitty asked. She looked around the room at the women eating silently. "Aren't you all angry? No one thought us worth saving. Don't you want to do something?"

"What do you suggest?" Kate asked.

"I suggest we leave here and we go and talk to the reporters. They're outside. You can see them through the windows. We can tell them what happened and how we were not allowed in the lifeboats."

Kate shook her head. "Very few people were allowed in the lifeboats, Kitty. There weren't enough boats."

As she said the words, Kate realized that it was the first time she had truly understood the reality of what she had seen. Looking down from the deck of the *Carpathia*, she had seen thirteen lifeboats. Why so few? With two thousand passengers on the *Titanic*, thirteen lifeboats, even if they had been loaded properly, would never have been enough.

She thought about Senator Smith marching on board the *Carpathia* and issuing subpoenas. He was going to hold a hearing. He wanted to blame someone, preferably Sir Bruce Ismay. Well, Ismay was odious enough, but was he responsible for the number of lifeboats?

"I hear the reporters will pay money for a story," Kitty said. "We're all going to need money." She squinted at Kate. "But maybe not you. You're different, aren't you, with that snooty expression on your face? You were in second class, weren't you? Don't suppose you want to be in here with us."

"I wasn't in second class."

"So you were down on your luck and slumming?" Kitty asked. "But you got a seat, didn't you? You were something special. Some of the women in our boat had to row. Did you have to row?"

Maeve tugged at her sister's sleeve. "Kitty, don't. There's no point. We're here now."

"But Da's not here, or Liam or Finnan."

Tears welled up in Maeve's eyes, but Kitty ignored her sister's distress. Kate knew how Kitty felt. She had been in Kitty's position once, not very long ago. She knew what it was to constantly stoke the fires of anger until there was no room left for grief or compassion.

"Row to the other boat," Kitty said. "That was just a game, wasn't it? Pointing at some starlight and telling us to row. There was nothing there."

"I saw light," Freya said. "We all saw light. A ship. Just there."

"It was a trick to make us row," Kitty said. "If there was another ship, why didn't it come? Why did we have to wait for morning?"

Something stirred in the back of Kate's memory: the Countess of Rothes asking about another ship. *We were told to row towards it.*

A shrill whistle blast interrupted Kate's reverie. Three women in Salvation Army uniforms marched into the hall and arranged themselves at the center of the room in such a way that no one could hide from their benevolent but watchful gaze.

The tallest of the trio introduced herself. "I am Major Evelyn Sullivan, and this is Captain Veronica Rich and Private Elspeth Dorman. We are here to take care of you. As soon as you've eaten your breakfast, you will be able to take a bath, and we have clean clothes for all of you thanks to the generosity of the women of New York. We also have a fund that will pay for you to go on from here to your original destination with a small amount of money in your pocket."

Her announcement was greeted by a babble of concerned voices. "You will kindly translate for each other," Major Sullivan said. "Make sure that everyone understands." She raised a finger and wagged it at one group of women, who seemed even more agitated than anyone else, if that was in fact possible, considering the level of agitation in the room.

"We will make special accommodations for you Jewish ladies," the major said. "The Hebrew Immigrant Aid Society will become responsible for you."

The major's assurances did nothing to lower the volume of the women's voices, and the major resorted to blowing her whistle in short, agitated bursts until at last silence was achieved.

"Ladies," she said, "I know you are all upset—"

"The devil she does," Kitty muttered under her breath.

"—but," the major continued, "you are not yet landed immigrants. You will not be required to go to Ellis Island, but you will all be interviewed. You will remain here while we discover who you are and where you are to go, and we will locate any relatives among the men who have been saved." She waved an imperious finger. "Translate for each other now. I will wait."

"Prisoners," Kitty hissed.

"No," Maeve said. "We're going to be all right. Remember the man we talked to, the one who came on board the *Carpathia*. He said he knew who we were and he would make sure we go to Washington, to our cousin's house."

"And have you seen him since?" Kitty asked. "Of course not. He's forgotten about us, or perhaps he didn't believe us. Maybe saying that our cousin works for some grand senator was too much for him to believe. If Da were still alive, he could tell him, and maybe he'd believe, but the devil we know the name."

"Senator Smith," Kate said.

Kitty glowered at her. "Are you making fun?"

"No," Kate said. "The man who spoke to you was Mr. McKinstry, who is Senator Smith's personal aide, and your cousin is employed by Senator Smith. I can assure you that Mr. McKinstry will come back for you. He won't forget."

Maeve's face brightened, but Kitty could not, or would not, let go of her anger and suspicion. "And how are you after knowing such a thing?"

"I was with the senator when he came on board."

"Then what are you doing here?" Kitty asked.

Kate shook her head. "It's a long story, but I'll get it sorted out, and then I'll make sure that Mr. McKinstry comes for you."

Kitty rose abruptly to her feet, pushing back the benches and rattling the cups and plates. "You're touched in the head. You came here like everyone else, and now you're trying to pretend you're better than all of us."

The major's whistle shrilled again. "All right, ladies, that's enough." She pointed a stern finger at Kitty. "Sit down, girl."

"I won't."

"Sit down, or I'll set you down myself. We'll have no hysterics here. I will inform the immigration officials of anyone who gives me trouble, and you will be refused entry to the United States. Do any of you want to go back across the Atlantic?"

A blanket of silence smothered the room as Kitty slowly returned to her seat.

Kate studied the major's face. Her features were long and narrow, in keeping with her height, but her face, framed by a Salvation Army bonnet, was not unkind. Kate did not read hostility in her expression, only something very close to fear. Major Sullivan was afraid of a riot.

The three days on board the *Carpathia* had given the immigrant women a chance to see how many first-class women had been saved, and even how many first-class men. As they had huddled together on board their rescue ship, they had shared their experiences, and some, such as Kitty, had turned grief into anger. Now they had arrived in their promised land, but they were still not free. They were still locked up, as Kate suspected they had been locked up on the *Titanic*. Major Sullivan was going to need more than a whistle to keep these people under control.

Captain Veronica spoke into the hostile silence. Not only was her voice pleasant, but it held a hint of an Irish accent. "Just one more day," she said. "You'll all have a nice hot bath and a chance to wash your hair and put on clean clothes. We'll come and take all of your particulars and pass them onto the immigration officers. We're going to make this as easy as possible. I know the reporters are outside, but they can't help you."

"Think yourselves lucky you're not on a barge to Ellis Island," Major Sullivan added. "Now finish your breakfast, and we'll make a start on the paperwork."

Kate helped herself to a slice of toast. When she explained her situation to the major, she would surely be released, but she had no idea where she would go next. Nothing had changed since last night. She still had no money and no prospect of obtaining any. She thought a hearty breakfast, a bath, and a change of clothes would be a good idea.

The Waldorf Astoria
New York
Senator William Alden Smith

Bill took a deep breath as he entered the luxurious meeting room at the Waldorf Astoria. Despite his protests, representatives of the press and eager spectators had been admitted. He had been awake most of the night, preparing challenging questions for Bruce Ismay and the crew of the *Titanic*. He hoped to impress upon Ismay the seriousness of appearing before representatives of the US Senate. Now, instead of confronting Ismay in an atmosphere of quiet intensity, he felt as though he were part of a three-ring circus.

He surveyed the audience: ladies in fashionable hats, reporters with notebooks, gentlemen in expensive suits, and of course, Eva Trentham in her wheelchair. She was seated in the front row, with Bridie standing by with refreshments and smelling salts, not that Eva was ever likely to faint.

Unfortunately, he could see no sign of Kate, the girl who had been the witness to Joe Bayliss serving the subpoenas to the crew.

Her signature could prove to be important. She would have to be found. He scanned the room for a glimpse of Joe and saw him standing against the back wall. As he met Bill's eye, he shook his head. No, he had not yet found Kate, and he had not found the logbook.

Senator Newlands sat down in the seat beside Bill and leaned forward to speak quietly. "Phone message from the president."

"Well, thank goodness. He's finally decided to take notice of what's going on," Bill said.

Newlands shook his head. "He's giving us forty-eight hours."

"What do you mean?"

"Diplomatic pressure from the British," Newlands said. "Taft will only allow us two days to ask questions and hold British citizens against their will. After that, you will have to release them."

"I can't do this in two days," Bill protested. "I won't even get to the bottom of Ismay's story in two days."

Newlands leaned back in his seat. "Well, you'll have to try, because that's as long as we have."

"Did you try to explain?"

Newlands grimaced. "I didn't speak to him personally. He's still not speaking to anyone. Hilles is doing his dirty work for him and fending off the British. All Taft cares about is finding out what happened to Archibald Butt."

Bill groaned. "There's more there than meets the eye," he said.

Newlands pulled a pair of glasses from his pocket and set them on the end of his nose. "Let's see what we can find out," he said.

Bill shook his head. "I don't care what happened to Butt. I want to know who was giving the orders that sent them at full speed through an ice field. If it's all right with you, I'll ask the questions."

Newlands nodded. "It's your show, Smith. You go ahead. I'll jump in if I have anything to add."

"Very well."

From the corner of his eye, Bill saw Will McKinstry turn to a fresh page in his notebook. A stenographer would keep the official record; the reporters would no doubt pick and choose what they recorded; but McKinstry would know what to write down and what to leave out—what to revisit tomorrow and what questions had been asked and answered.

Bruce Ismay sat alone on one side of the long table, facing the dozen officials arrayed on the other side waiting for his explanation—waiting to assign blame. All around him, the spectators radiated hostility. The newspapers had already found their villain, and Ismay would have to work hard to change their minds. It did not help that he was such an unattractive figure with his too-small eyes and his too-black hair.

Bill leaned forward, hands on table. The witness had been duly sworn. *Let the games begin.* Bruce Ismay remained seated.

"Mr. Ismay," Bill said, "for the purpose of simplifying this hearing, I will ask you a few preliminary questions. First, state your full name, please."

"Joseph Bruce Ismay."

"And your place of residence?"

"Liverpool."

Bill was momentarily diverted by the answer. So that explained Ismay's unusual accent: slightly Irish but with undertones of something else, and everything overlaid by an education that had tried to obliterate any regional accent. It was not an attractive voice and not one that would endear itself to the reporters, who would have to strain to understand him.

"And your age?"

"I shall be fifty on the twelfth of December."

Bill could see no gray in Ismay's hair, but it was hard to believe that the man was only fifty years old. It would seem that the loss of the *Titanic* had aged him, etching lines on his face and creating bags beneath his eyes.

"And your occupation?" Bill asked.

"Shipowner."

If only that were true, Bill thought. If only Bruce Ismay owned the *Titanic* lock, stock, and barrel, the inquiry could stop now. But of course, he didn't personally own the ship, and it would take more than a few questions to find out who did.

"Mr. Ismay, are you an officer of the White Star Line?"

"I am. I am the managing director."

"And as such an officer, were you officially designated to make the trial trip of the *Titanic*?"

"No."

Bill glanced down at Newlands, who raised his eyebrows. Now the real questioning would begin, with Ismay trying to wriggle out of any responsibility for the actions of the crew. Bill knew he would have to ease into it, but he would get there.

"Were you a voluntary passenger, Mr. Ismay?"

"A voluntary passenger, yes."

"Where did you board the ship?"

"Southampton."

Bill had his own memories of Southampton, a bustling port on the south coast of England where liners arrived from all over the world. He had arrived there himself along with Nana on their first transatlantic voyage.

Ismay was speaking again, his tone conciliatory. "In the first place, I would like to express my sincere grief at this deplorable catastrophe. I understand that you gentlemen have been appointed as a committee of the Senate to inquire into the circumstances. So far as we are concerned, we welcome it. We court the fullest inquiry. We have nothing to conceal and nothing to hide."

A bead of sweat formed on Ismay's forehead. Bill waited for him to wipe it away, but Ismay was far too canny to do any such thing. He leaned back slightly in his chair, trying to appear relaxed.

"She left Belfast, as far as I remember—I am not absolutely clear about these dates—I think it was on the first of April. She underwent her trials, which were entirely satisfactory. She then proceeded to Southampton, arriving there on Wednesday, the third, and leaving again at twelve noon on the tenth."

Ismay pulled a paper from his pocket and looked inquiringly at Bill. Apparently, he intended to read from notes he had made. Bill wondered who had assisted in making the notes. Was it a crew member, or did Ismay have the elusive logbook? Bill waited. He would bide his time.

"We arrived in Cherbourg that evening, having run over at sixty-eight revolutions," Ismay said. "We then proceeded to Queenstown at seventy revolutions and embarked the mails and the passengers."

Ismay didn't say it, but Bill knew what kind of passengers had embarked at Queenstown. This was where the Irish immigrants, the bulk of the steerage passengers, had embarked to join the Hungarians and Scandinavians who had embarked in Cherbourg. The lower decks of the *Titanic* would now be filled with penniless men, women, and children eager to start life again in the New World.

Ismay made no mention of these passengers and continued to

read from his notes. "The first day's run was four hundred and eighty-four miles. The second day, the number of revolutions was increased to seventy-two, and on the second day, our run was five hundred and nineteen miles. On the third day, the revolutions were increased to seventy-five, and we ran five hundred and forty-nine miles. The weather during this time was absolutely fine, with the exception, I think, of about ten minutes of fog one evening."

Bill looked at the faces of the spectators. Surely they were all imagining the same thing. They may not understand what exactly was meant by "number of revolutions," but they could imagine the result. The great ship was steadily increasing speed, plowing through the Atlantic under clear blue skies, while the wealthy wined and dined under crystal chandeliers, and the less wealthy ate hearty meals and danced to their own music.

Ismay sat forward in his chair and spoke without any prompting from Bill. "The accident took place on Sunday night. What the exact time was, I do not know. I was in bed myself, asleep, when the accident happened. The ship sank, I am told, at two twenty. That, sir, I think is all I can tell you."

No, Bill thought, *that is not all you can tell me. You are going to tell me a great deal more than this.*

Ismay smoothed the paper he had taken from his pocket. The spectators murmured. Bill waited.

Ismay cleared his throat and looked across at Bill. His eyes narrowed, and his focus was sharp. His voice contained no traces of his former conciliatory tone. Bill nodded. Now it would begin.

"I understand," said Ismay, "that it has been stated that the ship was going at full speed. The ship never had been at full speed. The full speed of the ship is seventy-eight revolutions. She can work up to eighty. So far as I am aware, she never exceeded seventy-five revolutions. She had not all her boilers on. None of the single-ended boilers were on. It was our intention, if we had fine weather on Monday afternoon or Tuesday, to drive the ship at full speed. That, owing to the unfortunate catastrophe, never eventuated."

Bill looked at Newlands. Newlands nodded. It was time to discover exactly how Ismay had managed to save himself.

"Mr. Ismay, will you describe what you did after the impact or collision?"

The bead of sweat returned to Ismay's forehead. "Well, Senator, I presume the impact awakened me. I lay in bed for a moment or two afterwards, not realizing, probably, what had happened. Eventually, I got up and walked along the passageway and met one of the stewards, and said, 'What has happened?' He said, 'I do not know, sir.' I then went back into my room, put my coat on, and went up on the bridge, where I found Captain Smith. I asked him what had happened, and he said, 'We have struck ice.' I said, 'Do you think the ship is seriously damaged?' He said, 'I am afraid she is.' I then went down below, where I met Mr. Bell, the chief engineer, who was in the main companionway. I asked if he thought the ship was seriously damaged, and he said he thought she was, but was quite satisfied the pumps would keep her afloat."

Ismay paused. The bead of sweat dripped onto the paper in front of him. He seemed not to notice.

"I went back onto the bridge. I heard the order given to get the boats out. I walked along to the starboard side of the ship, where I met one of the officers. I told him to get the boats out."

Ismay's face was pale with remembering, the newly formed lines on his face seemed to etch themselves deeper. In one terrible moment, when he had heard the order given to break out the lifeboats, Ismay had reacted by giving his own orders to an officer, and everything had changed. He had sworn he was just a voluntary passenger, but now he was admitting to giving orders.

"What officer did you meet?" Bill asked.

"That I could not remember," Ismay replied.

Maybe he knew he was in a trap of his own making. Maybe he did remember but would not say, or maybe that officer had died along with so many others of the crew.

"I assisted as best I could, getting the boats out and putting the women and children into the boats," Ismay said with pleading in his voice. "I stood upon that deck practically until I left the ship in the starboard collapsible lifeboat, which is the last boat to leave the ship, so far as I know." He dabbed at his forehead with a white handkerchief and sat back in his chair. "More than that I do not know."

Joe Bayliss

Joe slipped quietly out of the room. He had heard as much as he needed to hear for the time being, and he had no need to watch Bruce Ismay squirming under Bill's questioning. For Joe, the outcome was obvious. Bill was not asking questions because he needed to know the answers—he already knew the answers. He just needed to give Ismay free rein to speak, and Ismay would condemn himself. He may say that Captain Smith was in sole command of the *Titanic*, but his words betrayed him. Obviously, the captain had consulted with him. Equally obviously, Ismay wanted to see how fast the *Titanic* would go under a full head of steam.

As for the newspaper reporters, scribbling away on their notepads, they had no interest in the give and take of the senator's questions. They had heard what they wanted to hear. Ismay had given orders to break out the lifeboats, and Ismay had found himself a seat in one of them. He had saved himself while others had drowned.

Joe passed through the small salon where Guglielmo Marconi himself waited for his turn to give evidence. From what little Joe had seen of the man who had invented the equipment that had sent the *Titanic*'s distress call, Marconi was simply waiting to receive accolades. No doubt about it, Joe thought, Marconi's invention had saved the day. So what if there were rumors that he was trying to make the newspapers pay for a story from Harold Bride, the surviving operator? No harm in making a little money when there was money to be made, and Bride was still in the hospital and needing all the help he could get.

Captain Rostron, from the *Carpathia*, was seated beside Marconi, maintaining a stoic silence. Here was another man who would have no need to defend himself. Rostron was the hero of the hour, and no one could say differently. The fact that any of the survivors were alive was because Rostron had raced to their rescue. Kate had seen him in action.

He thought of Kate. She had been present when Cottam had brought the news of the collision. She had seen everything Rostron had done. If anyone doubted anything that had occurred on the *Carpathia*, she could be called as a witness—if only he knew where she was. More significantly, she was the witness to the *Titanic* officers receiving their subpoenas, and that meant she had to be found.

He pulled a cheroot from his pocket as he made his way to the service entrance, where he could avoid the throng of reporters and spectators. He lit a match by scraping it on the heel of his boot and stood for a moment drawing on the cheroot and thinking about Kate.

"Excuse me."

Joe looked up to see a small man with thinning brown hair and an ill-fitting suit looking at him with a worried frown. "I beg your pardon, sir, but could you tell me if this is the entrance I should use? I've been called as a witness, and I have no wish to push my way through the crowd. It would not be appropriate, you see."

British, Joe thought, and striving for an upper-class accent. He considered the man's obviously borrowed suit and the shadow lurking deep in his eyes. They all had that shadow—all those who had survived the sinking.

"You can come in this way," Joe said. "I'll escort you. What's your name, and what's your business?"

"Alfred Crawford, sir. Bedroom steward, first class."

Joe nodded. "Oh yes, I know who you are. In fact, I'm the person who called you. You're late. You should have been here an hour ago. Where is your police escort?"

"Well," Crawford said, "as for being late, I had to wait for someone to bring me clothes on account of having nothing clean or right for a place like this. I had a policeman walking with me, but I lost him round the front of the building because of the crowds out there, so I nipped around the back here to see if I could get in this way."

"I'll take you in," Joe said.

Crawford hesitated. "Begging your pardon, sir, but why would anyone want to talk to me?"

"You've been talking to reporters," Joe said, "and the senator heard about it."

Crawford sniffed and searched in his pocket for a handkerchief. "Sorry, sir. I have a cold—you know, from being on the water."

Joe offered him a handkerchief from his own pocket and waited until the steward had blown his nose and stowed the handkerchief.

"Those reporters are like blooming vultures," Crawford said. "I just told them what I knew. I didn't mean to make trouble."

"Of course you didn't," Joe said soothingly. "The problem here is the story you told the reporters about Mr. and Mrs. Straus. We don't

127

want any wild rumors taking hold, and so we will try to nip them in the bud. If you're telling the truth, there'll be no problem, but instead of talking to reporters, you'll have to talk under oath. Do you understand?"

"It's God's honest truth," Crawford declared.

"Then you have no problem."

Joe ushered Crawford into the service entrance and paused for a moment. "Where are your officers, Mr. Crawford? Are they still at the hotel where we put the crew?"

"No, sir. I think they're all coming here. They were like me, waiting for clothes, and then they'll have to get through the crowds and the reporters, but they're on their way."

"Well, that's good to know," Joe said as he ushered Crawford into the meeting room.

Bill, along with Senator Newlands and a number of officials, was still seated at the table. The spectators were chatting among themselves, and Ismay was nowhere in sight. *Hiding in shame*, Joe thought. *He'll be hiding for the rest of his life if he's not careful.*

"Blimey," said Crawford, who seemed to have abandoned his attempt at high-class English. "There's a lot of people, ain't there? Wish I hadn't said nothing."

"Just tell the truth and you'll be all right, but if it's not the truth, Senator Smith will know."

Joe signaled to Bill and brought Crawford forward in front of the long table and a phalanx of official faces. The spectators sat back in their seats and fell silent.

Bill rose and leaned forward. He looked at Crawford for a long moment and then smiled.

"What is your full name?"

Crawford's voice trembled. "Alfred Crawford, sir."

"And where do you reside?"

"In Southampton, England."

"How old are you, Mr. Crawford?"

"Forty-one, sir."

"And what is your business or occupation?"

"Bedroom steward."

"How long have you been going to sea?"

"Since 1881, sir."

Joe, taking up his position against the back wall, considered

Crawford's answer. It seemed that the bedroom steward had been at sea since he was little more than a child.

While Bill continued his questioning, Joe let his thoughts return to his most pressing problem—the logbook. The only way to be certain of the ship's speed at the time she hit the iceberg was to read the log. Knowing the speed of the ship would give Bill a chance to fix blame and declare that the sinking was no act of God but an act of recklessness caused by Bruce Ismay. If the logbook had survived, it would surely be in the hands of a crew member. Or maybe not literally in their hands—maybe under a mattress or beneath a pillow.

Joe pulled in his wandering thoughts as he sensed a change in the spectators. Bill had completed his preliminary questions. He was coming to the meat of his initial interrogation.

"Mr. Crawford, did you know Mr. and Mrs. Straus?"

"Yes. I stood at the lifeboat where they refused to get in."

"Did Mrs. Straus get into the boat?"

"She attempted to get into the boat first, and she got back again. Her maid got into the boat."

"What do you mean by 'she *attempted* to get in'?"

"She stepped onto the boat, onto the gunwales, sir. Then she went back to her husband. She said, 'We have been living together for many years, and where you go, I go.'"

Joe heard a collective sigh from the spectators and saw the reporters scratching at their notepads. So this was the story Crawford had been called to confirm. Isidor and Ida Straus, wealthy beyond belief, had chosen to die together on board the sinking ship. He understood why Bill had elected to call Crawford as a witness. This was a story that would catch the public's imagination and consolidate support for the hearings.

Bill changed the subject but continued his questioning. Joe was not surprised. He knew how Bill's mind worked. He had called Crawford to tell one particular story, but he hoped that Crawford would have more to say. He had been present at the launching of a lifeboat. What had he seen?

"The starboard boats were lowered before ours were," Crawford said. "We were on the port side, number eight boat, on the port side."

"Who superintended the loading?" Bill asked.

"The chief officer superintended, and myself."

"And the lowering?"

"Captain Smith, sir."

Joe felt renewed tension in the air. Crawford's answer had caught everyone's attention. It seemed the captain himself had been supervising the loading of lifeboats.

Bill frowned. "The captain of the boat personally superintended the loading and the lowering of number eight boat. Did he superintend the loading and lowering of any other boat?"

"I think he went to number ten boat. I could not see that being lowered into the water. He gave us instructions to pull to a light that he saw and then land the ladies and return back to the ship again. It was the light of a vessel in the distance. We pulled and pulled, but we could not reach it."

"But you didn't go back to the ship?" Bill asked.

"No, sir. We all took an oar and pulled away from the ship. A lady—I don't know her name—took the tiller. Four men took the oars and pulled away. We kept pulling and trying to make a light, and we could not seem to get any closer to it. We kept pulling and pulling until daybreak. Then we saw the *Carpathia* coming up, and we turned around and came back to her."

The shadows of painful remembrance deepened on Crawford's face, and he swayed slightly on his feet. Senator Newlands leaned toward Bill and spoke softly. Bill looked at the steward as if finally noticing the man's distress and waved for Crawford to be seated.

The steward sat and wiped his face with Joe's handkerchief. Perhaps tears, perhaps perspiration—the room was very warm.

Bill continued his questions.

"Mr. Crawford, so far as you observed, was there any struggle to get into the lifeboats, by men or women?"

"No, sir, none whatever."

"Was the ship sinking at this time?"

"She was making water fast at the bows. Yes, sir, she was sinking."

"Thank you for speaking to us," Joe said. "I think we can—"

Crawford interrupted with sudden passion in his voice. "I heard the crash, sir, and I went out on the outer deck and saw the iceberg floating alongside."

The look on Crawford's face told Joe that the steward would never forget what he had seen that night. He had spent almost his entire life at sea, but nothing had prepared him for that iceberg.

Joe retreated from the hearing room. He relit his cheroot and stepped out into the service area behind the hotel. Fortunately, the rain of the night before had given way to broken clouds that promised sunshine by later in the day. He leaned against the low wall that separated the yard from the street and tried to bring his mind to bear on something that had been troubling him—something that Crawford had said.

He gave us instructions to pull to a light that he saw and then land the ladies and return back to the ship again. It was the light of a vessel in the distance.

Crawford had seemed an honest enough man, and Joe could not imagine what the steward would gain by inventing such a story. Perhaps it was not Crawford's invention. Perhaps it was Captain Smith who had made up the lie in an attempt to calm the terrified ladies. Already the newspapers were creating a heroic myth of wealthy gentlemen stepping calmly aside and allowing the women and children into the boats, but Joe suspected that calm had not truly prevailed as the ship had begun to list and the crew had scrambled to uncover the lifeboats. It was quite possible that Captain Smith had conjured up an imaginary light in the near distance. By telling the terrified passengers that a vessel was nearby and help was just a short distance away, he had managed to control the loading of the lifeboats and get them safely away. The light could not have come from the *Carpathia*—she had still been well over the horizon—and radio messages placed all other vessels at a greater distance.

Joe shrugged. No one would ever know what Captain Smith had done or thought as he had gone down into the icy water along with his ship. Crawford thought he had seen the light, but every survivor had spoken of the brilliance of the stars and the fact that their light reflected in the water. *No*, Joe thought, *let the light be a white lie told by the captain—something to set the oarsmen rowing away so they would not be caught in the* Titanic's *suction as she went down.* The man was gone now, and his lie had done no harm and maybe a great deal of good.

"Sheriff Bayliss!"

Joe dragged his mind back from the far reaches of the Atlantic and saw a man walking toward him. The man was not at first familiar, but the dog was a creature not easily forgotten. Wolfie the otterhound was being held on a tight leash by a tall young man in a dark suit. His hair was combed, and his beard was neatly trimmed. It took Joe a moment to realize that the dog walker was Danny

McSorley, the Marconi operator who had sailed on the *Titanic* as a passenger.

Joe took a step forward and shook Danny's hand despite the fact that Wolfie threatened to trip him in his eagerness to sniff at Joe's boots.

"Well," Joe said, "you're looking a lot better. I see you still have Mrs. Trentham's dog."

"He's mine now," Danny said with a rueful grin. "She didn't want him. She never really wanted him. She just wanted to annoy the Countess of Rothes by insisting on keeping him. Now that we're ashore, Mrs. Trentham doesn't know what to do with him. He's the only one, you see. We think he was being brought here with a female so they could be mated, and that way, he would be valuable. All alone, he's nothing but a big, hairy, unhousebroken hound."

Danny pulled on the leash to lift Wolfie's head away from Joe's boots. "I spent the night at Mrs. Trentham's house, and it's no place for a dog like Wolfie. Too many things for him to break or chew on, and too many housemaids for him to frighten. So I took him and we left. The Marconi company wired me some money, and I bought this suit to look smart and respectable, and then I came here to see if anyone could tell me how to find Miss Kate. I didn't have a chance to say goodbye to her."

Joe shook his head. "She's not here, and you're not the only person who needs to find her. She was a witness to me serving subpoenas on the *Titanic's* officers." He hesitated, looking down at Wolfie and then back at Danny. "That animal won't be welcome on an omnibus or a cab, but I'm sure he can use a good long walk. We have to assume that Kate has gone with her employers."

Danny gave him a glance of mingled relief and puzzlement. "She has employers?"

"Yes. She's a governess."

"Well, that's interesting," Danny said. "So she wasn't a first-class passenger?"

"No. I suppose she was working her passage to Europe."

"And she isn't employed by Mrs. Trentham."

"No. She was just helping the old lady," Joe said, "and now we don't know where to find her. I was planning to go to the Van Burens' house myself. I have attempted to telephone and received no reply, but you could go for me if you have the time. I have something else to look for, and I think that now is as good a time as any."

Danny nodded thoughtfully. "I had planned to go to Washington, but I can do this before I go."

"I thought you were headed for Canada," Joe said.

"I am, but there's something I have to do in Washington first."

"Wouldn't you rather see New York City?" Joe asked. "A young man like you won't find much to do in Washington."

Danny shrugged. "Maybe I'll see New York after I've done …" He hesitated and looked at Joe quizzically. "Is it easy to see the president?"

Joe laughed. "He's a big man. You can't miss him."

"But is it easy to talk to him?"

"I don't know," Joe said. "I've never tried. Senator Smith talks to him all the time, but that's different."

Danny nodded. "Maybe I'll ask the senator to help me. Meantime, give me the address for Miss Kate, and I'll go and find her."

Joe watched thoughtfully as Danny strode away with Wolfie at his heels. He wondered if he should tell Bill about Danny's sudden interest in talking to the president. He shook his head. Bill had enough on his mind.

☐

CHAPTER TEN

Senator William Alden Smith

The spectators had been silent for some time. Albert Crawford's story of Ida and Isidor Straus waiting serenely for death had brought an abrupt ending to the circus atmosphere, and a shadow lingered in the room. Perhaps it was the effect of Crawford's humble presence, so small and unpretentious in his borrowed suit, or perhaps it was his simple words: "I saw the iceberg." As the steward sat there wiping his nose, it seemed that everyone in that room could see the iceberg and feel its chill.

Bill knew that he was taking a risk in calling his next witness, but it had to be done. Time was short, and he was making very little progress. He would have to talk to the man who was already a hero in the British newspapers—the man who had kept the small flotilla of lifeboats afloat during the long, cold night—the most senior officer to survive. Charles Lightoller.

Within moments, Bill knew that Lightoller was making a favorable impression on the spectators, especially the ladies, and if he was not careful, Lightoller would make him look like a fool. The officer answered every question in a quiet but firm voice with a warm, friendly rural accent. He was polite, professional, and every word he spoke revealed how little Bill knew of the sea and how foolish Bill was in his questioning. The questioning began well enough.

"What is your name?"

"Charles Herbert Lightoller."

"How old are you?"

"Thirty-eight."

"What is your business?"

"Seaman."

Such a simple answer, Bill thought. The sea was the entirety of this man's professional life. He didn't boast of his status; he simply spoke of the sea. He did not try to put his position above that of anyone else. He was a seaman—enough said.

Bill would have to begin by forcing the man to acknowledge that he had some responsibility for the ship. He was not just a seaman. "What position do you occupy?" Bill asked.

"Second officer of the *Titanic*."

While Bill took Lightoller through a long series of questions about the sea trials of the *Titanic*, he could feel the audience, and even his own committee, becoming restless. The man answered each question, but each answer led to another question, and Bill was soon lost in a flurry of replies about the intricacies of preparing a ship like the *Titanic* for sea trials. Lightoller spoke with authority about days spent in Belfast Lough, turning circles and adjusting the compass. He professed no knowledge of engine tests, stating quite clearly that was the business of the chief engineer, and somehow making Bill feel a fool for asking.

He looked at the man standing at attention behind the committee table. Lightoller had been given an opportunity to sit, but he had chosen not to. He was not a conventionally handsome man—stocky and broad faced—but every eye was fixed on him, and some of the ladies were actually fanning themselves.

"Mr. Lightoller," Bill said, "would you describe a life belt?"

Lightoller raised his eyebrows, and Senator Newlands leaned across the table and seemed to offer Lightoller a sympathetic wink. Nonetheless, Bill waited while Lightoller described a life belt in unnecessarily minute detail.

"So," Bill asked, "have you ever been in the sea with one of these on?"

"Yes, sir."

"Where?"

"From the *Titanic*."

"In this recent collision?"

"Yes, sir."

"How long were you in the sea?"

"About an hour."

Lightoller spoke the words in the same businesslike tone he had used for all of his responses, but Bill, and probably everyone else, would know what they meant. An hour in the frigid water was almost more than a body could bear. The man who stood calmly now had been very close to death. *Well*, Bill thought, *I suppose we are closing in on the important questions now.*

"What time did you leave the ship, Mr. Lightoller?"

"I didn't leave it."

"Did the ship leave you?" Bill regretted the words as soon as they were out of his mouth.

"Yes, sir."

Bill watched the shadow that crept into Lightoller's eyes and softened his tone. "Did you stay until the ship had departed entirely?"

"Yes, sir."

The shadow retreated from Lightoller's eyes to be replaced by stoic resignation as Bill poked and prodded at the man's memory, asking if he had seen Ismay, asking where the captain had been, asking how the boats had been uncovered. Finally he returned to the moment that the *Titanic* had taken her final plunge into the depths.

The shadow returned deep and dark, and seemed to fall not only over Lightoller but over the entire room. Lightoller turned his head away and focused his eyes on something that no one else could see.

"The ship lunged forward, and a great wave rolled up over the bridge. I turned my back on the ship and dived forward into the icy water. I swam towards the starboard, not knowing why, not knowing why I should swim at all, for there was surely no hope of rescue for me."

Bill held his breath. He could see it for himself. The ship sinking by the bow, the people scrambling upward, trying to save themselves for one last moment, one last precious breath, and Lightoller turning his back and diving into the sea.

"As the vessel sank," Lightoller said, "I found myself drawn by suction towards an airshaft on the roof of the officers' quarters. The sea was pouring down the shaft, and I was riveted to the grating, unable to escape. I closed my eyes and recalled the words of the Ninety-First Psalm: 'He shall give his angels charge over thee.' And then a great explosion of hot air belched up from the shaft, and I found myself surfacing next to an overturned collapsible lifeboat. I grabbed the rope and thanked God. I drifted with the collapsible and watched. The *Titanic's* bow plunged deeper, and her stern rose ever higher into the air. The smokestack toppled over with a crash and a spray of sparks onto the people struggling in the water."

"Did it injure any of them seriously?" Bill asked.

"Does it matter?"

"Did it kill anybody?"

"I cannot tell."

Newlands leaned across the table, and his voice was an angry hiss. "That's enough, Smith."

Bill nodded and took a deep breath to compose himself. "We'll break for lunch," he said.

"I think you had better."

"But I'm not done with Lightoller. He's a brave man, no doubt about it, and a natural commander, but that doesn't make him immune from questioning."

Newlands picked up his notepad. "Just be careful. If you raise too much sympathy for him, Ismay will get swept along with him. It's obvious you're not going to get Lightoller to say anything about Ismay—first, because he's a company man, and second, because I don't think he knows anything. Obviously, he was too busy getting the lifeboats out to worry about anything else. You'll do better asking the passengers."

Bill spread his hands in a gesture of helplessness. "You know the score, Newlands. Two days, that's all. After that, the passengers will all scatter, and I'll have to send the *Titanic* crew home. I can't keep them forever." He looked across at Will McKinstry. "Any other word from the president? Any change of mind?"

"No, sir. Nothing. He's still keeping his door closed."

Newlands shook his head. "I don't know how he plans to run an election campaign from behind closed doors. He'll have to come out sometime." He rubbed his hands together. "Come on, Smith, let's go to lunch. We have a table at the Palm Court."

Bill turned to his secretary, who seemed ready to follow along with him to the restaurant. "Will, what happened about the Irish family I asked you to find for my wife? Was there anyone saved?"

"It's possible," McKinstry said. "I found two girls, sisters. They were in a bad way, having lost their father and, I believe, a couple of brothers, but they said their father had talked of taking them to Washington, said they had a relative who worked in the house of someone in government. They didn't know you by name, Senator; they scarcely remembered their own names, poor little things, but they seem to be a possibility. The names matched. They are Maeve and Kitty McCaffrey, or so they say, and those are the names we were looking for."

"Well, where are they?" Bill asked. "They didn't send them to Ellis Island, did they? They've been through enough without ending up in that grim place."

"They were taken in by the Salvation Army," McKinstry said. "They have the men in one hostel and the women in another. They are locked up for the time being."

"Locked up?" Bill asked. "Why would anyone lock them up? They're not criminals."

"We don't know that," McKinstry warned. "They've no paperwork and they could be anyone. Immigration will have to sort them out and make sure they match with the passenger list. They promise to be quick about it, but of course, they'll mostly be charity cases even if they're allowed in—women without husbands, and children without fathers, and whatever little treasure they may have accumulated will have gone down with the ship. It's a sad case, Senator. I went in among them on the *Carpathia*. I have never seen such grief."

Bill rubbed a weary hand across his eyes. "I know, Will, and I promise you we'll get to the bottom of what happened, but we have to start at the top. If I can't pin the blame on Ismay and the whole thing is judged to be an act of God, no one will get a penny. As for the girls, we'll send them on to Washington. Maybe they're Molly's relatives or maybe they're not, but Nana will find a place for them. At least we can do that much. Go and send a telegram to her and tell her the girls are coming."

McKinstry frowned. "One more thing, Senator."

"Yes?"

"I saw a great deal of anger among those steerage folk. They say they were locked belowdecks. We need to nip that talk in the bud, sir, or we'll have an Irish rebellion on our hands. We don't need this to reach Boston."

"We don't need it to reach anywhere," Bill said. "We've enough Irish here in New York City to set off a rebellion."

He stood for a moment watching McKinstry walk away to send the telegram. He thought that Nana, at least, would be pleased with his decision and hoped that the two girls truly were Molly's relatives. He thought of the afternoon ahead and the questions he would have to ask. Not only must he deal with Ismay's slippery answers and Lightoller's quiet heroism, but he also had to avoid mention of the very late arrival on deck of the steerage passengers. That was a subject that would have to be approached carefully at a later date, once the steerage passengers had dispersed. Tempers were running high now, stoked by wildly speculative newspaper articles. He wished he had more time. Forty-eight hours was not enough time to even scratch the surface.

Eva Trentham was the first person he saw when he walked into the Palm Court. She sat at a small table in the center of the room. Although she was the only person seated at the table, she was not alone. Bridie, now wearing a nurse's gray dress and white cuffs, stood behind her wheelchair, and various representatives of New York society paused to speak to Eva as they proceeded to their own tables. Bill refused to catch her eye. She had helped to bring this hearing about, but he would not answer to her—not now, not ever.

Newlands led the way to a secluded table set among the potted palms, which were the main feature of the restaurant. Bill sank into his seat, and a waiter appeared at his elbow almost immediately.

"Whiskey and soda," Bill said. Nana did not approve of lunchtime drinking, but Bill needed a drink. He admitted to himself that he had not done well with Ismay. The man was arrogant and unlikable, but very firm in his testimony that he had not been responsible for the running of the ship. As for Lightoller ... Bill shook his head. The Englishman had made a fool of him. No, that was not true—Bill had made a fool of himself. He should never have given Lightoller a chance to describe his actions as the ship had gone down. He had left an indelible impression of bravery—going down with the ship, surfacing in the icy water, and recalling words from the Psalms. Who could condemn a man like that? Bill knew he would have to recall him after lunch and find a way to bring his actions into question.

The waiter brought him his whiskey and soda, and Bill took a long swallow to take the unpleasant taste from his mouth.

"Stop here, Bridie. Yes, right here."

Bill looked up and saw that Bridie was maneuvering Eva Trentham's wheelchair to a position beside his table. He rose instinctively to welcome her.

"Oh, sit down, sit down," Eva croaked. "I don't want to be shouting up at you for everyone to hear."

Bill returned to his seat and took another long swallow of his drink. "You know Senator Newlands?"

"Of course I do. I know everyone. Now, let's get straight to the point. Ismay is going to be a dead end, isn't he?"

"No, of course not. I'll recall him."

"And he'll continue to deny everything," Eva said.

"No doubt he will," Bill agreed, "but we'll have to break him down."

"He was a rat leaving a sinking ship," Eva said, "and if you dig around, you'll find he wasn't the only rat. I saw a few rats myself. Unfortunately, being a rat is not a crime, and you can't drag them all in and humiliate them—you don't have time."

"We need the *Titanic*'s sailing orders," Newlands said. "Without them, we have nothing."

Bill shook his head, hoping that Newlands would understand that they had no need to share this information with Eva. This was a Senate investigation, not an afternoon tea salon.

"Well," Eva said, "the captain's gone; the first officer's gone; and you got nowhere with Lightoller this morning, so where will you find these orders?"

"We're undertaking a search for the ship's logbook," Newlands offered. "We believe it will prove that she was proceeding at an unsafe speed."

"Well, of course she was," Eva sniffed. "If her speed had been safe, she wouldn't have run into the damned iceberg." She looked at Newlands's shocked face. "Yes, I swear sometimes. In fact, I swear quite often. I haven't always been a lady. I'm going to leave you to eat your lunch now, but I have one more name for you."

Bill stared down at the tablecloth, willing her to go away, but

Newlands waited with an eager expression.

"J. P. Morgan," Eva said. "It was his ship. He'll know if they were going for a crossing record."

"J. P. Morgan is in France," Bill said wearily. "He did not even sail on the *Titanic*. We'll never get him here to testify."

"Issue a subpoena," Eva growled.

Bill shook his head. "He won't come."

"Oh, really," Eva hissed. "I never took you for a quitter, Senator. I am very disappointed." She turned her head to look at Bridie. "Push me, woman. I have nothing more to say here."

Eva retreated to her table, and the waiter arrived with soup. Bill ordered another drink. Newlands raised his eyebrows.

"Impossible woman," Bill said.

"But she's not wrong. J. P. Morgan would be quite a catch."

"If we destroy him, we destroy our whole financial system," Bill said. "I'm not calling him. Ismay will be enough for our purposes."

Bill had taken only one spoonful of soup before he felt the presence of someone else at the table. He looked up and saw a handsome woman in a black dress, accompanied by a boy of about seventeen, wearing a black tie and a black mourning band on his sleeve. Once again Bill and Newlands rose to their feet.

"Please forgive me for interrupting your meal," the woman said. "I'm not accustomed to introducing myself, but I no longer have a husband to do that for me. I am Mrs. John Thayer, and this is my son, Jack. I think you know … knew my husband."

"Yes, of course," Bill said. "I did."

"We are sorry for your loss," Newlands added. "Your husband was a fine man."

"Yes, he was," Mrs. Thayer agreed. "I don't mean to keep you for long, but I don't suppose we will be called to give testimony, and so I want you to hear for yourself what my son has to say about Sir Bruce Ismay."

Bill looked at the boy, tall and gangly, more of a man than a child. "I'm sorry about your father," he said with sudden real sympathy. He remembered how it was to lose a father.

"Thank you, sir."

Mrs. Thayer gave her son a gentle push. "Go ahead, Jack. Tell the senators what you saw. Don't be shy."

"I was with Dick Williams, sir, and the ladies, our mothers, had already gone in the lifeboats."

"Why didn't you go with them?" Newlands asked.

Jack straightened his shoulders. "I'm seventeen years old, sir. It was women and children only."

Newlands nodded. "I see."

"We were running along the deck," Jack said. Bill thought that his calm words failed to convey the panic the two boys must have felt as they watched the lifeboats leaving and saw the water rising above the lower decks.

"There was a crowd," Jack said, "and we saw Sir Bruce."

Bill waited.

"He was pushing," Jack said. "You see, the purser, he had a gun, and he was firing it to keep the people away so he could load the lifeboat properly."

"A gun?" Newlands said. "This is the first I've heard of guns."

"That's how Sir Bruce got in that lifeboat."

"You're saying he forced himself in at gunpoint?" Bill asked.

"Yes, sir."

"And you," Bill asked. "How did you get into a lifeboat?"

Bill saw a shadow creep across Jack's young face. He was beginning to know what that shadow meant. Young Jack had a story he needed to tell.

"I didn't get into a lifeboat," Jack said. "I waited. We were all there, waiting. Masses of us. Just hanging on until the last breath. And then I sat on the rail and I jumped. The water was freezing, and I was so cold that I couldn't swim."

Mrs. Thayer caught hold of her son's arm. "You don't have to say anything else, dear."

"No," Bill said. "Let him speak. He needs to say it, and we need to hear it. What happened next, son?"

"I just stayed there," the boy said, "and watched her, watched the ship. There was light all around her, like she was on fire and shining up from under the water. And then I bumped into this overturned boat, a collapsible, and I climbed on top with the other men."

Bill noted the hint of pride in Jack's voice as he included himself with the other men. On that night, he had grown from a boy into a man. If he had gone with his mother to the lifeboats, he would still have been a boy, but not now.

"We could see the people on the *Titanic*," he said, "clinging to her deck like swarming bees. She rose way up into the sky, and then she fell."

Mrs. Thayer nodded to Bill. "We just wanted you to know," she said.

"What about your friend Dick?" Newlands asked.

"Dick Williams," Jack said. "I think he's going to be all right. He couldn't find a place on the upturned collapsible, so he was in the water for a long, long time. His legs are frostbitten."

"The doctor on the *Carpathia* wanted to amputate them," Mrs. Thayer said, "but he wouldn't let him. He said he would recover, and I think he will. He's up and walking. He's a very determined young man." She turned away with tears in her eyes. "Come along, Jack."

Newlands watched them depart. "Seventeen years old," he said, "and he owns the Pennsylvania Railroad. Will you call him as a witness? He spoke of the purser firing a gun."

Bill resumed his seat. "It's not enough for young Jack to say it. We need proof. I'll get Joe Bayliss on it and see what he can uncover. We need to know who was doing the shooting and why."

"And what will we do this afternoon?"

"We'll have Lightoller back, and this time, I won't have any heroic speeches from him. I want to know what really went on when they loaded the lifeboats, and then I want to talk to the radio operator from the *Carpathia*. The man from the *Titanic* is in the hospital. They say he stayed at his post even as the ship went down. I can't afford to interview any more heroes, and I'm not having him brought out in a wheelchair. Cottam, from the *Carpathia*, can tell us what he knows, and we'll only call the *Titanic*'s man if we have to, and when he's not in a wheelchair."

"Be careful," Newlands said. "We're looking into a tragedy, but if we can find heroes to praise, why not praise them?"

"Because praising heroes won't bring results. I will not allow the newspapers to see the White Star officers as heroes. The fact is they ignored radio messages and ran their ship into an iceberg. I'm not interested in what they did afterward—I want to know what happened before they hit the damn thing. I want Ismay."

"He's not going to tell you anything."

Bill turned his attention back to his food. "Someone will," he said, "if the president gives me time to ask enough questions."

West Village, New York
Joe Bayliss

Joe strode in through the front door of the sailors' hostel on Jane Street. He felt better for having stretched his legs on his walk across the city, but the ever-present noise, the polluted air, and the press of the crowded streets reminded him why he tried to avoid cities. He set aside his longing for the clear waters of Lake Michigan, with its sand dunes and pine-studded bluffs, and looked around at the gloomy dark-paneled lobby.

He thought that maybe the hostel's cramped accommodation would be suited to the *Titanic*'s ordinary crew members, but the ship's officers were no doubt accustomed to something finer. So far they had not complained, but that was probably because they expected to go home, if not tomorrow, then the day after. He leaned across the reception desk and struck the bell. An elderly man with sailor tattoos on his arms and crinkles around his eyes from staring too long at distant shores came out of the inner office. Joe flashed his badge.

"What?" the old sailor said. "You want to arrest someone here? No criminals here."

"I want to see the rooms where the *Titanic*'s officers are staying."

"Up the stairs, third floor. You'll find some of the crew up there, but the officers are all out."

Joe nodded. Of course the officers were all out; that was why he had chosen this moment to arrive. The officers were all at the Waldorf Astoria, waiting to be called as witnesses.

"We could do without those officers," the old sailor said. "They shouldn't be here. They made a fuss. Didn't want to mix with the crew."

Joe raised a querying eyebrow. "The officers didn't want to mix with the crew?"

"Said it wasn't right. Said they should have separate accommodations. If you ask me, they're lucky to have anything at all. Lucky to be alive."

"Yes, they are," Joe agreed. "Give me the room keys, and I'll see myself up."

"They won't like it."

"That's my problem, not yours," Joe said. "If they complain, you can tell them I'm acting on behalf of the US government, and if they don't like that, they can complain to their ambassador. Meantime, I am going to look in their rooms."

Joe ascended the stairs with the bundle of keys in his hand. The hallways were cramped, with cell-like rooms on either side and daylight seeping in through windows at the end of each corridor. When he reached the third floor, he saw that a number of doors were open and a knot of disheveled men stood in his way.

Joe was prepared to flash his badge and exert his authority, but the men who turned to face him showed no sign of aggression. They were unhappy, traumatized no doubt, but not dangerous.

"Step aside, please," Joe said.

A short man with a thatch of untidy brown hair and the beginnings of a beard looked at him with an expression that was almost pleading. "Have you come to tell us we can go home?"

"No. I'm sorry. That's not what I'm here for."

"I don't know why they want to keep us. It ain't like anyone's going to ask us any questions. We don't know nothing. The captain says we're sinking. The officers say get in a lifeboat and row, and that's all we done. We don't know nothing else."

Another man, this one with a bandaged hand and a cut over one eyebrow, shook his head. "You're wrong, Hemming. They're not done with us. I mean, they called Crawford, didn't they? He got a paper, and he had to go."

"A bedroom steward," Hemming said. "What they gonna learn from a bedroom steward?"

"He was a first-class steward," the other man replied. "They just want to know what the nobs were doing when the ship was sinking. They don't care about us."

"Are you all just regular seamen?" Joe asked.

"You could say that," Hemming said. "I'm a lamp trimmer." He indicated the man with the bandaged hand. "Fred Clench is an able seaman; Moore is a fireman; Frank Evans is another able seaman; and Fleet, well …" He pointed at a small, dark-haired man who seemed unwilling to look Joe in the eye. "Fleet was the lookout," Hemming said.

"Didn't do a very good job," Evans muttered.

"We didn't have no binoculars," Fleet complained.

Joe made a mental note. The lookout had had no binoculars—that was something to tell Senator Smith.

"Do you know when we're going home?" Hemming asked. "We don't know nothing, and we want to see our families."

"Do our wives even know we're alive?" Evans added. "They're probably thinking we've all gone down to a watery grave."

"What am I going to tell my mum?" Clench asked. He looked at Joe with watery eyes. "My brother, George, was on board with me, and he's gone. How am I going to tell her that I didn't look out for him?"

"Yeah, well, someone should have been looking out," Evans said. He looked at Fleet. "That's the lookout's job, isn't it, Fleet?"

"It wasn't my fault," Fleet mumbled.

"Can you do anything for us?" Hemming asked. "We ain't been paid, and we ain't going to be paid. Our pay stops when the ship goes down, and we need to go home and get another ship, or we need to make some money here. There's a whole lot of reporters out there willing to pay money for our stories, but our officers say we can't speak to them."

"They ain't really our officers," Clench said. "Think about it. If White Star ain't paying us, then Lightoller and Lowe and all ain't really our officers. We should just go outside and talk."

"If we do, we'll never get a berth from White Star ever again," Fleet said.

"Well, you won't," Hemming said, "on account of you not seeing the iceberg."

"I did see it," Fleet grumbled. "I called it out."

Joe slipped his hand into his pocket and pulled out a roll of dollar bills. He peeled off five one-dollar bills. "Here's a dollar each. Go on outside and buy yourselves something to eat, but don't talk to the reporters. If I find that any of you have talked to a reporter, I'll issue a warrant for your arrest, and you'll never go home. Do you understand me?"

Hemming eyed the money suspiciously. "You can't arrest us."

"Yes, I can. I'm a federal marshal. Take the money and go."

The men looked at each other, and finally Hemming nodded. "We'll take it." He held out his hand. "Come on, lads. Let's go and see the city."

Joe waited until the men had clattered down the stairs in their borrowed shoes, and then he sorted through the bunch of keys. He opened the first door and began his search.

Greenwich Village, New York
Danny McSorley

Danny surveyed the row of imposing brownstone houses and considered how fortunate he was not to live in one of them. Maybe some would think them very fine, with their grand front steps and fancy wrought-iron railings, but he could only see that they were squeezed together and sharing walls. In that respect, they were no different from the workmen's cottages at home in Borrowdale.

He considered walking along the side alley and presenting himself at the service entrance. He was disheveled and damp from his long walk across the city in a light, drizzling rain, and Wolfie was certainly not at his best. Although Danny had fed Wolfie a sausage he had purchased from a street vendor and allowed him to drink from a horse trough, Wolfie was not happy. The source of the hound's unhappiness was Danny's insistence that they keep moving instead of allowing Wolfie to investigate each and every intriguing new scent. On their walk through the varied city neighborhoods, they had encountered a flood of odors, from spicy Italian cooking to the inevitable stink of drains and privies. Wolfie wanted to trace them all to their sources.

Danny straightened his tie and smoothed back his hair. He was not going to the back door. He was here on business from the US Senate. He imagined that Joe Bayliss would not go to the back door, and therefore, neither would he.

He tied Wolfie's leash to the wrought-iron railing. "Wait here."

Wolfie flopped down onto the sidewalk and lowered his head between his paws. Apparently, he was in need of a rest. Danny, on the other hand, was filled with energy at the thought that the lovely Miss Kate was just a few steps away. She was within reach, both in terms of distance and in terms of social standing. She was not a rich first-class passenger; she was a governess. She was a member of a respectable profession, and so was he.

He was grinning as he walked up the steps and knocked on the door. When no one came to answer his knocking, he knocked again. Now he could hear voices on the other side of the door.

A man's voice was bellowing angry questions, and a woman's voice was providing answers.

"What do we pay the damned servants for," the man shouted, "if I have to answer the door myself?"

The woman's voice was shrill. "They're not here. We have no servants. You sent them all away when we went on the cruise."

"Well, I'm not answering the door," the man—Danny assumed he was Mr. van Buren—insisted.

Danny knocked again. He had no intention of leaving, and he would keep knocking until the two people behind the door resolved their argument.

To his surprise, the door opened suddenly while the man and woman were still arguing. He looked down and saw two childish faces looking up at him—a girl and a boy who shared the same round, well-fed faces, small dark eyes, and dull brown hair.

"It's a man," the boy said, turning away to talk to his parents.

The girl pushed past her brother and caught sight of Wolfie. "He's brought a dog. Is it for us?"

"What? No! No dogs."

The master of the house turned with a furious expression on his face. The expression changed a little as he took in Danny's height and width. When he was fourteen years old, Danny had achieved a growth spurt unrivaled by any other member of his family. Although his sudden expansion upward and outward had removed any possibility that he would make a living from the narrow coal seam worked by the miners of Borrowdale, it had its advantages in serving as a wordless threat to anyone who wanted to pick a fight with him. Mr. van Buren took a step backward and adjusted his expression.

Danny smiled at the little girl. "That's my dog. He's not for you, but you can go and pet him if you like."

The mother came forward at once. "Brigitta, don't you dare."

She scuttled past Danny and caught her daughter's hand. She turned to the boy. "Come with me, both of you. This is men's business."

"Not really," Danny said. "Just wanted to know ..."

Mrs. van Buren dragged her children away, with Brigitta still whining that she wanted to pet the dog, and Danny was left face-to-face with the master of the house.

Van Buren was a doughy-looking man, pudgy faced and soft bellied. His eyes were pale and protruding, and his lips were thick and seemed unnaturally moist. Danny tried to imagine Kate voluntarily spending time in the company of this man, or the two children, whose whining voices still reached him from somewhere within the house. How desperate must she be to submit herself to this family?

"I'm looking for your governess, Miss Kate Royston," Danny said firmly.

Van Buren pursed his unpleasant lips. "What do you want with her?"

"It's official business," Danny replied. "I would like to speak to her immediately."

"So would I," Van Buren sneered, "but she's not here."

Danny checked his momentary disappointment. "When will she return?"

Van Buren shook his head. "Never. She'll never show her face around here again, ungrateful little ..." Something in Danny's expression caused Van Buren to fall silent. When he regained his voice, his tone was somewhat milder but still suspicious. "What kind of official business are you on? You don't look very official to me, and that dog is no police dog."

"I'm here on behalf of the sergeant at arms of the US Senate," Danny said. "Miss Royston is to be questioned as a witness."

"Witness to what?" Van Buren asked.

"The *Titanic*," Danny replied.

"She didn't see anything," Van Buren sniffed. "She was on the *Carpathia*. You're in the wrong place, young man. Now take that mangy dog and go."

"Not until I've seen Miss Royston."

"She's not here," Van Buren repeated. "She was never here."

"But she left the *Carpathia* with you and your family."

Van Buren grimaced. "She did not. I offered to take her with us and let her stay the night here, and I left to secure a cab, but she never joined us."

"You mean she never left the ship?"

"I don't know what she did. I told her where to meet us, and we waited for her, but she never came, and I haven't seen her."

"Do you have any idea where she may have gone?"

Van Buren's lip curled impatiently. "No, I do not. I know nothing about her. She answered an advertisement I placed in the newspaper and seemed qualified for the position. I asked her nothing about her private life. In fact, I barely spoke to her." He leaned forward and spoke confidingly. "Attractive young woman like that … well, you know how it is. My wife didn't want me in close proximity."

"Perhaps your wife could tell me—"

"My wife is fully occupied with the children," Van Buren declared, "and she knows nothing of Miss Royston's comings and goings. We waited for her, and she never came. That's all I can tell you, and I'll thank you to get yourself off my doorstep and your dog off my sidewalk."

Danny retreated down the steps. He could find nothing to like about Kate's employer, but he had believed him when he'd said Kate was not in the house. It was obvious that Mrs. van Buren was reluctantly looking after the children herself.

His thoughts turned to the chaos that had reigned as the *Carpathia*'s passengers had disembarked and forged a path through the jostling reporters and anxious relatives. For some reason, Kate had followed the Van Buren family down the gangplank, but instead of seeking the safety of their waiting cab, she had set off in another direction. Where could she possibly have gone on such a night in the wind and rain, and carrying her portmanteau?

He untied Wolfie's leash and set off on his return journey. He walked slowly with his head down and his thoughts churning. He was painfully aware of the bloodstained letter he carried in his pocket. His promise to a dying man could not be ignored, and because of that promise, he could not stay in New York. He had not found Kate today, and now it seemed that he never would.

The Waldorf Astoria
Senator William Alden Smith

Senator Newlands leaned across the table and coughed discreetly to draw Bill's attention. Bill turned away from Harold Cottam, the *Carpathia*'s radio operator, and bent down to hear what Newlands had to say.

"Don't drag this out, Smith," Newlands whispered. "You ask too many questions."

"I have to ask before he forgets or changes his mind."

"He seems like an honest young man," Newlands said, "and he's done nothing wrong. You're losing sympathy."

"I'm not here for sympathy. I'm here for facts."

"It's an inquiry, not a court of law, and we only have another day and a half at the most. At this rate, we'll run out of time before we run out of witnesses." Newlands scowled impatiently. "Get on with it, or I'll start asking the questions myself."

Bill turned back to Harold Cottam, noting the concentration on the young man's face. Newlands was right, of course, Cottam was doing his best to make order out of the chaos of that terrible night when the *Titanic* had sent her distress call to any ship that could hear her. This man, only twenty-one years old, had been at the heart of the chaos, sending and receiving and monitoring messages to discover which vessel had the best chance of reaching the sinking liner.

"Mr. Cottam," Bill said, "what were your instructions?"

"The captain told me to tell the *Titanic* that all our boats were ready and we were coming as hard as we could come, with a double watch on in the engine room, and to be prepared when we got there with lifeboats. I got no acknowledgment of that message."

"Whether it was received or not, you don't know?"

"No, sir."

Bill tried to put himself in Cottam's place. He had sent a message of reassurance to the *Titanic*: *We are on our way. We're ready to help you.* And the response, as the *Carpathia* had changed course and fired up her boilers, had been silence.

"Just so we all understand," Bill said. "When you received that last call from the *Titanic*, that her engine room was filling with water, you say you acknowledged its receipt and took that message to the captain. Did you acknowledge its receipt before you took it to the captain?"

"Yes, sir."

"Then, after you had taken this message to the captain, you came back to your instrument and sent the message that you have just described?"

"Yes, sir."

"And to that you received no reply?"

"No, sir."

"And you never received any other reply?"

Cottam's voice was bleak. "No, sir."

"Or any other word from the ship?"

"No, sir."

"Very well. I think I will just let you stand aside for a while, but we may want you in the morning. Will you be here?"

Cottam gave him a wry smile, and Bill realized the futility of his question. Of course Cottam would return in the morning. He was under subpoena. He was going nowhere until Bill was finished with him. Bill was painfully aware that his questioning of the captain and crew of the *Carpathia* was delaying the ship's departure from New York. Hundreds of passengers were waiting to resume their interrupted cruise of the Mediterranean. The Cunard Line was losing money. Bill was making enemies in high places, and yet he could not shake the feeling that there was something still to be discovered— something that would point to the real reason for the sinking of the *Titanic*.

The reporters were the first to leave the room, rushing for the doors while the spectators gossiped and gathered their belongings. He wondered what the newspapers would make of the day's testimony. Crawford's story of Ida and Isidor Straus would form a tragic symphony. Lightoller, with his stiff upper lip and precise recall, would no doubt be lauded. Although Bill had spent the afternoon firing questions at Lightoller on where and when he had received warnings of ice, how fast the ship was moving, who had taken the ice warning to the bridge, none of that would erase the second officer's moving testimony. Neither, Bill thought, would it erase the stupidity of his own question when Lightoller had described the ship's funnel falling in a shower of sparks among the people struggling in the water. Had it hurt anybody? Of course it had. Had it killed anyone? Who could say? Did it even matter? The people in the water had already been as good as dead.

Well, Bill thought, they still had Ismay's testimony to chew on. Ismay had made a very poor impression. The reporters would have plenty to say about him.

McKinstry closed his notebook. "Do you still want me to call Mr. Bride, the operator from the *Titanic*?"

"Is he out of the hospital?"

"I understand he can be brought here."

Another hero, Bill thought, but he would have to be questioned. Despite Lightoller's protestations, it was obvious that the *Titanic* had received ice warnings from surrounding shipping and equally obvious that they had been ignored.

Bill looked up and saw Joe Bayliss looming in the doorway, an immovable rock as the departing spectators flowed around him. He tried to read the expression on his friend's weathered face, but Joe's craggy features gave nothing away.

When the room was finally empty, Joe stepped inside.

"Well?" Bill asked.

"You owe me five dollars."

"Why?"

"The cost of getting rid of some of the nosiest members of the *Titanic* crew."

"The officers are all here at the Waldorf," Bill said. "I have them standing by, ready to be called. I suppose I should send them away now."

"Well," Joel said, "if you're looking for the logbook, you'd better undertake a search of their clothing before they leave here, or maybe take a look in Ismay's room. The log is not at the seamen's hostel. Really, there's nothing much there. Those poor devils have nothing but the clothes they stand up in."

The sheriff pulled a cheroot from his pocket and struck a match against his boot. A woodsman to the last, Bill thought.

"I've sent young McSorley searching after our missing subpoena witness, Miss Kate Royston. If he doesn't locate her, do you want me to have a word with one of my Pinkerton buddies? After all, we may need her."

Bill thought he saw real concern on Joe's face. "Have you gone soft?" he asked.

"She seemed like a fine young lady, and I think she was traveling alone. I don't see how she could have disappeared. I'm worried about her."

Bill shrugged. "Let's wait a while before we bring in the Pinkerton men. If they start sniffing around, so will the journalists. I'm sure McSorley will find her. He seems a competent fellow."

"I suppose so," Joe grunted. "Sorry about the logbook, but I have something else for you."

"What?"

"I spoke to the lookout. His name is Frederick Fleet, and he let slip that he had no binoculars up there in the crow's nest. The other crew members didn't seem real happy with him, but they closed ranks when they could see I was interested. Maybe if he'd had binoculars, he could have seen the iceberg sooner."

"And," Bill said, "maybe if they hadn't been going so fast, or if they'd listened to the ice warnings, they would not have been in the ice at all. This was no accident, Joe. This was criminal carelessness. I know it, but I can't prove it."

"So what are you going to do?"

Bill shook his head. "I don't know. I've called the *Titanic*'s junior radio operator for tomorrow. The poor lad's been in the hospital ever since he arrived here, and they're going to bring him down here in a wheelchair. It won't look good. I'll have to go easy on him. If I can't prove that Ismay was in fact giving the orders, I'm going to come out of this with nothing, or maybe less than nothing. If I keep on like this, getting nowhere, I'm going to lose the support of my own constituents. This is not paving the road to the White House for me."

"Senator."

Bill turned to see Will McKinstry standing behind him. "Take a break, Will. You've been scribbling away all day."

"There's a lady, sir, a first-class survivor, who would like you to take her statement. She has something to tell you. She's staying here at the Waldorf. Would this evening be convenient?"

Bill shrugged. "Why not? I'm not doing anything else. You'd better come with me, Joe. I may need a sworn witness."

"Meantime," Joe said, "I think we all need a drink."

CHAPTER ELEVEN

Salvation Army Hostel
New York
Kate Royston

Kate waited on a hard wooden chair in the drafty hallway. She attempted to control her impatience. Major Sullivan had made it very clear that no one would leave the hostel until tomorrow, so it didn't really matter how long she had to sit here. At least she now had clean clothes and she'd bathed and washed her hair. She picked at the ugly green dress she'd been given—donated by some New York matron with more money than fashion sense. Kate had inherited her mother's innate sense of style, and she knew very well that green was not her color and ruffles were not her style. In fact, ruffles were no one's style. This dress was ten years old at least.

She fidgeted restlessly. The dress was at least made of a good-quality fabric, but the donated underwear was stiff and scratchy, and had most likely been starched. She sighed. It seemed as if a lifetime had passed since she'd been a girl who owned silk underwear and fashionable dresses. Nothing was left now to remind her of that life, except for her useless vanity, which made her unwilling to even look at herself in a mirror in this hideous travesty of a dress. Worst of all, she still didn't have a plan for what she would do when she was released tomorrow. The major had said something about giving the survivors a little money and a ticket to an onward destination, and that would certainly be useful to everyone except Kate. Kate was not a survivor of the *Titanic*. Kate was in a mess of her own making.

The door opened, and Kitty McCaffrey emerged and slammed the door behind her. "The cheek of it," she said. "Never in all my life have I been treated like that."

"Why?" Kate asked. "What did they do to you? I thought they were just going to ask your name and your destination, and check your health."

"Check my health indeed," Kitty fumed. "Do they think I'm a cow in a barn? If they think they can do that to my little Maeve, they have another think coming."

"What happened?"

"You'll find out," Kitty said as she flounced away, a furious figure in a baggy black dress several sizes too large that trailed on the floor as she walked.

The door opened, and Captain Veronica poked her head out. She smiled encouragingly from beneath her Salvation Army bonnet and then raised her voice in an alarming shout. "Do you speak English?"

"I do," Kate shouted back.

Captain Veronica's voice resumed its usual, good-natured tone. "Oh, good. You're next, my dear. Come in and take a seat."

Kate entered a large room, empty of all furniture except for a small desk and two chairs just inside the door and an arrangement of screens in one corner.

Captain Veronica sat at the desk and indicated that Kate should sit in the other chair. She consulted a dog-eared sheaf of papers set on one corner of the desk. She smiled and picked up a pencil. "What's your name, dear?"

"Kate."

"Kate what?"

"Katherine Elizabeth Royston."

"I see."

Captain Veronica studied a list she had selected from the file. "Your name is not here." Her kind smile remained unchanged, although she cocked her head to one side curiously. "This is the list of survivors we have from the radio operator on the *Carpathia*. It seems he overlooked you."

"No, he didn't. I talked to him."

"You talked to him?"

"Yes. I was there when the radio message came from the *Titanic* and—"

Now Captain Veronica was frowning. "No, that's not right, dear. You're confused. You could not have been with him. You were in a lifeboat, weren't you?"

"No, I wasn't. I was never on the *Titanic.*"

"Oh dear," Captain Veronica whispered, "you really are confused. Have you had a bump on the head?"

"Yes, I have," Kate confirmed. "I was seeing stars for a few minutes, and I can still feel it."

"Well, there you are, then," said Captain Veronica. She shuffled the papers on her desk. "Now, here's a list of all the passengers on the *Titanic.* Let's find you on that list, and we'll see what to do about you. You said your name is Katherine Elizabeth Royston?"

"Yes, I did, and—"

A loud female voice rose from behind the screen and interrupted Kate's answer. "Next! Send in the next woman."

Captain Veronica stood up and placed her hand on the small of Kate's back. "That's you," she said. "Go on in and do what the nurse says, and while you're in there, I'll look through the passenger list. We'll soon have this sorted out."

She moved her hand to Kate's elbow. "Go along and don't make a fuss. All the ladies have been through this inspection."

What am I going to do? Kate asked herself as she walked reluctantly across the room. Tomorrow morning, come what may, she would walk out of the doors of the Salvation Army hostel and onto the streets of New York. Then what?

"Everything off down to your shift, and unpin your hair."

The nurse's voice barely registered with Kate. She heard the words, but they meant nothing as Kate frantically weighed her very few options. Where could she find a friendly face in New York? Perhaps Eva Trentham—

"Come along, girl. Take off your dress, or I'll do it for you. Don't you speak English?" This question was asked in a loud, hectoring voice and broke through Kate's whirling thoughts.

Kate finally took note of the sturdy middle-aged woman who confronted her with hands on ample hips.

"Yes, I speak English."

"Well, that's a mercy. Now take off your dress and let me look at you."

"I'm all right. I don't need a nurse."

"I'm not here to nurse you. I'm here to make sure you're not bringing any of your foreign diseases into the United States."

"I'm not an immigrant. I don't need to be examined."

"None of that nonsense. Take off your dress, or I'll do it for you."

"I'm not an immigrant," Kate repeated.

Captain Veronica peeped around the screen. "She says she had a blow to her head."

The nurse stepped closer and studied Kate with cold indifference. "Sit on that chair and let me look."

The instruction was accompanied by a fierce shove that propelled Kate onto a wooden chair. The nurse's fingers scrabbled through her hair, pulling out pins and releasing Kate's heavy braids. She spoke over Kate's head. "You're right, Captain. She has quite a bump."

Captain Veronica's voice was sympathetic. "Well, then, it's no wonder she's talking nonsense."

"I'm not talking nonsense," Kate insisted.

The nurse's fingers continued the exploration of Kate's hair. "That's not for me to decide. At least you've no head lice. Now let me look at the rest of you. You'll not leave this room until I've examined you, so take off that dress."

Kate gave in to reluctant acceptance. Talking to the nurse would not bring any results. The nurse had no power to release her. If she wanted to go free, she would have to accept the indignity of the health inspection. She would have to allow this nurse, with her cold, calloused fingers and suspicious scowl, to examine her. She stood up, unbuttoned her dress, and let it fall to the floor.

"Underwear," the nurse said.

"What about it?"

"If you have any drawers on, take them off."

"Why?"

"Venereal diseases," the nurse said. She turned to the table behind her and snapped on a pair of yellow rubber gloves. "Syphilis, gonorrhea, and the like."

Kate clutched at her shift. "Don't touch me."

The nurse stood with folded arms. "Do you want to be released from here or not?"

Because she could think of no alternative, Kate lifted her shift, untied a ribbon, and stepped out of her underwear.

As she submitted silently to the kind of indignity that she had not imagined possible, Kate thought of the other women in the hostel— the women who had cried all night. They, too, had been marched into this room and faced this formidable nurse. Apparently, this was normal. This was what the immigrants would have faced at Ellis Island. This was what it took for them to be admitted to the United States.

At last the inspection was over. Kate buttoned her dress and followed the nurse's instruction to return to Captain Veronica. Unfortunately, Captain Veronica was not alone. A stern-faced man, resplendent in a navy-blue uniform with bright brass buttons, stood beside her.

"This is Sergeant Cassidy of the New York City police," Captain Veronica whispered apologetically. "I had to tell him."

"Do you still insist that your name is Katherine Elizabeth Royston?" Cassidy asked.

"I do."

"That name is not on the passenger list."

"That's because I was not a passenger. I was not on the *Titanic*."

"Hmm."

The sergeant studied her intently, and she returned his gaze defiantly, examining him as he examined her. If he was going to study her in her ugly dress and unpinned hair, she was free to study him. She could find nothing reassuring or welcoming in his pale, suspicious eyes or in the set of his mouth beneath a thin gray mustache.

"And you say you were a passenger on the *Carpathia*."

"I was."

"Katherine Elizabeth Royston was indeed a passenger on the *Carpathia*," he said, "but that is not who you are. Katherine Royston came ashore and was passed through by our officers last night. You, however, came ashore with all the other immigrants two hours later. I don't know who you are, but I know what you are."

With the indignity of the nurse's examination still fresh in her mind, Kate could not control her fury. "You know what I am?" she repeated. "Let me tell you, Sergeant Cassidy, you do not know what I am. I have friends in high places, and ..." She stammered to a halt.

She had once had friends in high places but not now. Now she had no friends, no permanent address, and no place to go. She stared back at Cassidy's cool, appraising eyes. "You think that just because I was picked up from the street, that I'm a ..." She hesitated again as her mother's disapproving face took shape in her mind. *Katherine Elizabeth, we do not use such words.* She finally said the word. "You think I'm a prostitute."

Cassidy shook his head. "No, I don't. I think you're something else entirely. We've been told to be on the lookout for someone like you. It stands to reason on a big ship like the *Titanic* that someone could slip on board and hide. You had it all worked out, didn't you? You knew there'd be a great crowd waiting for her to dock and you could choose your moment to slither away, and you might have gotten away with it if the *Titanic* hadn't gone down."

The sergeant's jaw tightened, and his voice held cold malice. "You took the place of some honest woman, letting her drown while you stayed dry."

"What are you talking about?"

"Stowaway," Cassidy said.

"I'm not a stowaway. Don't be ridiculous."

Cassidy ignored her protest. He seemed to be dredging up an idea from the back of his mind. His eyes were now cold stones. "No, not just a stowaway—a spy."

Kate and Captain Veronica spoke in unison. "Spy?"

"Yes. I think we've caught ourselves a spy. This explains everything."

"I'm not a spy," Kate protested. "What on earth could make you think that?" Her mother resurfaced in her mind as Kate cast off the last vestiges of the humility that had been forced upon her. She was a lady again, heir to a fortune, daughter of the most powerful man in the county. Her tongue dripped contempt. "My good man, that is an absurd notion. If I am a spy, on whom do you think I am spying?"

"I'm not your good man," Cassidy replied, "and I think you were spying on Major Archibald Butt."

Kate shook her head. "I don't even know who he is."

"Oh, yes, you do." Kate could see that Cassidy was warming to his theory. "It's been in all the papers. Major Butt was on a diplomatic mission on behalf of the president. The official word is that he was on a mission to the Pope, but that's not what the papers say. They say he was on a mission to the German kaiser."

Kate heard Captain Veronica's sharp intake of breath followed by a soft whisper. "Sergeant Cassidy, you are going too far."

Kate turned her head. "He's making this all up. I was a passenger on the *Carpathia*. I can produce all kinds of people to prove what I say."

Captain Veronica bit her lip. "Well, my dear, we saw you coming down the gangplank with the *Titanic* immigrants."

"I was not coming down. I was trying to get back on board."

"And why would you do that?" Cassidy asked.

Kate was silent. What answer could she give? *Because I'm penniless? Because I had nowhere to go? Because I no longer have a job? Because I can't face my father's shame?* She had held those words prisoner for so long in the back of her mind that it was a relief to finally release them as thoughts, but she was not ready to say them aloud. She thought that she would never be ready for that.

Captain Veronica tugged at her arm. "Say something, Kate. You have to explain yourself."

"She can explain herself at her trial," Cassidy said. His pale face was now flushed, and his eyes were glittering in excitement.

He's just a fool, Kate thought, *an ambitious nobody, but he has the upper hand at the moment.* She appealed to Captain Veronica. "I know people who will identify me," Kate said. "If someone could go and talk to Senator Smith at the Waldorf Astoria—"

Cassidy shook his head. "I'm not going to interrupt that man's important work, although ..." He hesitated, his eyes narrowing to slits as he looked at her. "If I can bring him a spy ..."

"That's right," Kate said urgently. "Take me to him."

"No," Cassidy said thoughtfully. "That's not the way to do this. For all I know, Senator Smith is up to his neck in this business. He's a politician, and I don't trust politicians."

Cassidy reached into his pocket and pulled out a set of handcuffs. Kate felt a cold shiver run down her spine. This was no longer a stupid misunderstanding. This was real. He was going to take her to jail unless she could bring herself to tell him who she was, and who her father had been.

"There are other people who can identify me," she said. She never wanted to see those people again, but she had no choice. "I come from Royston, Pennsylvania. Anyone there can tell you who I am."

And what I am and how far I've fallen. "They know I'm not a spy," she said.

"But that's the whole point of being a spy, isn't it?" Cassidy said with a hint of satisfaction at his own wit. "You can't be a spy if everyone knows you're a spy—stands to reason. I'm taking you with me."

Captain Veronica stepped in front of Kate. "That's enough, Sergeant. You have no evidence that this poor woman is a spy. You don't even have any evidence that she's a stowaway."

"You'd do best to stay out of my way," Cassidy said, "and let me do my job."

"It is not your job to harass poor confused women."

"She's not confused. She knows just what she's doing. She may have fooled you, but she hasn't fooled me. I'm locking her up, and she can stay locked up until she comes in front of the judge."

He reached out with a sudden, practiced movement and grabbed Kate's right hand. She felt the cold metal of the handcuff and heard the click of the lock. She flung herself away from him, with the handcuff dangling from her wrist. As Cassidy lunged toward her, the outer door banged open, and three women tumbled into the room and tangled themselves around Cassidy's feet.

Kate had only a brief moment to assess the situation. Kitty McCaffrey and Private Elspeth were locked in a fierce tug-of-war, with Maeve as the prize. Private Elspeth had lost her bonnet; Kitty's hair had become unpinned; and Maeve was apparently still wet from her bath. They were a tangled ball of wet hair, petticoats, curses, and prayers, alarming enough to stun even Cassidy into sudden stillness as they rolled around at his feet.

At last he found his voice, a loud, hectoring voice. "Now then, what's all this?"

"You're not to touch my sister," Kitty shouted. "None of you are to touch my sister."

"I'm not interested in your sister," Cassidy complained. "Now get out of my way."

Captain Veronica waded into the fray as Cassidy aimed a couple of vicious kicks at the struggling women. "That'll be enough of that, Sergeant. That's no way to treat these women."

Kate realized that this was her one and only moment, and she dashed through the open door and along the corridor. She tried several doors before she found one that would open. She ran desperately into a small room dominated by a tall sash window that allowed light to spill in from the streetlamp outside. She tugged at the bottom pane and was relieved when it slid smoothly upward for a few inches. She tugged again. Obviously, the person who used this room was accustomed to cracking the window open for fresh air but not cracking it wide enough to allow an escaping spy to flee the hostel.

The dangling handcuff clattered against the window frame as Kate heaved again, gaining a few additional inches. Was it enough? Only one way to find out. As she poked her head and shoulders out of the window, it occurred to her that she did not know what floor she was on. Had she gone upstairs for her health inspection, or downstairs? Her panicked mind could not remember. She hung for a moment half in and half out of the window, looking at the top of the streetlight a few feet below. So she was not on the ground floor, and if she didn't want to land on her head from a considerable height, she should have climbed out feetfirst so she could hang from the windowsill.

Did she have time to scrabble backward, turn around, and reinsert herself in the gap? Once Cassidy was free of Maeve and Kitty, he would come for her, and even he was smart enough to start trying doors to see which one would open.

She peered down at the dark, shadowy ground and thought she could discern shrubbery. With a quick prayer for a nice thick privet hedge and not a spiky barberry, she slithered forward and let herself fall, hoping she could manage to somehow turn in the air and land on her back.

She was only partially successful. She managed a slight turn to avoid diving headfirst into the privet hedge, and she took the brunt of the fall on her right shoulder. She bit her tongue to avoid screaming as her arm with the dangling handcuff became entangled in the branches. She felt as though it had been wrenched from its socket, but she had no time to give in to the pain. She tugged the bracelet free and stumbled to her feet.

Evening had already fallen across the city, but she was still trapped in the light from the streetlamp. She looked along the street. Gaslights blossomed at regular intervals, but side streets promised darkness. And what else or who else? Cradling her right arm with her left hand, she darted across the street and into the nearest alley.

Mrs. John Stuart White's Suite
The Waldorf Astoria
Senator William Alden Smith

Bill accepted Mrs. White's offer of a whiskey and soda with some relief. He could see Will McKinstry looking enviously at the cut-glass tumbler. McKinstry was reaching the end of a long, hard day, and no doubt he would soon be suffering from writer's cramp. It wouldn't be for much longer. Bill wished he could take more time, ask more questions, call additional witnesses, but he was well aware that patience was wearing thin on the part of the survivors. He couldn't keep them in New York forever. Taft would surely recover from his melancholy any day now, and Bill would face a political price for tweaking the tail of the British bulldog.

Mrs. White sat in a wingback chair with her leg propped on a hassock. Apparently, she had fallen while boarding the ship in Cherbourg. And yet, Bill thought, she had managed to get herself into a lifeboat. Miss Young, Mrs. White's paid traveling companion, sat meekly in a corner, and a maid bustled through the sitting room and into the bedroom. All three women were survivors, but a young manservant who had traveled in Mrs. White's entourage had been lost. Mrs. White had expressed his loss as a matter of course—of course he had been lost, being a man and not a woman or a child.

"I wonder," Bill said, "if you could tell me anything about the behavior of the officers and the crew. Did you see anything bearing upon the discipline of the officers or crew or their conduct that you would like to speak of for the record?"

Mrs. White shot him a shrewd glance. "So you have found nothing in your own questioning? I have not been downstairs to listen for myself, on account of my leg injury, but rumor has it that the *Titanic*'s officers are proving difficult nuts to crack."

"They are very careful in what they say," Bill agreed, "as are the company officials."

Mrs. Smith sniffed contemptuously. "Well, I have no need to be careful. I can speak the truth."

"Of course you can."

"But," Mrs. White continued, "let me first say that I have every praise for the *Carpathia*'s captain and crew. They were kindness itself to each and every one of us."

"We are preparing a commendation for Captain Rostron," Bill said. "We understand what he did."

"Unlike Ismay," Mrs. White said.

Bill glanced at McKinstry to make sure that he was still taking notes. "Do you wish to say something about Mr. Ismay?"

"I know of many women who slept on the floor of the smoking room on the *Carpathia*," Mrs. White said, "although I was not one of them. However, that man occupied one of the best rooms on the *Carpathia*, with a sign on the door saying 'Please do not knock.' Please do not knock indeed. Who does he think he is?"

"And what of the crew?" Bill asked.

Mrs. White settled herself more comfortably in her chair. "I've read the newspapers, Senator, and they speak of the bravery of the men, but I don't think there was any particular bravery, not at first, because none of the men thought the ship was going down. We were not properly informed. We were told that we should row a short distance away to the light we saw, and while we were away from the ship, repairs would be made, and we could return."

"And you had no notion that the ship was sinking?" Bill asked.

Miss Young spoke softly from her seat in the corner. "Not until the end, and then it was dreadful. So quick. There one moment and gone the next, and people in the water screaming."

"Is there any more you can tell me about the crew and the officers?" Bill asked.

"I can't speak about the officers," Mrs. White said, "because I did not see them. There were no officers in my lifeboat, only crewmen, but they were not sailors. They had no notion of how to row. I had to tell one of them how to put the oar in the oarlock. He said he'd never had an oar in his hands before. When I suggested we go back and pick up more passengers, he refused. He said we would be overwhelmed."

"How many were in your boat?"

"Only twenty-two. We could have had so many more."

Mrs. White was still speaking, but Bill's thoughts were elsewhere. He imagined himself in that lifeboat. It was a boat built to carry sixty-five or even seventy passengers but somehow it had been launched with only twenty-two people on board. He thought of the people, maybe as many as a thousand, struggling in the freezing water. The sailor, for all his ignorance of how to handle an oar, had made the right decision. If they had approached and offered hope to the drowning people, they would have been swamped, and another twenty-two people would have been added to the list of victims.

"It was a dreadful thing," Miss Young said quietly. "We heard the yells of the steerage passengers as they went down. To think that on such a beautiful starlit night, and with all those Marconi warnings …"

"What do you know of the Marconi warnings?" Bill asked, dragging his mind away from the dreadful scenes playing out in his head.

"We read what was written in the newspapers, but really, even without the Marconi, the captain should have known," Mrs. White said. "Everybody knew we were in the vicinity of icebergs. It was terribly cold. I made the remark to Miss Young on Sunday morning, didn't I?"

Miss Young leaned forward to speak. "She said we must be very near icebergs to have such cold weather."

Mrs. White flapped her hands angrily. "If I, using nothing but my own common sense, could tell we were in the vicinity of icebergs, how could the crew not know?"

"How indeed?" Bill said.

He drained his tumbler and heaved himself to his feet. McKinstry followed him from the room, and the two men stood together for a moment, gathering their thoughts. Bill was tired, not physically but emotionally. He could no longer find a way to organize his thoughts. He had begun the day filled with righteous indignation and every intention of breaking through Ismay's reserve and showing him to be the coward he undoubtedly was. He imagined himself as a heroic figure pointing the finger of blame squarely at the chairman of the White Star Line, proving negligence and obtaining compensation for the suffering of so many.

Now, after all that he had heard, his sense of righteous indignation was wavering, replaced by a secondhand vision of the ship sinking and the hundreds of people struggling in the water, their screams fading as their breath froze in their lungs.

Tomorrow he would depose the *Titanic*'s one surviving radio operator, a young man who had stayed at his post after all hope had gone. He would call the surviving officers, and no doubt they would all be cast from the same mold as Lightoller, with stiff upper lips and shadowed eyes that concealed the nightmare within. What would he even ask? What was left to say?

His questions felt like insults. He had not stood on the deck of the doomed ship and watched the last lifeboat being rowed away, or chosen to dive from the roof of the officers' quarters into the frigid ocean. He was not one of the men who had stepped back to allow women and children into the lifeboats. He had not joined the orchestra to play music to drown out the terror or stood beside a stoker while water rose around his feet. He had not even joined in the drinking in the salon among those who had hoped to allay their fears with alcohol.

He turned to McKinstry. "You're free, Will. Go on down to the bar. I won't need you again tonight."

"You're sure?"

"Quite sure, Will."

"And what about tomorrow? What should I prepare for?"

"Radio messages. We'll see who was saying what about the ice."

"And after that?"

"After that, we're done."

"But Ismay—"

"We'll have to let him go. We'll have to let them all go. I can't justify keeping them here. All we're doing is providing gossip for the newspapers. We've heard nothing useful. It was a tragedy, Will, and I don't know if it could have been avoided." He sighed. "I think that maybe this inquiry insults the memory of hundreds of brave men and women."

He extended his hand to McKinstry. "I'll see you in the morning, Will. I'm going to phone my wife."

McKinstry nodded. "Good night, sir."

Bill unlocked the door of his suite, kicked off his shoes, and sat down on the bed. He placed the call to his home and went to the small drinks cart to mix a whiskey and soda. He would have to be careful. One more drink would buoy him up enough to talk to Nana, but any more after that, and the black dog of depression would show up uninvited, tail between its legs, hounding his every thought. He could not afford to let that happen. He imagined that the black dog's littermates were already camping out in the president's office, but they could not both play host to the unwelcome hounds.

The telephone jangled. "Senator, I have your wife on the phone."

"Thank you."

Nana's voice sounded distant and tinny. He wished she had come with him to New York. Well, maybe not. She would not have liked listening to the testimony. She would not have wanted to be among the doyennes of New York society occupying the front seats at the hearing. On the other hand, he had good news for her.

"Did you receive McKinstry's telegram?" he asked. "He thinks he's found two girls from Molly's family."

"I did," said Nana, "but I'll say nothing to Molly until we're certain. And if they're not in fact her relatives, I'll find a place for them somewhere. One way or another, I'll take care of the poor little mites."

"It's a tragedy all around," Bill said, knowing that *tragedy* was not a strong enough word but unable to find another word. For something like this, there were no words. "I'll be finishing up tomorrow, and I'll come straight home."

"What do you mean?" Nana asked. "Surely you're not finished already."

"No, I'm not finished, but it's all the time I'm allowed," Bill said.

"Allowed?" Nana repeated. "Since when do you do only what you're allowed? Shame on you, William. People are waiting for answers. What happened? Why did it happen? What's to prevent it from happening again?"

"Nana—"

"No," Nana said angrily. "You are not finished. You have letters, Bill, from your constituents and from all over the country, and even telegrams."

"What do you mean?"

"I mean that when Richard LaSalle went into your Senate office this morning, he could hardly open the door for all the sacks of mail stacked up beside it."

"Sacks," Bill repeated. "Sacks of mail?"

"Yes, Bill, sacks of mail from people who are cheering you on. They want you to see this through. They're not satisfied."

"But—"

"I don't mean wealthy, important people," Nana said. "I mean ordinary, everyday voters—immigrants who are now citizens and know what it's like to come across the Atlantic. Everyday people who want to see justice done."

"I'm not sure what justice would look like."

"Then make yourself sure," Nana snapped.

For a moment, he heard nothing but crackling on the line, and then Nana spoke again. "Bill, are you feeling depressed?"

Even though she could not see him, Bill sat up straighter. "No, Nana, I am not depressed. I have been asking questions and receiving very little in the way of answers. I am not at all sure that I can pin this on Ismay and—"

"No one says you have to pin it on Ismay."

"Apart from Eva Trentham."

"Eva Trentham is not president of the United States," Nana declared. "Now, Bill, it would be good if you could find someone to blame, or at least someone who the general population can despise, but the important question is, what can you do to make sure this doesn't happen again? Think about it, Bill. We are populating this country with immigrants from all over Europe. They all have to cross the Atlantic to get here. I don't care so much about floating palaces like the *Titanic*; I'm thinking about people like Molly, who just want their families to arrive safely from Ireland, where they are currently starving to death. What can you find out about this tragedy that will prevent it from ever happening again?"

"Ships have always sunk," Bill said.

"Yes," Nana agreed, "but we didn't always know about it. This is a new age. Instead of just disappearing and nobody knowing anything, the *Titanic* sent messages, and Cape Race picked them up, and then the *New York Times* picked them up, and then everyone knew what was happening. It was as though we were all watching, Bill. This great ship was going down right in front of us. We have to know why."

CHAPTER TWELVE

The Men's Bar
The Waldorf Astoria
Sheriff Joe Bayliss

Joe was usually quite happy to lean against a bar, but tonight he was restless. The fact that this bar was in the Waldorf Astoria and the drinks cost a small fortune was not the source of his discomfort. Bill had provided a generous allowance from government funds, and Joe was happy to spend the government's money.

The barman, a middle-aged man with dark Italian features, wiped the counter with a wet rag and picked up Joe's empty glass. "Another one, sir?"

Joe pulled out his pocket watch and checked the time. Eight o'clock. Bill was late, and Danny McSorley was very late. He decided to wait a little longer. He knew Bill would turn up eventually, but Danny McSorley was an unknown quantity. It should not take him so long to track down Kate at her employers' residence. Perhaps she was refusing to return with Danny. Perhaps he would have to go and fetch her himself, but not tonight. She was not the kind of young lady who would appreciate a gentleman caller at this late hour of the night. He shook his head. He was not a gentleman caller; he was an officer of the law—not the same thing at all. He would have to wait until tomorrow.

The Men's Bar was a dim refuge where he could not even glimpse the street outside, but he knew what would be happening out there in the gathering dark. Streetlights would be coming on, and the crowd of reporters waiting outside the Waldorf would be thinning a little. They'd had their news for the day, and they would be off to their offices to file their copy and create tomorrow's sensational headlines. He wondered what they would make of the day's testimony and Bill's relentlessly detailed questioning. Rostron of the *Carpathia* would be the hero; Ismay would be the villain. But he thought that the reporters and the public would be disappointed in the lack of sensational revelations. He picked up his drink. Perhaps, he thought, there was nothing more to be revealed.

The barman, with his wet rag, had moved to the other end of the counter. He looked up and caught Joe's eye. "Yes, sir?"

"Have you been in here all day?" Joe asked.

The barman, still swiping with the rag, made his way toward Joe. "Yes, Sheriff, I have."

"You know that I'm a sheriff?"

"Yes, sir, I know that you are Sheriff Joe Bayliss. You are helping Senator Smith, yes?"

His accent and the theatrical way he flourished his bar rag confirmed Joe's suspicion that the man was Italian, a recent immigrant. No doubt he had come across the Atlantic on a ship not unlike the *Titanic*. He could see no harm in asking for the man's opinion. He looked at the man's name tag. Tony, of course.

Joe laid a five-dollar bill on the counter. "So, Tony," he said, "I'm sure you can't help overhearing things that are said in here."

Tony slid the bill into his pocket. "Yes, Sheriff, I hear things."

"What do you hear about the inquiry?" Joe asked. "What are people saying when they come in here?"

Tony glanced around the room and then quietly sidled away to the end of the counter, where the lights were dim. Joe followed.

"They say it's a lot of talking," Tony said. "Just talking."

"What do you expect?" Joe asked impatiently. "Dancing?"

"No, no, of course not, but this is a tragedy, a terrible thing where many people died, but your boss, your senator Smith, he is so calm. His questions are dull and uninteresting. He does not allow for … for …"

"Speculation?" Joe asked. "Storytelling?"

"For emotion," Tony said. "When the people like the English

officer talk about the ship sinking and the people crying out, your senator says nothing. He just moves to the next question. We do not see the people; we just see questions. And now he is finished, yes?"

"Finished?" Joe asked. "What makes you think we are finished?"

"The officers, the Englishmen, are going home."

"How do you know that?"

Tony glanced along the bar and around the room. It seemed that no one needed his services at that moment. Joe rapped on the bar. "What do you know about the Englishmen?"

"The officers of the White Star came in here today, about two hours ago. Four of them sat at the table over there in the corner. At first they were very quiet. I think they are sad men, you know, because they have lost their friends and their ship."

"And their logbook," Joe muttered.

"Sir?"

"Nothing. Keep talking."

"Well, I brought them drinks. Rum—a lot of rum. They are sailors, eh? They drink rum, and they begin to talk loud. Loud enough for me to hear."

"And what did they say?"

"That they were going home. They talked about a ship named the *Lapland* that would take them home. And then Mr. Ismay, he came to talk to them."

"You know Mr. Ismay?" Joe asked.

The barman nodded. "Of course. I have seen him here in the bar, drinking with other business gentlemen, and I have seen his picture in the papers. He is the man who saved himself, huh? He saved himself and let the ship sink."

"What did he say to the officers?"

"I don't know. They stopped talking and listened to him, and then he shook hands with all of them, and he left. And then very soon they left—no more rum, no more loud talk. I think they do not like him, but he is their boss, eh?"

"He says that he is not," Joe replied, "but I think that is a technicality." He looked up and saw Bill making his way into the room with a surprisingly cheerful bounce in his step and a slight grin beneath his neat gray mustache.

Joe waved to him, indicating the corner table where the White Star officers had previously been sitting, and then he picked up his glass and nodded to Tony. "Bring the senator a whiskey and soda."

"Yes, sir."

"I've just been talking to Nana," Bill said as Joe sat down. "The telephone is a wonderful thing, isn't it? Do you know what she said?"

Joe raised a finger to his lips. "The barman here likes to listen, and he likes to talk, so be careful. I just picked up an interesting piece of information myself."

"Oh yes?"

"Apparently, the officers were in today and saying that it's all arranged for them to sail on the *Lapland*. She's leaving the day after tomorrow. Is it true? Are you really letting them go?"

Bill raised his eyebrows and his eyes gleamed. "The president only allowed us to hold them for two days, and tomorrow is the second day, so of course they think they're going home."

Bill fell silent as Tony arrived and set a tumbler in front of him. Joe waited until Tony had returned to the bar before he spoke.

"Why are you looking so damned cheerful, Bill? It seems to me that you're getting nowhere."

Bill raised the glass to his lips. "Thank you for the vote of confidence, Joe."

"That was not a vote of confidence," Joe growled. "They're leaving. The British will hold an inquiry, but by then they'll have had time to get their story straight and—"

"They're not leaving," Bill interrupted.

Joe glanced toward the bar. "The barman heard them himself."

"Oh, I'm sure he did, but they're still not leaving. We're all going to Washington. McKinstry is writing out the subpoenas now, and you can serve them. We are going to take all the time we need."

"You mean Taft's changed his mind?"

"Taft hasn't changed anything," Bill said. "Nana called and told me that we have sacks of mail."

"About what?"

"About the inquiry. People are writing and phoning and telegraphing from all over the country. They want to know what happened. It doesn't matter anymore what Taft wants or says. I don't care if he can't get his chin off his desk and pay attention to the country—I have the people behind me, and I'm going to continue. We'll take the whole lot of them, crew, officers, witnesses, to Washington and have a full-blown Senate inquiry, and I'm going to keep them until I have all the answers I need."

Joe shook his head, still trying to take in the meaning of Bill's words. Joe was a lawman and Bill was the politician, but even Joe could imagine that there would be diplomatic repercussions. It was one thing to hold the British crew for a few days, but to subpoena them and take them to Washington was an entirely different matter, and Bill expected Joe to serve the subpoenas. Was that even legal? He was beginning to wish himself back in Michigan. Bill had always been a friend, and Joe had always trusted his judgment, but this was different.

On the other hand, if Bill managed to find out what he wanted without also plunging the country into a war, then he would be well on his way to the White House, and who would not want a friend in the White House?

Bill interrupted Joe's train of thought. "This would have been so much easier if you had found the logbook."

"Well, I didn't, and that's all I can say about it. I searched the officers' rooms, and I spoke to a few of the crew. I'm pretty sure the log is at the bottom of the Atlantic, or if it isn't, it's going to be."

Bill shrugged. "It can't be helped. I'll ask about it just to put them off their stride, but I agree with you that it doesn't exist any longer. I don't really need it to make the case that the *Titanic* was running full steam through the ice field. Now that I have all the time I need, I can prove it without the log. We know the Marconi operators on other ships were talking to each other and sending ice warnings to the *Titanic*, and we can subpoena their testimonies. Lightoller can lie as much as he likes, but I'll have him, and I'll have Ismay."

Joe took out his watch and looked at it. Bill glanced up. "Are you expecting someone?"

"Yes, I am. Young Danny McSorley, who was helping out Cottam on the *Carpathia*, should be back now. I sent him out to find Kate Royston, and he's not back yet."

Bill waved a dismissive hand. "First time in the big city. He's probably gotten himself lost. He'll turn up. Meantime, I need you to do something."

Joe looked at his watch again. Surely McSorley should have been here by now. "I thought I might go myself and look for Miss Royston."

Bill gave a sharp laugh. "You're no more at home in New York than McSorley is. It would be the blind leading the blind. He'll find her—don't worry. And I have something else for you to do tonight. I need you to keep an eye on the *Titanic*'s crew. They'll have to be under constant watch until we can get them out of New York and down to Washington. Every time I turn my back on them, I expect to find they've slipped on board a boat and they're heading for England. It won't be the same in Washington. There'll be no escaping me once I get them away from the docks."

"What about McSorley?"

"I'll wait here for him. I'm going to need him to come to Washington. He spent a couple of days helping Cottam on the *Carpathia*, so he may be able to shed some light on the confusing messages that Cottam was sending. The newspapers reported that the *Titanic* was under tow to Halifax. Where did they get that from? It had to be a message from *Carpathia*."

"Or perhaps they just made it up. Rumors are easy to get started," Joe said. He drained his glass and stood up. "Find someone else to watch the crew," he said. "I'm going to find that girl." He returned Bill's quizzical grin with a hard stare. "She's a witness. We need her."

Bill's response was cut off by the sound of a commotion breaking out in the lobby, beyond the entrance to the Men's Bar. It was not the sound of an impending bar fight—Joe was very familiar with that sound. This was the sound of squealing women and affronted gentlemen. He turned to look and saw a bevy of ladies picking up their skirts and running toward the grand staircase while their escorts made angry harrumphing sounds. He soon recognized Danny McSorley, tall and disheveled, standing helplessly as Wolfie joyfully shook water from his coat and onto the fine furnishings and the fine people.

Normally, the sight would have brought a grin to Joe's face, but not this time, because he could see at once that Danny was alone. He had not found Kate.

Kate Royston

Kate's only plan was to put as much distance as possible between herself and Sergeant Cassidy. She ran with no destination in mind, her route determined by the need to avoid streetlights. When she finally paused to draw breath, she was in an alley that ran behind a substantial house, where gaslights shone from the ground-floor windows.

As she leaned against the backyard fence, sobbing for breath, she thought she heard music being played somewhere nearby. With blood pounding in her ears, and the sound of her own gasping breaths, it was very hard to make out the tune or even the instruments. She fought to calm herself and listen carefully. The music was not coming from the house, and it was not orchestral music. Trumpets and drums, she thought, like a brass band playing a summer concert in the park.

She was suddenly very homesick for days that would never come again. She gasped at the stab of memory that carried her to a hot summer night beneath the gazebo, sitting between her mother and father in the seats of honor. She had been so happy then, listening to the brass band playing patriotic music while the long twilight faded and fireflies danced among the trees. She closed her eyes and tried to warm herself with the memory. She saw the faces she knew so well and the people she had trusted—the apothecary who had dispensed drops for her mother's headaches, the banker who had kept her father's money safe, and the school teacher supervising the children as they played in the school yard. She could not play with the children—that would not be appropriate—but she could always watch them and wonder what it would be like to be poor and have to wear faded hand-me-down dresses and ugly leather shoes.

The thought of dresses and shoes snatched away the warmth of her memory and dragged her back to her present reality. She, who had pitied girls in washed-out dresses and clumsy pigtails, was wearing an unspeakable ruffled gown, damp and sticky from the sea mist that hung over the city, and she was without even a shawl to put over her head unbraided hair. And one thing was certain—those people in what was left of that town would never again offer her a seat of honor.

She straightened up and forced herself to focus beyond her misery and fear. Why was a brass band playing on a night like this and in a place like this? The sound was moving away, with the big bass drum beating out a militant rhythm. "Onward, Christian Soldiers." Salvation Army—it could not be anything else. Where were they? She stumbled to the end of the alley and looked out on a broad avenue with streetlights marching away into the mist-laden distance.

The band gathered followers as it marched up to the steps of a building that occupied a corner position and advertised itself with a single gaslight above its double doors. The smell of ozone in the air was replaced by a welcome wafting of food odors—stew or maybe soup. For a terrible moment, she thought she had somehow circled back to the Salvation Army hostel where she had been arrested, but that wasn't the case. That hostel had been a tall, forbidding building, and this building was a single story, maybe a church.

The band had drawn a small crowd, mostly men in cloth caps and ragged overcoats, and a few women bundled into scarves and shawls. Kate looked past the building, with its welcoming light, to the broad avenue beyond, where she could see the mist-shrouded shapes of great houses. Where was she? She had a little knowledge of New York City. She had come here with her mother for an eighteenth-birthday shopping spree, and it was also here that she had stayed with the Van Buren family while they prepared for their departure on the *Carpathia*. None of those memories meant anything now. How could she know where she had run to when she didn't know where she had been when she had started running?

The band completed its rendition of "Onward, Christian Soldiers" with a flourish of trumpets and a final thundering boom from the bass drum, and one of the bonneted soldiers of Christ flung open the doors of the building. Light flooded out onto the street and illuminated the hungry faces of the ragtag group waiting patiently at the foot of the stairs.

"Come in, come. We have food for all."

The woman who spoke was young, maybe younger than Kate, and her face, which some people might have thought plain, was made beautiful by her sincerity. Whoever she was and however she had come to take up the black bonnet and plain cape of a soldier in the Salvation Army, her calling was real. It seemed that she truly loved the dregs of humanity who had washed up against the steps of this building.

She stood at the top of the steps and looked down at Kate. "Please come in."

Could she know? Kate wondered. Was there some kind of telegraph sending signals across New York from one refuge to another, warning that a dangerous spy was on the loose? *Keep a lookout for a crazy woman in a green dress, no hat, no coat, and no idea where she is going.*

Kate moved warily to the bottom step, and all she could think was *Soup*, and all she could see was a long trestle table with an oilcloth covering and bowls of soup and bread.

"Come along, dear. Don't be afraid. Jesus loves you."

Kate nodded. "Yes, I know."

The girl's voice was soothing. "The Good Shepherd moves through the city, seeking his lost lambs. Whatever you've done, you can be forgiven. You can start again. We have a hostel—"

"No!" Kate stepped back and would have lost her footing if the girl had not caught her arm. Oh, she was strong, just as strong as Captain Veronica and Private Elspeth. What did they feed these women? Definitely something more than the meat of the Gospel.

"I can't stay," Kate said.

"But you're cold and wet, and your dress is …"

"Ugly."

"No, I don't mean ugly. We do not concern ourselves with fashion and outward appearance. It is just unsuitable for a night like this. Come inside. We can find a coat for you and somewhere for you to sleep."

"I won't go to your hostel," Kate said, "and you can't make me."

"Of course not. Come inside and have some soup, and we will talk after you've eaten."

"Don't want to talk."

"Very well. If you won't talk, will you let me pray for you? I'm Private Helena."

Kate began to form a hearty dislike for Private Helena, who stood in the way of Kate snatching a piece of bread and running with it in her hand. She couldn't shake the feeling that Private Helena was quite capable of taking her prisoner and returning her to the hostel and thus to the custody of Sergeant Cassidy.

"I'm not coming inside," Kate said sullenly.

"Then I will stand outside with you. Jesus will not abandon you, and I will not abandon you."

Something welled up inside Kate at those words. What did Private Helena know about being abandoned? Had she ever been abandoned by an entire town of people? Did she know what it was like to have nowhere to go and no one to trust?

"I have to go," Kate said.

"Go where?"

Kate glared at her. Private Helena was becoming quite obnoxious. "I don't know where. How can I know where I'm going when I don't know where I am?"

"You're at the Salvation Army Mission on Park Avenue," Private Helena said patiently. "Where are you trying to go?"

"Good question," Kate said. "Well, let me tell you where I'm not going. I'm not going to your hostel, where they lock up immigrant women and do unspeakable things to them."

Private Helena fluttered her hands. "I don't believe—"

"Believe it," Kate snapped. "I was there and I know. So I'm not going back, and I'm not coming close enough for you to lay your hands on me. I'm not going to the Van Burens, because they are no longer my employers, and I can't go back to the *Carpathia*."

"I really think you should come with—"

"No, I will not." Kate shouted loudly enough to drown out her own thoughts, loudly enough so that she did not have to answer the question that was spinning around in her head. *Where am I going? Who do I trust? I really want a piece of bread. My feet hurt. I'm cold.* She picked just one thought out of the confusion of thoughts. Sheriff Bayliss had been kind to her, and if she could find him, he would keep her safe from the likes of Sergeant Cassidy. In fact, if he knew what was going on at the Salvation Army hostel, how the immigrant women were being treated, he would kick all of them into the middle of next week. She was dimly aware that her thoughts were not holding together in any sensible way, and the smell of soup was not helping. She should move away from temptation. She should go to … to … the Waldorf Astoria.

Apparently, Kate had spoken the last two words aloud. "Did you say the Waldorf Astoria?" Private Helena asked.

"Yes. This is Park Avenue, is it?"

"It is."

"Therefore, the Waldorf Astoria is somewhere along here."

"About half a mile," Private Helena said, "but they won't let you in."

"Half a mile in what direction?"

Private Helena pointed, and Kate looked at the wide avenue stretching away into the mist that ate the streetlamps and the outlines of the grand houses.

"That's where I'm going," she said.

"You really shouldn't."

Kate was suddenly calm again. For the first time in a year, she had a real plan. It was not a particularly sensible plan, but it was good enough for the moment. Instead of running away, she would be running toward someone or something. She was dimly aware that she had made a very large leap of faith in believing that Sheriff Joe Bayliss would be the answer to all her problems, but he had winked at her, and that meant something. Or maybe it meant nothing. She couldn't tell. She could barely think, but at least she would be on the move again, running along the broad avenue, past the mansions of the rich and famous, to the place where someone would finally recognize her and bring her in out of the cold.

Her legs were tired and her feet hurt, but she picked up her skirts in a way she had not done since she was ten years old, and sprinted away from Private Helena. She ran, glancing over her shoulder, until the light from the mission was lost in the mist. She slowed, listening for following footsteps, but heard nothing. Light spilled from the grand houses on either side of the avenue, and she found no shadows to hide her, so she walked with her head up and her back erect, as she had been taught.

She may not look like a lady, but she could act like one, couldn't she? Perhaps that would be enough to overcome the sorry state of her clothes. The Waldorf Astoria would be a formidable obstacle for someone in her condition. Even when she had come here with her mother and been dressed in her newest and most fashionable clothes, the thought of entering the hotel had been intimidating. Well, a lot had happened since then, and she would not be intimidated. She did not even know if Joe Bayliss was staying at the hotel, but surely Senator Smith would be there, so perhaps she should ask for him.

Bright lights, brighter than the light from the houses, pierced the mist ahead of her. She could hear traffic now—the rumble of automobile engines, the clop of horse-drawn vehicles, and the murmur of many voices. As she drew closer, she could see the facade of the great hotel, with lights in the windows of its many stories and brighter lights spilling out onto the sidewalk. Shadows moved within the brightness, a mass of people milling and churning with no apparent purpose and held in place by a cordon of police officers.

She crept forward cautiously, hardly daring to step into the light.

She felt like a wild animal approaching a campfire. One of the waiting men turned his face toward her, and she cringed but stayed in place as she recognized him. Carlos Hurd of the *St. Louis Post-Dispatch*. So these were all reporters waiting for a story. Well, she thought as she made an attempt to smooth her hair and straighten her dress, she had a story for them. She would tell them what was happening at the Salvation Army hostel and how innocent girls were being subjected to humiliating inspections. Even better than that, she could tell them what Kitty had said about being locked belowdecks on the *Titanic*. That was a story that would sell newspapers.

She hesitated for one more moment, surprised to find how profoundly her experience had changed her point of view. There was something obscene about holding the inquiry here, at the most luxurious hotel in New York, as if the only lives lost had been the lives of rich people.

A police officer loomed over her. "Move along, girl. Go on, be off with you."

Kate stood her ground. It was obvious that she would not succeed in getting past the police cordon and into the lobby, so she would have to find someone out here to identify her. She needed the man from the *St. Louis Post-Dispatch*.

"I want to talk to that man," Kate said. She tried to hide the dangling handcuff with her other hand as she pointed her finger at Carlos Hurd. "I have a story for him."

"Nobody wants to hear your story. Move along."

Some kind of commotion was taking place just inside the glass doors of the hotel. The reporters pressed forward. The policeman turned to look. Kate pressed past him and hurled herself at Hurd's back. He turned with a startled shout and pushed her away, but she clung to his coat.

He tried to shake her off, but his attention was on whatever was happening in the lobby. The reporters surged forward, and Kate dragged at Hurd's sleeve. He finally turned to look down at her, his face a mask of irritation.

"Get off me, woman."

"I have a story for you."

He tried to shake himself free. "I don't want your story."

"It's me!" Kate screamed. "I was on the *Carpathia*. Mrs. Trentham talked to you. I was there."

He hesitated and finally gave her at least some of his attention, although his eyes still flicked toward whatever was happening in the lobby.

"I'm Kate Royston," Kate said. "Please, you have to believe me. Champagne corks. You used champagne corks."

He stood still and made no effort to remove her hand from his sleeve. She saw recognition dawning on his face, and something else—calculation.

"What happened to you?"

"I'll tell you if you'll help me. It's a good story. It'll sell newspapers, but I won't tell it to you unless you get a message to Senator Smith."

Hurd shook his head. "Smith doesn't talk to anyone."

"Sheriff Bayliss," Kate pleaded. "If you tell him I'm here, I'll give you my story. You won't regret it."

Time stood still. If the reporters continued their shouting, she did not hear them. She heard only her own breath and saw only Hurd's face. Finally he nodded his head.

"All right. I'll tell him. He's just inside the door."

Kate gasped. She was so close, with nothing but a glass door to separate her from safety. She took a step forward, and this time, it was Hurd who grabbed her. "Oh no you don't. You promised me a story."

"I'll give it to you."

"I don't trust you. Come with me and tell me your story, and then I'll get hold of the sheriff or the senator or whoever you want to see."

Kate tried to break free, but Hurd's arm was around her waist. As he lifted her from her feet, she could see over the heads of the reporters and into the lobby, where a gaggle of uniformed doormen and bellhops were running in agitated circles. She caught a glimpse of brown and black fur. Wolfie raced toward the glass doors. The reporters who had crowded around the doors fell over each in their attempt to move away from the otterhound and his huge paws.

With a shout of triumph, a doorman leaped forward and flung open one of the doors. Wolfie hurled himself toward freedom. Hurd released Kate as the dog plunged into the crowd, sending them running in all directions. Kate, suddenly alone, stood her ground and watched as Joe Bayliss and Danny McSorley followed Wolfie through the door. Three figures seemed set to converge on the sidewalk in front of her. She couldn't decide which one to hug, but Wolfie relieved her of the decision as he leaped at her and covered her face with dog drool before pushing her to the ground and sitting on her.

Senator William Alden Smith

Bill's plans for an evening spent preparing his questions for the next day had vanished at about the same moment as Wolfie the otterhound had crashed out of the door of the Waldorf Astoria and into the arms of Kate Royston. Now Kate was in the bedroom of his suite, wrapped in a blanket and awaiting the arrival of Eva Trentham's maid with dry clothes. Joe Bayliss had already used his considerable lock-picking skills to remove the dangling handcuffs from Kate's right wrist.

Wolfie, who was apparently very taken with Miss Kate Royston, paced outside the bedroom door and perfumed the parlor with eau de wet dog, while Danny McSorley sat in one of the wingback chairs and showed no sign of departing for wherever he intended to sleep. Joe Bayliss was smoking a celebratory cheroot, with his long legs stretched out in front of him, and only Will McKinstry, scribbling away at the desk, showed any signs of preparing for the morning. Meantime, downstairs in the lobby, Carlos Hurd waited for the story that Kate had promised him.

Bill felt as though he had been pitched into the middle of a three-ring circus. He would undoubtedly receive a bill from the hotel for the damage to their lobby furnishings and for cleaning and perfuming the air in his suite. He had planned on spending the evening examining the radio messages that had sparked from ship to ship through the frigid air as the *Titanic* had steamed heedlessly toward New York. Now he was saddled with a disheveled young woman; a hairy dog; an apparently lovesick young man; Joe Bayliss, who seemed to have lost his head over Miss Kate Royston; and a demanding reporter, who had managed to make his way into the lobby.

"Sit down."

Bill looked at Joe in surprise. He sounded as if he were addressing a dog and not a senator, and then he realized the truth. Joe was in fact addressing the dog, in a tone that even Wolfie could not ignore.

The hound ceased his pacing and gazed at Joe with mournful brown eyes.

"Sit," Joe repeated, "or I'll make you sit."

Wolfie sat for a moment, gave a deep sigh, and rolled over onto his side, blocking the bedroom door. Well, Bill thought, Kate Royston's virtue was perfectly safe with Wolfie as her guardian. No one would get through that door without his permission.

Bill looked at the depleted supply of drinks on the polished mahogany drinks cart and spotted a bottle of beer. He looked from the beer to the dog and back again and decided to throw caution to the wind for once. There was something endearing about the great shaggy dog, and Bill had never been an unkind man. He tipped the contents of the ice bucket into the water jug and filled the bucket with beer. Wolfie eyed him with interest. Perhaps he was no stranger to strong drink. Who could say? Who really knew anything about him?

He set the bucket on the floor and waited until Wolfie had heaved himself to his feet and buried his nose in the beer before he looked at Danny.

"So, how come he didn't drown?" he asked.

"The animals were kept down on F deck," Danny said. "I've heard people say there were polo ponies, and some dogs that were too big for the cabins, and a whole flock of fancy chickens. I suppose there were cats somewhere too, to keep the rats down."

"Rats are supposed to be first to leave a sinking ship," Joe said.

"Well, they didn't go in the lifeboats," Danny replied. "At least, not the four-legged rats."

Bill made a note to ask Danny how he had ended up in a lifeboat. He could not imagine Danny pushing women and children aside to make room for himself, so there must be some other story to tell.

"It took a while, you know, for us to realize she was really going down," Danny said. "The corridors were filling with water, and it was creeping up the stairs, probably up that grand stairway in first class, but I didn't see that. Anyway, I suppose someone thought it would be cruel to leave the animals locked in with no chance to escape, although I can't say the same for the immigrants ..."

Bill crossed to the cart and refilled his whiskey glass while he thought about what Danny had just said. The animals had been let loose but not the immigrants. Could that be the truth?

Danny reached down and patted Wolfie's head. Wolfie eyed the bucket and licked foam off his beard. "Just minutes before we went under," Danny said, "I saw a pack of dogs running loose on the deck. They didn't know what was happening, poor beasts. They were just running, you know, for the fun of it, and I suppose old Wolfie fancied a swim. He must have flung himself over the side and just started swimming. He has a thick coat and webbed feet, and he made a distance away from the ship before she sank, or he would have gone down with the suction. Mrs. Trentham saw him swimming and insisted on saving him. She's a very determined woman."

"Yes, she is," Bill agreed. He sipped his drink and enjoyed the silence that had settled over the room. Wolfie rolled back on his side with a satisfied grunt, and Bill saw that Joe's eyes were drooping. He turned his attention back to the radio messages, now printed out and lying on the desk. He understood very little of Marconi's new technology or the rules and regulations governing the use of radios on board ships. He was not even sure that there were any rules, but he could not forget what Nana had said. *Everyone knew what was happening. It was as though we were all watching. This great ship was going down right in front of us.* These radio messages were the only truth he had. Everything else was subject to human interpretation.

He picked up the printed papers and studied them. One thing was obvious, even to his untrained eye. The *Titanic* had not been alone on the ocean. Any number of ships, large and small, had been plying the shipping lanes, and they had all been aware of the proximity of icebergs. Along with congratulations to Captain Smith on his command of his new ship, they had sent precise warnings with longitude and latitude. What had happened to those warnings? Who had read them? More to the point, who had taken notice of them? Why was the *Titanic* the only ship to have the tragic misfortune of striking an iceberg?

Tomorrow Bill would question Harold Bride, the *Titanic*'s remaining radio officer, a hero who had stayed at his post until the end. He would be brought into the room in a wheelchair—a tragic figure probably more deserving of a medal than a reprimand. Bill shook his head. What questions could he ask that would not make him look like a bully and Bride look like a martyr?

He picked up a message and read it aloud. "'Captain, *Titanic*—Westbound steamers report bergs, growlers and field ice in forty-two degrees north from forty-nine degrees to fifty-one degrees west, twelfth April. Compliments—Barr, SS *Caronia*.'" He picked up another. "'Captain Smith, *Titanic*—Have had moderate, variable winds and clear, fine weather since leaving. Greek steamer *Athinai* reports passing icebergs and large quantities of field ice today in latitude forty-one degrees fifty-one minutes north, longitude forty-nine degrees fifty-two minutes west. Wish you and *Titanic* all success—Commander, SS *Baltic*.'"

He set the paper back on the desk. "I have no idea what this means."

McKinstry shrugged. "It seems simple enough, Senator. The other ships were warning Captain Smith about the ice."

"Yes," Bill snapped, somewhat irritated by McKinstry's tone of voice, "I understand what it says, but what does it mean? What is the radio operator supposed to do with such a message? How close were those ships? Was the ice in the shipping lanes, or was it miles away? I'm not a sailor, Mr. McKinstry, and I will not be made a fool of."

Danny McSorley rose from his seat and walked across to the desk. He picked up another message. "'From *Mesaba* to *Titanic* and all eastbound ships. Ice report in latitude forty-two degrees north to forty-one degrees twenty-five minutes north, longitude forty-nine degrees west to longitude fifty degrees thirty minutes west. Saw much heavy pack ice and a great number large icebergs. Also field ice. Weather good, clear.'"

Bill tried to snatch the paper, but Danny held on to it. "I know what this means, Senator. I'm a Marconi operator. I'm on my way now to serve at a land station, but I've done my time on board ships. I can tell you what you need to know."

"Really?"

"Yes, Senator. I'm employed by the Marconi company. I know what I'm talking about."

"All right," Bill said. "If you were on duty and you took a message like this, what would you do with it?"

"I would take it to the bridge, and the officer of the watch would mark the position of the ice on the chart."

"And then what?"

"Well, then they would be sure to avoid the ice."

"That sounds too simple," Bill said warily.

Danny nodded. "Sometimes avoiding is not possible, and in those circumstances, the ship would stop." He picked up another paper. "Now this one is a different matter. This is a message the *Titanic* operator was asked to relay on behalf of another ship."

"I don't understand," Bill admitted.

"Sometimes a Marconi operator, if he has time, will relay a message on behalf of another vessel. This one is from the *Amerika* and is intended for the Hydrographic Office in Washington, DC. Steamship *Amerika* via *Titanic* and Cape Race, Newfoundland, to the Hydrographic Office, Washington, DC. *Amerika* passed two large icebergs in forty-one degrees twenty-seven minutes north, fifty degrees eight minutes west, on the fourteenth of April." Danny looked at Bill with a sad shake of his head. "This is truly unfortunate. No one did anything wrong, but …"

"But what?" Bill asked.

"A message like this is considered private," Danny said. "It's not addressed to anyone on *Titanic*, and all the operator has to do is relay it as a courtesy. Obviously, Bride sent it on to Cape Race, as requested, and didn't report it to the bridge. I don't suppose he took the time to really read it or consider what it meant for the *Titanic*."

"But it was a warning," Bill protested.

Danny shook his head. "He didn't see it that way. It was just a message for Cape Race. He had no reason to take it to the bridge. If he had done that, and if those bergs had been on the chart, everything would have been different, but he didn't, because it wasn't up to him."

"What about these other messages?" McKinstry asked, stabbing a finger at the papers on the desk. "Did he ignore them? Here's one from the *Californian* at eleven p.m. 'I say, old man, we're stopped and surrounded by ice.'" He set the paper down again. "Apparently, the captain of the *Californian* thought it was not safe to move. What would the Marconi man do with a message like that?"

"It would be taken to the bridge," Danny said. "All messages regarding navigation are taken to the bridge." Danny took the paper from McKinstry's hand and studied it. "Eleven o'clock," he said. "The operator was working late."

"What do you mean?" Bill asked. "Surely he would work all night."

"Not if he was the only operator on board. The *Californian* is a small freighter. She probably has only one operator, and he wouldn't be expected to work a twenty-four-hour shift." He continued to stare at the paper. "Harold Cottam on the *Carpathia* told me that it was only by good luck that he heard the *Titanic's* SOS. He was getting ready for bed and just turned his equipment on for a moment. If he had gone straight to bed, he would not have known anything until the next morning, and it would have been too late." He placed a hand over his mouth and stood for a moment as if struck dumb. When he finally spoke, his voice trembled. "I would not be alive. We couldn't have lasted much longer in the lifeboats, and no one else was anywhere near. The *Californian* didn't come up on us until late in the morning, when we were all aboard the *Carpathia*."

Bill turned away. Seeing Danny warm and dry, and hearing him suggest that the animals had been released out of pity but not the immigrants, reminded him that these messages were not just a code to be deciphered; they were the warnings that could have saved everyone on board if they had been heeded.

Danny shuffled through the papers again and picked up another message. "This is from the same ship, the *Californian*, at six thirty p.m., about the time the first-class passengers on the *Titanic* were dressing for dinner. 'Latitude forty-two degrees three minutes north, longitude forty-nine degrees nine minutes west. Three large bergs five miles to southward of us.'"

He leaned over McKinstry's desk. "Give me a pencil and a piece of paper."

McKinstry raised his eyebrows and looked up at Bill.

"I have a terrible suspicion," Danny said. "Let me show you."

McKinstry rose, and Danny took his place at the desk and began shuffling through the papers with fierce concentration. He did not even look up when the bedroom door opened and Kate appeared, wrapped in a blanket. Bill, a happily married man, could not ignore the fact that the mysterious Kate Royston was a true beauty. Her dark hair had dried in ringlets, and the warmth of the blanket had brought a flush to her cheeks and a sparkle to her eyes. Bill looked away and told himself that the beauty was illusory—she was probably flushed with fever and glassy-eyed with exhaustion. That was what he would say to Nana if she should happen to ask his opinion. He wished that Eva's maid would hurry her arrival and remove one of the many distractions from the room.

Danny was now making a sketch on the borrowed paper, drawing lines and scribbling names while he shuffled the pile of messages. Finally he looked up. "He was there," he said. "He was really there."

"Who was where?" Kate asked.

Danny glanced at her but scarcely acknowledged her presence as he drew another line. He looked past Kate and spoke to Bill. "Can you get your hands on a chart?"

"Not at this time of night," Bill said, "but in the morning, we can get one. What have you discovered?"

"I've discovered that another ship was very close by. That's why we were told to row towards the light."

Bill shook his head. "It's my belief that Captain Smith gave that instruction so that the people would have some shred of hope. He told them to row toward a light so they would row away from the ship and not be caught in the suction as she went down. It was a lie told for a good purpose."

"No," Danny said fiercely, "it wasn't a lie." He spread the paper on the desk and beckoned Bill forward. "Let me show you."

Danny had drawn a rough circle on the paper. At the center of the circle, he had written the ship's name: *Titanic.* "I can show you better on a chart," he said, "but this is good enough. If I take the rough position of each ship that sent a warning or responded to the *Titanic*'s SOS, I can make a map." He pointed to the names he had written on his sketch. "Here are the *Virginian,* the *Baltic,* the *Mauretania, Mesaba, Athinai, Caronia,* and the *Carpathia.* You can see that the *Carpathia* was the closest."

Bill looked down at the sketch and pointed at a mark Danny had made close to the center of the circle—very close to the *Titanic.* "What is that?"

"I believe it's the *Californian,*" Danny said through gritted teeth. "I believe he was not more than ten miles away."

"No," Bill said. "You must be wrong."

Danny shook his head. "I will need a chart of the area, just to be certain, but this is how it looks to me. I know where he was at six thirty, because he gave his position, and at eleven thirty, the operator said they were stopped and surrounded by ice. I also know that the *Californian* was bound for Boston, so she was traveling westward, and that means ..." He paused for a moment and then printed the word *Californian* next to the mark he had made on the map. "She was here. The *Californian* was no more than ten miles away while the *Titanic* was firing rockets, sending out distress signals, and launching her lifeboats."

Kate pushed her way forward. "The Countess of Rothes said they saw a light," she said, "and so did some of the Irish girls. Even Mrs. Trentham said they were rowing toward a light."

Bill stared down at Danny's sketch and tried to rearrange his thoughts. Tomorrow he would talk to the radio operators, but what would he say? If Danny McSorley was correct, and if the *Californian* was in fact only ten miles from the *Titanic*, everything would change, and the public would find a new focus for their outrage. Perhaps he would even be able to file a criminal charge. He shook his head. He could not afford to go forward without proof and make a fool of himself, especially as it would mean taking the focus away from Ismay's actions.

He had to find a witness—someone from the crew of the *Californian* would have to be persuaded to talk.

He looked up and found that Joe was already on his feet. "I guess I'm going to Boston," he said. "Let's hope the *Californian* is still in port."

☐

CHAPTER THIRTEEN

April 20, 1912
The Waldorf Astoria
New York
Kate Royston

Entering the hearing room at the Waldorf Astoria, Kate was suddenly self-conscious. It had been many months since she had worn such colorful clothing. She had become accustomed to the anonymity of her gray governess dress and the feeling that she could blend in anywhere as a governess or a lady's maid, but now she wore a walking skirt of fine bright blue wool, a high-necked lace blouse, and a fitted navy-blue jacket. Her hair was curled and pinned beneath a broad-brimmed hat, and she even wore a pearl brooch at her throat. The clothes were modest by the standards her mother had set as fashionable, but they were, nonetheless, very fine clothes, and they fit her well, considering that they were not made to measure but hastily purchased.

Last night, she had been reluctant to leave the senator's suite at the Waldorf Astoria. Sparks of excitement and urgency had seemed to crackle through the air around the makeshift desk where the Marconi messages had lain in a tumbled heap. She had been torn between listening to the calm certainty of Danny McSorley's explanations and the gruff determination of Sheriff Bayliss's threats against the captain of the *Californian*. Wrapped in a soft blanket and warmed by several glasses of brandy, she had felt as though she had been watching history being made. The world would read about this tomorrow, but last night, she had already been the possessor of secrets that would have to be teased from reluctant witnesses.

Unfortunately, the senator had been far too much a gentleman to allow her to remain in his suite after a suitable escort had been found to take her to Eva Trentham's house, and so she had been driven through the deserted, rain-soaked streets and been delivered into the hands of Bridie and Eva.

Despite the excitement of the night before and the whirl of her own excited thoughts, she had somehow managed to fall so soundly asleep that Bridie had to shake her awake.

"Dressmaker," Bridie said impatiently, pulling back the covers. "Herself wants you smartly dressed. It will be ready-made clothes— no time for anything bespoke—but there'll be something for you in a city this size and with a purse as heavy as Mrs. Trentham's, and there's a whole bevy of dressmakers waiting downstairs for you."

As soon as Kate was dressed to Eva's satisfaction, a footman arrived to convey Eva first to a motor vehicle and then through the front doors of the Waldorf Astoria. After that, Kate was given the task of pushing Eva's wheelchair, as Bridie had been left behind.

Kate paused to admire the lobby, which she had only glimpsed the night before, but Eva had no time to waste.

"Just push," she said impatiently. "I want to be in the front row of the meeting room. We've already missed the morning session while I found you something to wear."

"If you sit there, other people won't be able to see around you," Kate commented as she studied the room.

"Not my problem," Eva said. "Here. Put me here."

Kate set aside an ornate chair and parked Eva's wheelchair close to the middle of the front row. Having made certain that Eva was satisfied with her position, Kate sat down beside her.

Eva reached out and snagged a passing gentleman to her side. He looked shocked at the preemptory summons until he recognized her and greeted her with a courteous nod of his head.

"Mrs. Trentham."

"What did we miss this morning?" Eva asked.

"Radio operators," the gentleman informed her. "Interesting stuff about ice warnings and such, but Senator Smith was quite … well … very … long-winded in his questions. Far too many details."

Kate allowed herself a small, smug smile as she thought of the unsuspecting captain of the *Californian*.

Eva turned to look at her. "What are you smiling about? There's nothing new to be learned from radio operators. They won't have anything to say about Ismay. He's the one they should be talking to."

Kate bit her tongue. She had not shared any information with Eva about Danny McSorley's discovery. Eva had no idea that Ismay was not the only person who was facing public humiliation. So long as Joe managed to get to Boston before the *Californian* sailed, Captain Stanley Lord was going to have some questions to answer.

Kate hurriedly changed the subject, leaning across to Eva and saying, "Thank you again for taking me in."

"I don't know why you left," Eva said. "Why did you have to go running all over New York? You could have accompanied me from the boat. No one would have said anything."

"I didn't know you wanted me to—"

"Then why didn't you ask instead of running off?"

Kate didn't offer a reply out loud, although she whispered the question in her own mind. *Why didn't you ask me to stay? If you needed me, why didn't you say so?*

"Oh well," Eva said. "You're here now, and this is going to be much more fun than having Bridie with me. She's a good woman, but she can't make up a fourth at bridge. I'll keep her with me until my leg is healed, and then we'll ship her off to Chicago. After that, well, the world is our oyster. We'll have to go to Europe, of course, but you will not be jumping ship in Gibraltar or throwing yourself at impoverished Spaniards. Perhaps you should marry a title. It makes for a good start and never fails to impress. On the other hand, perhaps you shouldn't marry anyone, or at least not until your looks begin to fade. I will enjoy seeing you break hearts."

Kate turned her face away, afraid that Eva would read her confused expression. She wasn't sure she wanted Eva to plan her future, whether it meant finding her a titled husband or keeping her around so that Eva could watch men's hearts breaking. She did not currently have any other plans, and she had enjoyed her night in a comfortable bed. She was still enjoying the feeling of silk underwear and fine linen, but she could not shake the memory of her night at the Salvation Army hostel, the ragged women, and the humiliating health inspection, from scratching through her hair for lice to being examined for venereal disease.

The hearing room had not been set up to resemble a courtroom. The two senators, Smith and Newlands, sat at a long table, with other officials arrayed around them. The witness was apparently expected to simply sit on the other side of the table. Nothing in the room gave the impression of a criminal hearing. No one here was accused of a crime, or at least not yet.

Kate searched for Ismay, but she could not find him among the fashionable ladies and gentlemen seated around the room. She did, however, recognize Carlos Hurd sitting with a group of reporters. He had already accosted her as she had made her way into the hotel, insisting that she provide the story she had promised. She was still mulling that over in her mind. She was not going to tell him anything of what had transpired in the senator's suite last night, with Danny declaring that the *Californian* had been a mere ten miles away when the *Titanic* had sunk.

She did not see Danny here now. Perhaps he would not be permitted into the hotel again in light of the amount of damage Wolfie had inflicted during his brief visit. Perhaps he had already left for Washington, although she could not imagine why he wanted to leave the lights of New York City.

She turned her attention to the deal she had struck with Carlos Hurd. What could she tell him to fulfill her side of the bargain? Perhaps he would like to hear how the immigrants had been locked belowdecks. Maybe he already knew. Well, she would tell him again. If he didn't like it, he wouldn't have to print it, but she would have fulfilled her promise.

A hush fell over the room as Senator Smith rose to his feet. He waited until the last whisper had died away and then took a paper from Will McKinstry. He took his time about removing reading glasses from his pocket and settling them on his nose. He had not needed glasses last night. *This,* Kate thought, *is pure theater. I wonder what he will say.*

The senator cleared his throat and looked over the top of his spectacles. "Ladies and gentlemen, members of the press, I have been asked to make a public statement. Before doing so, I request that no representative of the press or other person shall ask any question of me before beginning or during my statement or after I have finished. What I say, I desire reported accurately, and I wish the public to know that this statement is the only official utterance I shall make before resuming our inquiry in Washington."

Kate heard the whisper rustling through the room. "Washington? Who is going to Washington? What does he mean?"

Senator Smith took another paper from McKinstry and set it on the table. "This list will be provided to the press, and I have no need to read it aloud here. All these witnesses, along with officers and crew of the *Titanic*, have been summoned to appear in Washington on Monday morning at ten o'clock. At that time, this investigation will be resumed, and no further testimony will be taken at this hearing."

The audience gave an audible groan. They had come to witness a spectacle, but apparently, they were to be disappointed. The whole three-ring circus, as Smith had called it, was moving to Washington.

"The object of this committee in coming to New York coincident with the arrival of the *Carpathia* was prompted by the desire to avail ourselves of firsthand information from the active participants in this sad affair," Senator Smith said.

Once again he looked over the rim of his spectacles. "Our course has been guided solely by this purpose—to obtain accurate information without delay. Information had been received that some of the officers of the *Titanic*, and the managing director of the White Star Line, who are British subjects residing in England, desired and intended to return to their homes immediately upon arrival at this port. We concluded that it would be most unfortunate if we were deprived of their testimony for any indefinite period, and felt that their removal beyond the jurisdiction of our authority might complicate and possibly defeat our purpose."

"Well," Eva said, her voice carrying in the stunned silence. "He certainly showed them, didn't he?"

"Yes," Kate whispered. "I was there. I saw what he did. I was with him when he first met Sir Bruce Ismay. It was not a pleasurable meeting."

Eva smiled happily. "Of course not. Push me out of here, Kate."

"But he's still talking."

"I don't need to hear what he's saying. We have to make reservations on the train to Washington while they are still available, and we will have to obtain the very best hotel rooms in Washington before someone else does."

Kate did not move. Maybe Eva would try to scold her, but Kate was not ready to leave. She needed to hear what the senator would say next.

"In closing this statement," Senator Smith said, "I desire to acknowledge our debt of gratitude to the representatives of the press for their marked consideration and courtesy in this most trying situation. I wish to assure them that everything that has transpired of public interest has been entirely in their presence and that this course will be pursued, so far as I am concerned, in the future hearings before the committee."

Before Senator Smith could resume his seat, the representatives of the press, apparently not reassured by what he had said, were on their feet.

"What does the president say?"

"The British will protest?"

"What are you trying to prove?"

"Do you have new information?"

Senator Smith shook his head, scooped up his papers, and took Senator Newlands by the arm. He departed through a side door, leaving McKinstry to hand out the list of witnesses who would be summoned to Washington.

"Get a paper," Eva demanded. "Go on, Kate. Get me a list."

Kate pushed her way through the throng, almost losing her hat as she squeezed between the gentlemen of the press and finally managed to grab the only remaining sheet of paper. By the time she returned to Eva, the room was already emptying.

Eva held out a grasping hand. "Show me. I want to see how much trouble he's going to make."

Kate held the paper away from Eva as she skimmed the list. She was surprised at the amount of pleasure she felt in reading one of the names. Danny McSorley had been summoned to Washington. He was going to get his wish.

As Kate handed the list to Eva, she became aware of two figures approaching her. She recognized Carlos Hurd but not the woman at his side. She had already met Mrs. Hurd on board the *Carpathia*, and this person was not Hurd's wife. She was a tall, big-boned woman with iron-gray hair pulled back beneath a small, unfashionable hat. She wore a skirt and jacket of mismatched tweeds and held a notebook—another reporter.

"Miss Royston," Hurd said, "this is Myra Grunwald, one of my associates at the newspaper. She has been assigned to your story."

"I don't have a story," Kate said impatiently while keeping one eye on Eva, who was studying the list of witnesses and alternately smiling and grimacing.

"You promised me a story," Hurd insisted.

"Yes, yes, I know. Well, here it is. I spent a night at the Salvation Army hostel, and I talked to the immigrant women. They say they were locked belowdecks and only broke free at the very last moment. That's my story. You can also add that female immigrants who enter the United States are subjected to humiliating so-called health examinations, and someone should put a stop to it. Now, if you will excuse me, I need to take Mrs. Trentham home."

"No, you don't," Eva said, looking up from the list. "What sort of humiliating examinations are you speaking of?"

"I'll tell you later," Kate hissed.

Myra Grunwald gripped her pencil and gave Kate a long, searching examination from the top of her hat to her new shoes. When she spoke, she revealed a deep voice and a slight hint of a German accent. "We have already obtained stories from steerage-class passengers, Miss Royston. As for the Salvation Army, well, it is not wise to speak ill of them. They do good work."

"I was not speaking ill of the Salvation Army, Miss Grunwald. I was speaking of immigration officers."

The reporter gave her a bleak smile. "You may address me as Myra, Miss Royston. I do not have any interest in announcing my marital status by the use of a prefix."

"Oh, I like that," Eva said. "You're quite right, Myra—a woman should not be identified by whether or not she has a husband. Yes, very good." She looked up at Kate. "Push me, Kate. We have to be on our way."

"Not yet," said Myra. "Miss Royston, I am not interested in the immigrant story. I am interested in you."

"Why would you be interested in me?"

"Because you are a mystery. Mr. Hurd found you on board the *Carpathia*, where you say you acted as a governess, but he thought it was obvious that you came from money, even wealth. He suspected that you were involved somehow with Mr. Cottam the Marconi operator, but we have seen no evidence of that since the *Carpathia* docked. However, you were seen on board the *Carpathia* in the company of Senator Smith and Sheriff Joe Bayliss. Another mystery?"

"No," Kate said. "There's no mystery."

Myra held up a finger to silence Kate. "Last night," she said, "you appeared outside the Waldorf Astoria, dressed in rags, soaked to the skin, and frantic to tell your story to Mr. Hurd so that he could confirm your identity. You were running away from someone, weren't you?"

Kate tightened her grip on the wheelchair. "I have told you all that I intend to tell you."

"You have told me nothing."

"Because it's none of your business."

"I am a reporter, and everything is my business. Your name is familiar, Miss Royston. I have read it somewhere before, possibly in my own newspaper." Myra looked up at the ceiling and appeared to be deep in thought.

Kate watched her with a sinking heart. She inched the wheelchair forward. "We have to go."

Myra refocused her eyes and gave her a predatory smile. "It is only a matter of time, Miss Royston. I shall consult my newspaper's archives, and I will see you in Washington. By the time I arrive, I will know all about you. *Auf wiedersehen, fräulein.*"

The San Francisco Call
April 22, 1912

64 BODIES OF TITANIC VICTIMS FOUND

The first bodies were reported and recovered from latitude 42.1 north, longitude 49.13 west. The cable repair ship MacKay Bennett ... *was the first to flash the news to the signal station at Cape Race that salvage was already begun.*

Halifax Morning Chronicle
May 2, 1912

With the exception of about 10 bodies that had received serious injuries, their looks were calm and peaceful—Dr. Thomas Armstrong, ship's surgeon on the Mackay-Bennett.

☐

PART THREE
WASHINGTON, DC

New York Times
April 22, 1912

The officers and men subpoenaed to appear before the committee are incommunicado and under surveillance at the Hotel Continental. The fact that they are under surveillance was not advertised by the committee, but was admitted tonight by one of the Senators prominently identified with the investigation, who also explained why it was impossible for newspaper men to see or interview the officers or crew.

"No one will have a chance to talk with any member of the Titanic *party tonight," said Senator Smith. "I think it would be highly improper for anyone to seek statements from these witnesses before they give their testimony on the stand before the committee."*

CHAPTER FOURTEEN

April 21, 1912
The Willard Hotel
Washington, DC
Kate Royston

Kate sat on a velvet banquette in the hotel lobby. She had been to any number of fine restaurants and hotels in Philadelphia and New York in the company of her mother and father, but she had never been to Washington, and she had never been anywhere quite as magnificent as the Willard Hotel. Although she was dressed in the best evening gown that could be obtained at very short notice, she felt homely and insignificant amid the marble splendor of the Willard, set within sight of the White House and the Capitol Building and bustling with the comings and goings of men of power.

She was waiting now for Bridie to bring Eva down in the elevator. She knew that as soon as Eva arrived, she would be able to bathe in the glow of the old lady's social standing, and nothing would be said about her rather ordinary ivory gown, more suited to a Sunday afternoon tea than dinner in Washington's most expensive hotel.

She shrank back into the shadow of an enormous aspidistra in a gilded vase as a side door opened and admitted a contingent of gentlemen with suitcases. From her hidden position, she was able to observe the surreptitious arrival of Sir Bruce Ismay and Philip

Franklin, along with two other gentlemen. She glanced toward the front doors, where she could see a large contingent of reporters lying in wait for the arrivals from New York. They were obviously unaware that their quarry had eluded them. Several hours earlier, when Kate had arrived with Eva, Bridie, and one of Eva's footmen to carry the luggage, the reporters had looked at them in disappointment.

"I'm surprised they don't want to talk to me," Eva had remarked. "If they only knew what I know, they'd be all over me."

"What do you know?" Kate asked impatiently. She was tired from the train journey and uncomfortable under the scrutiny of the press. Where was Myra Grunwald? When was she going to arrive to challenge Kate with the newspaper headlines of just a year ago?

"I know that J. P. Morgan is hiding in fear," Eva said, "but Bill Smith will drag him out of his burrow, and then we shall see."

Now, as Kate watched Sir Bruce Ismay scurrying across the lobby to the bank of elevators, she wondered why Eva couldn't be satisfied with making this man's life miserable. Why was she so determined to also ruin the life of J. P. Morgan? Wasn't it enough that, whatever the verdict of the Senate committee, Ismay would never hold his head up in public again? He was already ruined. He had been branded as a coward and would be forever forced to bear the burden for the fifteen hundred people who had died on his ship.

As one elevator car spirited Ismay away, another car arrived and disgorged Eva in her wheelchair, attended by Bridie in a nurse's uniform and a footman carrying a traveling rug over one arm. Eva's wispy white hair had been teased into a bun and adorned with a jeweled pin and a tall red feather to match her red velvet dress. Looking at her as she approached, Kate could see the shadow of a once-beautiful woman. Even now, there was something endearing about the twinkle in Eva's eyes. Of course, Eva didn't want anyone to find her endearing—she wanted people to be terrified of her—but Kate was coming to hope that a soft heart lay beneath the sharp exterior, and it would soon be revealed.

Kate rose to meet the entourage and felt Eva's eyes sweeping the length of her body, from the modest pearl brooch in her hair to the ruffled hem of her dress.

"We have to find a dressmaker," Eva said. "You're sufficiently youthful and pretty that you can pass muster in a dress like that, but we will need to dress you in something brighter and better fitting if you are to break men's hearts."

"I wasn't planning on breaking hearts," Kate protested.

"We shall see," Eva said enigmatically. "Push me, Bridie."

Kate followed the procession into the dining room and found it to be almost the twin of the dining room in the Waldorf Astoria, with potted palms and a glass ceiling. The room was bright with electric lights that glinted on polished silverware and crystal glasses set on snowy-white table linens. Moving between the tables, Kate wondered if this was how dining had been on the *Titanic*.

As they approached their table, Kate saw that they were not going to be dining alone. Two men rose to their feet as Eva and her entourage arrived. The footman busied himself removing one of the chairs. Bridie pushed Eva's wheelchair into place and then took up a position behind the chair. The footman took several steps back from the table, where he remained like a rather grim statue, holding the traveling rug.

In any other circumstance, Kate would have laughed at Eva's showmanship, but instead of laughing, she found herself able to proceed with renewed confidence. Her dress was very plain and her jewelry almost nonexistent, but she was with Eva Trentham, and Eva was putting on a show with Kate as only a minor player. The overwhelming effect of their arrival, intentional or otherwise, was that all eyes were on Eva and not on Kate. Kate's dress was irrelevant.

The two men remained standing as Kate took her seat between them.

"Major Arthur Peuchen and Colonel Archibald Gracie," Eva said. "Survivors."

Unwilling to stare directly into their faces, Kate looked at them from beneath lowered eyelashes. They were not youthful men, but neither had they settled into the comfortable middle age that would strain a waistcoat. Major Peuchen appeared to be the picture of health, but Colonel Gracie was pale. Kate had read the interviews these two men had given to the *New York Times*. The major had been assigned the task of rowing a lifeboat. He had not been in the water. On the other hand, the colonel had spent the night in the water and stayed afloat by clinging to the overturned collapsible lifeboat. No wonder he was pale, and no wonder his body trembled.

"And this," Eva said, "is Miss Katherine Moorhouse, who was

very kind to me on board the *Carpathia*."

Kate looked up sharply and met Eva's bland, innocent stare as the two gentlemen settled into their seats. She felt herself blushing with guilt. Why had Eva decided to invent a name for her? Was she now expected to become Katherine Moorhouse and live forever under an assumed name? She busied herself spreading the linen napkin on her lap and consulting the menu. Could Eva do this? she wondered. Could she just give Kate another name and swipe away all the memories that went with the name of Royston? Surely it could not be so simple.

The dark-haired gentleman with melancholy eyes, who Eva had introduced as Major Peuchen, leaned forward. "How are you now, Mrs. Trentham? We understand that you had an unfortunate landing on board the *Carpathia*."

"Yes, I did," Eva agreed. "All would have been well if only Ismay had been willing to offer a hand."

"On the *Carpathia*?" Major Peuchen queried. "Perhaps you mean on the *Titanic*."

"No," Eva insisted. "I would not have been injured at all if Ismay had come forward to give me a hand. He just stood there and watched while I struggled to come on board."

"Because of the dog," Kate said, without realizing that she had spoken aloud. "You can't blame him for that. It was the dog that caused the problem."

Eva looked down her nose at Kate. "I don't know why you would say that, Miss Franklin."

Kate's anger began to rise. If Eva was going to invent a name, she should at least try to remember what name she had invented, and if she was going to blame anyone for her broken leg, she should blame herself, not Sir Bruce Ismay. He was certainly an unlikable man, but he was not responsible for everything that had happened to Eva.

Kate's anger leaked out in the form of a hissing whisper. "If the *Carpathia*'s crew had not saved you," she said, "you and the dog would both have fallen into the boat below. You can't blame Ismay for everything."

"He was standing there watching," Eva snapped back.

"I blame Captain Smith," Major Peuchen said smoothly.

"For breaking my leg?" Eva challenged.

"For all of it."

Kate lifted her head and stared at him. He had spoken words that had been spoken by no one else. So far it had seemed that Captain Smith's reputation was to remain unsullied. He had done all that a captain should do, including following his ship to the bottom of the Atlantic, but now Major Peuchen was actually blaming him for everything that had happened.

Colonel Gracie made a harrumphing sound at the back of his throat. "Now come along, Arthur. This will never do. We don't speak ill of the dead."

"Maybe you don't," Major Peuchen said, "but I will. Captain Smith was never any good. I don't know why he was given the command. He was popular with the society crowd, a great man to have at your dinner table, but as for commanding a ship like the *Titanic*, well ..."

"No, no," Colonel Gracie said, his pale face flushing, "this will never do. You can't speak like this."

Eva's eyes were alight with excitement. "Let him speak any way he likes," she insisted. "We have all been through a simply terrible ordeal, and I for one refuse to sit back and say nothing when there is blame to be apportioned. I am quite sure that Senator Smith agrees with me, and that is why we are all here to speak to the Senate committee."

Colonel Gracie shook his head vehemently. "Ismay was pushing for speed," he said. "He wanted to show what his ship could do. Well, he showed that, didn't he?"

"And Captain Smith was a very poor seaman," Major Peuchen responded. "He managed to collide with another vessel before we even left the harbor in Southampton. My goodness, he surely should have known that a ship the size of the *Titanic* would create a wash leaving the pier, but he showed no awareness. Boats were snapping their mooring lines all around us, and we just sailed on, not even caring."

"It is difficult," Colonel Gracie said, "for a ship the size of the *Titanic* to come to a stop or even change course, especially in a harbor like Southampton. What would you expect him to have done, Arthur?"

"I pity the people on board the *New York*," Major Peuchen replied. "Smith snapped their mooring lines and sent them drifting without power. She was almost under our bow."

"I agree it was an inauspicious start to the voyage," Colonel Gracie responded placatingly.

"Inauspicious!" Major Peuchen's voice took on an angry tone. "Yes, I would certainly say that it was. I don't doubt Ismay will bear the blame for all of this, but I don't believe it. Smith escaped blame by going down with his ship. Ismay was not so fortunate."

Kate lowered her lashes and looked surreptitiously at the men on either side of her. They were both becoming red in the face. She looked at Eva. Eva's smile was pure satisfaction. Kate sighed. Eva knew exactly what she was doing in inviting these two men to share a table. She had expected a disagreement, and she had what she had expected. Kate suspected that if the two men had been alone, they would have come to blows. Only rigorous social training kept them in their seats and speaking in low voices.

It occurred to Kate that either one of these men could be accused of doing exactly what Sir Bruce Ismay had done—they had survived. She looked around the dining room, occupied mainly by men in evening dress and only a very few women. She had no doubt that most of these men had also somehow saved themselves, some without even getting wet. And, she asked herself, what of Danny McSorley? Was it wrong for him to be alive? What had he done to save himself? The warm feeling that had come from expecting to meet him in Washington suddenly turned cold. Had Danny taken the place of a woman or a child? Did he bear any blame?

She stared down at the tablecloth and wished for the meal to be over even before the waiter had set the first dish in front of her.

The cold consommé was just one of many dishes. Each dish was no doubt excellent, but for Kate, the food turned to ashes in her mouth as she grappled with an inescapable reality. Sir Bruce Ismay was just one of many men who had saved themselves. If he truly had nothing to do with the speed of the ship, and if the captain had been incompetent, how did it feel to be blamed for all those lives? When would the blaming stop?

Kate fought back tears. She could see her father's face set in a mask of despair and hear her own voice whispering to him. *It's not your fault. They can't blame you. You didn't know.*

But they had blamed him, and this was the result. This was why she was here, on Eva's charity, waiting for Myra Grunwald to recover a memory.

The White House
Washington, DC
Senator William Alden Smith

The president's door was open. Taft was seated at his desk, and Charles Hilles was standing beside him. The windows were open, admitting a light breeze that promised rain and made little progress against the lingering odor of new construction..

Bill took the open door as an invitation and stepped inside the office. "You wanted to see me, Mr. President?"

Taft looked up. Bill saw that the president had not yet set aside his melancholy. If anything, he looked worse than he had the last time Bill had seen him. Although the president's belly was still a massive mound, causing him to sit far back from his desk with his legs spread wide, he seemed to have lost weight in his face. His cheeks were drooping, and the skin beneath his eyes was dark and baggy.

Taft waved Bill to a seat and waited until Bill was sitting down before he dismissed Hilles. "Five minutes," he said as his secretary reached the door. "Come back in five minutes. We have no time to waste today."

Hilles exited, and Taft looked at Bill ferociously. "Your *Titanic* hearing is not the only thing happening today," he said accusingly.

Bill kept silent. He was not the one who had asked for this meeting, and therefore, he was not the one who should be accused of wasting time.

Taft gestured to the papers on his desk. "Everybody wants something," he said. "They want me to go after Roosevelt, you know. Go after him with hammer and tongs, they say. Make him sweat." He shook his head. "I can't do it. I'm not ready. Losing Archie has knocked the stuffing out of me." He looked at Bill with mournful eyes. "It's true, isn't it? There is no hope of finding Major Butt alive."

"No, sir, there is no hope."

"And what was he doing at the very end?"

"Witnesses say that he helped with the lifeboats until the last one was launched. There were a number of gentlemen who behaved with courage, and I can assure you that Major Butt was one of them."

Taft pursed his lips. "Is it possible," he asked, "that the sinking was intended as a way of making sure Major Butt did not deliver his message?"

Bill took a deep breath and held it for a moment while he considered the answer to Taft's question. "Well, Mr. President," he said slowly, measuring his words, "if someone had wanted to assassinate Major Butt, they could have done it at any time. He was apparently out and about, eating in the restaurant, walking on the deck, exercising in the gymnasium. There would be no need to sink the entire ship just to harm the major."

Taft rubbed his chin, his expression gloomy. "It was an important message," he said eventually. "There's going to be a war in Europe unless we do something about it."

"I'm not sure there is anything we can do," Bill said, "except make sure that we are not involved. It will be Europe's war, not ours."

"It will be Britain against Germany," Taft said. "The king against the kaiser, even though they are cousins, and it will affect trade, if nothing else. I was trusting Archie to bring me news, but now he's gone." He looked at Bill with watery eyes. "Have they found his body yet?"

Before Bill could answer that question, Hilles returned with a yellow telegram form in his hand.

Taft looked up. "Not now, Mr. Hilles."

"I'm sorry, sir, but this is urgent. Another telegram regarding the Mexico situation. You will need to make a decision."

Bill turned his attention to Hilles. "What Mexico situation?"

Taft lifted a despairing hand. "Go ahead and tell him. He's a senator, and maybe he has an answer."

"We have a situation in Mexico," Hilles said. "Americans are being held prisoner by a bandit chief in Chihuahua. The president is being pressured to send in the marines."

Bill looked at Taft and saw that he was not even listening. He turned back to Hilles. "If the president sends in the marines, we could find ourselves in a war with Mexico."

Hilles nodded and leaned down to speak softly to Bill. "Perhaps you could talk to him. He seems to be unable to make a decision. We also have a miners' strike in West Virginia, and the railroad workers in New York are threatening to down tools. The president has a number of decisions to make."

"Well, I can't make them for him," Bill hissed. "He needs to pull himself together."

Taft looked up and focused his eyes on Bill. He ran a hand through his hair. "I know you have your eye on the White House," he said. "Now you see what I have to deal with. Do you think you could do better than me?"

Bill decided that silence would be the best response. *Yes, I could handle it better than you*, he thought. *I wouldn't give in to mourning over one man's life, and I would certainly get out on the campaign trail before Roosevelt has a chance to steal the election.*

Taft straightened his shoulders, and his eyes strayed to the pile of papers on his desk. "About this hearing," he said, "and the people you are bringing to Washington."

"Yes?"

He laid a hand on the papers. "I have messages here from the British. They are deeply offended by the tone of your questions to Ismay and the British officers."

"That is not my concern."

Taft poked a finger at Bill. "The British newspapers are holding you up as a figure of scorn."

"I am not concerned with the British press; I am concerned with apportioning blame for the great tragedy that robbed you of a friend and robbed this country of some of its greatest leaders of industry."

Taft nodded. "Fine words, Bill, but you'll need more than words. So this fellow Ismay—can you pin the blame on him?"

"I am going to try. He's a very reluctant witness, but I'll have the truth out of him."

"I hope so," Taft said solemnly, "because if you get this wrong, you can give up any hope of sitting in this chair."

Hilles coughed discreetly from the doorway, and Bill rose to his feet. His mind was already on the committee members gathering in the new Senate hearing room, on the witnesses waiting to be called, and on the ace he had up his sleeve.

Boston Harbor
Sheriff Joe Bayliss

Joe was more accustomed to dealing with the ships and sailors that plied the Great Lakes, but now he felt perfectly at home leaning on the counter of a dockside bar in Boston. Through the open door, he could see the *Californian* snugged up against the pier, with her deck hatches open and longshoremen unloading her cargo. A trio of sailors was stationed in the bow, half-heartedly chipping paint under the supervision of an officer.

He watched as two men came down the gangplank and approached the bar. The anxious expressions on their weather-beaten faces told him that these were the men he was expecting. He signaled the barman to bring a bottle and three glasses, and then he lit a cheroot and made himself comfortable.

The elder of the two men was first to speak. "You Sheriff Bayliss?"

"I am."

"So you're a policeman, are you?"

Bill heard a trace of Scottish in the man's accent. Evidently, this was James McGregor, the ship's carpenter.

"No," he said, "I'm not a policeman. I'm an officer of the court, and I'm not here to arrest you, if that's what you're worried about, Mr. McGregor."

"How do you know my name?"

"Lucky guess," Joe said. He looked at the other man. "You must be Ernest Gill."

"So what if I am?"

Joe pushed the bottle toward them. "Take a drink, Mr. Gill, and calm down. I'm not here to make trouble, but I will if I have to."

Gill poured himself a drink and eyed Joe suspiciously. "What do you want?" he asked.

"Well," Joe said, "it has come to my attention that Mr. McGregor told a story to a newspaper reporter about seeing a ship in the early hours of April fifteenth. Is that true, Mr. McGregor? Did you see a ship?"

"Maybe," McGregor said as Joe slid the bottle toward him. "The reporter made it worth my while."

Joe nodded. "I'm sure he did, Mr. McGregor, but you won't get the same consideration from me. What you will get from me is a ride to Washington to testify before the Senate committee investigating the sinking of the *Titanic*. If you tell the truth, nothing else will happen to you, but if you don't …"

"It's the truth," Gill said. "I'll swear to it. We're telling the truth. We saw a ship, only it weren't the fifteenth; it were the fourteenth, because it wasn't yet midnight. It was four minutes to midnight when

I seen it."

Joe poured himself a drink. "That's very precise. Are you always so sure of the time?"

"Not always," Gill said truculently, "but I am this time, because at five minutes to twelve, I was working with the fourth engineer at a pump that wouldn't work. While we were interested in our work, we forgot the time, and I looked up, and I said, 'It's five minutes to twelve, and I haven't called my mate Mr. Wooten to come on duty. I'll go and call him.' And I got to the ladder to climb out of the engine room and get on deck. That took me one minute to get up there, so it was four minutes to midnight, like I said."

Joe studied Gill's face and was reassured to read an expression of frustrated honesty. He relaxed, convinced now that he was not on a wild-goose chase.

"Was the ship moving at the time?" Joe asked.

Gill shrugged. "I didn't notice, what with rushing to call my mate."

"We were drifting," McGregor said. "Not underway, just drifting."

"So you were also on deck?" Joe asked.

McGregor nodded and looked down into the depths of his glass.

"I went along the deck," Gill said, "and I could see her a way over, a big ship and a couple of rows of lights. She wasn't any small craft, not a tramp, nothing like that. I didn't think then that she was a White Star boat; I reckoned she must be a German. Anyways, I dived down the hatch, and I went and called my mate, and that's the last I saw of it."

Joe refilled his glass. "Are you sure that's the last you saw of her?" he asked.

Gill nodded. "I didn't see her again, but I saw rockets."

"She was firing rockets," McGregor said. "That's what I told the reporter. It's no lie. A big ship firing rockets, and not ten miles away."

"So first you saw the ship, and then later you saw rockets, but you couldn't see her lights."

"That's right," Gill said. "It was about half an hour later, after I'd called my mate and come back on deck, and I seen rockets. No ship, just rockets."

Joe watched the smoke drifting idly from his cheroot for a moment before he spoke. "What made you say that you saw a

German ship?"

"I dunno," Gill said. "I mean, that's where we sometimes see a German ship coming and going from New York, and the *Frankfurt* was somewhere out there, so I just thought, well ..." He stuttered into silence for a moment.

"It was the *Titanic*," McGregor said flatly. "We all agree it was the *Titanic*, and if it wasn't the *Titanic*, why have we been told not to talk about it?"

"Why indeed?" Joe said.

"It's not right," McGregor said, "and that's why I spoke to the reporter."

"And because he paid you," Joe commented.

McGregor shook his head. "Someone had to say something."

Joe turned to Gill. "What else did you see?"

"I didn't see nothing after the rockets, but I heard Mr. Evans, the second engineer, saying that more rockets went up after I turned in, and they reported her to the captain. Seems they tried to signal her with the Morse lamp, but they didn't get no reply. And then Mr. Evans asked why the devil they didn't wake the wireless man."

Joe suppressed a shiver as he thought of Harold Bride on the *Titanic*, sending desperate messages into the night as the ship sank lower and lower into the water, while just a few miles away, the officers of the *Californian* did not think to wake their wireless operator.

"If you were concerned about the rockets," Joe said, "why didn't you take your concern to the bridge or the officers of the watch?"

McGregor gave a short bark of a laugh, and Gill grimaced. "I couldn't do that, sir."

"It's not our business to notify the bridge or the lookouts," McGregor said, "but they couldn't have helped but see the rockets."

"I went to bed," Gill said softly. "I turned in immediately after. I supposed the ship would pay attention to the rockets. I didn't know nothing else until six forty, when we got our orders. 'Turn out to render assistance—the *Titanic* has gone down.' We saw her, sir. We saw her lights and we saw her rockets. We saw her sinking."

Joe straightened up and drained his glass. "What is the name of your captain?"

"Captain Lord. Stanley Lord."

Now Joe had what he had come for. He called for the bartender to bring the bill.

"What do we do now, sir?" Gill asked.

"You pack your bags while I go and talk to your captain. I'm taking you all to Washington."

The Russell Senate Office Building
Washington, DC
Senator William Alden Smith

As Bill stepped out of his car in front of the gleaming white facade of the Russell Senate Office Building, he was swarmed by reporters.

A familiar face emerged at the front of the pack. Carlos Hurd of the *St. Louis Post-Dispatch* had wasted no time in transporting himself to Washington. Now he stood in the watery spring sunshine, notebook in hand, eyes eager.

"Senator, where are the crew of the *Titanic*? Are they here?"

"They are in Washington," Bill admitted.

"Where are they staying?"

Bill shook his head. "Do you really expect me to tell you? Let me just say that they have arrived in Washington. They came in a special car from New York and were escorted by my own personal aide, Mr. William McKinstry."

"Are they under guard?"

"The sergeant at arms has a man with them for their own protection."

"Protection from what?"

"I imagine they're being protected from you, Mr. Hurd," Bill said. "Now let me pass. We have important work to do."

When Bill attempted to climb the stairs to the main doors, another man barred his way. This man also had the look of a reporter, although his attitude was not quite as combative. Bill paused to allow him to ask his question.

"Will you be discussing compensation for the victims, Senator?"

Bill's anger flared. "Of course we will be discussing compensation. That is why we are here." He waved a hand at the reporters pressing in on him. "If you would stop looking for sensational stories, and if you would stop listening to lies, you would understand what we, as a Senate committee, are doing."

He searched the crowd, looking for unfamiliar foreign faces. The American press may well understand, but the foreign press would have to be told. "Here in the United States, we have an act called the Harter Act, and this act allows victims of maritime disasters to sue for compensation if—and only if—negligence can be proved on the part of the shipowner. That is what we are about here. Now please let me through."

"What about the immigrants? We heard some of them were shot."

Bill rounded on the questioner, recognizing an Irish accent. "Well, I have heard no such thing."

"Because you haven't asked, and you won't ask, will you?"

"My colleagues and I will ask every question we believe to be relevant, and you will be allowed to listen to the answers."

He was pleased at the surprised murmur from the reporters. "We will hold the hearing in the Caucus Room," he said. "It will hold several hundred people, and there will be a reserved area for members of the press."

He pushed forward and climbed several steps until he was able to look down on the crowd. "We will have no star-chamber proceedings," he declared. "The country has a right to know the truth about this terrible disaster, and we'll ascertain the truth if we possibly can. The doors will be opened shortly. The sooner you let me go, the sooner we can start the proceedings."

He nodded to a police officer stationed at the top of the steps, and the doors swung open to admit him and closed again to keep out the reporters.

He found two of his fellow senators waiting for him. Francis Newlands grinned. "Star-chamber proceedings," he said. "Where did you get that from?"

"My wife suggested it," Bill said. "It's an infamous British court known for its secrecy and unfair judgments."

Newlands continued to grin. "You really are out to tweak the British bulldog's tail, aren't you?"

"Yes, I am," Bill agreed.

Senator Jonathan Bourne joined in the discussion with a somber face. "Don't let the British insults get under your skin. We can't give in to their demands."

"I wasn't aware they had made any demands," Bill commented.

"They want their people back," Bourne said.

"They'll have them back when I'm finished with them," Bill responded grimly. "I am determined to get to the bottom of this."

Newlands shook his head. "I'm on your side, Smith, but I doubt if anyone will ever get to the bottom of this affair. We'll do our best, but the rumors are flying thick and fast, and I don't see how we'll ever rein them in."

"And that," said Bill, "is why we have to do this now, with no further delay. Memories will change with time, and some of these people are susceptible to outside pressure. I'm not saying they will lie outright, but ..."

"I think they will," Newlands said. "I'm willing to bet that the stories we heard in New York will have changed already."

Bill looked up as Will McKinstry approached, with his footsteps echoing along the marble corridor.

"Good morning, McKinstry."

"Good morning, Senator. We are almost ready. I have the witnesses sequestered in the small meeting room, and we're in the process of seating some of the survivors in the Caucus Room. We'll want them in place before we admit the general public."

McKinstry paused and gave Bill a hangdog stare. "Mrs. Trentham is here with her entourage."

"Her entourage?"

"Her nurse, her footman, and young Miss Royston. I must say that Miss Royston is looking far better than she did in New York. She's quite the young lady now."

Bill nodded. "I'm not sure what to think about that girl. She's hiding something. I suspect that she's running away from someone."

"A husband?"

"No. She's too young."

"How young is too young?" Newlands interjected. "Jacob Astor's widow is a girl of twenty-one. He was almost twice her age."

"Does anyone know how she is?" Bill asked. Now that the subject had come up, he thought he should glean some information to take home to Nana, who was very interested in the affairs of New York society.

"I understand she's at home in the New York mansion with the drapes closed and the doctors in attendance. The family is relying on her to safely produce an heir, although she has some months to go."

Bourne shook his head. "A sad affair. I sometimes wonder about

215

this business of women and children first. We lost some splendid fellows from the *Titanic*, and the stock market fell two points overnight. Surely there should be some other measure to use in loading lifeboats."

"I have to agree," Newlands said. "I read some of the reports in the New York newspapers, and from what I can tell, some of the boats were launched half-empty because there were no women and children to put in them. It makes no sense."

Bill drew in a sharp, disapproving breath. "If we give in and allow 'every man for himself,' we will be no better than savages. If you will excuse me, gentlemen, I will go and greet Mrs. Trentham." He pulled a watch from his vest pocket and glanced at it. "We shall commence in ten minutes."

Bill followed McKinstry along the echoing corridor and up a short flight of steps into the splendor of the Caucus Room. The drapes on the floor-to-ceiling windows stood open, allowing daylight to flood the room and reflect off the gold-leaf decorations on white marble walls and columns. He shivered slightly at the sight of row upon row of chairs lined up to face the dais where he and his fellow senators would sit. The hearings at the Waldorf Astoria had been cramped and impromptu, but this was different. This room solemnly reflected the serious intent of the committee. Bill thought of the sacks of mail in his office. The people of the United States wanted the answers he had promised to provide.

He studied the dais and the chair he was going to occupy. He wondered how long he would be able to continue the inquiry. Taft would not stay forever wrapped in melancholy. Any day now, maybe even today, he would emerge from his grieving and begin to ask questions.

Mrs. Trentham was entrenched in the front row, just as she had been in New York. Kate Royston sat beside her, looking quite fetching in a broad-brimmed hat trimmed with silk roses and a dress of gauzy pink fabric. He fixed the details of her couture in his mind, because he knew Nana would ask questions.

Eva wasted no time in coming to the point. "Who will be first?" she asked. "Will it be Ismay? You'll need to skewer him early on, before he has a chance to lie his way out of the corner."

"He may not be lying," Kate said quietly.

Eva turned on her. "Of course he's lying. I know what kind of man he is. Cut him down as fast as you can, Senator, and we can move on to Mr. Morgan."

"Mr. Morgan will not be here."

"You can subpoena him."

"I have no evidence," Bill insisted.

"Well, find some."

Bill clasped his hands tightly behind his back, resisting the temptation to clasp them around Eva's throat, or at least to grasp the wheelchair and wheel it from the room.

"We will begin with Mr. Franklin, the American representative of the White Star Line," he said.

Eva shook her head. "No one wants to hear from him. He wasn't on the ship."

"That doesn't mean he wasn't giving orders," Bill said. "If they were to try for a speed record, the orders would have been given before they left Southampton."

Bill looked up as the doors opened to admit a trickle of people. They were well dressed, the ladies in extravagant hats, the gentlemen with bristling mustaches and starched collars, but their eyes were haunted, and their faces still held the shadow of their memories. Survivors, he thought, come to relive the horror.

He turned away, but Eva caught the sleeve of his coat with a grip as clawlike and as tenacious as a bird of prey's. "You need to meet these people."

"I don't have time."

"Of course you do," Eva said. "They are passengers from first class. They have influence. Now, let me see ... Do you know Sir Cosmo and Lady Duff-Gordon?"

"I've heard of them, but I don't know them."

Eva beckoned to Sir Cosmo and Lady Duff-Gordon, and they approached with wary expressions on their faces. It occurred to Bill that Eva was taking full advantage of her wheelchair confinement to order people around. She no longer had to make any effort of her own. She was now in the queenly position of summoning people to her side, and she was loving it.

Bill had, of course, heard of the Duff-Gordons and their scandalous marriage. Nana had been at pains to make sure he knew all about it and to ask him for a report on what Lady Duff-Gordon was wearing, in the unlikely event he had a chance to meet her. He could almost hear Nana's voice. *She's a divorcée, Bill. She can't even be received at court, but I doubt she cares. She makes her own money as a fashion designer, although I'm told it's not dresses she designs but lingerie. Very expensive but very risqué.*

He studied Lady Duff-Gordon. She was a slim, attractive woman with dark hair and a black dress that clung sinuously to her frame. As all her possessions had been lost along with the *Titanic*, he could not imagine where she had obtained such a fashionable garment at such short notice.

Her Scottish husband, Sir Cosmo Duff-Gordon, had the look of a sportsman and the complexion of a man accustomed to tramping the moors. On first sight, he did not look like the kind of man who would marry a divorcée, or have any interest in dress designs, but he and his wife were actually clasping hands, and he looked at her with besotted affection.

As Bill extended his hand to Sir Cosmo, he saw that the Scotsman was giving him a wary look that verged on fear.

"You don't intend to call us, do you?" he asked.

"No," Bill said. "I have subpoenaed the witnesses I need."

Lady Duff-Gordon smiled at her husband. "You see, *chéri*. He doesn't intend to make trouble for us." She smiled at Bill. "I'm afraid your newspapers have been most unkind to us. It is not our fault that there were so few people in our lifeboat. It is not something that we arranged, and I do not intend to apologize for the fact that my dear husband is alive when so many men are not. He waited and I waited with him, and he did not get into the lifeboat until we were quite certain that there were no other people waiting."

Bill wondered what the newspapers had said about Sir Cosmo Duff-Gordon and his wife. Obviously, there was more to this tale than Lady Duff-Gordon being a divorcée and a designer of lingerie. He made a mental note to ask McKinstry. He had been too busy preparing to question Bruce Ismay and the officers of the White Star Line to even formulate questions about what had happened in the lifeboats. Those questions could wait, because whatever had occurred in the lifeboats had not caused the *Titanic* to sink. They were not the focus of his inquiry.

"Oh, look," said Lady Duff-Gordon. "There's that young man who was in the lifeboat with us."

Bill saw that Danny McSorley was approaching. For once, he was not accompanied by Wolfie. Danny's name was on the list of witnesses to give testimony about Marconigrams sent from the *Carpathia*. He really should not be in this room. He should be sequestered with the other witnesses. It was some years since Bill had practiced law, but he still knew he needed to keep witnesses separate.

He heard someone draw in a sharp breath behind him. He turned to see that Kate Royston was on her feet and facing the Duff-Gordons. "Are you sure he was in your lifeboat?" she asked.

Lady Duff-Gordon smiled. "Why, yes, of course. How could I forget any detail of that awful night? He was in our boat, and he seemed to be a very nice young man."

"I don't think so," Kate said breathlessly. "No, I really don't think so."

Bill stared in amazement as Kate turned on her heel and fled the room.

Danny stared after her with a bemused expression on his face, but he made no move to follow her. He ignored the Duff-Gordons and stepped close to Bill.

"Senator," he said softly, "I need you to do something for me."

Bill shook his head. "I never interfere in affairs of the heart."

Danny looked after Kate's fleeing figure. "No, nothing like that," he said. "I don't know what I've done to offend her, but it's not important. Well, not important at this moment."

"I see. Well, what do you need?"

"I need to talk to the president."

"The president?" Bill queried. "The president of the United States?"

"Yes. President Taft. I need to talk to him."

"Why?"

"I can't tell you that."

"Well, if you can't tell me, I can't arrange it. We don't let just anyone into the White House to talk to the president."

"I need to talk to him," Danny said stubbornly.

"No," Bill said. "You need to leave this room and go and sit with the people I have subpoenaed."

He raised a hand and summoned one of the policemen who were guarding the doors. "Take Mr. McSorley to the small caucus room, and then I suppose you'd better open the doors and admit the members of the public."

"There's an awful lot of them, Senator," the policeman said.

"It's a big room."

The policeman shook his head. "Not big enough. We'll do our best to keep them under control. You'd better go and join your colleagues before the rush."

As Bill followed Danny and the policeman from the room, he heard the sound of the doors opening behind him. He turned quickly and saw a tidal wave of people scrambling into the room, pushing and shoving at each other and climbing over chairs in order to get seats. Police whistles blew; women screamed; and men roared.

Bill hurried from the room with his mind reeling. This was not an inquiry. This was a Roman circus with a mob howling for blood.

CHAPTER FIFTEEN

Kate Royston

Kate wiped away her tears and stared in astonishment as she saw the size of the crowd jostling for position outside the Russell Senate Office Building. Those who were not crowding the steps had taken up viewing positions at the tall windows by climbing onto the window ledges and craning their necks to see inside. *Bloodsuckers*, she thought. *How can they find entertainment in tragedy?* If any of them had actually felt the biting wind from the ice field and seen the lonely huddle of lifeboats adrift amid the ice floes, they would not now be laughing in excitement at the prospect of hearing the details. If they had heard the terrible cries of the survivors as they had been brought on board the *Carpathia*, they would hang their heads in shame instead of pushing and shoving to obtain a better view of the bereaved. Would they act this way at a funeral?

The words of the Reverend Mr. Dayton crept from the place in her mind where she kept her most bitter memories.

She saw the minister's long, disapproving face as he ushered her into his office.

"I don't think you should remain here, Kate. Is there somewhere you can go? Will someone take you in?"

"My father's maiden aunt, Great-Aunt Suzanna, is in Pittsburgh. I'll go to her. She's never approved of my father's marriage, and we've had no contact, but she's the only relative I have. She'll have to take me in."

The Reverend Mr. Dayton unlocked a drawer in his desk, removed a small cash box, and counted out a few notes. "For your train fare."

"Oh, no, I don't need—"

"I think you do."

"I have my mother's jewelry. I can sell it or pawn it."

The Reverend Mr. Dayton shook his head. "Not in this town. Take the money and buy a ticket to Pittsburgh. I'll take you to the station. I have a closed carriage. You won't want people to see you." He lowered his voice to a whisper. "We'll bury your father tonight, privately."

"And the headstone?" Kate asked.

"No headstone. We don't want to arouse bad feelings."

"Maybe you should just bury him at the crossroads and be done with it," Kate snapped.

"Maybe we should," he said.

Kate stumbled to a halt, blinded by tears of memory. The crowd pressed in around her, and she felt herself falling. Before she could hit the ground, a strong hand took hold of her arm and pulled her back to her feet.

"Steady on, Miss Kate."

She looked up into the craggy face of Joe Bayliss, who stood as firm as the Rock of Gibraltar in the midst of the seething crowd.

Suddenly embarrassed, she groped for words of explanation for the blind panic that had sent her running from the Caucus Room, but he was not listening. He set a firm arm around her waist, lifting her almost off her feet, and led her through the throng and up the steps to the doors of the Senate building.

"I can't go back," she insisted. "Please, Sheriff. I can't go back."

He ignored her, or maybe he didn't hear her. He growled a greeting to the police at the door and ushered her into the comparative calm of the marble corridor.

"I can't go back in there," Kate protested.

Joe released his grip on her waist and turned her to face him. "Where do you want to go?"

"I don't know," she wailed.

She caught his fleeting glance of exasperation, but his voice was kind. "We'll go to Senator Smith's office," he said. "You can wait there while I fetch Mrs. Trentham."

"Oh, no, don't do that. I don't want to see her."

The exasperation was more than fleeting this time. "Well, who do you want to see?"

"I don't want to see anyone."

He returned his arm to her waist and propelled her along the corridor. "I'll fetch the Irish nurse," he said. "She can take care of you."

He hurried her through an open doorway into an outer office and pushed her gently into a wooden chair. "Sit there, Miss Kate. This is Senator Smith's office, and no one will disturb you. Just wait here for the nurse. Don't go outside again."

Kate stared down at her lap, listening to the sound of Joe's retreating footsteps as he strode away along the marble-floored corridor. When she could no longer hear his footsteps, she could still hear his voice speaking to her as though she were a troublesome child being told to wait for her nanny. *Just wait here for the nurse. Don't go outside again.*

She listened to the distant muffled voices of people going about their business in the Senate building. She glanced at the open door. She didn't have to sit and wait like a child. If she could find a service exit, she should be able to leave without anyone noticing. She stood up, smoothed her dress, and adjusted her hat. This time, she would walk instead of run, and she would keep her tears under control until she could ... could what? Where was she going?

"Well, now. What's all this about?" Bridie Conley's voice broke through her thoughts, and Kate looked up to see the Irishwoman standing in the doorway with her hands on her hips.

"I don't need you," Kate said. "I'm leaving."

Bridie shook her head. "No, you're not. Herself wants to see you."

"Herself?"

"Mrs. Trentham. She says I'm to bring you to her."

"I don't want to see her."

Bridie raised her eyebrows. "Did I ask you if you wanted to see her?" she said. "It's not a matter of what you want. She says I'm to bring you and not take no for an answer." Bridie reached into the pocket of her apron and produced a handkerchief, which she handed to Kate. "Wipe your eyes; blow your nose; and come with me."

"I don't think you should speak to me like that," Kate replied, suddenly resentful of Bridie's tone.

"And how should I be speaking to you?" Bridie asked. "You're a grown woman with a job to do for Mrs. Trentham. Sure, and the world would be a terrible place if every person with a job to do felt free to run away crying like a child whenever they fancied. She wants to see you, and you're to come with me, and that's all there is to say about it."

Kate dabbed at her eyes with the handkerchief as fresh tears welled up and trickled down her face.

Bridie shook her head and raised her eyes to the heavens. "Look at you, in your pretty new dress and your smart new hat. What do you have to cry about? That's what I'd like to know."

"Well, I—"

Bridie waved away Kate's attempt at an explanation. "Don't tell me. Tell herself."

Kate reluctantly followed Bridie along the corridor toward the sound of voices from the Caucus Room.

"Are they still asking questions in there?" she asked.

"They'll be asking questions from here till kingdom come," Bridie replied, "and still they'll have no answers. 'Tis only God can tell us why. No need to be listening right now. Mrs. Trentham is in the ladies' retiring room, and very nice it is."

Bridie arrived at a door bearing a discreet sign indicating that this was for ladies only. She pushed the door open and ushered Kate through into a carpeted sanctuary lit by clerestory windows and electric lights with pink silk shades. Eva's wheelchair had been placed in the center of the room, where the light from the high windows illuminated the angry expression on her face. Kate stood before her, clasping and twisting the handkerchief Bridie had given her.

"Stop doing that," Eva said firmly. "You look like a five-year old. If you've finished drying your eyes, stop playing with that handkerchief. Put it away."

"I'm sorry," Kate said.

"Sorry for what?"

"For leaving you and for Bridie having to run after me."

"Is that all you're sorry for?"

"I should have stayed," Kate said, "but I was upset."

"I see." Eva's voice was cold. "And what were you upset about?"

"About …" Kate looked around at the chintz-covered armchairs. "Do you mind if I sit down?"

"Yes, I mind. Stand there and tell me what has you so upset."

"It was Danny, Mr. McSorley. The Duff-Gordons said that he had been in their lifeboat. I suppose I hadn't thought about it before. I mean, I hadn't asked how he came to be rescued, but now I realize he took the coward's way out. He got in a lifeboat. He took the place of a woman or a child. I thought he was better than that."

Eva sniffed disapprovingly. "And for that reason, you ran out of the Caucus Room, where people were reliving a terrible tragedy?"

"I was upset."

"Upset!" Eva declared. "You were upset, were you?"

"I was disappointed in Danny."

"And so you ran."

"No … well, yes."

"Because you were disappointed that Danny McSorley had not drowned along with all the other gentlemen?"

"No, it's not like that."

"I think it is," Eva said. Her face was flushed and her voice was low and dangerous. "You were not there. You have no idea what happened or under what circumstances young Danny was put into a lifeboat, and yet you presume to judge his actions. You presume to call him a coward."

"I didn't call him a coward."

"Yes, you did. You have made up your mind that any man who did not fling himself into the water is a coward. You are as bad as the newspaper reporters. How dare you presume to judge? You cannot judge, because you were not there."

"Senator Smith is judging," Kate muttered.

"What was that? Speak up."

"Senator Smith is judging," Kate repeated.

"Senator Smith is asking questions," Eva said, "and attempting to find the truth. Did you ask any questions?"

Kate stared down at the floor, feeling like a child and fighting back renewed tears.

"So," Eva hissed. "Is that how you intend to go through life? Do you intend to just run away from your problems?"

"I don't do that."

"Don't you?" Eva snapped. "You were running away when I

found you on the *Carpathia*, weren't you? I don't know what you're running from, but let me tell you that running away is a bad habit."

"I'm sorry."

"Don't apologize to me. It doesn't matter to me if you run away. I can always replace you. Apologize to yourself for being so weak."

Kate's eyes prickled, and she was mortified to feel teardrops slipping from beneath her eyelids and sliding down her cheeks.

"Oh, sit down," Eva said impatiently, "and tell me what you're really crying about. Are you really so attached to Danny McSorley?"

"No. It's not just him. It's everything."

"By 'everything,' I assume you mean whatever had you running in the first place. You'd better tell me what it is."

"I can't."

"If you don't tell me, someone else will. Probably that reporter woman who is trying to remember what she read about you in the newspaper."

After a year of silence, Kate could not speak the words. If Myra Grunwald unearthed the story and spoke the words that Kate could not speak, that would be soon enough. Meantime, she could only look at Eva and shake her head.

Eva sighed impatiently. "Very well. I only hope that when I do find out, I will discover that your current tears are justified. The survivors of the *Titanic* have come through a night of desperation and loss, and should not be subjected to seeing you cry because a young man has not come up to your expectations."

"That's not why—"

"Good." Eva waved a dismissive hand. "I will not ask you to justify yourself, but I will offer you some advice. Running away is no solution to anything, and you should never do it again. You have to face your demons, Kate. You can never outrun them. I don't ever want to see you do that again. Do you understand me?"

"Yes, ma'am."

"Very well. Now go and fetch Bridie to push me."

Kate found Bridie waiting in the corridor outside the retiring room and walked behind her as she pushed Eva back into the Caucus Room. Bridie walked with a straight back and shoulders stiff with resentment. Kate wondered how long it would be before the Irishwoman forgave her.

Eva's and Bridie's words had stung. Kate tried to justify her actions. Surely if Bridie and Eva knew why Kate was running, then they would understand and forgive her, maybe even find her justified. She longed to tell them. *It's not about Danny McSorley; it's about my father. I'm not a coward, but I had to run. I couldn't live with the hostile stares and the blame.* She wondered how long it would be before Myra Grunwald retrieved the newspaper clippings from March 1911 and what Myra would do with the information.

Kate looked up at the dais, where Senator Smith was on his feet, interrogating a witness. The man before him turned toward Kate as she helped Bridie to move chairs and accommodate Eva's wheelchair. He was a very ordinary-looking middle-aged man sporting the large mustache popular with men of his age. His mild blue eyes were fixed on Kate for a moment, and then he turned back to the senator. His posture was relaxed. Apparently, this man was not under any suspicion. He was simply a passenger with a story to tell.

Eva turned in her seat and queried the people behind her. "Who is he?"

"Charles Stengel. First-class passenger."

Eva nodded and leaned sideways to speak to Kate as she settled into her seat. "He's a no one. So I wonder why he's here."

Senator Smith shot an angry glance at the interruption and continued his question. As always, his voice was without emotion, but his questioning was relentless.

"Mr. Stengel, I understand that wagers were made by you as to the speed of the ship."

Stengel shook his head. "I would not say wagers," he responded, "but as is usual in these voyages, there were pools made to bet on the speed that the boat would make, and at twelve o'clock, after the whistle blew, the people who had bet went to the smoking room and came out and reported she had made five hundred forty-six nautical miles. I figured then that at twenty-four hours to a day, we made twenty-two and three-quarter knots, but I was told I was mistaken, that I should have figured twenty-five hours."

Senator Smith frowned. "Twenty-five hours for the day?"

"Yes, Senator, on account of the elapsed time, I believe, which made it almost twenty-two nautical miles an hour. At the same time, a report came from the engine room that the engines were turning three revolutions faster than at any time on the voyage."

"And what time was that on Sunday?"

"I should say about between one and two o'clock Sunday afternoon."

"Did you have occasion to consult with anyone as to, or did you familiarize yourself with, the speed of the ship after that time?"

"Not after that time, any more than I called my wife's attention to the fact that the engines were running very fast. That was when I retired, about ten o'clock. I could hear the engines running when I retired, and I noticed that the engines were running fast. I said I noticed that they were running faster than at any other time during the trip."

Smith's eyes glittered as he leaned toward the witness. "How could you tell that?"

"Just through being familiar with engines in the manufacturing business."

Smith seemed disappointed. Perhaps he had been hoping for an expert opinion, not just a vague speculation.

"Where were you, Mr. Stengel, when the accident happened?"

"I had retired. My wife called me. I was moaning in my sleep. My wife called me, and says, 'Wake up; you are dreaming,' and I was dreaming, and as I woke up, I heard a slight crash. I paid no attention to it until I heard the engines stop. When the engines stopped, I said, 'There is something serious; there is something wrong. We had better go up on deck.' I just put on what clothes I could grab, and my wife put on her kimono, and we went up to the top deck and walked around there."

Stengel paused. Kate could see only the back of his head, but from the sudden stiffness of his posture, she imagined the shadow of memory creeping across his face.

"There were not many people around there. That was where the lifeboats were. We came down to the next deck, and the captain came up. I supposed he had come up from investigating the damage. He had a very serious and a very grave face. I then said to my wife, 'This is a very serious matter, I believe.' Shortly after that, I heard the order given to the stewards to arouse the passengers, but I heard another passenger later complain that the stewards were not doing that."

Smith turned sharply as another of his committee members leaned forward across the table to ask a question. "You say that the stewards were not arousing the passengers?"

Smith turned back to Stengel. "What do you say, Mr. Stengel?

228

Why would someone say that?"

"I think I know the cause. The crew calmed the passengers by making them believe it was not a serious accident. In fact, most of them, after they got on board the *Carpathia*, said they expected to go back the next day and get aboard the *Titanic* again. As for the stewards not arousing the people, well, even the stewards were not told how serious the accident was, because the officers did not want to spread panic. The stewards would have done their duty, but the stokers, if they heard, would have come up and taken every boat."

A murmur spread through the people seated in the Caucus Room and out into the people behind the open windows. Smith shook his head slowly. "Is that your belief, Mr. Stengel?"

"It is the judgment of the officers," Stengel replied. "It is what they thought would happen."

"And what did you do?" Smith asked.

"I had seen the grave look on the captain's face," Stengel said, "and so I went back to my stateroom and put a life preserver on my wife, and then she tied mine on."

Kate tried to picture Mr. Stengel and his wife alone in their cabin, helping each other into the life vests. *Did they have any idea what was to come?* she wondered.

"We went back up to the top deck," Stengel said. "Then I heard the orders given to put all the women and children in the boats and have them go off about two hundred yards from the vessel."

"And who gave that order?"

"It seemed to me an officer. Of course, I was a little bit agitated, and I heard them, and I did not look particularly to see who it was. While they were loading the lifeboats, the officers or men who had charge of loading the lifeboats said, 'There is no danger; this is simply a matter of precaution.' After my wife was put in a lifeboat, she wanted me to come with them, and they said, 'No. Nothing but ladies and children.' And so I remained behind."

And yet you are here now? Kate thought. *Why are you here now?* Was this yet another man who had saved himself at the expense of others?

"I turned toward the bow, although I do not know what led me there," Stengel said with a note of awe in his voice, "but there I found a small emergency boat with three people, Sir Cosmo Duff-Gordon and his wife and Miss Francatelli. I asked the officer if I could get into that boat, as there was no one else around. He told me to jump in, and so I did."

Stengel turned his head and looked at the tall windows of the room, through which the outside spectators were clearly visible. "He told me to jump in," he repeated. "There was no one else there. No ladies."

"Did anyone else enter your lifeboat?" Smith asked.

Stengel turned back from glaring defensively at the spectators. "A young man, a Marconi operator. He jumped in as we were being lowered."

"How did that happen?"

"I am not sure. There had been some kind of altercation on the deck above, and gunshots. I saw a man—an officer, I think—lean from the deck above and give the order to let the Marconi man into the boat."

"Do you know who the officer was?"

"I do not."

"Did this young man, this Marconi man, say why he should be allowed in the boat?"

"He did not."

"Do you know who fired the weapons?"

"No, Senator, I do not."

"Could the Marconi man have fired the weapon?"

"I cannot say."

Kate sprang to her feet. Was Danny McSorley a murderer? In her mind, she was already fleeing the question, holding up her skirts and running down the long marble corridor, seeking open air. Eva's hand emerged from the embroidered shawl that covered her lap and grasped Kate's skirt. Kate looked down and met Eva's steady gaze. *You have to face your demons, Kate. You can never outrun them.*

Kate closed her eyes and allowed a memory to surface. A cold, clear moon illuminated the graveyard and the hastily dug grave. The Reverend Mr. Dayton hurried through the prayers.

"We therefore commit this body to the ground, earth to earth, ashes to ashes, dust to dust."

The earth had been cold as she had waited to cast it onto her father's coffin. Voices echoed in the valley below. They knew what she was doing, and they were coming. She released the soil, and it fell silently into the deep darkness.

The Reverend Mr. Dayton's voice trembled on the edge of fear.

"Go now, Kate. As fast as you can."

The demons climbed up the valley from what remained of the town. They followed her as she fled to New York, and lay in wait for her on board the *Carpathia*. They were here now, filling her with restless suspicion and urging her to run again. She took a deep breath, pulled her skirt from Eva's grasp and resumed her seat. This time she would not run.

Senator William Alden Smith

Senator Smith leaned back in his chair and beckoned to Will McKinstry. "Tomorrow," he said, "I want to use the smallest meeting room, with seating for no more than a handful of spectators."

"But you said you wanted the proceedings to be open to the public," McKinstry reminded him.

"I did," Bill agreed, "but I was wrong. I can't make any progress in this atmosphere, with people trying to climb through the windows, and a constant babble of conversation."

He looked at the shabby young man who had replaced Charles Stengel in the witness chair. Stengel had been a willing witness, eager to tell his story, but this witness was an entirely different matter.

He gestured toward the new witness. "This fellow is playing to the gallery," he whispered. "He's been told to make me look like a fool, and he's succeeding. The British press will have a field day with this. See to it that we have a small room, and from tomorrow on, there will be no spectators, just a handful of reporters."

"What about survivors?" McKinstry asked. "We can't keep them out."

"First come, first served," Bill said, "but no one else."

"And Mrs. Trentham and her coterie?"

Bill looked across at Eva Trentham, ensconced in the front row. The flighty young woman from the *Carpathia* had returned to her side with a tearstained face and a distinctly disheveled appearance. The comings and goings of Eva and the nurse and the girl from the *Carpathia* had disrupted the meeting and broken his concentration, but he could not discount Eva's political influence. He still needed her on his side. "You'd better save a place for her," he agreed. "There'll be hell to pay if we try to keep her out."

McKinstry retired to his seat at the rear of the dais, and Bill returned his attention to Frederick Fleet, the *Titanic*'s lookout. Fleet wore a cocky grin on his weather-beaten face. At twenty-four, he had been at sea almost half of his life, and he'd spent four years as lookout on the *Olympic* before gaining a post on the *Titanic*. Bill regretted that he had elected to be the person who would question Fleet. The young sailor should have been questioned by someone else, preferably someone with naval experience.

He looked down at his notes and proceeded to the next question. "Did you board the *Titanic* from Southampton or from Belfast?"

"I fetched her round from Belfast on the lookout," Fleet said with a grin, "and I stayed on the lookout from Southampton."

"And where were you stationed in the performance of your duty?"

Fleet shrugged. "Like I said, sir, I was on the lookout."

"You were on the lookout at the time of collision, meaning you were in the crow's nest?"

Fleet raised his eyebrows. "That's what I said."

Outside the window, someone laughed. Bill tried to ignore the laughter and persevered with the dogged line of questioning that was the only tool available to him. He knew of no other way to arrive at the truth, but he was beginning to doubt that Fleet would ever tell the truth. Perhaps the young man had not been directed to lie, but he certainly had not been directed to be helpful.

"Can you tell me, Mr. Fleet, how high the crow's nest is above the boat deck?"

Fleet shook his head. "I have no idea."

"Can you tell how high above the crow's nest the masthead is?"

"No, sir."

"Do you know how far you were above the bridge?"

Fleet shook his head vigorously. "I'm no hand at guessing."

"I don't want you to guess," Bill said patiently, "but if you know, I would like to have you tell."

"I have no idea."

From the corner of his eye, Bill saw that Senator Duncan Fletcher, from Florida, was leaning forward impatiently.

"You must have some idea," Fletcher said.

Fleet pursed his lips and rolled his eyes up to look at the ceiling as if in deep thought. "No," he said finally, "I do not."

"You must know whether it was a thousand feet or two hundred feet," Fletcher insisted.

Fleet shrugged. "No, sir, I do not."

Fletcher leaned back in his seat, and Bill returned to his notebook. "What time did you go on watch on Sunday night?"

"Ten o'clock."

"And were you told to keep a sharp lookout for ice?"

Fleet looked at Bill suspiciously. Perhaps no one had prepared him for that question. "Yes," he said reluctantly. "I was told."

Bill made a note on his notepad. One very small victory. Fleet had finally admitted that he had been told to look out for ice.

"And did you see ice," Bill asked, "and did you report it?"

"I did," Fleet said. "Just after seven bells, I saw a sort of shadow on the water, like a black mass, and I rang three bells and reported an iceberg right ahead."

Senator Fletcher leaned forward again, and his voice was sharp and serious, the voice of someone who expected to be obeyed. "How far away was this black mass when you first saw it?"

Fleet's face paled. "I have no idea, sir, but I reported it as soon as ever I seen it."

"But you can't tell me how far away it was?" Fletcher persisted.

"No, sir."

Bill began to wonder whether Fleet was being evasive or whether he was, in fact, somewhat lacking in brains. Perhaps he had misjudged the young Englishman. Maybe he was not being evasive; maybe he really could not measure distances.

"Mr. Fleet," Bill said, "could you tell how many ship's lengths you were away? *Titanic* ship's lengths."

"No, sir. No, I couldn't."

"Well, how large did the iceberg appear to be when you first saw it?"

Fleet's voice was on the edge of panic. "I don't know, sir."

Bill tried again. "Was it the size of an ordinary house? Was it as large as this room?"

"No. It didn't appear to be very large at all."

"Well," Fletcher interrupted angrily, "how large did it get when it struck the ship?"

Fleet buried his face in his hands for a moment. When he looked up, his eyes were shadowed. "When we were alongside," he said quietly, "it was a little bit higher than the forecastle head ... Fifty feet, I should say."

Bill stared down at his notebook for a moment, realizing that there was something that Fleet was not saying. Why had he not seen the iceberg sooner? Was it because of the ship's speed, or was there another reason? He remembered Joe's report from his meeting with the crewmen. *I spoke to the lookout. His name is Frederick Fleet, and he let slip that he had no binoculars up there in the crow's nest.* How could he have forgotten such important information? "Mr. Fleet, did you have binoculars in the crow's nest?"

Fleet shook his head. "We asked for them in Southampton, and they said there was none for us."

Bill felt a moment of triumph. Perhaps this was it. Perhaps he had found the Achilles heel of the White Star Line. "Who did you ask, Mr. Fleet?"

"We asked Mr. Lightoller, the second officer, and he said there was none for us."

"Suppose you had glasses," Bill persisted. "Could you have seen this black object at a greater distance?"

"We could have seen it a bit sooner."

"How much sooner?"

Fleet lifted his head defiantly. "Soon enough to get out of the way."

☐

CHAPTER SIXTEEN

Senator William Alden Smith

Bill looked up and saw Joe Bayliss in the doorway. He set aside his notebook and reached into his desk drawer for a bottle and two glasses.

Joe dropped into a chair and stretched out his long legs. "They're here," he said. "I have a man watching the two crewmen, and another watching Captain Lord. They're not going anywhere, but I suggest you get them into the witness chair sooner rather than later. Lord is not happy at being called."

Bill poured a generous measure of Jim Beam and pushed the glass across the desk. "What do you think?" he asked. "Was Lord really close? Did he just sit and do nothing while the *Titanic* went down?"

Joe shrugged. "The two crewmen say they saw a big ship with her lights blazing, and Lord says that's not so."

"Why didn't someone wake the radio operator?"

"I don't know. You'll have to ask him."

Bill poured himself a glass and sat back in his chair. "What do you think, Joe?"

"I think it's up to you to find out." Joe sipped his drink. "Of course, even if Lord and the *Californian* were just over the horizon, even if they were only ten miles away from the *Titanic*, the *Californian* didn't cause the sinking. Lord and the *Californian* are a distraction at best; they are not the story you're looking for. You're grasping at straws, Bill."

Bill studied his old friend. Was this the time to say what he really thought, or should he maintain the confident facade he had been displaying for the past two weeks? He had been certain that careful questioning would reveal the story he wanted to hear, but now he wasn't so sure. His meticulous, patient interrogation of the survivors had raised more questions than answers. Time and again, he had found himself immersed in the chaotic scene they painted for him. He stood with them on the deck of the sinking ship while steam shrieked from the boilers, drowning out all coherent speech. He joined in their desperation at finding only a handful of hastily uncovered lifeboats. He felt the panic as officers and gentlemen insisted that women and children take the few seats available. He heard the courage of men who told their wives, "I'll be along shortly. Don't worry."

At times, he descended to the bowels of the ship, where the stokers continued to feed the boilers and immigrants struggled to unlock the gates that kept them from the boat deck. He was in the radio room, where Harold Bride and Jack Phillips, up to their knees in icy water, hunched over the radio, sending the same message again and again. He was even with Bruce Ismay as he looked around and found no ladies to occupy the seats in the last collapsible lifeboat.

Bill shook his head. "I can't stop now, Joe, but I need a diversion to buy me some more time. I have to find something to keep the press at bay and keep the president from closing me down, and I'm going to give them Lord. I'll let them chew on that while I try to find more evidence."

Joe took a long swallow of his drink before he spoke. "What if you don't find what you're looking for?"

"I have to."

"But if you can't …"

"Then there'll be no compensation for the families." Bill allowed frustration and anger to take hold. "I thought you were with me, Joe."

Joe rose from his chair and set the glass carefully on Bill's desk. "I'm interested in the truth, Bill. What are you interested in?"

As Bill attempted to form an answer, Joe raised a hand to silence him. "No, don't tell me. I don't think I want to know. I'll see myself out." He turned as he reached the door. "By the way, what do you know about the Marconi man Mr. Danny McSorley?"

Bill shrugged. "I know nothing about him."

"He wants to see the president."

"I know he does, but does he say why?"

"No."

"The president is not seeing anyone. I'd like to keep it that way until we finish our inquiry."

"Whatever you say," Joe growled. "I'll see you in the morning."

Bill slumped in his chair and listened to the steady pace of Joe's departing footsteps as the sheriff strode away along the marble corridor. The footsteps stopped abruptly, and Bill heard a snatch of muffled conversation before Joe's footsteps resumed marching away into the distance while lighter, more uncertain footsteps drew closer.

Bill barely had time to open the desk drawer and stow the bottle and the two glasses before Bruce Ismay shuffled into view. The Ismay Bill had seen on board the *Carpathia* had been a proud and angry man, and the Ismay he had questioned in New York had been calm and supercilious. The Ismay now standing in his doorway was a shadow of his former self. He seemed to have lost weight. The luster was gone from his dark hair, and his eyes were red and tired. For a moment, Bill was tempted to open his desk drawer and offer the Englishman a drink, but the lawyer in him resisted the temptation. This was not a legal trial, but he still thought of himself as the prosecutor and Ismay as the accused.

"Mr. Ismay."

"Senator."

"What can I do for you?"

"You can put an end to this farce and release my crew."

"Your crew? As you have testified that you were not responsible for the operation of the *Titanic*, I am surprised you now take responsibility for her crew and call them *your* crew."

Ismay's eyes flashed. "Common decency calls me to defend these men, who are being kept here against their will and against the will of the British government."

"I have had no official complaint from your government."

"His Majesty's government has complained to your ambassador in London. Action will be taken if we are not released."

Bill's heart sank as he understood Ismay's words. Taft could not continue to ignore an official complaint made to the ambassador.

Ismay sat without being invited. "Time is running out, Senator, and you have nothing."

"On the contrary," Bill replied, "I have accumulated considerable evidence that the *Titanic* was driven through the ice field at reckless speed on your instructions."

"You have no proof."

"I have the word of witnesses."

"You have the word of passengers, who are people with no knowledge of the sea. You have a man who thinks the engines were running fast but admits he knows nothing about marine engines. You have a couple of society ladies who misunderstood the information in a radiogram. You have not persuaded even one officer to tell you the ship's speed, and you do not have the logbook. No one has reported seeing me on the bridge. You have nothing."

Bill looked longingly at his desk drawer. He was in no mood for verbal fencing with Bruce Ismay. He needed a drink; he needed a bath; and he needed to go home.

"Your lookout had no binoculars," he accused.

Ismay nodded his agreement. "Yes, I heard about your questioning of Fleet. The man is obviously a fool who is unable to tell the difference between two hundred feet and a thousand feet. The *Titanic* was equipped with binoculars. All he had to do was ask, but he didn't ask." Ismay's face suddenly flushed red with anger. "Are you saying that it's my fault? Do you think that I take personal inventory of the equipment in the crow's nest? I am no more responsible for Fleet than I am for the missing logbook."

"I am not so sure that the logbook is missing," Bill interrupted.

Ismay sighed. "It makes no difference. If you could find the logbook, it would not tell you what you want to know. Your president was most unwise in putting this inquiry into the hands of politicians. If you had a serving merchant marine officer on your committee, he would have told you that the daily log is not kept in a logbook."

"What do you mean?"

"The daily log is kept in the scrap log, which is nothing but a sheet of paper affixed to the chart table. At the end of the watch, the numbers are neatly transferred to the official log. Give it up, Smith. You're not looking for a company logbook; you're looking for a single scrap of paper that floated away on the waves or went to the bottom of the ocean. You'll never find it."

Bill's voice trembled on the edge of fury as he stared into Ismay's small, deep-set eyes. "Did you destroy it?"

Ismay stared right back at him. "No, Senator, I did not. If I had it, I would show it to you, and you would see that it is nothing but instructions and notes taken by the officer of the watch. The navigation of the ship is the captain's business, not mine. Can't you get it into your thick politician's head that I was not responsible for anything that happened?" He leaned back in the chair. "What do you really want from me, Smith?"

"I want compensation for the victims."

Ismay shook his head. "No, you don't. This isn't about compensation. This is about your ambition. You don't care about the victims. You're just playing games for the benefit of the newspapers and your voters." He lifted his hands in a despairing gesture. "You've got everything you'll get from me. You've ruined my reputation, and—"

"You ruined your own reputation when you took a seat in a lifeboat."

"It was the last lifeboat," Ismay said quietly, "and there were no women or children anywhere near it. I acted on impulse. If you had been there, Senator, you might have done the same thing."

Bill intended to speak, but the words would not come. He was suddenly unsure of himself. If he had seen a space for himself in that half-empty lifeboat, what would he have done?

"I hear you've found another man to ruin," Ismay said.

"What are you talking about?"

"Lord, of the *Californian*. I hear you're about to ruin his reputation."

"I intend to ask him questions."

Ismay rose wearily from his chair. "It's just another way of getting at me, isn't it?"

Bill looked at Ismay in genuine puzzlement. "I don't understand."

"Of course you do," Ismay sneered. "The *Californian* is part of the Leyland Line, and the Leyland Line is part of International Mercantile Marine, and I am the chairman of International Mercantile Marine. This is just another way of destroying me."

Ismay loomed above Bill's chair, his face twisted in contempt.

"How many more people do you intend to ruin, Senator? Do what you like. You won't find your scapegoat. Only one man is responsible for the loss of the *Titanic*, and he's dead. He went down with his ship. Isn't it time to leave the living alone and start speaking ill of the dead?"

Capitol View Guest House
Washington, DC
Sheriff Joe Bayliss

Joe sat on the front porch of the guesthouse as the dawn sky turned from pink to blue. As he puffed on his cheroot, he watched the flow of traffic along Delaware Avenue and came to the conclusion that the automobile was now king of the road. Even his enjoyment of his fine Kentucky cheroot was blunted by the gasoline fumes that accompanied the clattering automobiles and omnibuses. He had been here for far too long, and he was homesick for the cool, clean air of Lake Michigan. It was time to go home. Once he reached Sault Ste. Marie he would stay there, and he would never again involve himself with politics and politicians. Bill could finish the hearings without him. One of the Pinkerton men could keep an eye on Captain Lord, and Joe could get the next train to Chicago. He looked longingly up the road toward Union Station. Just a short walk, and he would be on his way.

His thoughts of home were interrupted by a chorus of Klaxon blasts, a squealing of brakes, and an angry warning shout. He looked up and saw that a woman had managed to bring traffic to a halt as she made her way across the road. The woman wore a bright blue skirt and a navy jacket. Tendrils of black hair escaped from her feathery blue hat as she ran across the road and up onto the sidewalk in front of the guesthouse.

Joe grinned. He really could not help himself. It seemed that Kate Royston was always running and always causing chaos. He stepped down from the porch and caught Kate's arm as she stood panting for breath.

She turned her face toward him. Her cheeks were flushed; her eyes were bright; and she was definitely the prettiest thing he would see today.

"Are you all right, Miss Kate?"

"Yes, of course I am," she said impatiently as she made a futile attempt to tuck her hair back under her hat. "I'm not used to automobile traffic."

"Neither am I," Joe agreed. "Where are you going? Would you like me to walk with you? You really shouldn't be out on your own."

"I'm perfectly capable of being on my own," Kate replied.

Joe said nothing, but his raised eyebrows were met with a grin.

"All right, Sheriff, I admit that this is the third time you've had to help me stand upright." She shook her head, and another ringlet escaped from her hat. "I'm really not like this. I don't usually require the assistance of a lawman to help me stand."

"Of course not," Joe agreed. "May I ask where you are going?"

Kate indicated the front porch of the guesthouse. "Up there," she said. "I want to talk to Danny McSorley. He's staying here, isn't he?"

"He's in the backyard," Joe said, "with the dog. I'll show you the way." He stubbed out the cheroot and offered Kate his arm. "I think you should hold on to me."

She took his arm, and he led her along a flagstone path toward the back of the guesthouse.

"Does Mrs. Trentham know that you're out here?" he asked.

Kate withdrew her hand from his arm. "She's not my keeper. I can go wherever I want."

"Of course. I wasn't suggesting—"

"Yes, you were. I suppose you think that I would be nothing without her."

Joe shook his head. "No, of course I don't think that, but I was under the impression that you had no family to help you."

Kate stopped walking and stood for a moment, staring at the ground. When she looked up, she had tears in her eyes. "You're right, Sheriff—I have no family, and without Eva Trentham, I am nobody. And no, she doesn't know I'm here. She won't be up and dressed for at least another hour, and that's why I came over to see Danny. I have to ask him something."

"Well," Joe said, "while you're asking, will you please ask him to tell you why he wants to see the president?"

"The president? Really?"

"Oh, yes. He's quite insistent. I thought he'd be off to Newfoundland now that Senator Smith has moved on to a new line of questioning, but he won't leave until he's seen the president."

They rounded the corner of the house, and Danny McSorley came into view, throwing a stick for Wolfie, who didn't seem to understand the object of the exercise.

"He's been trying that for a couple of days," Joe said, "but that dog's not a land retriever. He's a water dog. That's why he was swimming around the *Titanic*. He was probably trying to retrieve something he fancied. Wolfie doesn't belong in the city any more than Danny does, or any more than I do. I'm going to deliver Captain Lord to the hearing room, and then I'll take my leave of Washington."

"Oh no!" Kate made no attempt to hide her disappointment. "I thought that you would ... I mean, Eva thought that you would ..."

"Would what?" Joe asked, looking down at Kate, whose face had flushed to a fetching shade of pink.

"Nothing. Nothing at all. I'll just speak to Danny, and I'll go back to the Willard."

"Will you need me to see you safely across the road?"

"No, I will not."

Joe watched Kate as she marched across the lawn toward Danny and Wolfie. He thought about the flush on her cheeks and her obvious disappointment, now followed by equally obvious irritation. Surely it was not possible that Kate had formed some kind of attachment to him. He knew that women, against all common sense, sometimes found him attractive. Several society beauties had told him that he represented a challenge. He was a grim wild beast they would like to tame. Kate wouldn't think that way, but Eva Trentham was not above playing that kind of game. Perhaps she had been putting ideas into Kate's innocent young head.

Wolfie took his nose out of the bushes and fixed his eyes on Kate. He wagged his tail and turned his attention to retrieving the stick that Danny had thrown. Apparently, he would not retrieve for Danny, but Kate was a different story.

Danny's face lit up with delight at the sight of Kate tripping lightly across the lawn, and Kate returned his broad smile. Joe set aside his previous thoughts of Kate. Whatever Eva Trentham may have up her sleeve, Kate's mind was fixed on Danny. He observed the way that the tall young Viking stood in blond contrast to Kate's petite build and dark hair. Kate laughed as Wolfie trotted up with the stick, and Danny laughed with her.

Joe spun on his heel and walked purposefully back to the front door. Once inside the paneled front hall, he slipped into the morning room, where he had a view of the backyard and the two young people. He quietly lifted the sash window and pulled up a chair, taking care to conceal himself behind the heavy red drapery. He felt no guilt in listening in on Kate's conversation. He was not, he told himself, listening to Kate; he was listening to Danny. As a representative of the law, and a sworn deputy of the Senate sergeant at arms, he had every right to find out what Danny was saying. Danny was an Englishman, a foreigner, and yet he wanted to have a private audience with the president, and he would not explain his reasons.

Danny McSorley

Danny watched the smile fade from Kate's face as Joe Bayliss walked away. Her eyes followed the sheriff's tall form until he disappeared into the house. When she turned back, her face was set in a serious expression. Wolfie made an attempt to attract her attention by offering her his stick, but she ignored him.

"Mr. McSorley," Kate said in a soft but determined voice, "you know that I've been able to hear all the testimony given to Senator Smith."

Danny looked down curiously at the top of her head, which came only just above his shoulder. Perhaps she wanted to tell him something that she'd heard, something he would not have been able to hear for himself. He would have preferred to talk about something else, but if she wanted to talk about the testimony, then that was what they would talk about. He was willing to talk about anything she wished, so long as she remained with him in the garden. "I haven't heard everything," Danny said, "because witnesses are supposed to be kept separate, like at a real legal trial, but I've read the newspapers and I've talked to other people. It's not really possible to keep anything secret, is it?"

Even as he spoke the words, he thought of the secret he was keeping. The only way to keep a secret was to tell no one, and he had told no one.

"I met Sir Cosmo Duff-Gordon and his wife," Kate said. "They were in your boat, weren't they?"

Danny tried to keep his voice steady as he replied. "Yes, they were."

He knew he should say more than just three words if he wanted to keep Kate with him in the garden, but memory surrounded him like a sinister mist, curling around the rosebushes and spring flowers, and turning the lush green lawn into cold gray ocean. Would it always be this way? he wondered. Would the names ever cease to trigger memories and set him adrift in the darkness, chilled to the bone and listening to the shrill of an officer's whistle somewhere impossibly far off?

He forced himself to return to the garden and the sunlight. "I thought the Duff-Gordons were rather unpleasant," he said. "There were just the three of them, Sir Cosmo and his wife and the secretary woman. And then there was the man who sells machinery, Mr. Stengel. He was all right, I suppose, but the three stokers they put in the boat were useless."

"And what about you?" Kate asked. Her voice was still strangely cold, perhaps even accusatory. Her posture had become rigid, her shoulders stiff, and her face pale.

"What about me?" Danny asked.

"What were you doing in the boat?"

"Not much," Danny said. "I took quite a tumble getting into the boat and banged my head. I was out of action for a while. I didn't even see the ship go down."

"Didn't you?" Kate said.

Danny was puzzled by the ice in her voice. It was as though he had done something to offend her, but he could not imagine what that could be. Surely she should understand that he had no wish to recall all the horrors of the night. Nonetheless, if she wanted him to speak, he would speak.

"When I came round, Sir Cosmo was making the stokers row. He said we were supposed to go towards a light that everyone could see. Mr. Stengel was very upset. He wanted us to go back, because there were still people in the water. Sir Cosmo refused. He promised the stokers money if they would keep rowing. He said that if we went back, the boat would be swamped and we'd all drown."

"And what did you do?" Kate asked.

"Well," Danny said, "I was confused, you know, and I'd banged my head."

"But what did you do?"

"I didn't do anything. I suppose I agreed with Sir Cosmo."

"You agreed not to pick up any more people?"

Danny hesitated. He didn't want to paint himself into the picture she was surely imagining. He didn't want to say why he had gone along with Sir Cosmo. It was not just that Sir Cosmo's arguments were, unfortunately, sensible and realistic; it was that Danny was under orders. *Stay alive! Take this to the president.*

"Is that true?" Kate asked with a shrill edge to her voice. "Did you agree not to pick up any more people?"

"No, no, it wasn't like that. But we had to wait until … uh … well, we waited until there were fewer people."

"You waited until most of them had died," Kate accused.

Danny took a step back. She was angry. What right did she have to be angry? What right did she have to pick and prod at his already guilty conscience? "No, it wasn't like that," he snapped. "We were drifting, you see, and it wasn't long before we lost sight of the people in the water—"

"If there were any left alive," Kate interrupted.

"I suppose you could say that."

"I am saying that."

"Well," Danny continued, doggedly hanging on to his self-control, "we could hear an officer's whistle, so we rowed toward the sound and found the other lifeboats."

"The ones that were full," Kate said.

"No. They weren't all full, but some people were transferred out of the boats that were too full into ones that had seats. I don't understand why you're asking me these questions. You've heard the testimony."

"Yes, I have, and now I begin to understand."

Danny felt his self-control slipping. "What do you understand? What will you ever understand? You're one of those women, aren't you? You think that any man who preferred stepping into a half-empty lifeboat to diving into the freezing ocean is to be branded a coward and a monster. Why don't you just give me a white feather?"

Kate's voice rose to an angry shout. "Did you shoot someone?"

Danny took a step back and stared at the angry red spots on Kate's cheeks. "Did I shoot someone? What kind of question is that?"

"Well, did you?"

"No, of course I didn't."

"That's not what Mr. Stengel says."

"Mr. Stengel says that I shot someone?"

"He says that he heard a shot, and then suddenly an officer was leaning over the rail and telling Sir Cosmo that he had to let you into the boat. Obviously, you shot someone so you could get a place in the boat."

Sheriff Joe Bayliss

Watching from behind the curtain, Joe saw that Danny was clenching his fists. If Kate had been a man, there was no doubt that she would now have been flat on her back with a bloody nose.

Danny took a long, deep breath. His voice was cold with controlled rage. "I'm sorry you think so little of me, Kate. Do not expect me to dignify your question with an answer. I trust you can find your own way back to your lodgings."

Joe shook his head in disappointment as Kate clamped her mouth shut, turned on her heel, and ran from the garden. *Running again,* he thought. *Always running.* He thought of going out to the sidewalk and making sure she crossed the street without incident, but at the rate she was running, she'd be across the road before he reached the front porch.

He stepped away from the window and went out into the hall to intercept Danny. He was in time to see Danny and Wolfie coming in through the back door.

Danny didn't wait for Joe to speak. "I'm sick of this," he declared. "I'm going to the White House."

"Why?"

"To see the president."

"They won't let you in."

"They will if you come with me."

"I can't come with you now. I have to accompany Captain Lord to the hearing."

"Another scapegoat for your American press," Danny said.

Joe shook his head. "I think he was close by, Danny, and so do you. I think his crew saw the *Titanic* and he did nothing."

"That's a serious charge," Danny said.

"Well," Joe said, "I think I heard another serious charge—something about you shooting someone."

Danny was easily equal to Joe's height and well able to stare him in the eye. "Why were you listening?"

"I couldn't help it. I was in the morning room. Your voices carried."

"So what are you going to do? Who are you going to believe?"

"I'd believe you if you gave me an explanation," Joe said. "I understand why the young lady is concerned. We've had several reports of gunfire."

"I wasn't firing."

"So who was?"

"I believe it was Officer Lowe."

Officer Lowe, Joe thought. *Yes, that sounds possible.* Fifth Officer Lowe had been a slippery witness, and Joe suspected that he'd withheld a great deal of information. "Did you see Lowe fire his weapon?"

"No, I didn't see him fire it, but I saw him with a weapon. I was on the boat deck with Major Butt when ..." Danny shook his head. "I'm sorry. I can't say any more."

"Why not?"

"I can only speak to the president."

Joe wanted to shake the young Englishman, although he suspected that Danny would not take well to being shaken and would probably return as good as he received.

"Why," Joe asked, "do you want to see the president? Does it have something to do with Major Butt?"

"Would it make a difference?"

"Of course it would. The president is practically paralyzed with grief over the major. If you have something to tell him—"

"I do. Can you help me?"

Before Joe could reply, he heard heavy footsteps on the stairs and looked up to see Captain Lord descending the staircase. Unlike the *Titanic*'s officers, who had dressed in borrowed civilian clothes to give their testimony, Stanley Lord was arrayed in his dress uniform and carried his cap tucked under his arm.

"This is all nonsense," Lord declared as he reached the bottom step. "If your Senator Smith carries on like this, there will be war."

Joe heard Danny's sharp intake of breath and turned away to

speak to him. "He's exaggerating, lad. There'll be no war."

Danny pulled on Wolfie's leash and turned toward the kitchen. "Don't be sure about that," he said softly as he walked away.

The Willard Hotel
Kate Royston

Kate straightened her hat and brushed dog hair from her skirt before she entered the lobby of the Willard. When she approached the desk, the clerk looked up and recognized her immediately.

"Miss Royston."

"Yes?"

"I have been asked to tell you that the Countess of Rothes is waiting for you in ... uh ... she's ... uh ... she's waiting for you in the smoking room." His last words came out in a rush of disapproval.

Grudging amusement momentarily dissipated Kate's fog of anger and disappointment. She was well aware that ladies rarely entered the dark-paneled smoking room that adjoined the gentlemen's bar, but obviously, Lucy Noël Martha Leslie, Countess of Rothes, was not someone who could be restricted.

Maintaining an air of calm, as though the visit of a countess were an everyday event, Kate thanked the clerk for the message and turned toward the smoking room. Perhaps the countess was in Washington to attend the Senate hearings, but why would she want to talk to Kate? Their interaction on the *Carpathia* had been interesting, but they were hardly friends.

Kate walked across the lobby and into the tobacco-scented smoking room, with its groupings of wingback chairs. She found the countess comfortably ensconced in a leather chair, smoking a thin black cigarette adorned with a gold band. With her blonde hair and pale blue traveling costume, the countess stood out like a beacon amid the heavy furnishings and the scattering of dark-suited gentlemen.

The countess waved an elegant hand to Kate as she entered the traditionally masculine enclave. Fragrant smoke wafted from the countess's cigarette as she gestured toward an adjoining armchair.

"Good morning, Miss Royston. Would you care for a cigarette?"

Struck speechless by the countess's appearance and the fact that some of the chairs in the room were occupied by powerful men, Kate could only shake her head.

The countess smiled. "Sit down, Miss Royston. May I call you Kate?"

Kate reluctantly took a seat. Why couldn't the countess sit in the elegant lobby like any other well-bred lady? Why was she insisting on invading this bastion of male privilege?

"May I call you Kate?" the countess asked again.

Kate could only whisper her answer. "Yes, of course."

"And I shall be Noël. No need to stand on ceremony when we have, after all, shared underwear and nightclothes."

Kate blushed. "Really, I don't think that's—"

"You don't think that's an appropriate subject of conversation?" Noël asked. "You are no doubt correct, Kate, but someone has to do something about the atmosphere in this room. All these stuffy old gentlemen need to be shaken out occasionally, like dusty oriental carpets. Are you sure you won't have a cigarette? They are Sobranie Black Russians, the very best tobacco."

"No, thank you. I have never smoked."

Noël grinned. "No, I suppose you wouldn't. When I see you now, in fashionable clothing, walking and talking like a lady, and entering this room with the appropriate diffidence of a well-bred young lady, I realize that I misjudged you. I was told you had boarded the *Carpathia* as a governess, and I assumed you were one of those unfortunate young women who have been educated above their station. Now I see that is not the case. I think you have fallen suddenly from a comfortable, if somewhat bourgeois, station in life, and you have been unable to pick yourself up."

Kate's heart began to pound. Noël's suppositions were very close to the truth.

"It's ironic that you should have found a refuge with Eva Trentham, whose situation is the opposite of your own," Noël continued. "Eva Trentham started with nothing—some would even say less than nothing. It's a long climb from poor Irish immigrant to the richest woman in America."

"But she's not Irish," Kate protested.

The countess smiled and shook her head. "That's what she'd like you to think, but I've made it my business to find out who Eva Trentham is and why she will stop at nothing to ruin J. P. Morgan. It's her single-minded passion that's dragged Senator Smith into holding these hearings. She's the one who is egging him on day after day, although anyone with half an eye can see that he's ruining his political career and making himself a laughingstock overseas."

Kate sat forward on the very edge of her seat. She had not thought to question Eva's background. Eva had climbed the social ladder with a series of marriages to wealthy men, but had she really been a penniless immigrant like Kitty or Maeve? The countess was right about one thing—Eva's determination to destroy J. P. Morgan. Kate had suspected that the financier had at one time destroyed the business enterprises of one of Eva's husbands, but perhaps the feud had a different root.

The countess leaned back in her seat and blew a perfect smoke ring. She watched it drift away before she returned her attention to Kate. "What do you know of the Irish potato famine?"

Kate's mind drifted back to Miss Arbroath's Academy for Young Ladies and the minuscule amount of practical information that had been imparted to her along with her study of pianoforte, French, and embroidery. "People starved," she said, "and the Irish came here to find work and food."

Noël nodded. "Well, that's a place to start, although it certainly doesn't do justice to the plight of the Irish. Here is what I now know. Padraig O'Donnell and his pregnant wife, Evelyn, were brought to ruin by the famine, and so they came to America in 1855 as immigrants aboard the sailing vessel *Caiton*. They sailed from Galway, and when they reached Boston, Evelyn gave birth to a baby girl."

"Eva has a child?" Kate asked. "She has never said anything about having a daughter."

Noël abruptly stubbed her cigarette in a cut-glass ashtray beside her chair and left it to smolder sullenly as she leaned forward and lowered her voice to a whisper. "She no longer has a daughter."

August 1856
Newport, Rhode Island

"Rory says we can go with him on his boat this afternoon, and we'll catch us some fish," Padraig said. "It's good fishing even in the harbor, and a light wind to cool us down and move the boat. Wouldn't you like to have some good fresh fish? A nice piece of cod, perhaps."

Evelyn sighed. "You only have one half day a week to be home, and already you want to go out."

Padraig looked around at the cramped room that served as bedroom, kitchen, and nursery. "I can't stay in here. I need fresh air, and so do you, mavourneen. Come with me. Rory won't mind."

Evelyn looked at her infant daughter and saw that the child's face was flushed and her soft baby ringlets were sweat soaked and clinging to her scalp.

"She'll be all right," Padraig said, catching up the baby and tucking her in the crook of his arm. "She'll sleep better after an afternoon out."

Without waiting for Evelyn to respond, he carried the baby out of the door and down the steps to the street level. Evelyn followed closely behind, feeling instant relief as the fresh sea breeze ruffled her hair.

The harbor was alive with the white sails of boats, from square-riggers to sturdy fishing vessels to the sleek racing yachts of the wealthy families who kept laborers like Padraig busy building summer homes along the cliff tops.

Rory's boat was reassuringly sturdy, and Rory himself was gray haired and fatherly, reminding Evelyn of her own father. The two men pushed the boat down the beach into the water, and the four of them sailed smoothly away from the shore. Soon they were drifting peacefully in the slight swell. With Padraig and Rory occupied in sailing the boat and hauling in fish, Evelyn relaxed in the sunshine and watched contentedly while Shelagh played at her feet. It was almost like being home again, before the potato crop had rotted in the fields, before the dreadful hunger, and before the eviction. Evelyn closed her eyes.

Kate kept her eyes on Noël's face, knowing that she was about to tell of some great tragedy—some awful reason why Eva no longer had a daughter, and why Eva's hatred for J. P. Morgan could not be assuaged.

"James Pierpont Morgan," Noël said, "liked to be called Pierpont. He was a sickly young man who had spent several years recovering from rheumatic fever. He spent the summer of 1856 at his parents' Newport mansion, with the idea he would take up sailing, the one sport he could take part in despite his weakness. After all, what could be more suited to a sickly rich whelp than standing at the helm of a yacht and ordering healthy people around? He was out on the water that afternoon, on board his personal yacht. No one knows for certain what happened, but one can assume that his lack of experience coupled with his insistence on being in control led to disaster."

Kate looked at Noël's troubled face. She thought of young Eva, or Evelyn, as she had then been called, relaxing in the sunshine with little Shelagh at her feet and Padraig reeling in fish for supper. She painted a careless smile on Pierpont Morgan's face as he steered his monstrous yacht, with its massive sails stretched taut by the wind. She imagined Morgan pressing for more speed, driving with reckless abandon, oblivious of the small fishing boat and its Irish occupants.

"Only Evelyn survived," Noël said. "The two men and the baby were gone. It was all kept very quiet. Pierpont was sent away to school in Germany, and Eva was offered payment for her silence."

"Did she take the money?" Kate asked with a suspicion already forming in her mind.

"Oh, yes. I am told that she demanded a considerable sum for her silence." Noël removed another gold-tipped cigarette from her purse and struck a match from the match holder beside the ashtray. She drew deeply on the cigarette and watched the tendrils of smoke curl upward.

At last she resumed her story. "Some would have expected Evelyn O'Donnell to return to Ireland and maybe use the money to help her starving relatives, but I think you and I know better than that. What Evelyn did was purchase a ticket on a liner bound for Italy, and in Italy she remade herself, emerging eventually as the bride of the Conte di Lombardia-Parma, an extremely elderly aristocrat with no close relatives to protect him from the machinations of Evelyn O'Donnell. She had invested the money from the Morgan family into dressmakers, hairstylists, voice coaches, and private tutors. When she finally launched herself on society, the poor old count did not stand a chance. Within a year of the wedding, the count was dead, and Eva was a widowed contessa with a title that gave her entrée into American society."

Kate thought suddenly of Bridie Conley and realized that Eva may have fooled everyone else, but the Irishwoman who was now attending to Eva's intimate personal needs had not been fooled. She knew who Eva was and where she had come from.

"So," Noël said, "now you know why we are all here, taking part in Senator Smith's farcical hearing. It's all bait to lure J. P. Morgan away from his French villa in order to defend his investment. If he is ruined by the disaster that struck his ship, it won't be because Eva Trentham cares about the *Titanic* survivors, it will be because he killed her husband and her child."

"You don't think that …" Kate could not complete her sentence.

"Do I think that Eva Trentham engineered the sinking of the *Titanic*?" Noël said. "Is that what you wanted to say?"

"Do you?"

"I wouldn't put it past her," Noël said, "but as a practical matter, I can't see how she could have done it. The ship was supposed to be unsinkable. Even if she somehow persuaded Captain Smith to drive recklessly through an ice field, she still couldn't have known that the *Titanic* would sink. No, Kate, I don't think we can blame Eva Trentham for this."

Noël leaned forward and lifted the silver coffeepot from its tray. "Have some coffee, Kate. I know this is all a shock, and a quick cup of coffee will set you up for the next shock I have in store for you."

"You know something else?"

"Drink some coffee. You are going to need it. You do drink coffee, don't you?"

Kate nodded, and Noël poured a dark liquid unlike anything Kate had ever seen before from the coffeepot. "Americans don't really know how to make coffee," Noël said. "Out on the Scottish moors, we drink it thick and black, the way God intended. I had them make a double brew. Have to do something to get the morning started."

Kate took the cup and sipped tentatively. Noël watched her intensely. The coffee was hot and bitter, and Kate had to force herself to swallow.

"You don't like it?" Noël asked.

"I'm not used to it," Kate whispered, unable to regain her full voice as the piping hot liquid made its way down her throat.

Noël sat back in her chair. "You don't have to drink it if you don't want to. I'm not here to encourage you to take up bad habits. I'm sure Eva Trentham will take care of that once she gets you to Europe. Are you still planning to go with her now that I've told you who she really is?"

"I don't know. I don't know what to do."

"Well, you'd better make up your mind," Noël said. "Senator Smith isn't going to string these hearings out much longer. The president will recover his wits any day now and ask what on earth is going on. Try the coffee again; take a good mouthful. It will give you strength for what I'm going to tell you."

Kate took another slow sip of coffee. She began to savor the bitter flavor. She eyed Noël's cigarette. Perhaps she should try one. She could no longer be the girl who ran from every new experience, and she could no longer be the kind of girl Danny McSorley would take to Newfoundland. Where had that thought come from? Had she really planned to go with him? Well, that was definitely over.

Noël was already speaking. She kept her voice low and glanced occasionally at the partially hidden gentlemen smoking their pipes and cigarettes as they perused the morning papers. "Your bag was stolen when you left the *Carpathia*, wasn't it?"

Kate nodded her head, surprised by the change of subject. "Yes."

"I'm glad to say it's been found, with all its contents."

Kate took a celebratory gulp of her coffee, the taste beginning to grow on her. The countess reached into her reticule and produced a thick envelope. "Your travel papers are intact. Here are your identification papers and your ticket."

Kate looked down at the envelope. If these were her travel papers, she was no longer beholden to Eva, who was determined to find a forger who would create fake documents and a new name for Kate. With these papers, Kate could continue to be herself. She was surprised at how good she felt. Of course, her name was irretrievably linked to a scandal, but it was still her name, and one day, she wanted to be able to use it. Maybe she would still travel with Eva under a false name, but having her own documents would give her a secret sense of freedom.

"How did you get this?" Kate asked.

"Just a lucky chance," Noël said. "Your bag was not stolen by some casual thief who intended to pawn the contents. It was stolen by, or maybe sold to, someone who saw an opportunity to take passage on the *Carpathia*. When the *Carpathia* was ready to resume its journey to the Mediterranean, a woman attempted to board using your ticket and your travel papers."

Kate swallowed her coffee in one burning gulp as she stared at the countess. "Who? Why?"

Noël dismissed Kate's questions. "It's not important. The important thing is that Mrs. Broomer, the chief stewardess, recognized your name and recognized that the passenger attempting to board was not the Kate Royston who had been so helpful to her and to the doctor." Fragrant smoke wafted from Noël's cigarette as she lifted her hand in a triumphant wave. "You are more memorable than you realize, Kate. Well done."

"I don't really want to be memorable."

Noël's voice was a short, sharp snap. "Stop it. Stop hiding behind a humble facade. It serves no purpose. Drink your coffee and allow me to continue. You will recall that I gave you my card in case you needed me, and it is because my card was found in your portmanteau that your possessions were delivered to my New York house. I, of course, knew where to find you. New York society is abuzz with the news that Eva Trentham has found a new companion. Wagers are being placed as to how long you will be able to last before the old harridan dismisses you."

"I have to stay on her good side," Kate said. "If I don't go to Europe with her, I don't know where I'll go." *Newfoundland. I could go to Newfoundland. No, don't be ridiculous.*

"Don't you have a home to go to?" Noël asked.

Kate bit her lip, remembering a solid brick house with a wide front porch and steps leading down to the lake. Daffodils would be giving way to tulips by now, and the apple trees would be in bud. The fire had been a year ago, and the flowers would have had time to recover. Nature would always win.

Kate steadied her voice and changed the subject. "Surely you didn't come all this way just to bring my portmanteau. You could have had it sent on by train."

Noël grinned. "I came out of curiosity. I've read the accounts in the newspapers, of course, but I don't believe everything I read. I wanted to see for myself and maybe offer testimony of my own."

"Is your husband with you?" Kate asked.

Noël laughed. "Oh, no, of course not. He's out in the heather, shooting things. He prefers to live the life of a Scottish earl. We often go our separate ways. Of course, being a man, he did offer me his opinion."

"And what is his opinion?"

"He tends to believe that the whole thing will be dismissed as an act of God. He's right, of course, in believing that the case for compensation will be hard to prove. I'm not interested in compensation for myself. I took my jewel case with me onto the lifeboat, and so I lost nothing but a few clothes. Others were not so fortunate. If the poor creatures in third class are to be compensated,

Senator Smith will have to prove that the *Titanic* was inherently unseaworthy and that Captain Smith risked his unseaworthy vessel by taking it at reckless speed through the ice field."

"Did you meet the captain?" Kate asked.

Noël nodded her head. "Oh, yes, I dined at his table. He was a charming gentleman, and I have not heard a word spoken against him. Sir Bruce Ismay, on the other hand, is the current bête noire of the American press. Any claim that is made against the White Star will depend on holding Ismay responsible for the running of the ship, and then the blame will climb up the corporate ladder until it reaches J. P. Morgan himself."

"Giving Eva the revenge she's been looking for," Kate whispered.

"Exactly," said the countess. "What do you think, Kate? You've been watching. Who would you hold responsible?"

Kate tried to formulate an answer that would not cause the countess to accuse her of being too hesitant, uncertain, or meek. She gritted her teeth as she replied. "It's hard to say. Senator Smith is determined to place the blame on Sir Bruce, but I'm not sure he's correct. I am not convinced that Ismay was responsible for the boat's speed. He didn't come across well when he testified. He is really quite obnoxious."

Noël nodded. "Yes, I recall his behavior on the *Carpathia*. He certainly didn't endear himself to anyone."

"But is that enough?" Kate asked. "Just because he is unlikable, does that make him responsible?"

Noël shrugged. "Senator Smith is a politician, and he's stuck his neck out a long way. He has to find someone to blame." The countess stubbed out her cigarette and fixed Kate with a long, hard look. "That brings me to the reason I am talking to you. I could have just sent your bag up to your room and let matters rest, but I found something interesting among your clothing."

Kate frowned, remembering the contents of her bag. Surely there was nothing of value beyond her passport. Her gray governess gown was of no value to anyone. She had a few underclothes and almost nothing else.

"I gave your clothing to my maid to be laundered," Noël said, "and she, of course, washed the apron you had been using in the infirmary."

"I suppose we should return that to the *Carpathia*," Kate muttered.

"That's not the point," Noël said. "My maid discovered a piece of paper in the pocket."

Kate had a flash of memory. Sir Bruce Ismay standing on the deck of the *Carpathia* with his hands in his pockets. When he gestured to the officer on the deck, he pulled his hands from his pockets. A paper fell to the deck, and Kate caught it before it was stepped on by the crew working to lift the survivors. She called to Sir Bruce, but he failed to answer as he hurried away, and she put the paper in her pocket.

She looked at Noël. "Is it something important?"

"Yes, I think it is. I would say that it is the very thing that Senator Smith is looking for. I believe that what Sir Bruce had, and what you picked up, was a page from the *Titanic*'s scrap log."

Kate drew in a sharp breath. "Senator Smith has been asking questions about the logbook. He doesn't know who has it."

"I don't suppose anyone has the actual logbook," Noël said, "but you have something more valuable. You have the sheet on which the officer of the watch made notations. It is quite possible that you have the sheet that will tell us the speed at which the *Titanic* was traveling. This may settle matters once and for all."

Kate shook her head. "Why do you say that I have it? I don't have it; you have it."

"I would sooner have a viper under my nightgown," Noël said. "It was in your portmanteau; it is your responsibility. Leave me out of this. I'll ride and shoot with the best of men, and I'll dance a fandango until my legs give out, but I will not involve myself in the dispute between Eva Trentham and J. P. Morgan."

"Is he so terrifying?" Kate asked.

"He owns us," Noël said. "My husband's estate is mortgaged to him, as is half of Europe and most of the United States. I know of only two people who are not afraid of him."

"And who are they?"

"Eva Trentham, because she knows his deepest secret, and people like you, Kate, who have nothing and therefore have nothing for him to take. That sheet of paper is yours, not mine. Depending on what it says, you can use it to ruin Ismay, and therefore Morgan, or you can throw it away, and no one will ever know for sure what happened on the bridge."

"And if I throw it away, there will be no proof of anything?"

"It will be one of history's great unanswered questions," Noël said. "It's up to you."

CHAPTER SEVENTEEN

The Russell Senate Office Building
Washington, DC
Senator William Alden Smith

Bill ran his hand through his hair and across the stubble on his chin. He knew that he was not looking his best. He was representing the United States Senate and was responsible for finding the cause of the worst maritime disaster on record, but he had spent the night pacing his office and dozing in his chair. He had not even found time to go home and change his clothes. He had not bathed. He could feel the disapproval of his colleagues. They no doubt thought his interest in the *Titanic* was verging on a dangerous obsession. Any day now, the president would rouse himself from his melancholy and insist on ending the inquiry. It was surely time to send the crew of the *Titanic* home and allow the British to take over responsibility. But somehow, exhausted as he was, Bill was not ready to let go. Surely something good could be salvaged from the disaster—some lesson that could be learned and applied to the transatlantic shipping routes.

He rose wearily to watch Captain Lord entering the Caucus Room, and he remained standing as Lord placed his hand on the Bible and swore an oath to tell the truth. He was well aware that he was not in a courtroom and Captain Lord was not bound by anything other than his honor to tell the truth.

The master of the *Californian* was a tall, thin man with blue eyes and thinning hair. Despite his apparent youth, his eyes had the hooded squint of a man who had spent many years gazing at distant horizons. His expression was somber but not wary. Bill imagined that Stanley Lord would be hard to intimidate and even harder to shame. Would it come to that? he wondered. Would he be forced to shame Lord into admitting that he had not come to the aid of the *Titanic*?

Bill resumed his seat and looked out at the small audience. Eva Trentham was in her usual place in the front row. Today she wore a kingfisher-blue jacket and a hat adorned with peacock feathers. Now that she was fully rested from her ordeal on the *Titanic*, it was possible to see why she had been the toast of the Gilded Age. Even in old age, she was an arresting figure. Kate sat beside her, wearing a navy jacket, a feathered hat, and a worried frown. Joe Bayliss stood against the back wall with his gaze swiveling between Captain Lord and Kate as though uncertain which of the two would make a break for it.

Bill consulted his notebook, smiled at Lord, and asked his first question. He was not under the illusion that he could take Stanley Lord by surprise. Lord knew why he had been summoned, but it would take time to reach the point where Bill could ask for the answers he really needed. Meantime, he would begin with standard questions.

"What is your full name, sir, and where do you reside?"

"Stanley Lord. Liverpool, England."

"And what is your business?"

Lord's chest seemed to swell slightly. "Master mariner."

Bill remembered Lightoller, the man whose heroism had captured the hearts of the New York newspapers. Lightoller had merely called himself a seaman. Lord apparently had no intention of appearing humble.

Bill glanced at his notes, skipped a few of his intended questions, and gestured for Lord to be seated. He had a feeling that his questions would take quite some time. Lord sat back in his seat, apparently relaxed.

"Where were you and your ship on the fourteenth day of April last?" Bill asked.

"Forty-two, forty-seven."

Perhaps Lord intended to reveal Bill's ignorance of marine

navigation. Bill would not be intimidated.

"Would you be more specific, please?"

Lord produced a leather-bound book that he had carried in with him. He opened it and flicked through the pages. "Forty-two north and forty-seven west."

Bill knew he would have to rely on the experts seated behind the senators to tell him the meaning of those numbers by plotting them on a chart he kept in his office. He continued his questioning.

"Are you reading from the log of the *Californian*?"

"I am."

So Lord had brought his logbook into the inquiry. If he was willing to read from it, either Lord was supremely confident that he had done no wrong, or the log had been altered. Bill knew that the game was only just beginning.

"Captain Lord, what other entries have you in the log, of your position on that date?"

Lord flicked the page. "At six thirty, we had forty-two degrees five minutes and forty-nine degrees ten minutes as having passed two large icebergs. The next entry was seven fifteen: 'Passed one large iceberg, and two more in sight to the southward.'"

"And," Bill asked, "did you attempt to communicate with the vessel *Titanic* on Sunday? Is that entered in your log?"

"It is. We communicated at ten minutes to eleven."

"A.m. or p.m.?"

Lord raised his eyebrows impatiently. "P.m."

"What was that communication?"

"We told them we were stopped and surrounded by ice."

"Did the *Titanic* acknowledge that message?"

"Yes, she did. I believe their operator told my operator he had read it, and told him to shut up, or stand by or something, that he was busy."

Bill thought back to what he had heard in New York. Both Bride of the *Titanic* and Cottam of the *Carpathia* had said the same thing. The *Titanic*'s operator had been impatiently resisting incoming messages, declaring that he was too busy working Cape Race on behalf of the passengers. Bill made a note on his notepad. At some time very soon, the whole question of rules governing Marconi operators would have to be considered. The Marconi was a new and wonderful device, but its use would have to be codified and regulated. Perhaps the *Titanic* would not have collided with the iceberg if the radio operator had been able to concentrate on incoming messages instead of using his time to send personal messages for first-class passengers.

Bill realized that the room had fallen silent waiting for his next question. "Captain Lord, do you know the *Titanic*'s position on the sea when she sank?"

"I know the position given to me by the *Virginian* as the position where she struck an iceberg: forty-one degrees fifty-six minutes and fifty degrees fourteen minutes."

"And so," Bill said, "figuring from the *Titanic*'s position at the time she went down, and your position at the time you sent this warning to the *Titanic*, how far were these vessels from one another?"

Lord shrugged. "Approximately nineteen and a half miles."

Bill tried to ignore the shocked murmuring rising from the senators beside him. He had taken a gamble, and it was about to pay off. Lord sat in the witness chair looking smug and admitting that his ship had been less than twenty miles away from the *Titanic*.

"Of course," Lord said, "the *Titanic* was moving, but we were stopped altogether."

"What did you stop for?"

"We stopped so that we would not run over the ice."

"And you notified the *Titanic* of your condition?"

"Yes, of course. We always pass the news around when we get hold of anything like that. I didn't know exactly where the *Titanic* was, but it was a matter of courtesy."

So far, Bill thought, the captain of the *Californian* had said nothing to incriminate himself. He had been close to the *Titanic*, and he had stopped his ship because he was surrounded by ice. The *Titanic* had ignored his warning message and continued on her way to New York. Lord had been cautious; Captain Smith had been foolhardy. Or so it appeared. Or perhaps Smith had been under orders from Ismay to break the speed record.

"Did you see the *Titanic*?" Bill asked.

Lord shook his head. "No, sir."

Bill glanced at Joe and then back at Lord. This was not what the two crewmen from the *Californian* had reported. "Did you see any signals from her?" Bill asked.

"No, sir."

"You say that you were twenty miles away at the time she sank."

"Yes. I was stopped and surrounded by ice."

"And the *Carpathia* was fifty-three miles away."

"That is what I've been told."

"So, Captain Lord, how long did it take you to reach the scene of the accident, from the time you steamed up and got underway Monday morning?"

Lord consulted his logbook. "'Six o'clock, proceeded slow, pushing through the thick ice. Six twenty, clear of thickest of ice, proceeded full speed, pushing the ice. Eight thirty, stopped close to steamship *Carpathia*.'"

"Am I to understand that the *Carpathia* coming from fifty-three miles away was at the scene of the wreck when you arrived?"

Lord looked at Bill with cool blue eyes that showed no sign that he understood the weight of Bill's words, that the *Carpathia* had come fifty-three miles through the ice field and still arrived before the *Californian*. Could the man really be so unaware of what he had done, or did he truly believe that he had done nothing wrong?

"The *Carpathia* was taking the last people out of the lifeboats when I arrived," Lord confirmed.

"Captain Lord," Bill said, trying to keep his tone neutral, "did you see any distress signals on Sunday night, either rockets or Morse signals?"

Lord shook his head. "No, sir, I did not. The officer on watch saw some signals, but he said they were not distress signals."

"Not distress signals?"

"No, Senator, they were not distress signals."

"And yet the officer on watch reported them to you. Why is that?"

Lord closed the logbook and leaned back in his seat. "I think you had better let me tell the story myself."

"I wish you would," Bill replied grimly. "Please, Captain Lord, tell us your story."

"When I came off the bridge at half past ten," Lord said, "I pointed out to the officer on deck that I thought I saw a light coming along, and it was a most peculiar light, and we had been making mistakes all along with the stars, thinking they were signals. We could not distinguish where the sky ended and where the water commenced. You understand it was a flat calm. He said he thought it was a star, and I did not say anything more. I was talking with the engineer about keeping the steam ready, and we saw these signals coming along, and I said, 'Do you know anything?' He suggested it could be the *Titanic*, as he thought she was close by, but I told him what I had seen was too small to be the *Titanic* and it did not even look like a passenger liner.

"We went ahead and signaled her with the Morse lamp, but she did not take the slightest notice of it. We saw her lights go out, which meant to me that she had made a turn and was pointing north. I could see her red port light. We signaled her every fifteen minutes from ten thirty until one o'clock, and she did not take the slightest notice. After that, I decided to turn in for the night."

Bill tried to put himself into the scene. He had made several transatlantic crossings, alone and with Nana. He remembered standing on deck at night and feeling the utter isolation of being a creature of the land adrift on the vastness of the ocean—an alien being who could neither swim nor fly to safety. He stared at Lord's weathered young face. This man had not been lonely or alien. This man saw himself and his ship as part of a network of oceangoing vessels and was no more surprised to see the distant light of another ship than Bill would be surprised to see the passing of a train on a parallel track. Lord had signaled. The other ship had failed to reply and had apparently sailed away over the horizon.

And yet, Bill thought, the *Titanic*'s survivors were told to row toward a light that some had seen on the horizon. Had that been a comforting lie, or was there more to this?

Bill looked up and caught Joe Bayliss's expression. The sheriff certainly thought that there was more to the story.

"Before I fell asleep," Lord continued, "the second officer came to my cabin and told me that the ship we had seen was firing rockets. He claimed to see four white lights at three-minute intervals, but he heard no explosions. We agreed that they were most probably company signals, maybe some form of celebration. I again instructed the second officer to keep signaling, and then I went to sleep."

The audience murmured as Bill confirmed Lord's statement. "You went to sleep?"

Lord smiled. "Yes, Senator, I went to sleep. I have a faint recollection of awaking to hear the apprentice opening my room door, opening it and shutting it. I said, 'What is it?' He didn't answer and I went to sleep again."

The smile left his face, and for the first time, he seemed to realize how damning his words could be. Everyone in the room knew now that somewhere close by the *Titanic* had been sinking and more than a thousand people had been drowning, but Lord had apparently known nothing. Despite the words of the second officer and the apprentice, Lord had continued to sleep. Bill wondered if the captain of the *Californian* had been drunk. It was always a possibility. She was a British ship, and British sailors were very fond of their ration of rum.

Before Bill could formulate another question, Senator Fletcher rose to his feet and leaned forward across the table.

"Captain Lord, let me ask you a question with reference to that steamer you say you saw before you ... uh ... retired for the night. What was her position in reference to your ship?"

Lord swiveled his eyes to look at Fletcher. "Pretty near south of us, four miles to the south."

"To starboard or port?" Fletcher asked.

"When he was coming along, he was showing his green light on our starboard side, before midnight. After that we slowly blew around and showed him our red light. He appeared to stop until one o'clock, and then he started going ahead again."

"Was he ever any closer to you than four miles?"

"No."

"And were you able to tell what kind of ship it was?"

Lord glanced around the room and then back at Fletcher. "We were of the opinion that it was an ordinary cargo steamer. We saw no tall funnels and just one masthead light."

Bill turned to look at the members of his committee. They were all leaning forward in their seats. Obviously, they were transfixed by Lord's testimony, but what did they believe? Had Lord truly seen the *Titanic* and failed to act, or had he seen a small cargo steamer plowing her way toward a European port with a sleepy lookout who had failed to see the *Californian*'s Morse signals? But why fire rockets, if there were rockets? Where was the truth in this tale?

Senator Bourne leaned forward on this elbows and stared down at Lord. "Captain Lord, did you or your crew hear anything, perhaps the sound of a siren or escaping steam? The *Titanic*'s survivors speak of a great noise."

Lord shook his head. "No, we heard nothing."

Bourne looked at Bill and shook his head. It seemed that he had heard enough. Bill looked at the other members of his committee. Senator Fletcher was still on his feet.

"Captain Lord, from the log which you hold in your hand, and from your own knowledge, is there anything you can say further which will assist the committee in its inquiry as to the causes of this disaster?"

Lord shook his head. "No, sir, except that in the morning, we saw a yellow funnel steamer about eight miles away."

"Do you have anything further to say which will assist the committee?"

"No, sir, there is nothing. Only that it was a very deceiving night."

Bill studied Lord's face for a long moment, seeing how Stanley Lord had been remade in the past few minutes. Lord had entered the hearing room with the air of a man determined not to be browbeaten by a committee made up of hostile Americans, but his face had changed as he recalled details of that long April night. His eyes were shadowed now, and his face had been painted with lines of regret, maybe of doubt. He would not say, and maybe he could not even allow himself to think, that he had been a mere ten miles away from the *Titanic*.

Bill shook his head. The captain was ruined, of course. Perhaps Lord had been unaware, or perhaps he had chosen to act wisely for the safety of his own vessel. It would seem that his ship had been more or less trapped in the ice and unable to move without danger. If the *Titanic* had in fact been in trouble nearby, what could Lord have done by pushing through the treacherous ice in the dark? Everyone knew the *Titanic* was unsinkable, and therefore, whatever the trouble, it could wait until morning, when Lord could see his way through the ice.

I've ruined him, Bill thought as he closed his notebook, *and for what purpose?* He knew he could not go on this way, wondering if he was serving as anything other than an instrument of Eva Trentham's war on J. P. Morgan. He needed time to think. He needed to go home.

He turned to the other members of his committee. "Thank you, gentlemen. We are adjourned until ten o'clock tomorrow morning."

Bill tripped in his hurry to leave the dais and be free of the usual press of reporters, who seemed to flow toward him in an unrelenting tide. He felt a steadying hand on his elbow and saw Joe Bayliss chewing on an unlit cheroot and regarding him with curiosity.

"Finishing early?" Joe asked.

"To be honest, Joe, I don't know how much more of this I can take."

"I thought you made progress."

"Well," Bill snapped, "I'm glad you think so, because I don't. So far, I've proved nothing."

He took Joe's silence as assent and allowed the sheriff to bulldoze a path through the press of politicians and reporters. With his mind reeling, he barely heard the questions being hurled at him. How could he answer their questions when he couldn't answer his own questions?

Joe pushed open the outer door of Bill's office and ushered him inside. Bill was heading straight for his inner office and the bottle he kept in his desk drawer when he realized that the office was not unoccupied. A tall blond figure, a Viking in everything except his clothing, rose from a chair in the corner.

"Mr. McSorley wants to see the president," Joe said, "and he refuses to leave until you help him."

Bill shook his head in frustration. "Mr. McSorley, we are finished with your testimony. You've been very helpful, but we don't need you any longer. You should make your arrangements to travel to Newfoundland. There's nothing left for you to do here."

"Well," Joe said, winking at Bill, "there's the question of Miss Kate. I think that young Danny is—"

"No, I am not," Danny interrupted dismally. "I have nothing left to say to Kate. She made it clear what she thinks of me. In fact, she made it very clear what she thinks of any man who did not go down with the *Titanic*. We're all cowards."

"That's not true," Bill said.

"I'm afraid it is," Joe said solemnly. "It is now considered an act of cowardice for any man to have saved himself. With the current level of hysteria on the subject, I expect to see women handing out white feathers on the streets."

"But that's nonsense," Bill argued. "I agree that there were some men who behaved poorly, but the fact of the matter is that many of the lifeboats had empty seats. If a man saw one and stepped in ..."

He stopped speaking, allowing his argument to die away as he realized what he had said. He had spent the past week publicly humiliating Bruce Ismay for the crime of taking a seat in a lifeboat.

But this is different, he thought. Ismay wasn't just a man who saved himself; he was the reason the ship had gone down in the first place.

Bill was seized with an overwhelming desire to go home and talk to his wife. Nana would help him chart a path through these troubled waters. Her instincts were not just political and social; they were also highly moral. She would warn him if he had gone too far, wouldn't she?

Danny interrupted Bill's train of thought. "I didn't want to get into a boat. I was going to wait with the other men, but then Major Butt—"

Bill's mind snapped back into focus. "How is Major Butt involved?"

"I can't tell you. I have to tell the president and only the president. That's what he said. I know Miss Kate thinks I'm a coward. In fact, she seems to believe that I shot someone in order to get into a lifeboat, but I didn't, and I'm not a coward."

"Why don't you save yourself a lot of trouble and tell me what Major Butt said?" Bill asked. "I'm a United States senator. I can be trusted with state secrets."

"I know my instructions," Danny said, "and I'm not leaving here without seeing the president, and that's all there is to it."

"We can deport you," Joe offered grimly, "or arrest you as a spy. We could find a way to make you talk."

Bill shook his head, angered by Joe's words and suddenly aware how little he had done to help the stranded Englishman. "Stop it, Joe. We won't need to do anything like that. I'll arrange a meeting for you, Mr. McSorley, on condition that I am also present."

Danny nodded. "I think that would be all right. Shall we go now?"

"No," Bill said, his irritation returning. "We can't just walk into the president's office. Good heavens, man! Would your government allow me to walk into Buckingham Palace and talk to the king without an appointment? We will go in the morning. Sheriff Bayliss will accompany you to the White House, and I will meet you there."

Danny grinned with relief. "Thank you, sir."

"After that," Bill said, "I suggest you take the next possible passage to Newfoundland. I won't need to take additional testimony from you. The afternoon train will take you to New York tomorrow, and from there you can board a packet steamer to St. John's. I believe there is a regular service."

Danny's face was suddenly suffused with color. "I would like to see Miss Kate before I leave."

"Whatever for?" Bill snapped. "Does she also have a message for the president?"

"No, sir, of course not."

Joe grinned sardonically and poked Bill's arm. "There's more to life than sinking ships and state secrets," he said. "Give the boy a chance."

The Willard Hotel
Kate Royston

Kate wanted desperately to lock herself in her room and examine the contents of her portmanteau. Eva had already purchased a whole wardrobe of clothing to replace the items that had been stolen, but Kate still wanted to touch and hold her own few possessions—all that was left of her previous life.

She followed Bridie as Bridie wheeled Eva into the parlor of her suite. "If I can be excused," Kate said, "I'd like to—"

"Why are you in such a hurry?" Eva asked. "Don't you want to celebrate?"

"Celebrate? What do we have to celebrate?"

"Captain Lord," Eva said, rubbing her hands together. "We can celebrate that the man is such a coward that he refused to move his ship. I know he saw the *Titanic*. I don't believe any of this talk about seeing some other ship. I know what his crewmen said. They saw the *Titanic* and they did nothing. He said it himself. He went to sleep. We were out there, drowning, and he went to sleep."

"And you want to celebrate that?" Kate asked.

"I want to celebrate the fact that the *Californian* is a Leyland liner, and therefore, she's J. P. Morgan's responsibility. I'll have him for this, Kate. I swear that I will."

If Kate had not heard Noël's account of Eva's feud with J. Pierpont Morgan, she would have thought the old woman had finally lost her senses. Eva's eyes were bright with a kind of evil delight, and spittle gathered at the corners of her mouth as she chortled. Her voice had changed, taking on the faintest hint of an Irish lilt. Perhaps Kate would not have noticed before her conversation with Noël, but she noticed now. She glanced in Bridie's direction. Had Bridie also noticed?

"Smith has him on the ropes," Eva declared. "It'll be a quick one-two punch—a punch from the US Senate and another one from the British tribunal. He'll have to answer for what he's done."

"But ..."

"But what?"

Kate bit back her words. She had almost admitted that she knew Eva's story, but even knowing the story could hardly excuse Eva's jubilation. Fifteen hundred people were newly dead, their families still in mourning, but Eva's joy was grounded in revenge achieved for the death of three people nearly sixty years before. For Eva, the sinking of the *Titanic* was just another stepping stone to her own vengeance.

Kate thought of the travel documents stowed safely in her purse and wondered how long she would have to wait until she could find a way to leave Eva. The thought of spending any additional time with the vicious old lady was almost as bad as the thought of spending time with Great-Aunt Suzanna.

She fingered the pearl brooch at the neck of her blouse. Eva had said it was a gift. Those were not her actual words. *It's just a cheap trinket; you might as well keep it. By the time I've finished grooming you, men will be giving you diamonds.* She wondered what a pawnbroker would give her for it. She knew it wasn't a high-quality piece, but perhaps it would bring a couple of dollars, and a couple of dollars could buy a third-class ticket to New York. But then what?

One step at a time, she told herself. *See how much you can get, and then see what you can do.* She leaned forward to speak softly to Eva. "I have a headache. Would you mind if I go to my room?"

"Go wherever you like," Eva said expansively, "but be back in time for dinner. Tonight I think we will have champagne." She flicked her fingers at Kate. "Off you go."

Kate hurried along the corridor and into her own room. She locked the door behind her and stood for a moment contemplating the battered leather portmanteau. At last she lifted it onto the bed and unfastened the straps.

Slowly, fighting back tears, she removed the contents of her portmanteau. Noël's maid had packed the scant few belongings with care. Here was the gray dress Kate had worn a year ago on the train to Pittsburgh. It had once been very fine, but now it was a shadow of its former self, still showing the marks where Kate had later removed the lace and the beadwork. Great-Aunt Suzanna had sneered at the original adornments.

"So you come here in a fancy dress and tell me you have nothing."

"The house burned. This is all I could retrieve."

"Do you expect me to clothe you as well as feed you?"

"I didn't know where else to go."

Kate stared down, seeing the fancy lace corset she had worn on her flight from home a year ago. She could almost laugh at her naiveté in thinking she should truss herself up in a corset before fleeing the smoky ruins of her home. She would have done better to search for the silver candlesticks that had once adorned the mantelshelf in the parlor.

She moved the corset aside and saw the cheap undergarments reluctantly purchased by Great-Aunt Suzanna.

"Your mother was a fool with money. Don't expect fine things here."

Kate shook her head to clear away the memory of her great-aunt's sour face and grudging hospitality. Only once had she seen Great-Aunt Suzanna smile, and even that smile had been followed by sneering resentment.

"I won't be staying here, Aunt. I'm going to New York to take up a position as a governess."

"Do you expect me to pay your fare?"

"No, Aunt. I have pawned my mother's jewelry."

"You didn't tell me you had jewelry. You told me you were penniless. You're full of deceit, just like your mother. Well, be gone with you."

There had been no supper that night, and no breakfast in the morning.

Kate knew that she was wrong to wallow in bitter memories. She could never return to the grim old house in Pittsburgh—not after the final goodbye at the kitchen door as Kate had buttoned her cape and prepared to go out into the smoky morning air. Great-Aunt Suzanna, watching her leave, still wore her nightcap, and her face twisted in contempt.

"I always suspected that my nephew was not your father. Your mother was a—"

Kate did not wait for the word to be spoken. Her hand shot out of its own accord, cutting off Great-Aunt Suzanna's parting words and leaving a bright red imprint on the old lady's cheek.

Kate dragged her mind away from the bitter memory of Pittsburgh. She was not there now, and she would never go there again. The Willard's chambermaid had opened the window to air the room. Kate breathed in the clean afternoon air and looked around at the elegant furnishings. She had come a long way from that grim mansion in Pittsburgh, but she was still a prisoner. Great-Aunt Suzanna and Eva Trentham had almost nothing in common, but each one had held her captive. No, she thought, it was not the women who imprisoned her; it was her own poverty. She had been a prisoner from the moment her father had taken his own life and left his only child to cope with the aftermath.

She reached into the bag and took out the sturdy brown envelope that rested on top of the folded apron from the *Carpathia*. So this was it. This was the paper that Sir Bruce Ismay had carried in his pocket.

The envelope had not been sealed. Kate opened it and pulled out the single sheet of crumpled and stained paper. She studied the scribbled notes and numbers. Was this the evidence that would destroy Eva's enemy? And if it did, who else would it destroy? The paper felt heavy in her hand, as though its importance was reflected in its weight. Only one other person knew that this paper still existed, and that person wanted nothing to do with it. What had the countess said? *I'd sooner have a viper under my nightgown. It was in your portmanteau; it is your responsibility.*

She wondered why Ismay had taken the paper. Maybe he hadn't taken it; maybe it had been given to him. Perhaps someone, possibly Captain Smith himself, had given it to Ismay for safekeeping. *Take this as proof you did nothing wrong.* Was it possible that the captain had been thinking of Ismay's fate even as the ship had been going down? Why hadn't the captain given it to one of the officers? The answer was obvious. Captain Smith could not have known that any of his officers would be saved, because he had trusted them to put the safety of the passengers first. They would not have left the ship until the ship had left them. But Ismay had not been under the same restraint. Kate wondered if everyone had misunderstood Ismay's actions. Was it possible that Captain Smith had ordered Ismay to save himself and take the evidence with him?

Kate's mind was whirling. The paper presented so many possibilities, including the possibility that Ismay was innocent of all the charges brought against him. She shuddered. She knew what it was for one man to be blamed for the death of many. She imagined Ismay's shock when he had reached the safety of the doctor's cabin on the *Carpathia* and discovered that he no longer had that important scrap of paper. Did that account for his behavior on board the ship? She imagined him locked away in the cabin while women pounded on the door, demanding justice. He'd had nothing to say to them, because he'd no longer had proof of his innocence, and he had known what would happen next.

She realized that she was creating a house of cards. She could not translate the scribbled notes into anything meaningful, and she needed to find someone who could. She made a mental list of people who should not be trusted with the information. Lightoller seemed a noble and truthful man, but he was an officer of the White Star Line, with loyalty to his employers. Senator Smith needed to prove Ismay's culpability in order to justify holding the Senate hearings and outraging the British government. Joe Bayliss was a good man, but he was not a sailor. He would not understand the notes. Eva, of course, was so filled with the need for revenge that she would not entertain any truth that did not fit in with her plans. Kate's mind flashed back to Senator Smith's suite at the Waldorf Astoria, where Danny McSorley had turned numbers on Marconigrams into positions on a makeshift chart. Danny was landlocked now, but he'd served his time at sea. He would know what this meant.

She thought of their conversation early in the morning. She could barely recall what she'd said to him in her righteous anger and suspicion, but she knew she'd accused him of cowardice. In fact, she had accused him of shooting someone in order to take their place in a lifeboat.

She folded the paper and returned it to its envelope. Without allowing herself any more time to think, she stuffed the envelope into her beaded purse, alongside her recovered documents. She settled her hat firmly on her head, tucking away a few stray tendrils of hair, and stepped out into the corridor.

Even as she descended in the elevator, Kate was not certain that she knew where she was going. She crossed the hotel lobby and stepped out through the revolving doors into bright afternoon sunshine. If she turned right, she would be a short walk from the Capitol View Guest House, where she could find Danny McSorley.

Of course, she would have to apologize for her previous behavior if she expected any assistance from him. *No*, she told herself, *I am not wrong. He saved himself, and that must mean he took a seat in a lifeboat that could have been given to someone else. And don't forget, Mr. Stengel said he heard gunshots.* She stood on the sidewalk, stoking the fires of her justifiable anger until she had convinced herself that she would sooner rip out her tongue than eat humble pie with Danny McSorley.

A fresh breeze whipped at her hat and distracted her by tugging at her hatpin. As she paused to replace the pin, she found her temper cooling along with the breeze. Perhaps she was being unreasonable. Perhaps she should speak to Danny again. Maybe he had a reasonable explanation for his behavior. She remembered her father's words in the hours before he had ended his own life. *If only they would stop shouting and let me explain. It wasn't my fault, Kate.* Kate stared down at the sidewalk with tears prickling behind her downcast eyes as she thought of her father. No one had been willing to listen to him, and he had found the only way to stop the shouting.

With her mind made up, Kate turned to the right. The brown envelope, with its incriminating scrap of paper, seemed to add disproportionate weight to her purse. She wanted to be rid of it. She wanted to give it to someone who would understand. If that meant apologizing to Danny, that was what she would do.

She took a step off the curb and immediately felt a firm grasp on her arm. She caught a whiff of strong tobacco smoke and turned to see Sheriff Bayliss standing beside her with a cheroot clenched between his teeth.

"I am not going to run out into the traffic," she said impatiently. "I don't need any help to cross the road."

Joe tucked her hand into the crook of his arm. "Don't make a fuss. Don't do anything to draw attention to yourself; just walk with me like we're going for an afternoon stroll."

"No, I won't. I'm going—"

"Yes, you will. This is official business." Joe pulled the cheroot from his mouth and gestured toward two figures hurrying along the sidewalk. "That's Ismay and Lightoller up ahead, and I'm following them. Stay with me, and they won't suspect a thing. I'm just taking an afternoon walk with a pretty girl on my arm."

"Why are you following them?"

"Because that's the road to the train station, and they're in time for the afternoon train to New York."

"But why would they …?"

"Because the *Majestic* is sailing out of New York on the morning tide."

CHAPTER EIGHTEEN

Sheriff Joe Bayliss

Joe had no trouble keeping Ismay and Lightoller in view as they approached the classic white marble facade of the new Union Station. Ismay walked with the sluggish pace of a middle-aged man who had spent too much time behind a desk, and Lightoller walked with a slight limp and a hitching of his right leg. *Old injury*, Joe wondered, *or something he acquired in the sinking?* Joe had occasionally been forced to swim in the cold waters of Lake Michigan, and he knew the way the cold affected the extremities. Lightoller's hands and feet, maybe his whole body, had no doubt been rendered numb by the bone-chilling cold of the Atlantic. He was probably still discovering cuts and bruises. In fact, it was a wonder that the man was still alive.

Joe felt a twinge of guilt about following Lightoller. He had no problem tailing a criminal, but so far as he could see, Lightoller was more of a hero than a criminal. Certainly, he had shown astonishing courage and leadership in saving as many people as he could and keeping the lifeboats together through the long night. As for Ismay, Joe could find nothing to admire in the White Star's chairman, but he was not convinced that Ismay had committed an actual crime. The more he listened to Bill's questioning of the survivors, the more trouble he had forming a firm opinion of anyone's guilt.

No, he thought, that was not quite true. Lord was guilty as sin of something, either knowingly failing to respond to the *Titanic*'s distress signals or being drunk and unconscious in his bunk. Either way, Joe could find no sympathy for the *Californian*'s captain. However, he was not tailing Lord; he was tailing Ismay and Lightoller, and they were definitely up to something.

"Sheriff, what are we doing?"

Joe looked down at Kate, who was clinging to his arm and staring up at him in bewilderment. *Pretty as a picture*, he thought. If Lightoller or Ismay looked behind them, all they would see was old Sheriff Bayliss trying his luck with Eva Trentham's companion. They wouldn't be suspicious; they would be envious.

He felt a moment of shame. When he had grasped Kate's arm, he had not intended to do anything that would ruin her reputation, and perhaps this situation really would look bad to the casual observer. He wondered how it would look to Danny McSorley. Something like this could earn a fellow a poke on the nose, and McSorley looked capable of throwing a pretty good punch.

"Sheriff, stop!"

Kate was digging her heels in now and trying to bring him to a halt.

"Just walk with me," he urged.

"Think this through," she said.

He looked down at her. "I have thought it through, and I have decided they're trying to get out of the country."

"So where is their luggage?"

He stopped abruptly.

"They won't leave without their luggage," Kate said. "They may not have much, because most of it went down with the ship, but they'd surely have something. Look at them. They're both empty-handed."

Joe shook his head in bewilderment. She was right, of course, but why hadn't he thought of that? He knew the answer well enough. He was tired of this whole inquiry and impatient to bring it to a close. He'd had enough of careful questioning and cautious diplomacy. He wanted to arrest someone for the death of fifteen hundred people, and then he wanted to go home to Michigan.

"I don't know what to tell you, Miss Kate," he said, "but they seem to be determined to go inside the station. Why would they do that if they don't intend to catch a train?"

"I don't know."

"Well, then," Joe said, removing his hat and giving her a slight bow, "would you mind accompanying me inside so that we can see what they're up to? If it's not out of your way," he added.

"No," she said, "it's not out of my way. Perhaps we can do a deal."

"What kind of deal?"

"I'll come with you into the station if you'll come with me to the nearest pawnshop."

"Pawnshop?" Joe took a step backward. "What could you want in a pawnshop?"

"Money," she said.

"Doesn't Mrs. Trentham give you money?"

"No, not a penny. I think she's afraid that I'll run away if she gives me half a chance."

"And would you?"

"I don't know, but I'd like to have the option." Kate fingered a small pearl brooch nestled at the neck of her blouse. "This is all I have, and I want to pawn it or sell it."

"Miss Kate, I would lend you—heck, I would give you money if you needed it."

She shook her head. "No. I want my own money. I don't want a gift or a loan. Will you come with me?"

"If you want me to."

She tucked her hand back in the crook of his arm. "Good. Now let's go and see what these two gentlemen are doing. They've just gone inside."

Joe picked up speed, with Kate tripping along beside him to keep up with his long strides. When they stepped out of the afternoon sunshine into the vast, echoing ticket hall of the train station, he was in time to see Lightoller and Ismay meeting up with a group of half a dozen men, each of whom carried a small suitcase or duffel bag.

Joe abruptly released Kate's hand and strode across the tiled floor. "Ismay! Lightoller!" he shouted. "Stop where you are." His voice was swallowed up by a babble of voices echoing from the high domed ceiling, along with the hissing of steam engines, the clank of machinery, and the constant beat of hurrying footsteps. In all the commotion, Ismay and Lightoller appeared not to hear him.

To Joe's amazement, Kate ran ahead of him and seized Ismay's arm. The Englishman turned to look down at her. His brows drew together in a ferocious frown. She hung on to his arm, her face lifted toward him, her lips moving. The frown on his face turned to an expression of utter astonishment, and then Joe was beside him, his voice grim as thunder.

"Don't you dare touch her."

"I wouldn't dream of it," Ismay said coldly. "What do you take me for?"

"It's all right, Sheriff," Kate said. "It's not what you think."

Joe looked past Kate's worried face. "I think that he's trying to flee the country."

Ismay shook his head. "I wouldn't do that. I gave my word, as did Officer Lightoller. We are not going anywhere."

"Then what is this all about?" Joe asked. He looked at the worried faces of the other men. They were a sorry-looking bunch in ill-fitting clothes. He studied their sallow faces and their shadowed eyes, and then he knew. He turned to Lightoller. "This is your crew, isn't it?"

Lightoller fixed him with a steady blue-eyed gaze. "Yes, Sheriff, this is some of my crew. These men are my responsibility, not because they are White Star sailors but because they are my shipmates. What they have to say will have no bearing on the outcome of Senator Smith's hearings."

"What about the lookout?" Joe asked. "He had something to say."

"He's not here," Lightoller said. "Fleet is staying, and so am I. All the officers will remain here, but you don't need these men for your inquiry. For pity's sake, man, put yourself in their shoes. They have families waiting for them in England. They won't be paid for their time on the *Titanic*. I've managed to get them berths on the *Majestic*. They can work their way back to England and be back in Southampton with some money in their pockets. How much harm will it do if you let them go?"

"And you're not going with them?" Joe confirmed.

Lightoller shook his head. "I told you, I can't go home. I gave my word. My family will be all right. I've been through worse."

"Worse than this?" Joe queried. "Worse than having the ship sink under you?"

Lightoller shrugged. "I've never seen such loss of life, but I've learned the hard way that seafaring is a dangerous business. I've been wrecked on a deserted island, attacked by pirates, and had the coal cargo catch fire and burn the ship to the waterline. There's not much I haven't seen, but I've never seen anything like the way your newspapers and your Senator Smith have treated my crew. These men have done nothing but obey orders to get in the lifeboats and row as best they can. Is it their fault we didn't have enough lifeboats? Do you think they were in charge of fitting out the ship? What we have here is a steward, a laundryman, two stokers, a cook, and a greaser. What do you think should be done with them? What questions can they answer?"

He turned to Kate and gave her the benefit of his clear-eyed gaze and noble smile. She blushed. "It seems," Lightoller said in a suddenly persuasive tone, "that your newspapers have taken quite a liking to me. Perhaps they appreciate honesty when they see it. How will it look if you arrest me?"

"I'm sure he's not going to arrest you," Kate said. Joe noticed dimples on her cheeks as she smiled at Lightoller.

"Now wait a minute," Joe protested.

"Let them go," Ismay said gruffly. "You have me. Isn't that enough for you? Between me and Stanley Lord, you don't need any more scapegoats. You might as well let Lightoller go with them. He's not the one you want." Ismay's face twisted into a snarl. "Let them all go, why don't you? Send all the officers home. It won't make any difference. I don't know what I ever did to Senator Smith, but it's me he wants, and it's me he'll have."

"It's not Senator Smith who wants you," Kate said.

Joe looked at her in surprise. "What do you mean?"

"He's not behind this," Kate insisted. "This is all Eva Trentham's doing."

Joe shook his head. "No, Kate, I don't think so. Bill's his own man. He's not doing this for anyone except himself and the good of the shipping industry."

"And his own political future," Ismay sneered.

Joe felt his fist curling and uncurling. He was beginning to regret his sudden decision to involve himself in this case. Going aboard the *Carpathia* to stop Ismay from sneaking away had seemed the right thing to do. Finding Stanley Lord and bringing him to Washington had felt good. Now, seeing the contempt on Ismay's face, he began to wonder if he had been wrong. No one doubted that the British would hold an official inquiry, so why was Bill Smith using the power of the Senate to force an American inquiry? Surely there was more behind this than Bill's personal political ambitions, and why was Kate saying that Eva Trentham was the cause of all this trouble? Mrs. Trentham was a wealthy woman, whose name was known even in Michigan, but surely Bill Smith was not her puppet.

His eyes were drawn to the pearl brooch pinned to Kate's blouse. Was it true that the old lady had not given Kate a single penny for her labors? Somehow that thought offended him more than the thought of Bill dancing to Eva Trentham's tune. He knew from long experience that character was not revealed in extravagant gestures but in small daily kindnesses.

He said nothing as Ismay reached into his pocket and brought out a handful of dollar bills. "Here you go, lads," he said as he handed the money around. "Go and buy your tickets." He glanced at Joe. "Is that all right with you, Sheriff?"

Joe could not bring himself to disagree, and so he nodded. "I suppose so."

"I'll be going with the sheriff," Ismay said, "so I won't be coming to make sure you get on the train. I'm trusting you to do the right thing. Go home to your wives and families."

Joe stepped back and watched Ismay shake hands with the six men. He looked up at Joe again. "All right if Lightoller goes to the ticket office with them?"

Joe nodded again. He was having trouble finding the right words. He wanted to say that it was all right by him if Lightoller went all the way to New York and onto the *Majestic*, but that permission was not his to give.

Ismay watched as Lightoller shepherded his charges through the crowd of travelers toward the ticket windows. As soon as they had been swallowed up by the milling throng, he turned to Joe and released a long breath. So, Joe thought, despite the bluster, Ismay had been nervous.

"I suppose you'll want to escort me back to my hotel," Ismay said, with his usual, belligerent tone fully restored, "or will you call in one of your Pinkerton men? I know you've been having me watched."

Joe shook his head. "No, Mr. Ismay. You are free to come and go as you please. No one will be watching you or Mr. Lightoller."

Ismay nodded and cast a curious glance at Kate. "Very well. I'll leave you and your young lady to your afternoon stroll and—"

"Oh, no," Kate interrupted. "We were not … uh … strolling. No, nothing like that."

"If you say so," Ismay grunted.

Before he could turn away, Kate spoke again. "Mr. Ismay, I need to speak to you … alone. May I meet you in the lobby at the Willard in an hour's time?"

Ismay's eyes narrowed with suspicion. "Why would you want to meet me?"

"I have something of yours," Kate said.

"What?"

"Something you dropped."

"I didn't drop …" Ismay's voice died away. He stared at Kate with a baffled expression. "Were you on the *Titanic*?"

"No. I was on the *Carpathia*. I was helping the doctor when you came aboard."

"You're a nurse?"

"No. I was standing on the boat deck, taking names of survivors."

"And you have something of mine?"

"Yes."

Kate set her hand on Joe's arm and gave a slight tug. "We'll be leaving now, Mr. Ismay, and I will meet you in an hour."

Joe gave in to the force of Kate tugging at his arm. Suddenly he had gone from being the leader to being the led. He had no explanation for Kate's conversation with Ismay or the mixture of fear and hope that flashed across Ismay's face.

"Let's see what I can get for this brooch," Kate said. "I'm tired of doing what other people want me to do."

Kate Royston

Kate would not have done so well without Joe Bayliss standing beside her to negotiate. The pawnbroker had been scornful of the little pearl brooch. He had in fact sneered and attempted to convince her that the pearls were artificial and the setting was not gold. Joe had taken care of that problem with one long, withering look of his gray eyes. With the first hurdle out of the way, the second hurdle had been easier. The purchase price of the brooch—she did not wish to pawn;

she wished to sell—had risen by small increments every time Joe had loomed over the counter. Kate wished that it had not taken the presence of a man to bend the transaction in her favor, but she could not avoid that painful truth. For a year now, ever since the death of her father, she had been without a man to represent her interests, and she was fully aware that she lived in a man's world. Of course, the other side of the coin was the fact that women were not required or expected to fight in wars that men had started, and when a man crashed his ship into an iceberg, women were given seats in the lifeboats.

She walked back to the Willard with Joe Bayliss at her side and the comforting knowledge that she had a few dollars of her own tucked into her purse. If it took Joe's presence to get a better price, then that was what it took. With that business out of the way, she now faced the prospect of talking to Sir Bruce Ismay, and this was something she had to do alone. As a lawman, Joe could have no part of that conversation.

She thought back on the afternoon's events. She felt a flush of embarrassment at the way she had behaved with Lightoller. She had simpered. Yes, that was the word. When he had turned his steady blue-eyed gaze on her, she had simpered. How awful! Was this what Eva would expect of her? Was she supposed to simper and dimple her way around Europe in an attempt to have wealthy men fall at her feet? She couldn't do it. Lightoller had been a special case—the man exuded stoic heroism. She'd felt no desire to simper at Ismay, and definitely not at Joe.

What about Danny McSorley? No. He had made her blush and had made her heart flutter, but she had felt no need to be artificial—no need to exert her feminine wiles. Of course, that was before she had realized that he was a coward who had no reasonable excuse for taking a seat in a lifeboat. She supposed that she would never see him again, and that would be all right. The inquiry was winding down. People were being sent home, and Danny would soon be on his way to Cape Race. If it were not for his strange insistence on meeting the president, he would already be on his way. She imagined his life out there on the wild sea coast. He would be alone but not lonely, because every ship that passed would talk to him. There would be other people, of course—other operators, people who lived and worked nearby, passengers on the train from St. John's ... women.

Kate entered the hotel lobby, where ceiling fans dissipated the afternoon's heat and people spoke in hushed voices. She could hear occasional bursts of sound from the bar and the adjoining smoking room. Ismay would not be in there. If he intended to meet her, he would be where she had suggested—he had his reputation to consider. She searched the scattered groupings of armchairs and low tables. A woman sat alone, pouring tea from a silver pot. She lifted her head and their eyes met. Myra Grunwald of the *St. Louis Post-Dispatch*!

Myra set down the teapot and rose from her chair. Kate turned toward her. She might as well face the music. The expression on Myra's face, a mixture of sympathy and triumph, told Kate that Myra had found what she had been looking for. Now that she knew Kate's story, what was she going to do? Could Kate persuade her to concentrate on an exposé of the way immigrant women were mistreated and humiliated, or would she want to thrill the public with the next chapter in the story of Kate Royston and the Royston disaster?

"Young lady!"

Kate turned at the sound of the Englishman's voice. Ismay exited the elevator and hurried across the lobby. Myra turned her startled gaze toward him and then back to Kate.

"Excuse me," Kate said.

"I will talk to you later," Myra promised, or maybe she threatened. Just for the moment, Kate did not care about Myra and whatever Myra had discovered. She felt the weight of her purse, which now contained three things she had not previously carried. She had money; she had her travel papers; and she had the *Titanic*'s scrap log for April 14, 1912.

"Well," Ismay barked as he approached. "I suppose you'll want tea."

Kate shook her head. "No, thank you, Sir Bruce. Tea will not be necessary." She could not imagine taking tea with Ismay under the suspicious gaze of Myra Grunwald. She also could not imagine discussing the scrap log anywhere within Myra's hearing. She gestured to an intimate pairing of armchairs set by the window with a view onto Pennsylvania Avenue. "Over here," she said.

As Ismay stomped across the room, Kate looked back at Myra. The reporter lifted her teacup and saluted her. Well, she wasn't going to eavesdrop on the conversation, but neither was she about to go away. Kate set that issue aside temporarily. She would deal with Myra later—Sir Bruce Ismay was enough of a problem for the moment.

"Well?" Ismay said, standing over her as she settled into an armchair.

"Sit down, Sir Bruce, please."

Ismay sat. Kate could see that he was somewhat mollified by her intentional use of his title. So far, Senator Smith had treated him without respect, but Kate could see no point in being rude just for the sake of being rude. She didn't have to score points over Ismay. She already had the upper hand, and he knew it.

"Well," Ismay said, "out with it, young lady. Do you have something of mine, and what do you want for it?"

Kate was truly startled. How strange that she had not thought of money. Money made the world go around, and she really wanted some control over her madly turning world, and yet she had not thought of asking Ismay for money. "I don't want anything," she said. "I just want to know why you had it."

"And what is this 'it' that you refer to?"

"A piece of paper that fell from your pocket. I am told it is the scrap log of the *Titanic* for April fourteenth, taken directly from the bridge."

"And who told you that?"

Kate leaned forward impatiently. "Sir Bruce, I am trying to do the right thing here, although I am not sure what is the right thing. Can we start by being honest with each other? You came on board the *Carpathia* with a piece of paper in your pocket. The paper fell from your pocket, and I picked it up. That paper contains some notes and some numbers that mean very little to me and—"

"Why didn't you return it to me?"

Kate studied Ismay's face. He was angry, but she sensed relief behind his anger. Was he relieved that the paper had been found and now he could dispose of it himself?

"I tried to return it to you," she said, "but you walked away. You didn't hear me."

"It was chaos," Ismay said. "I watched those people coming up from the lifeboats, and it was chaos." He paused and seemed to choke on his next words. "I thought there would be more people … somewhere. I thought there was another ship. I never thought …"

He looked at her with anguished eyes. "They took me to a cabin, and I felt in my pocket for the paper, and … well, it wasn't there. I didn't know where it was."

"I'm sure that was a relief," Kate said.

"Relief?" Ismay queried. "Why would it be a relief?"

"To know that the evidence no longer existed," Kate said. "So you couldn't be blamed."

Ismay rubbed his hand wearily across his forehead. "But I am being blamed," he said.

Kate hesitated, suddenly realizing that she may have seen everything in reverse. She had convinced herself that Ismay was a coward who deserved everything that was about to happen to him. Her bad opinion of him had been formed the moment he had come aboard the *Carpathia*, warm and dry in his thick overcoat. It had increased when he'd locked himself in the doctor's cabin, and had been reinforced when Senator Smith had come on board to serve his subpoenas. Ismay was an ambitious tyrant who had forced Captain Smith to drive the *Titanic* at top speed through an ice field and had then taken the coward's way out by taking a woman's place in a lifeboat. She glanced across the room at Myra Grunwald, who sat drinking her tea and staring at her. She could give the whole thing to Myra. What a scoop that would be for a woman working in a man's world.

But what if she was wrong? What if the paper in her purse was not proof of Ismay's guilt? If the scrap log was proof of the reckless instructions he'd given to the *Titanic*'s captain, would Ismay really have taken it and kept it in his pocket? Of course, it was possible he had taken it to prevent anyone else from taking it. Even in the chaos of abandoning the ship, one of the officers may have thought to take the log, so Ismay had taken it. But why had he kept it? He'd had all night to watch the tragedy unfold, and yet he had kept the paper when he could have dropped it into the ocean. It was only when he had been unable to find the paper that he had locked the cabin door and refused to come out.

Her pulse quickened, and her heart seemed to hammer against her ribs as her whole view of the world slipped sideways and reassembled itself into a new pattern.

"Go ahead," Ismay snarled. "Give the damned thing to Smith, but don't expect him to use it. He'll just lose it somewhere, won't he?

He'll do anything to ruin my reputation."

Kate felt an overwhelming sadness as she looked at him. His unpleasant nature was written in every line of his face, and yet she had watched him handing money to the crew and making sure they took the train to New York. How could he be so unpleasant and so generous at the same time? She thought about Senator Smith's implacable, single-minded pursuit of the truth. What truth was he really seeking? Was it the truth of what had happened to the ship, or was it just a truth that would satisfy the American public and gain him votes? And all the time, Eva Trentham sat like a spider in the center of this web of blame, seeking revenge for something that had happened at another time and at the hands of another man.

Kate opened her purse and took out the envelope. "Take it," she said. "I don't know what to do with it, but you do."

Ismay reached for the envelope with both hands. His hands trembled as he opened the seal and pulled out a sheet of torn and crumpled paper. "Do you want to look at it?" he asked.

"I wouldn't understand it," Kate replied.

Ismay licked his lips. "I could explain it to you." He set the paper down on the low table. "These numbers are engine revolutions. Basically, they tell you the speed the captain was trying to achieve. These are navigation points, and these ..." He fell silent, staring down at the paper.

"What?" Kate asked. "What are they?"

"They're ice warnings. Notations of where other ships have seen ice, name of vessel and position, but ..." Ismay leaned back. "So that's how it happened," he said. "It's not on here."

Kate frowned in frustration as she looked down at the indecipherable columns of figures and scribbled notations. "I don't know what you're talking about."

Ismay stabbed his finger at the paper. "The *Mesaba*. She sent a warning. It's not on here."

"Are you saying," Kate asked quietly, "that the captain didn't know about the ice?"

Ismay shook his head. "It's not that simple. All these other numbers are positions where other ships saw ice. All I'm saying is that the *Mesaba*'s warning is not marked here."

"And who is responsible for that?" Kate asked.

Ismay shrugged. "How the devil would I know? Could be the

radio operator; could be the officer of the watch; could be the junior officer. I know it wasn't me. None of this was my responsibility."

"So when you took the paper, you didn't know what was on it?" Kate asked.

Ismay narrowed his eyes. "I knew that there were no instructions on there either given or signed by me," he said.

Kate tried to imagine the moment when Sir Bruce Ismay had snatched the scrap log. After days and days of listening to testimony, she had a pretty good picture in her mind of events on board the ship as *Titanic* had begun to list and then to sink. The air was filled with the shriek of the boilers venting steam while the stewards ran along corridors, knocking on cabin doors and calling people from their sleep. On the deck, sailors and officers argued about how and when to load the lifeboats and when to drop them eighty feet down to the water. Women refused to leave without their husbands; third-class passengers fought to be free of their imprisonment in the hold; and stokers and firemen swarmed onto the deck as the engine rooms filled with water.

Sir Bruce Ismay had said that he'd helped to load the lifeboats, but this paper told her something else. At some point in the terrifying time before the *Titanic* had sunk, Ismay had coolly made his way to the bridge and retrieved the scrap log. He had then worked his way back through the chaos on the deck and found a seat in a lifeboat. *He knew!* As he'd watched the disaster unfold, he'd known he would be blamed. Was it fair to blame him? Was anything fair? Was it fair for all those people to have died?

Kate rubbed her hand across her forehead, feeling the onset of a headache. She rose from her seat and spoke to Ismay as he struggled to rise. Always the gentleman, she thought, but was that enough?

"I'll leave this with you," Kate said, "but I don't think it will help you."

Ismay nodded. "I know. I've already been tried and found guilty in the court of public opinion. Maybe I should have just gone down with the ship, but I wanted to live. I'm not so sure now that my life is worth living."

Kate recognized the sullen despair on his face, and her heart seemed to rise up into her throat. "Don't talk like that," she whispered. "Think about your family."

"They'd be better off without me," Ismay muttered.

Kate reached out and touched his arm. She could feel no sympathy for him, but her heart ached for the family he was planning to leave behind. "It takes more courage to live than to die," she said. "Find your courage, Sir Bruce. It's not too late."

She turned away from him before he could answer her and fled across the lobby. From the corner of her eye, she saw Myra Grunwald setting down her teacup, but Kate kept running, dashing toward the stairs. She had to keep moving. She could not wait for the elevator. She heard Eva's voice in her mind. *You have to face your demons, Kate. You can never outrun them.*

CHAPTER NINETEEN

The Willard Hotel
Senator William Alden Smith

Joe Bayliss was waiting for Bill and Nana as they entered from the darkness of night into the bright electric lights burning in the lobby of the Willard Hotel. The sheriff greeted Bill with a perfunctory handshake and a brief nod to Nana.

"Thanks for coming. I'm sorry about disturbing your evening."

Bill, who had just emerged from the bath when the phone had rung, gave Joe a rueful smile. "It's all right, Joe. I don't blame you for phoning me. Mrs. Trentham is a very difficult old lady. What is this all about?"

"She believes that Kate Royston has stolen a valuable item from her, and she wants me to find Kate and arrest her."

"And what do you think?" Nana asked.

Bill looked at his wife. Her expression was as serene as ever, but her appearance was somewhat disheveled. She had dressed in a hurry and without the assistance of her maid. Her plans for what would happen when Bill emerged from a relaxing bath had not included putting up her hair and lacing herself into a corset and a stylish dress. The result of her haste was evident from the hair escaping from beneath her hat and a warm flush on her cheeks.

"I thought Mrs. Trentham had a nurse to care for her," Nana said.

"Surely she can take care of the situation."

Joe shook his head. "I'm not worried about Mrs. Trentham," he said. "I'm worried about Miss Kate. She's gone from her room, and she's left behind all the clothes that Mrs. Trentham bought for her. I've spoken to the Countess of Rothes, who is also staying here, and she told me that she had seen Kate this afternoon. As you know, Kate had her portmanteau stolen in New York, but it was recovered, and the countess brought it here. I've questioned the countess as best I can, but I think she's holding something back. She will only say that the bag contained Kate's clothes from the *Carpathia* and her travel papers."

"And you think there was something else?" Nana asked.

Joe nodded. "I think the countess knows more than she's saying, but I can't press her. She's committed no crime." He scowled. "And I don't believe that Kate has committed a crime. If she was going to steal, why wouldn't she also steal the clothes that Mrs. Trentham purchased for her? There is much more going on here than the simple theft of a brooch."

"I'll go and talk to Mrs. Trentham," Nana said. "Perhaps I can calm her down."

Nana took several steps toward the elevator, but Bill caught hold of her and held her back. "Not yet, dear. I think we need to ask Joe a few more questions."

Joe scowled impatiently. "The old lady is worth a fortune. If Kate wanted to steal something, it would be something more valuable than a little pearl brooch that's worth no more than a couple of dollars."

Bill looked Joe in the eye, expecting to see Joe's normal, hard-eyed stare, but Joe's gaze slid sideways. It was the action of a guilty man, or at least the action of a man who had something to hide.

"Joe, what is it that you're not telling me? Why are you so worried about Kate?

"I don't want Mrs. Trentham calling hotel security and the local police. It's obvious that Kate has a secret. She's running away from something and the last thing she needs is hotel detectives asking questions. If you and your wife can talk to Mrs. Trentham and calm her down, that will give me time to make my own inquiries," Joe said. "Kate didn't steal that brooch. Mrs. Trentham gave it to her. I want to know where Kate has gone in the middle of the night, and I don't want to see her arrested. She's not a thief."

Bill stared at his old friend. From the moment that Joe had first encountered Kate Royston on board the *Carpathia*, he had behaved toward her with unusual kindness. Joe was not a boorish man, and he was quite capable of good manners, but he rarely made friends and never showed favoritism. He seemed to have made an exception for Kate Royston, appointing himself to carry her luggage and act as her protector.

Bill chose his next words with care. He could see that Joe's emotions could easily boil over into anger, but he was not willing to confront Eva until he had all the facts, and Joe had not given him all the facts.

"You seem very sure about this," Bill said. "Do you know something about this brooch? Eva says it's valuable, but you say it's worthless. How do you know so much about it?"

"Kate told me it was a gift," Joe said.

Bill felt as though he were back in the Senate hearing room, questioning a reluctant witness. "And when did she tell you this?"

"This afternoon."

"Where were you, and why were you even discussing the brooch?" Bill asked.

Joe looked away and fixed his eyes on a point above Bill's head. "I was at Union Station, and I will not tell you why ... not yet."

"You were at the station with Kate?"

"She ... accompanied me."

Nana tugged at Bill's arm. "I don't think that the sheriff wants to discuss this here in the lobby."

"Maybe he doesn't," Bill said, "but I do."

"Forget about the station," Joe said, returning his attention to Bill. "All you need to know is that Kate told me the brooch was a gift, and I went with her to the pawnshop and helped her get the best price I could. She said Eva Trentham never gave her any money, but she did give her that brooch."

Bill shook his head in amazement. "I don't understand. Why were you and Kate strolling around Union Station together, and why would you escort her into a pawnshop? Have you lost your mind, Joe? You're a federal agent and she's a witness, and ..." He hesitated before speaking, but it had to be said. "Joe, you're old enough to be her father."

Joe's hand shot out and took hold of Bill's coat collar. The hard gray-eyed stare returned, not cold this time but flashing with anger. Nana was suddenly at Joe's side, her anger as hard as Joe's.

"Sheriff Bayliss, what do you think you're doing? Let go of him at once."

Joe released Bill's coat and took a step back. "You shouldn't have said that," he hissed. "You don't know what you're saying."

"I know that your relationship with that young woman, whatever that may be, is clouding your judgment."

"There's nothing wrong with my judgment."

"Oh, come on," Bill scoffed, the anger and frustration of the past few weeks rising to the surface. "From the moment you saw her on the *Carpathia*, you changed. You've been fussing and worrying over her ever since. Now you're telling me you went with her to pawn a stolen piece of jewelry. What do you expect me to think?"

"I expect you to think that I am concerned for her welfare."

"Unusually concerned," Bill said, unwilling to let the subject lapse.

Joe, taller by at least half a head, glowered down at Bill. "What are you suggesting? I've a good mind to put you in your place. Don't you dare talk about her like that!"

"Why not?" Bill responded. "What do you know about her? Nothing. You know nothing."

Joe reached out and poked Bill in the center of his chest. "I know all I need to know."

Bill poked back, jabbing Joe in the solar plexus, and found a hard slab of muscle. "Where is she from?" He jabbed again. "Why was she on the *Carpathia*? Why is she running away?"

On the third jab, Joe caught hold of Bill's finger in an iron fist and pushed him backward.

Bill felt a glorious rising of the emotions he had kept in check since the first word of the *Titanic*'s sinking. He was ready for this. He no longer cared that he had become embroiled in an unseemly scuffle in the lobby of the most expensive hotel in Washington. He was no longer a young man, but neither was Joe. Bill was quite sure he could land a couple of blows before Joe had him on the floor.

Nana stepped between them, laying one hand on Bill's chest and the other on Joe's shoulder. "Stop it," she hissed. "You're drawing attention to yourselves. There's a woman sitting over there who is taking in every word."

Bill glanced across the lobby and saw a middle-aged woman with an angular face and an unbecoming tweed suit. She was sitting alone and was staring at them with rapt, intelligent interest. A reporter. Definitely a reporter! Anger drained from him, replaced by the sudden awareness of his position. How much had she overheard? What would he read in tomorrow's newspapers?

Nana led the way across the lobby to the elevator bank, and Joe and Bill followed in guilty silence. The attendant slid open the ornate brass gates, and they entered without saying a word to each other. Aside from Nana's whispered instruction to the attendant that they should be taken to the fifth floor, they rode in silence. When they stepped out into the carpeted seclusion of the corridor, Nana barred the hallway, defying them to move past her.

"Get on with it," she said firmly. "Say whatever it is you want to say, and then we'll go and see Mrs. Trentham. I don't know what's going on with you two, but you need to put an end to it. Now you're both sulking like schoolboys."

Joe looked down at the top of Nana's head and then across to Bill. "You married a strong woman," he said. "You're a lucky man." He shook his head. "I'm sorry, Bill. What you said just struck me the wrong way."

"I shouldn't have said it," Bill agreed.

"No," Joe argued, "you have every right. I'm acting as a federal agent, and I stepped way beyond the limits of my position and made this personal. I'm not cut out for politics. We seem to be surrounded by liars, all except for Kate. I'm worried about her. I think she's the only honest person in this city."

Bill's temper flared again. "This is my city, Joe. Are you calling me a liar?"

Joe shook his head. "No, of course not." He shrugged. "I just want to make a couple of nice, clean arrests and go home. I had no idea what I was taking on when you asked me to help."

Bill nodded. "Neither did I, Joe." He thrust out his hand. "Thank you for everything. I couldn't have done this without you, and I didn't mean to imply anything about Kate."

Joe managed a wry smile. "I suppose I should be flattered that you think a pretty little thing like Kate would be interested in me." He looked at Nana. "I'm sorry, Mrs. Smith, for creating a scene."

Nana patted his arm. "Think nothing of it, Sheriff."

Joe's expression changed to one of concern. He looked at Bill.

"You don't think Kate misinterpreted, do you? It was a fatherly interest. You don't think that she ..."

Bill set aside his doubts. He could not say whether or not Kate had misinterpreted or even welcomed Joe's attention. He left those kinds of thoughts to Nana to sort out. It was certainly possible, and not even unusual, for a man of Joe's age to marry a young bride, and he was not convinced that Joe's attentions were strictly fatherly. Well, that was something for another day. For the moment, he needed to get Joe's attention back on the work at hand, and the best way to do that was to avoid any confusion in his feelings for Kate.

"I'm sure there was no misunderstanding, or she would have told you she was leaving," he said. "I think she had an interest in Mr. McSorley, but obviously, even that wasn't a strong enough interest to make her stay around."

"They fought," Joe said. "She accused him of cowardice because he managed to get into a lifeboat."

"There's a lot of that going around," Nana said. "It's really quite absurd. I can't think of anyone who would voluntarily dive into the water when there was a seat in a lifeboat."

Joe grinned. "You haven't met Charles Lightoller. He's a hero worthy of the monthly magazines. I expect we'll be reading about him in *American Boy* one day soon. I didn't think one man could have so many adventures."

Bill was not so sure that he agreed with Joe's assessment of Charles Lightoller, but he was interrupted before he could express his opinion. The door of Eva Trentham's suite opened with a bang, and Bridie Conley stood in the doorway with her hands on her hips.

"So, 'tis there you are," she said angrily, "and about time too. Herself has been giving me a devil of a time."

Nana pushed past Bridie and bustled into the room. Bill stood back while Nana's soothing questions were answered by Eva in angry shrieks.

Bridie leaned against the doorpost with her arms folded and a slight twitch of amusement pulling at her lips. "She's in a devil of a temper," she said, "but it's not about the brooch."

"Well," Bill said, "if Miss Royston has stolen—"

"She hasn't," Bridie said. "I was there myself when the old woman gave Kate that little geegaw. She said Kate could keep it, and there would be more jewelry to come. It's not a silly little pearl brooch that's got her upset."

"Then what is it?" Bill asked.

"It's the fact that Kate's gone. She's left behind everything Mrs. Trentham bought for her, and she's gone."

"Do you know where?"

Bridie shook her head. "I don't know where, but I know why."

"And why is that?"

"Because Mrs. Trentham will take you prisoner if you let her. I'm going to leave as soon as I can squeeze her for the money to buy a ticket to Chicago. She made me a promise, and I intend for her to keep it, but she's the devil for keeping people by her and not allowing them their freedom. Is that your wife that's gone in with her, Senator?"

"Yes, it is."

"Then you'd best go and rescue her. With the mood she's in, that old woman will chew her up and spit her out."

Joe grinned as he stepped past Bridie. "I think Mrs. Smith can look after herself. It didn't take her long to get me under control."

Bill followed Joe into the parlor. Although he hated to admit it, he was finding pleasure in the prospect of a dispute that was not about the sinking of the *Titanic*. He was tired of being meticulous and diplomatic and producing very little in the way of results beyond revealing the horror and chaos of that night at sea.

Eva had brought this mess into his life, and he was beginning to resent the time it was taking and the danger it posed to his political career. He actually looked forward to defying Eva and telling her Joe Bayliss was not at her beck and call and he was not going to arrest Kate Royston, because Kate was not a thief. Kate was simply a young woman who had tolerated as much as she could of Eva's venom and had decided to move on. He made a note to himself that he should ask Joe how much Kate had obtained for the brooch. Knowing the amount would give some idea of how far Kate had managed to flee, just in case he should ever need to find her again.

Eva was seated, as usual, in her wheelchair. Her hair was standing on end, and the rug that was usually placed across her lap had slipped to one side. Bill could see the plaster cast on Eva's right leg. Her bony old foot was uncovered, and her toes were blue from poor circulation. The fact that a hairbrush lay on the floor on one side of the chair and a fluffy white woolen sock lay on the other side was an indication that Bridie had done her best to make Eva comfortable, but obviously, Eva did not wish to be made comfortable.

Nana pulled up a chair and sat quietly for a moment while Eva called down the wrath of heaven on Kate's ungrateful head. She waited until the old woman's raging ended in a coughing fit, and then she went to the sideboard and poured a good slug of whiskey. Bill looked at her in amazement. Nana was not a drinker. Perhaps she had poured the drink for him. He certainly would like to have a drink. He looked hopefully at his wife, but she raised her eyebrows at him and handed the glass to Eva.

"Drink this, Mrs. Trentham, and tell us what this is really about."

"She stole from me."

"According to Sheriff Bayliss, she did no such thing. You gave her the brooch, didn't you? Come on now, admit it."

Eva took a hasty gulp of whiskey and glared at Nana. "So you're Bill's wife."

"Yes," Nana said with quiet dignity. "I have that honor."

"And he thought he could save himself by bringing you with him."

Nana shook her head. "My husband does not need to save himself, Mrs. Trentham. You are the one who needs to be saved."

Bill heard a sudden burst of laughter and looked around to see that Bridie Conley had returned to the room. "Saved, is it? There'll be nothing Baptist for that one, and no mass neither." She leaned toward Eva. "How many years is it since you've been to mass?"

Nana cocked her head to one side. "Are you a Catholic, Mrs. Trentham?"

"No, of course not," Eva hissed. "Why would I be a Catholic?"

"Because you're Irish," Bridie said.

Eva glared at her nurse. "You watch your tongue, woman. You know nothing about me."

"I know a Galway girl when I see one," Bridie retorted, "and I know it's many years since you've been to confession. Perhaps you should begin by confessing that Kate didn't steal your silly little brooch. You've got a ring on every finger and more diamonds than you know what to do with, so why would Kate steal some cheap pearl brooch? You want the sheriff to bring her back because you miss her."

"I do not."

"Yes, you do."

Eva pulled herself upright in her seat and patted at her wild hair. "Don't argue with me, woman. I'll have you out of here tonight, and there'll be no ticket to Chicago for you."

Bridie pursed her lips. "I'll have a ticket from you, or I'll be telling the newspapers what I know about you. I'll tell them about the names you call out in your sleep and the way you slip into the Gaelic when you dream."

"I do not."

Bill wanted to speak, but Nana quieted him with a small gesture. "Take some more of the drink and try to calm yourself," she said to Eva. "I know you're afraid."

"I am not."

"I know you feel helpless."

"Well, wouldn't you feel the same way if you had a broken leg and couldn't move, and the person who was supposed to care for you was threatening to leave, and the girl who could make you laugh goes running off, and goodness knows where she's gone?" Eva gulped her drink and began to cough again. Tears formed in her eyes, but Bill suspected that they were not because she had coughed.

"You're worried about her," Nana said.

Eva dabbed at her eyes with a corner of the blanket. "The girl has no more sense than a newborn babe. She had this wild idea that she would leave the ship in Gibraltar and somehow make her way across Europe. She is *virgo intacta*, but she wouldn't have stayed that way for long, would she? What does she have to sell except her body?"

"Yes, that would be a problem," Nana agreed, "especially at a naval base like Gibraltar. Sailors can be a problem."

Bill retreated to the side of the room, where he and Joe looked at each other in inarticulate masculine embarrassment. Bill had no idea that Nana could even carry on this kind of conversation. She was certainly saying things to Eva that she had never said to him.

"But she doesn't have to be in Gibraltar to get herself into trouble," Eva hiccupped. "She's such an innocent. She's not safe even here in Washington. Sheriff Bayliss has to find her."

"If I find her, I won't arrest her," Joe said. "I'll make sure she's safe, but I won't bring her back to you."

"I can ruin you," Eva snarled.

Joe shook his head. "You can't do much to me that I haven't

already done to myself," he said, "and I don't think you'll chase me all the way to the Soo."

Eva's response was cut short by a rapping at the door. Joe and Bill looked at each other, and Joe shook his head. The rapping was not the polite knocking of a well-brought-up young lady. This was a very determined knocking.

"Well, now," Bridie muttered. "Let's see who this is. Perhaps it's the priest come to hear Mrs. Trentham's confession."

"Don't be ridiculous," Eva said. "You don't know what you're talking about."

"If I don't get my ticket to Chicago ..." Bridie threatened.

Bill turned his back on the women and opened the door. The woman from the lobby stood outside, with her fist raised to knock again.

"Myra Grunwald, *St. Louis Post-Dispatch*," she said in a German-accented voice. "I can tell you where to find Miss Kate Royston. What can you tell me in return?"

Union Station
Washington, DC
Kate Royston

Kate ignored a fellow passenger's suggestion that she should put her possessions in the overhead rack. She pulled the bag onto her lap and gripped the handle with both hands, vowing that she was not going to lose her possessions ever again. She could feel the comforting crackle of the dollar bills she had tucked into her bodice, next to her skin. The train fare had cost almost everything she had, but she retained just enough money to make the final leg of the journey from the train station in Pittsburgh to the ruined house—provided she did not spend anything on food or drink throughout the long journey.

The long passenger compartment of the B&O slow train was filling rapidly with men, women, and children, loaded down with bags and bundles. She wondered where they were all going. She had not been in time to take the express train, and now she faced a long night in the crowded third-class compartment of the slow train, which would stop for passengers to embark and disembark at isolated stations throughout the night. She studied the ticket she was clutching as though her life depended on it, and perhaps it did. If she changed her mind, she could step off in Hagerstown, or Cumberland, maybe Meyersdale or Connellsville, or someplace in between. If she stayed on board, she would be in Pittsburgh by the time dawn had broken across the Allegheny Mountains.

Even now, with the train windows open and the sulfurous smell of coal drifting through the carriage, she shuddered at the thought of returning to the smoke and grime of Pittsburgh, but of course, she would not stay there. Nothing in the world would persuade her to call on her great-aunt Suzanna. Even starvation could not induce her to knock at Suzanna Royston's door to beg for a crust of bread. She would sooner die in the street than ask the old woman for anything.

She shook her head to clear her thoughts of her sour-faced aunt. Her time with Eva in New York and Washington now seemed like a dream, and the remembrances of first-class travel, satin sheets, and new clothes blew away in the face of her new reality. And what of the two men who had entered her life so precipitously? Danny with his Viking good looks and Joe with his dangerous eyes. They, too, would have to be banished from her thoughts—one a disappointment and the other an impossibility.

If she had ever intended to stop running and make a new life, this was a journey she would have to make alone. The small amount of money Joe Bayliss had obtained for the pearl brooch could have taken her back to New York, but she could not go there again and find work as a governess. As much as she hated the idea, there was only one place left for her to go, and that was the place where her father was buried in an unmarked grave. All she wanted now was for the train to start moving before she had a chance to change her mind, or before someone came to remove her and maybe even arrest her.

Once she reached Pittsburgh, she could disappear. Her small reserve of money would set her on a series of local trains and carry her up into the forested hills, where no one from Washington could find her—except maybe Myra Grunwald. By now Myra would know Kate's story, but surely Myra would not leave the frenzied newspaper scene around the *Titanic* inquiry to chase after a penniless girl whose tragedy had taken place a year ago. What were five hundred deaths compared to fifteen hundred?

The train rattled and clanked and moved a couple of feet. Was it time to go? She looked out of the window. No, the train was just repositioning itself, preparing to leap forward into the night like a horse positioning its feet for a jump.

She sat back in her seat, making herself invisible from the platform and silently prayed for the train to move. She knew that she really had nothing to fear. No one would come for her. No one would even look for her. Joe Bayliss had no idea of her background and would not expect to find her on a Pittsburgh train. He was a lawman; he could find out if he really wanted to, but why would he want to? What about Eva Trentham? No, she would not even try. Kate had proved to Eva that she could not be held prisoner. She had taken the one item that she could rightfully claim and left everything else behind. Eva would have no grounds to prevent her from leaving.

She gave a momentary thought to Danny McSorley before banishing him to the corner of her mind where she hid disappointments and bad memories. He had made her heart flutter, and she'd dreamed foolish dreams of a cozy house on the edge of the Atlantic, and tall, sturdy children with blond hair and blue eyes. But he was a coward. By his own admission, he had forced his way into a lifeboat. He was to be despised along with all the other men who had put their own lives first.

The train shunted forward again. Just a few more minutes, and she would be safe from pursuit. *Safe from pursuit,* she told herself, *but not safe from all danger.* In the morning, after changing trains in Pittsburgh and taking the narrow-gage railway up into the forested hills, she would be penniless and facing her greatest danger. She imagined walking the main street, past the bank and the hotel and Klebbert's Department Store. People would turn and stare. *That's her. That's Philip Royston's daughter.*

She shook her head. It was a foolish fantasy. The main street could no longer exist. The bank had burned; the hotel had been washed away; the department store had crumbled. No one would recognize her. Nothing was left but the smoke-blackened mansion on the hill and the unmarked grave of her father.

The carriage moved again. Doors slammed. A whistle blew. She was safe from pursuit now. She could look out of the window and watch the lights of Washington disappear into the distance while the dark bulk of the Alleghenies swallowed up the horizon ahead. It was done. She was on her way home.

CHAPTER TWENTY

The Willard Hotel
Senator William Alden Smith

Myra Grunwald appeared to be at ease as she sat in one of the Willard's satin-covered armchairs with her briefcase on her lap and her legs neatly crossed at the ankles.

"Well," she asked. "What are you prepared to offer me for what I have in here?"

Her German roots revealed themselves in her slight mispronunciation of the words "well" and "what," but Bill guessed that she had been in the United States for a number of years and her written words would not reveal any limitations.

"Why should I offer you anything?" Bill asked.

"Because I witnessed a very interesting exchange between you and Sheriff Bayliss in the lobby," Myra said. "I also have very sharp ears. I believe you have some dispute about Miss Royston, and it is possible you could have come to blows. I did not actually see you fighting, but my readers do not need to know that. I can describe your attitude, your raised voices, the way that you, Senator, poked—one could even say punched—the sheriff. I do not lie in my reporting, but words can be made to mean many things."

She opened the lock on the briefcase with a decisive, audible snap. "What am I offered for this information?"

Eva came perilously close to falling from her wheelchair in her eagerness to be heard. "Listen to me, woman—"

"You will not call me 'woman,'" the reporter commanded. "I am Myra Grunwald, and you will call me Myra because I do not wish to be identified as either a married woman or a single woman. These things are immaterial. I am a reporter."

"And I am—"

"I know who you are," Myra said. "What are you prepared to offer me for my information and my silence?"

"Name your price," Eva said. "I have plenty of money. I'm not interested in your silence—if these two men want to fight, that's their own foolishness. I want that girl returned and arrested."

Myra spread her hands. "I don't want money. Money is of no interest to me. I want information."

"Very well," said Eva. "Here is the information. Kate Royston stole from me. Report that."

"Details of petty thefts by unimportant young women are of no interest to my newspaper," Myra said. "I did not come for such a story."

Bill was surprised when Nana rose from her seat and walked across to stare down at Myra. "What did you come for? What did Miss Royston promise to give you?"

"A firsthand story about the Salvation Army's humiliating treatment of young Irish girls coming from the *Titanic*. Such a story would sell newspapers. We rarely can find any scandal involving the Salvationists."

"And did she give you that story?" Nana asked.

Bill sat back. If he had been on better terms with Joe, he would have winked at him conspiratorially, but Joe was currently a glowering fortress of offended pride. Bill had to be satisfied with knowing that Nana, with all the stubbornness of her Dutch forebears, was on the warpath. It would only be a matter of time before Myra produced the papers she was guarding.

"Miss Royston did not give me the story she promised," Myra said. "She owes me."

"I am surprised she made a promise that she did not keep," Nana said.

"I'm not," Eva growled.

Bridie stepped out from behind the wheelchair. "She offered to

303

tell the story," Bridie said. "I heard her myself. But this woman wanted something else. She thought she could find a scandalous story about Kate herself. She said it was only a question of remembering where she had heard Kate's name."

"And did you remember?" Nana asked.

Bill had trouble reading Myra's expression and concluded that the reporter was somewhat ashamed of her actions.

"Yes, I remembered, and I found the story," Myra said. "It's old news and no longer interesting. There was no need for the girl to run away again."

Eva waved a dismissive hand. "She's always running away. It's what she does best."

"I did not intend to publish it," Myra insisted. "The public are no longer interested in the Royston disaster."

Joe was suddenly alert, his tone aggressive. "What Royston disaster?"

Nana waved him into silence, her gaze focused on Myra. "You believe that the public want to hear a story that discredits the Salvation Army?" she asked.

"Of course they do. Bad news sells newspapers. Miss Royston's descent from the child of a successful businessman to a paid companion to the notoriously unpleasant Eva Trentham is not sufficiently bad news, and so no one would be interested. But the Salvation Army, well, that's a different story. A well-born young woman falls into their hands and is subjected to humiliation and—"

"You can hear that story from someone else," Nana said, keeping her eyes fixed on Myra.

Myra lifted her eyebrows. "How can that be, Mrs. Smith?"

"I have two young Irish girls in my house who were with Miss Royston at the Salvation Army hostel. They were witnesses to her escape and what led up to her escape." Bill frowned at his wife's statement and then remembered the two girls, relatives of the kitchen maid, who McKinstry had directed to Nana's kitchen. He had found them at the hostel where Kate had been held prisoner. Apparently, they were still at the house. He could not resist a grin. Nana had found a way out of their dilemma.

"What," Joe said between gritted teeth, "is the Royston disaster?"

Myra ignored him and extended her hand to Nana. Nana took it. Bill had never seen two women shake hands before. It struck him as unnatural, but Nana seemed perfectly happy with the gesture.

"We have an agreement," Nana said, turning to Bill.

"So where is she?" Eva asked. "Now that you two ladies have worked things out between you, you can tell me where Kate is. I want my brooch back."

Bridie leaned over the back of the wheelchair. "She didn't steal it and you know it."

"I still want to know where she is," Eva said sullenly.

"I do not know where she is now," Myra said, "but I know where she will go."

Eva leaned forward in her wheelchair. "Just go ahead and arrest her, Sheriff. A few hours in jail will have her talking."

Myra spread her hands. "Oh, yes, please feel free to arrest me, Sheriff, and I will feel free to write of the experience. 'German immigrant mistreated by Wild West sheriff.' That should make a good headline."

"I am not from the Wild West," Joe barked, "and I don't plan to mistreat you."

"No one ever plans to mistreat another person," Myra argued. "It usually happens when someone becomes unreasonably angry, and the cause of the anger is rarely mentioned in the argument. I watched you in the lobby, Sheriff. You are angry, but not with your friend Senator Smith. As for the senator, I wonder if perhaps Kate Royston has information that will help you, and that is why you also appear to be angry."

Bill grimaced. The reporter seemed to have an instinct for knowing words that had not actually been spoken. No doubt she was very successful at her job. "Miss Royston has no information that would assist my inquiries," he said stiffly.

"What a pity," Myra said. "I think you could use some new information before even the largest newspapers lose interest. This afternoon, I sat in the lobby and observed several interesting scenes. I saw Kate Royston enter the smoking room for a tête-à-tête with the Countess of Rothes, and later in the afternoon, I saw another tête-à-tête, this time with Sir Bruce Ismay. Would you care to comment on this?"

"No, I would not," Bill said. His mind was turning somersaults, and he was beginning to think of the girl from the *Carpathia* as an infernal nuisance. "My wife has promised to give you what you want, so just get on with telling us what is in those papers."

"It is nothing that will help with your inquiries," Myra warned.

"Will it help me find Kate?" Joe asked.

"Do you wish to find her?"

"Of course he does," Eva snapped. "I want her back."

Myra leaned back in her chair, and the expression on her face grew soft. "It is possible that I could continue to bargain with you and extract a higher price for this information, but I will not." She looked at Bill. "I will not do what you do, Senator. I will not use the death of so many for my own gain."

Bill found that he could not meet her accusing eyes. He knew that he could legally justify holding the *Titanic* inquiry. He had the voters behind him—people wanted to know what had happened—but was finding the truth his only motivation? As for Eva, what did she want from this inquiry except the perverse pleasure of making politicians dance to the jingling tune of her money? He stared down at the floor, unwilling even to look at Nana. Did this hard-bitten German newswoman have a better sense of right and wrong than any of the senators on his committee?

"Mrs. Smith, would you please read this?"

Bill looked up to see that Myra had handed a sheet of paper to Nana.

"You want me to read aloud?" Nana asked.

"Yes, if you would be so kind. I have read it too many times. My voice will not reveal the shock I found on my first reading."

Nana held out her hand. "Very well." She sat in an armchair, reached into her purse, and pulled out her reading glasses. She looked down at the paper and then back at Myra. "Is this a report from your newspaper?" she asked.

"No. This first report comes from the newspaper of Knox, a small town in northern Pennsylvania. It is dated March second, 1911, a little over a year ago. Please read, Mrs. Smith."

Nana settled her glasses on her nose and began to read. "'Royston, Pennsylvania, March first, 1911.'" She looked up at Myra. "The town is named for Kate's family?" she asked.

"In a way, it is," Myra said. "It is named for the Royston Pulp Mill, owned by Kate's family. Keep reading, Mrs. Smith."

"'Possibly five hundred persons, most of them women and children, are dead tonight,'" Nana read. She swallowed, took a deep breath, and continued reading. "'Their bodies were scattered through the valley by the two million gallons of water that, dashing faster than a mile a minute and foaming in a wall fifty feet high, swept down Loggers Run this afternoon from the broken dam of the Royston Pulp Mill and snuffed out this little town. The deluge was followed by fire.'"

Bill sensed movement, saw Bridie Conley crossing herself, and heard her whisper, "Holy Mother of God."

"'Royston is a wreck,'" Nana read. "'The living are hardly able to seek the dead.'"

Bill extended his hand. "Perhaps you should let me read. This is upsetting my wife."

Nana gripped the paper. "No, Bill. I'll read it." She returned her attention to the paper. "'The flood swept through Royston, crushing nearly every one of its five hundred houses. There was no warning. There came a roar and then the shock of the flood, the crash of the timbers, the screams of fear. On the crest of the wave rode a thousand cords of pulp mill timber. These hit houses and stores like a succession of battering rams. They riddled the flimsy frame homes of the mill workers and left great gaps in their sides. They struck unto unconsciousness the terror-stricken people seeking to swim the flood to safety. The water passed the town in a solid wall two miles in length. The course from the dam was down the valley of Loggers Run, along whose banks there are hundreds of houses this evening covered by the swollen river or wrecked.'"

Nana set the paper down on her lap and pulled a lace handkerchief from her sleeve. She lifted her glasses and wiped her eyes. "Another Johnstown flood," she said, "and yet we never heard of it in Washington." She flicked a finger at the paper. "Is this only reported in the smallest of papers? Does no one else care?"

"Over two thousand people died in Johnstown," Bill said carefully. "This, it seems, was only five hundred."

"*Only*," Nana repeated. "*Only* five hundred. How many will it take to make us care? Does it have to be more than the two thousand who died in Johnstown before the *New York Times* will report on it?"

What about the next shipwreck? Bill wondered. *This time, we cared because fifteen hundred people, many of them wealthy, died. How many people will it take next time? Will we only care if more than fifteen hundred people die?*

Nana wiped her eyes again and resumed her reading. "'Many

bodies are being recovered along the banks of the river. Some had been swept five miles below the town. Rescuing parties are busy fighting the flames tonight, seeking to save the bodies buried there from incineration. Many were imprisoned in houses washed onto high ground by the flood, but soon licked up within the fire zone. The Royston mansion, home of mill owner Philip Royston, stands on a hill above the flood and was undamaged.'"

Bill turned his head as he heard the clink of a glass behind him. Joe Bayliss was pouring whiskey into tumblers. "Poor little Kate," he said. "No wonder she was running."

"I could accuse that newspaper of yellow journalism," Myra said. "The writing is florid and unprofessional, but it is a true report, and I am afraid that it becomes worse for your friend Kate, much worse."

"How much worse could it be?" Joe asked.

"As reporters," Myra said, "we are trained to ask questions and report what we see. We are not to give opinions. Of course, when emotions run high and hundreds of people are dead, it is not possible to remain neutral. It is only to be expected that reporters will look for the most sensational stories, and there were many stories to tell in Royston, just as there are now with the *Titanic*." She shrugged slightly, as if trying to lift a burden from her shoulders. "We report what we hear, and people repeat what they see reported, and so one man's story becomes the story of many men. When one man points a finger, he is joined by many others."

"Are you apologizing?" Bill asked.

Myra shook her head. "No, Senator. I do not apologize; I simply report a fact to you. When one man points a finger, many follow where he points. You know this, Senator, because you have pointed your finger at Bruce Ismay and you see for yourself what has happened to that man."

"Nothing has happened to him," Bill blustered.

"He is ruined," Myra said, "just as Kate's father was ruined." She selected another sheet of paper. "This was reported less than twenty-four hours later in the newspaper of the town of Clarion, just a few miles away but with a far greater circulation. You will read, please, Senator."

Bill took the paper from her hand, cleared a lump from his throat, and began to read. "'The Royston dam, which collapsed on March first with great loss of life, was completed in December 1909 at a cost of eighty-six thousand dollars and was built to the specific design of Mr. Philip Royston to provide water to his pulp mill. It stood fifty feet tall and spanned a length of five hundred and thirty feet and was designed to impound two hundred and fifty million gallons of water.

"'Mr. Gregory Petrov, who was engaged by Mr. Royston to oversee the project, states that Mr. Royston rejected many of the safety features that Mr. Petrov wished to include in the final design. Mr. Royston stated that such features would prove too costly and that Mr. Petrov should find ways to save construction costs, specifically in the thickness of cement to be used and by avoiding the use of a cut-off wall that would prevent water from flowing beneath the dam and creating erosion. It is Mr. Petrov's opinion that these two cost-cutting measures led directly to the collapse of the dam with resulting loss of life.'"

Bill looked up from the paper. "Why should I believe this?" he asked. "It looks as if Mr. Petrov did a good job of diverting blame from himself."

"Yes, he did," Myra agreed. "He spoke to reporters when Mr. Royston would not. Mr. Royston shut himself away in his mansion with only his daughter for company and would not speak, not even to defend himself. The remaining citizens of Royston heard what Mr. Petrov had to say and marched up the hill to the Royston mansion. When Kate's father would not come out and talk to them, they set the building on fire, and so Mr. Royston died."

"You mean they burned him to death?" Nana gasped.

Myra shook her head. "No. He and his daughter fled from the townspeople and hid in the forest. It was several days later that Philip Royston took his own life, leaving his daughter alone in a hostile town."

"And that is why she began to run," Eva said.

Bridie crossed herself again, and Bill was not even surprised to see Eva mimic the action. He set down the paper. The air in the room was thick and heavy with guilt. He clenched his fists, pressing his fingers into his palms so that they could not move—so that they could not point even at himself.

CHAPTER TWENTY-ONE

The White House
Senator William Alden Smith

Bill had not slept. Shock and conscience had kept him awake. He ate an early breakfast and set out to walk to the White House. He hoped that a brisk walk in the clean spring air would clear his mind. For weeks, he had dwelled on the image of the *Titanic*'s passengers fighting for survival in the icy Atlantic, and now that image had been replaced by something new—something else he could do nothing about. Myra had accused the small local newspaper of yellow journalism, but Bill could not agree. The unknown journalist had painted a picture that Bill could not forget even as he added his own touches to the painting. He saw Kate and her father hiding in the forest and Kate waiting alone as her father stepped away into the dense undergrowth. He saw her being startled by a sudden gunshot, then running to the place where her father had fallen. That was the point where Bill's imagination failed him. He could not imagine what happened next or how Kate came to be on board the *Carpathia*.

He took a deep breath and made a determined effort to clear his mind of everything except the fact that Joe was supposed to bring Danny McSorley to meet with the president. He wondered how Joe had spent the night. Despite his denials, it was obvious to Bill that Joe had formed some kind of attachment to Kate Royston. Perhaps it was a fatherly attachment, and perhaps it was not.

He was relieved when Joe arrived on time, escorting Danny McSorley, who wore a dark suit, a dazzling white shirt, and a look of nervous anticipation.

"Well, here he is," Joe said, ushering the young Englishman in through the front entrance of the White House. "Is Taft ready for him?"

"Mr. Hilles is inside with the president. He'll let us know when we can go in," Bill said.

Joe studied his surroundings. "Never thought I'd find myself here," he said. He took a cheroot from his pocket, thought better of it, put it back, and gave a prodigious yawn.

"Didn't you sleep?" Bill asked softly.

Joe shook his head. "No, I didn't. How about you?"

"Couldn't get my mind off what that reporter said about pointing fingers," Bill admitted. "It doesn't change my opinion of Bruce Ismay—he's a damned unpleasant fellow—but that doesn't make him a criminal, does it?"

"How's your wife?" Joe asked.

"Upset," Bill replied. "Nightmares. I shouldn't have brought her with me last night."

Joe gave a short bark of a laugh. "We wouldn't have any information without her quick thinking. Women are stronger than we know. Think about all that Kate's been through, and still she keeps on going."

"Kate?" Danny interrupted. "What do you know about Kate? Do you know where she is? I'm sure Wolfie will want to see her before we leave."

"Wolfie?" Joe queried. "Are you taking that hound with you to Newfoundland?"

"Well, I'm sure I don't know what else to do with him," Danny said. "Mrs. Trentham doesn't want him, and he'll be no problem up there. We'll have plenty of space."

Bill allowed the silence to linger and waited for Joe to tell Danny what he knew about Kate, but Joe continued to ask questions about the dog. He was a rare breed, so where would Danny find a mate for an otterhound?

Danny shook his head. "I don't even know where I'll find a mate for myself," he said. "I really wish I could talk to Kate."

"She's left already," Joe said carelessly. Bill caught his eye for a moment, but Joe looked away and continued to destroy any hope McSorley might have of seeing Kate again. "No one seems to know where she's gone," he said, "not even Mrs. Trentham. Don't worry about her. If we find her, I'll tell her you wanted to say goodbye. She'll understand."

"I wanted to tell her that I wasn't a coward. Once I've told the president, I assume I'll be able to tell her why I had to get into a lifeboat."

"But she's gone already," Joe insisted. "She left last night. Don't worry about her. I'm sure there are plenty of girls in Newfoundland. There'll be a girl for you."

"Not the one I want," Danny muttered.

"Well," said Joe, "we can't always have what we want, can we? Have you made your arrangements to leave?"

"Day after tomorrow. I'll go by train to New York, and then I've a berth on a packet steamer, the *Prospero*, to St. John's. The Marconi office has made the reservation." He patted the pocket of his dark suit. "I have my ticket and a ticket for Wolfie. It will be strange to be back on the sea after what happened last time."

"You'll be fine," Joe said encouragingly. "The icebergs will have gone south by now." He thrust out his hand. "Good luck, lad. I don't suppose I'll see you again."

"No, I should think not."

The door to the president's office swung open, and Hilles stepped out. He looked at Danny suspiciously. "Is this him?"

"Yes."

"Canadian?"

"No. British."

Hilles continued his inspection. "He looks like a Viking," he said.

"I'm British," Danny repeated.

Hilles nodded. "Well, at least you have a decent suit. The president has agreed to see you, but you'd better not be playing any kind of game here. I'm only permitting this meeting because you have something to say about Major Butt. You'd better make it good and you'd better make it quick. The president is a busy man."

Danny nodded. "Yes, sir. I understand."

"I'm going in with him," Bill said. "That's what we agreed."

Hilles pulled Bill aside and spoke softly. "If you can do anything to get the president moving, I will be very grateful. The country is going to the dogs while he mopes around in there."

Bill shrugged. "I don't know the nature of the message, but McSorley is a decent kind of fellow and very insistent."

"And what about your cowboy friend?" Hilles asked, cocking an eyebrow in Joe's direction.

"He's leaving now," Bill replied.

Hilles nodded his response. "All right, then. You can go in. He'll see you now."

Bill ushered Danny into the gloom of the president's office. Although the morning sun was shining brightly outside, the drapes on the tall windows were partially closed, and the electric light sconces on the walls fought a losing battle with gloomy green wallpaper. Taft was behind his desk. Although it had been no more than a few days since their last meeting, Bill thought the president had lost weight in his face, if not in his body. His jowls drooped like those of a depressed bloodhound, and his skin had taken on a yellow tinge. *Oh God*, Bill thought, calling on the Almighty with complete sincerity, *let Danny have good news*. He regretted his prayer almost immediately. How could there be good news of Archibald Butt? The president's envoy was gone. Even his body was gone. He would not be seen again until the final day, when the sea would give up its dead.

"Mr. Taft."

Bill was suddenly aware that Danny was reaching into his pocket. For a horrified moment, he wondered if he had brought an assassin into the White House. Should he shout for help? Marines were stationed in the White House. Would they arrive in time?

Danny withdrew his hand from his pocket and deposited a bloodstained envelope on the cluttered surface of Taft's desk.

Taft sat up, suddenly alert. "What's this? Whose blood is this?"

"Some of it's mine, and some belongs to Major Butt," Danny said.

Taft pulled the envelope toward him with reverent fingers. "What's in here?"

"I don't know, but Major Butt died trying to bring it to you, and the captain himself put me in a lifeboat. My instructions were to stay alive and bring this to you without fail, and that's what I've done."

"And you say that some of this blood is yours?" Taft asked. He was sitting up straight in his chair now, and his eyes were gleaming with interest. Suddenly he was the man that Bill knew, the man who could beat Roosevelt.

"Most of it belongs to the major," Danny said. "He was gutshot."

Taft winced. "Tell me."

"Well, sir—"

"Sit down," Taft ordered. "You are too tall to be standing up. You too, Smith. Sit down, the pair of you, and tell me what this is all about. Why was this given to you?"

"Well," Danny said, "we knew we were going down. There was no two ways about it. She was going fast, but it was chaos, and it seemed like no one remembered the lifeboat drill. Some of the boats were away on the port side, and most on the starboard. Major Butt and the other gentlemen were helping. He was very brave, sir. He tried to get the women and children into the boats, but it was hard. A lot of shouting and a lot of people who didn't speak English, and there was the whole issue of the other ship."

"What other ship?"

"Some people said they could see the light of another ship and she was coming for us, but some said there was no such thing."

"We've had testimony," Bill interrupted. "We've found the blighter."

"I hope we shoot him," Taft said vehemently. "Why haven't I heard about this?"

Bill bit his tongue. *Because you haven't been listening.*

"Towards the end," Danny said, "when it was obvious that no one was coming for us and there were never going to be enough lifeboats, we saw a boat, collapsible A, going down the side of the ship. You see, that one wasn't kept on the deck; it was kept in davits for general use, but I don't think anyone had noticed it until then. Major Butt said he would have to try to get in. He said he was sorry, but he had a mission for the president and it was his duty to carry it through to the end. He wasn't a coward, sir."

"I know he wasn't," Taft interrupted.

"He could have insisted on going on any of the boats," Danny continued doggedly. "All he had to say was he was acting on the president's orders, but he waited until the last minute. I think he would have made it, sir, if it had not been for the officer with the gun."

"What officer with a gun?" Taft roared. "Smith, do you know anything about this? Did a British officer shoot Major Butt?"

Danny shook his head vehemently. "No, it wasn't like that. The third-class passengers had come swarming up on deck, and they were going to rush the boats. We were lowering the lifeboat. The officer, I think it was Officer Wilde, but I will not swear to it, fired along the side of the ship to keep them back. But you see, just as he fired, Major Butt moved to get in the boat, and the bullet took him in the gut."

"You know this for a fact?" Taft asked.

"Yes, sir. I've seen gutshots before. I've been in action against ... well, I've been in places where men have been shooting, and I know how it is. The major knew too. He knew he couldn't survive. He couldn't get up off the deck, let alone get down into a lifeboat. That's when he gave me the envelope. Captain Smith was there. He was watching. I think he knew the major had an important mission."

"Yes," said Taft gravely. "Archie had a very important mission."

"So Captain Smith told me to take the envelope and get down into collapsible A—by then it was in the water. I had to go down a rope. Major Butt couldn't have done it, sir. If I'd thought he could have survived, I would never have taken his place."

Bill stared at the young Englishman. "Why have you kept all this to yourself?" he asked.

Danny scratched at the top of his head for a moment. "Well, Senator, it was a secret. Major Butt said I should go to the president and no one else. I did tell you I needed to see the president."

"But you didn't tell me why."

"I was not clear as to who I should trust," Danny explained.

"I'm a senator," Bill hissed. "You could have trusted me."

"I didn't know that, sir. I don't understand the politics of your country. I was not sure of your party affiliation."

Taft's chair creaked as he leaned back in his seat. "I think he understands us perfectly well." He turned the envelope in his hands. "How did your blood get on here, young man?"

"I went down a rope," Danny said, "but it wasn't long enough. In the end, I had to jump. I banged my head. Heads bleed a lot, you see." An expression of regret crossed his face. "I wanted to tell Miss Kate what happened—how come I was in that boat with only those few people and none of them willing to help anyone else—but I couldn't say, could I? I had to let her think badly of me. I don't suppose I'll have another chance to tell her, this being a secret

315

meeting." He sighed. "Oh well, at least I'll have Wolfie."

Taft shook his head and looked at Bill. "Don't know what he's talking about, but I want you to make sure he's looked after. Give him a medal or something."

"I can't just—"

"I don't need a medal," Danny said. He leaned forward and frowned at Taft. "I'd just like to know that it was all worth it, Major Butt dying and everything."

Taft's puffy fingers pawed through the papers on his desk and retrieved a letter opener. "Let's see," he said.

"Sir," Bill protested, "you surely don't plan to expose state secrets."

"I plan to open this envelope," Taft said, "and when I have opened it, I will tell you what I plan to do next."

Bill had become so accustomed to Taft's morose apathy that he had almost forgotten how energetic the president could be when the mood was upon him.

With a deft stroke of the letter opener, Taft slit the bloodstained envelope and pulled out a sheet of heavy, embossed paper.

"German," Taft said. "So he managed to see him. Good old Archie. He got his meeting with the kaiser." The note was short, and Taft scanned it quickly before folding it and reinserting it in the envelope. Then he lumbered to his feet.

"War," he said. "There will be war. The kaiser will not promise peace, and so there will be war."

Bill forgot that Danny was still listening. "When? Does he say when?"

Taft shook his head. "No, he doesn't, but the kaiser warns me not to interfere. He says that the German immigrants he has sent to America will rise up if America goes to war against Germany." He slammed the letter down on the desk. "The cheek of it," he said. "How dare he threaten me!" He looked at Danny. "So, you're British?" he said.

"Yes, sir."

"I imagine your king will fight," Taft said. "It will be a bloody mess with or without German immigrants rising up and starting a civil war."

"What will you do?" Danny asked.

"Damned if I know," Taft replied.

He walked around the desk and extended his hand to Danny. "Thank you, young man. You've done a great service, and now you'd best be on your way. Newfoundland, isn't it?"

"Yes, sir. Cape Race."

"I shall think of you when next I receive a Marconigram forwarded on from your station," Taft said. "Good day to you. Safe journey."

Taft waited until the door had closed behind Danny before he spoke again. "All right, Smith. Time to be done with this inquisition of yours. Find someone to blame, and send everyone else home. Get it done quickly. We have work to do."

Bill closed the door of the Oval Office behind him and found Joe still hovering in the corridor.

"Where's McSorley?"

"Gone on ahead," Joe said. "Is everything all right?"

Bill shook his head. "No, everything is not all right. I'm supposed to find someone to blame and wrap up the inquiry. This has basically been a waste of time, Joe. Now that Taft is over his grief, he doesn't want to hear another word."

"And who will you blame?" Joe asked.

"I don't know," Bill replied. "I'm not even sure if it will make a difference. We haven't broken through to J. P. Morgan, and we've ruined Ismay and Lord, but we've achieved nothing."

"So you no longer need me?" Joe asked.

"No," Bill said morosely, "I suppose not. There's no point in subpoenaing any additional witnesses. We know what we need to know."

"In that case, I'll make my way back to Michigan," Joe said.

"When will you leave?"

"As soon as I can."

"Well," Bill said. "I … uh …" He found himself stumbling for words to thank his friend for all that he had done.

"Bill," Joe said, "did you know that poor Mrs. Astor is only eighteen?"

"Yes …"

"And Jacob Astor was forty-seven."

"Yes …"

"Good to know," Joe said. He pulled a cheroot from his pocket, struck a match against his boot, and sauntered away, leaving a trail of fragrant smoke.

Bill glanced at his watch and realized that the committee would soon be taking their lunch break. He mentally reviewed the list of witnesses who had been called for the morning session. Marconi would be given another chance to showcase his remarkable invention. Harold Bride, hopefully in better health, would assure them once again that he had passed all ice warnings to the bridge, and Harold Cottam would be back in the witness chair to tell of the warnings he had received on board the *Carpathia*.

Bill fought against an overwhelming feeling that he was wasting his time. Increasingly the witness statements had been one man's word against another man's word, or memory, and even memories were shifting on a daily basis. Now a new phenomenon had arisen: witnesses who simply could not be trusted at all. Yesterday the committee had been in recess for hours waiting for a witness who had been brought by armed guard from Cleveland. He had claimed to be Luis Klein, a *Titanic* crew member, and he had vowed that the captain and all the officers had been drunk at the time of the collision. Unfortunately, having installed Klein in a guesthouse, the marshal from Cleveland had failed to watch him, and the witness vanished overnight. Even more unfortunately, neither the crew nor the officers knew of anyone named Luis Klein.

As tired and irritated as he was, Bill had wondered whether some unfortunate fatal accident had overtaken that particular witness, or whether he was simply a confidence trickster who had never been at sea on the *Titanic*—a man from Cleveland looking for a free visit to Washington. Bill had wasted an hour of committee time questioning the crew and the passengers very closely about any suspicion of the captain and officers being drunk and had come away with the impression that none of them had been seen to touch a drink while the *Titanic* was underway. He had also come away with the impression that he had made a fool of himself … yet again.

He decided not to lunch at the Willard and stepped off the curb to call a cab. He would go home. Nana would be surprised to see him, but she would come up with something for his lunch, and he needed her company and her plain common sense.

He found the dining room empty and kitchen in turmoil. Myra Grunwald had arrived to question the two Irish girls, and according to a flustered Nana, things had not gone well. Kitty had become a spitting fury, and Maeve had dissolved into a puddle of tears. The end result was an empty table and no lunch for the senator.

Bill repaired to the parlor with the morning paper while Nana restored order. He read quickly through the headlines. Congressman Oscar Underwood of Alabama had won the Democratic primary in Georgia, defeating New Jersey governor Woodrow Wilson. Bill began to suspect that Taft would find himself running against Wilson for the presidency. He could only hope, now that the major question of Archibald Butt's fate had been answered, Taft would start to pay attention to his political future. He scanned on down the page. Only two days until the British Wreck Commissioner, in England, would open his own hearing into the sinking of the *Titanic*, but Bill was still holding Ismay in the United States. He shook his head. The British were growing impatient, and he was rapidly running out of time.

He flipped the page to the shipping news. The *Olympic*, sister of the *Titanic*, had docked in New York. He studied the grainy photograph. These two ships were said to be almost identical. *What if ...?*

He opened the kitchen door, steeled himself against the tumult within, and beckoned to Nana. "Will you come with me to New York?"

Nana bustled out of the kitchen. "New York?" she queried. "What would we do in New York?"

Bill ushered her into his study, where he could no longer hear the hubbub in the kitchen. "Every day," he said, "I question witnesses about what happened. Where were they on the ship? Where were the lifeboats? Where were the immigrant quarters, and how could they reach the boat deck? People give me answers, but I know that the best words they have cannot describe the scene. I can't see it in my mind, Nana. If I could go on board the *Olympic* and walk its decks, maybe the picture would become clearer. I have to bring this inquiry to a close, but I know I don't have the full picture."

"No one expects you to know everything," Nana said. "And you have other committee members."

Bill shook his head. "I'm the one who has to write the report. I have to put this tragedy into words, apportion blame, and find ways to make sure this never happens again. I wasn't on the *Titanic*, but I can go aboard the *Olympic*. What do you say? Will you come to New York?"

Nana frowned. "Why do you need me? Surely you should take one of the other senators."

Bill slipped his arm around his wife's waist. "I watched you at the Willard," he said, "and I saw you take on Eva Trentham and Myra Grunwald. You were stronger than I would ever have imagined. And then there was the conversation you had about what fate could befall Kate Royston in Gibraltar and—"

Nana buried her face in her hands. "You weren't supposed to hear that. Were you shocked?"

"Intrigued," Bill admitted. "I believe that I have underestimated you. I don't think I need some crusty old senator at my side; I believe I need my charming, surprising, and highly intelligent wife. What do you say? Will you come?"

Nana smiled. "When you put it like that, how can I resist? All right. Let's go and walk the decks of the *Olympic* and see what she has to tell us."

CHAPTER TWENTY-TWO

Loggers Run, Pennsylvania
Kate Royston

Kate allowed herself to fall asleep on the final leg of her journey, because the station at Loggers Run was now the end of the line. The train tracks that had run down into the town in the valley and along the riverbank no longer existed. Knowing that there was no danger she would sleep past her stop and end up far from her destination, Kate was finally able to relax. She had been vigilant on the numerous small trains that had carried her up into the hills far beyond Pittsburgh. If she had missed her connection at any of those junctions, she would have lost a whole day or maybe even two days, but now she had reached the point of no return. She had no choice but to leave the train.

Although she had bought nothing to eat or drink, the dollar bills had dwindled as she'd purchased connecting tickets. She had no money left to stay at even a modest guesthouse or to purchase so much as a cup of coffee. She definitely did not have enough to pay for a pony and trap to take her up to the house. This was it. She was once again penniless, but at least she was almost home.

The conductor roused her from a sound sleep when the train puffed into the final stop on the branch line.

"This is Loggers Run, miss. End of the line. Train can't go no farther."

She awoke with a start. Her neck was stiff from the way she had fallen asleep with her head on her portmanteau. She felt a twinge of pain as she turned her head to look out of the window at the familiar little station. The great flood had not come this way, and the station looked the same as ever. As a girl, this railway had been her magic carpet, transporting her to the glittering world beyond her valley. These were the tracks that had carried her and her mother as they had embarked on the journey that would take them to New York to buy fine clothing for her eighteenth-birthday ball. Here was where she had come a year ago, fleeing in shame and horror.

She rose clumsily to her feet, rubbing sleep from her eyes. She stepped down onto the platform, and the conductor handed down her bag. "I doubt you'll find a porter here, miss. The town's in a pretty bad way. You know about the flood, of course. Washed away the rest of the tracks. We can't go down into the valley."

"Yes, I know," Kate said. "Don't worry. I can manage."

Her bag was light and almost empty. She had a sudden memory of Joe Bayliss snatching the bag from her hand on the *Carpathia*.

"We'll move faster if I carry this."

She had been afraid of him then, of his lean, craggy face and his hard gray eyes. She had been even more afraid when Senator Smith had spoken. "The sheriff will take good care of your bag." A senator and a sheriff!

That was how it all began, she thought. If Joe Bayliss had not taken her bag and forced her to wait for him, she would not be here now. She would have left with the Van Buren family to spend the night, and in the morning, she would have taken her wages and gone in search of another position.

She stood uncertainly on the sidewalk, not taking in her surroundings but chasing what-ifs around in her head. What if the *Titanic* had not sunk? Would she now be trying to make her way across Europe on her own? What if Great-Aunt Suzanna had been kind? Would she have stayed in Pittsburgh? If Eva Trentham had not broken her leg, would Kate ever have met Danny McSorley? What if Joe Bayliss had not helped her to pawn the pearl brooch? What if the train station at Loggers Run had been destroyed and she could not reach the town of Royston? What if her father had not taken his own life? What if there had never been a flood? What if the dam had been properly constructed?

A loud hiss called her back to reality. The locomotive was getting ready to shunt the train back out of the station and reconnect it to the main line. The train was going where she could no longer go.

She stepped away from the shady refuge of the train station and looked at the narrow road ahead. She stood on a high point here, and the road curved away downhill. From the corner of her eye, she could see a tangle of washed-out railroad tracks, the obvious reason why the train could not go on down into the valley. If she walked a few hundred yards, she would reach the bend in the road and see the town, or what was left of it.

She walked slowly, allowing the afternoon sun to warm her stiff limbs. Up here in the hills that constituted the "icebox" of Pennsylvania, spring was always a late arrival. In Washington the trees had been in full leaf, but here she saw only a few tentative buds and a slight misting of green on low-growing bushes.

She sniffed the air, her nose searching for something else that was not there. The pulp mill stood several miles away from the town itself, but even the lightest of breezes from the east would carry with it the sulfurous odor of the mill as it turned wood pulp into paper. For the people of Royston, the odor had been an everyday reminder that the mill was making money for their wages. Today she smelled nothing but budding foliage. The mill was not running. The town was dead.

She turned the corner and looked down into the valley. The water from the dam burst had drained away now, and Loggers Run was attempting to return to its original bed. It was now nothing but a harmless trickle of water wending its way through the ruined town, dividing to flow around the remnants of the remaining bridge pillars, and diverting around the sturdy brick foundations of the Church of the Holy Sepulcher. What about the Catholic cemetery? What had happened to the dead buried there over the last century? Had they, too, been swept down the valley on the great wave of water? The Presbyterians, her people, had built their church and their graveyard above the dam. Kate's mother would rest in peace in her grave, and her father would still be lying nearby, unmourned and unmarked.

Main Street was still clearly discernible as a ribbon of cracked pavement threading through the chaos. Despite the fact that many of the houses were sitting askew or lying on their sides, the street was clear of debris and crowded with pedestrians. The First Bank of Royston had suffered scorched brickwork, and its windows were boarded up, but the doors stood open and people moved in and out. A clumsily lettered sign revealed the presence of Klebbert's Department Store, now housed in a makeshift barnlike structure. An old timber house leaning drunkenly askew declared itself as Royston Hotel. Kate lifted her eyes to the opposite bank of the creek. The floodwaters and the fire that had followed the flood had destroyed all signs of life on the hillside, replacing greenery and houses with mountainous piles of logs—the thousand cords of timber that had been intended for the pulp mill.

Kate reluctantly turned her gaze upstream, where once the cement dam had loomed over the town. She had never thought of the great wall of cement as anything dangerous, but she, of course, had lived above the dam. Her fine house stood alone at the far end of the lake, where she could enjoy the sight of weeping willows dipping their fronds in the water, and where her father kept a small sailboat for the entertainment of his friends. She had lived all her life in that house beside that lake without a thought for the millions of gallons of water held in check by one small cement dam.

The dam had not completely disappeared. Although great chunks of cement had broken away and crashed down into the valley, sections of the dam still remained, like great gaping white teeth in the tumbled landscape.

She let her gaze wander along the hillside. There had once been a path that skirted the main street and followed the contours of the land up to the Royston mansion. If it still existed, she could avoid walking through town, but what would that accomplish? Word of her return would spread quickly enough. She could see no point in hiding. *You have to face your demons, Kate. You can never outrun them.*

She lifted her bag and set off down the hill toward the town. In her plain overcoat, inconspicuous hat, and gray dress, she looked nothing like the elegant daughter of Philip Royston, but it would not take long for someone to recognize her. Strangers rarely came to Royston. She could see the road clear ahead and the path that would take her up the hill to her own house, or what was left of it. She wondered if anything remained of the elegant parlor, the wide, welcoming porch, and her father's wood-paneled study.

March 4, 1911

He had been drinking all day, and Kate did not know what to do. The father she loved and trusted, the man who had built a business that sustained an entire town, had vanished, to be replaced by a disheveled madman who paced the floor reading and rereading the front page of the two-day-old Knox Courier.

Kate ventured out onto the front porch. The setting sun was casting a golden light over the pall of smoke that shrouded the ruined town. A light breeze carried the stench of the still-smoldering buildings and the inarticulate sounds of anger and grief. Her reluctant footsteps carried her down the terraced steps and across the lawn to the weeping willow beside the lake. The spring-green branches that had so recently promised new life fluttered in the acrid wind and bent down to seek the cool waters of the lake, but the lake was gone, and in its going, it had destroyed everything in its path.

As the sun dipped below the horizon, the sounds rising from the valley gained shape and coalesced into an angry thunder of voices. Kate's father stumbled out onto the porch, suddenly sober, suddenly the father she knew.

"Go to your room, Kate, and pack a bag. Take only what you can carry, and take your mother's jewelry."

She hesitated.

"Now!" he thundered. "Do it now. They're coming for us."

"Who?"

His eyes were wild again. "The dead and the living. They are all coming."

Still she hesitated. "But it's not your fault. You didn't do anything wrong. Can't you explain?"

He waved a wild hand toward the valley and the rising chorus of voices. "They won't listen."

A year had passed since that night. Spring had returned to the valley, and so had she. She knew that she had no choice. She would no longer be the girl who ran away. She wondered what her life would now have been if she had never followed her father into the forest. She opened the vault in her mind where she kept her memory of that night, and she gave herself permission to examine it in the light of everything she now knew.

Her father had carried her bag into the forest just as Joe Bayliss had carried her bag on the *Carpathia*. From their hiding place, father and daughter had watched as people they knew, people who had always treated them with courtesy, rampaged through the house beside the vanished lake. When the first bright flames blossomed at the windows, Kate's father led her deeper into the forest. She still thought she was safe. She still thought that her father would somehow make matters right. She had not expected the gunshot.

When morning came, she did not return to the house. Her father had left her alone, but she could not leave him—not yet. Whatever he had done, he did not deserve to be left for the wolves and coyotes, and so she crept out of the forest and up to the church door, where the Reverend Mr. Dayton would surely know what to do. An unmarked grave and a burial in the dead of night.

She took a deep breath. A year had passed since then, and she was no longer that frightened girl who ran away in terror. She set out along the main street, firmly resisting the temptation to break into a nervous scurrying. In a town where most people were walking purposefully, a silly girl skittering from shadow to shadow would only draw attention to herself. She decided to walk at a steady pace and hold her head high. She was Philip Royston's daughter, but she had nothing to be ashamed of. No one had accused her of allowing faulty construction of the dam. She had been a child when the cement had been poured and the engineer's warnings had been ignored.

She passed the bank, the store, and the hotel without being recognized. She approached a small knot of men in suits. One of them held up a large sheet of paper, a drawing or plan of some kind. They blocked her path as they stared up at one of the ramshackle buildings. The building's stone foundation was still in place, but the rest of the building leaned precariously to one side. She recognized the color of the painted siding, and she could still make out some of the lettering. This had been the Sears and Roebuck Catalog Store, always busy with people coming in to purchase anything from baby clothes to cookstoves. The men spoke excitedly, and she felt a little of their excitement. They were rebuilding. The town of Royston was far from dead. She wondered if they planned to restore the pulp mill. She supposed that the mill now belonged to her, as her father's sole heir. Why had she never thought of that? Was it up to her to restore the mill?

A figure broke free from the knot of men, and she recognized the Reverend Mr. Dayton, the man who had helped her to flee the drowned town. His long face first registered puzzlement and then recognition. She searched the faces of the other men. She knew them all by sight and most of them by name. They were the ones who had come to her house the morning after the disaster to accuse her father. They were the ones who had shown him the newspaper.

She dragged her mind away from that dreadful remembrance. The Reverend Mr. Dayton was still speaking. "We've been looking for you. Where have you been?"

Where have I been? Kate thought. *How can I tell you of all the places I've been? I've sailed out on the North Atlantic to the very place where the* Titanic *sank. I've seen the survivors come on board. I've met the richest woman in America. I've fallen in love with a man who looked like a Viking and turned out to be a coward. I've done so many things that I cannot even list them, but none of them are important. The important thing is that I am here now, with the men who drove my father to suicide and burned my house, and I am going to face them. I am not going to run.*

New York Harbor
Senator William Alden Smith

Nana clutched at Bill's arm as they stepped out of the cab and stared up at the vast bulk of the *Olympic*. Bill could not repress a shudder as he saw the massive ship safely docked in the berth that had been intended for the *Titanic*. He remembered waiting on this shore in the cold, driving rain and seeing the *Carpathia* drop the *Titanic*'s lifeboats into the great gaping space that should have housed the White Star Line's mammoth new ship. That had been just a few weeks ago, but much had happened since then, and now he was here to try to make sense of what the survivors had told him.

"How could she sink?" Nana said softly. "How could anything so magnificent just disappear beneath the waves? Is she really *Titanic*'s twin?"

"Almost," Bill said. "There are a few minor differences, but basically the same hull and the same interior ... the same watertight bulkheads."

Nana shook her head. "All that magnificence gone in a minute," she said. "I suppose she's just lying on the seabed now. It's hard to even imagine. Beds, tables, people's luggage, just resting on the bottom."

"I don't think it's like that," Bill said. "From what people have said, she broke in two as she went down. I imagine the wreckage is scattered."

Nana shivered. "It doesn't bear thinking about." She looked up as a smartly dressed elderly gentleman approached along the busy quayside. "Do you suppose this is the man we're supposed to meet?"

Bill studied the approaching stranger. He had expected a White Star officer in uniform, but maybe this was a civilian manager or one of White Star's engineers, although he seemed rather too elderly for such a position.

"Senator Smith?" the man inquired.

"Yes. Good morning."

"Good morning, sir, and madam." The newcomer's voice was almost aggressively British, with the slight drawl created by an elite education. To Bill, it was a voice that declared the speaker superior to all others. The man had hardly said more than a few words, and already Bill felt offended.

The man extended his hand. "Captain Godfrey Fowler," he said. "I'm retired now, but I am happy to continue to represent the White Star Line. Captain Haddock would have welcomed you himself, but he is under considerable pressure preparing for the next departure."

Fowler made a sweeping gesture to encompass the activity on the dock and on the decks of the *Olympic*. "Food and beverage," he said, "coal, water, freight, trunks sent on in advance, livestock, all have to be loaded and tidied away before our passengers come aboard. I never commanded a ship of this size—we didn't have one this size in my day—but the process is the same. Why don't we go on board, and I'll show you around? What in particular did you want to see?"

Bill stared up at the ship that towered above him. What did he want to see? *All of it*, he thought, *but mostly I want to see what I can't see. I want to see where the bridge officers put the ice warnings. I want to see where Bruce Ismay cornered the captain and told him to increase speed.*

Fowler took Bill's hesitation as an invitation to devise his own tour schedule. He gestured to a gangplank, the only one not swarming with workers. "We'll go in here. This is the best way to reach the grand staircase and the first-class accommodations."

As he led them up the gangplank, he pointed to a broad promenade deck, where deck chairs had already been arrayed. "This is B deck promenade," he said. "On the *Titanic*, this deck was enclosed to make additional cabins. Sir Bruce Ismay had one of the parlor suites that were created in the remodeling." He turned his head to look at Bill. "How is Sir Bruce?"

"I believe he is well," Bill said stiffly.

Fowler nodded. "Unfortunate. Very unfortunate. Don't know what will happen to him now. It's just not on, you see. It's simply not on."

Bill assumed that the something that was "not on" was the fact that Ismay was still alive. He said nothing and allowed Fowler to lead them into the interior of the ship, where he stopped short in amazement. A stained-glass dome shed diffused light on a grand staircase ornamented with carved banisters and newel posts. The staircase led up to a landing, where it divided into two directions, leading, he thought, to the first-class cabins. He imagined how it would be every night at sea, when the rich and powerful, splendid in their evening clothes, descended to dine at tables set with crystal glasses, gleaming silverware, and starched linen tablecloths. He thought of Nana's words. The twin of this floating palace was now lying on the seabed. In time, it would be consumed by the ocean, but for now, perhaps the crystal glasses were still intact and the silverware had only just begun to corrode.

Nana tightened her grip on his arm. "I don't like it," she said. "It's so sad."

Fowler turned to her and his expression softened. "It is indeed, madam. We have found some difficulty in filling the ship's accommodations and even in signing on a crew. Assurances had to be made that such a disaster could never happen again."

"How could you ever make such an assurance?" Bill asked impatiently. "Am I to assume that the White Star Line knows exactly what went wrong and therefore can avoid a repeat performance?"

Fowler shook his head. "No, of course not. Speaking from experience, I would say it is not just one thing that went wrong, but many things—a chain of events leading to an inevitable disaster. I have offered to give my opinion at the British inquiry. In fact, I will be sailing on this ship when she leaves New York."

"And you're not afraid?" Nana asked.

"No, madam, I am not," Fowler said firmly. "The sea and I have an agreement."

Bill fixed the image of the grand staircase in his mind. He had not come here to see stained glass and elaborate woodwork, but he was glad to have seen what he had seen, because now he could paint his own picture of the night of April 14, when this staircase had been crammed with passengers from all classes. Some would have been wearing life jackets, but some would have refused to believe that anything was wrong. Gentlemen, facing the reality that they would not be allowed in a lifeboat, would probably have turned here at the foot of the stairs and gone into the smoking room and bar. A steward, holding to his post in the face of disaster, would have remained behind the bar, serving drinks—maybe drinking something himself.

"I want to see the lifeboats," Bill said abruptly. He suspected that Nana would like to peek into the cabins, but he felt an abrupt need for fresh air. Although the *Olympic* had already made a number of uneventful transatlantic voyages, he could not shake the shadow of the *Olympic*'s twin and the feeling that he was trapped in a magnificent coffin.

"The lifeboats," Fowler repeated. "Yes, I suppose that would be pertinent. Follow me, and I'll take you to the boat deck."

Bill's feeling of claustrophobia lifted as he emerged into the open air of the boat deck. From this position, he could see in through the windows of the bridge and the radio room. He glanced inside and saw no movement. No doubt all the officers were elsewhere, making sure everything was prepared.

Fowler pointed away from the bridge, toward a section of open decking where the lifeboats were housed. "This is our full inventory," he said. "Fourteen standard lifeboats, two emergency cutters, and four collapsibles. We keep the two cutters in their davits, ready to be lowered in an emergency."

"What kind of emergency?" Nana asked.

"Man overboard," Fowler said, "or perhaps to take someone ashore. They're rarely used."

Bill looked at the lifeboats, gleaming, like everything else, under a fresh coat of paint. "It's not enough," he said. "How many passengers are on the *Olympic*?"

"Usually around two thousand three hundred."

"But those boats would never carry two thousand three hundred people," Nana said.

Fowler nodded his agreement. "No, of course not, madam. The lifeboats are only intended to ferry passengers to a rescue ship."

"And if there is no rescue ship?" Nana asked.

"It is not something we usually envisage in this kind of vessel," Fowler admitted. "The ship itself, with its watertight compartments and greater buoyancy, is its own lifeboat in a way."

"In a way!" Nana sniffed.

A rather spiteful expression crept across Fowler's face. "Alexander Carlisle, the original designer of these ships, suggested somewhere between forty-eight and sixty-four lifeboats per ship. I am told that Sir Bruce Ismay raised the loudest objection to such a thing. He said they would only be obstructions on the deck and the presence of so many lifeboats would make the passengers nervous." He gestured at the lifeboats. "We have twenty, and that is more than is required by the law."

"Well, that's ridiculous," Nana declared. "There is something wrong with your law."

Fowler raised his distinguished eyebrows. "The lifeboat requirement is based on the tonnage of the vessel and not the number of passengers." He lowered his eyebrows again. "I think we should consider rewriting that law."

"Oh, we will consider it," Bill said.

The eyebrows were raised again. "It's a British ship under British law."

Bill could feel his anger rising. "It's a British ship carrying American passengers and entering American ports. I think we have some say in the matter."

Fowler shrugged. "Maybe so, Senator. I assume that will be within the purview of your committee."

Bill stared in silence at the lifeboats while the words of the survivors echoed in his head.

The ship lunged forward, and a great wave rolled up over the bridge. I turned my back on the ship and dived forward into the icy water.

I didn't get into a lifeboat. I waited. We were all there, waiting. Masses of us. Just hanging on until the last breath. And then I sat on the rail and I jumped.

I saw a pack of dogs running loose on the deck. They didn't know what was happening, poor beasts. They were just running, you know, for the fun of it.

It was like being in a nightmare. People screaming and shouting, the steam whistle shrieking, ropes tangled, immigrants locked down belowdecks, lifeboats launched sideways and upside down, and some of them half-empty, and all those people left behind.

"Bill! Bill!"

331

He returned from his nightmare vision to see Nana's worried face and realized that someone else was now standing beside Captain Fowler.

"This is Fred Barrett," Fowler said. "I've had him brought up from the engine room to speak to you. I didn't think your good lady would want to go down there among the oil and coal dust. Mr. Barret was on board the *Titanic*."

Barrett removed his cap to reveal dark eyes and a head of dark hair. His overalls were grimy. He extended his hand and then pulled it back to wipe it with a red rag. Finally, still unhappy with the state of his hands, he offered Nana a slight bow and nodded his head to Bill. "Fred Barret, lead stoker," he said.

"Oh my," Nana said. "Are you really going back to sea after all that you've seen?"

"It's my living," Barrett said. "Not much choice."

"I thought you would want to hear Mr. Barrett's story," Fowler said. "He had a very lucky escape."

"Yes, I did," Barrett declared. "I was right there, sir. I was right where that blooming iceberg came in. We were running hot, all but one engine fired up. I was talking to Mr. Hesketh, the second engineer, when the red light and bells came on, signaling us to stop the engines. I shouted to the men in the boiler room to shut the dampers, and then the water starts coming in, and pretty soon it's pouring in.

"I did my duty, sir. I went to help with boiler five, and then I got the order to go back to boiler six, but I couldn't, you know—the boiler room was full of water, all the way up. I heard the order for the stokers to go up topside, but Engineer Harvey told me to stay and get some lamps. So I got lamps, and by the time I went up, there were only two lifeboats left. I got into lifeboat thirteen, and we was going down the side when lifeboat fifteen came down on top of us, nearly drowned us all. I took charge for a while, being a crewman and all, but I think I passed out. I didn't know nothing until the *Carpathia* came up alongside of us."

Bill looked at Barrett and then at Fowler. What was he supposed to make of this interview? Barrett had told him nothing he didn't already know. He had only confirmed that chaos had reigned, or perhaps there was more to it than Fowler was willing to say.

"You say you were running hot?" Bill said.

"Yes, sir. Sunday afternoon, we had orders to light up three more boilers."

"And what does that mean in layman's terms?" Bill asked.

"Full speed ahead," Barret said. "We were doing seventy-seven revolutions."

"And do you know who gave those orders to light up the boilers?"

"Orders from the bridge," Barrett said. "All orders come from the bridge."

Fowler stepped in to dismiss the stoker. "Thank you, Mr. Barrett. Safe voyage."

"I should blooming hope so," Barrett responded, replacing his cap and walking away.

"Have you seen everything you wish to see?" Fowler asked.

"I'm not sure."

"Perhaps I should ask you if you have heard everything you need to hear. Has Mr. Barrett explained the situation in the boiler room to your satisfaction?"

When Bill failed to respond, Fowler led them back to the dock. He stood looking up at the great ship with a wistful expression. "I would have loved such a command," he said, "but Captain Smith had earned the right to the *Titanic*. He was retiring, you know. It was to be his last voyage. We all reach the point where we have to hand the reins to another, younger man. It is, as you can see, such a great responsibility."

Bill wanted to speak, but he sensed that he would learn more if he said nothing.

"Ship captains are masters of their own kingdom," Fowler said. "They give the orders. No one else gives the orders. No one!"

"So the order to light up the boilers came from …"

"From the bridge," Fowler said, "and from no one and nowhere else."

He pointed to a heavy truck making its way along the dock to stand beside the ship. "That's the mail truck. There will be seven postal workers on board *Olympic*, sorting mail throughout the voyage. The Royal Mail contract is a good contract. RMS means something. Royal Mail Ship *Olympic*. RMS *Titanic*. It's a responsibility. It's a contract to deliver the mail on time." He gave Bill a long, steady look. "On time," he repeated.

When Bill failed to reply, Fowler nodded to Nana. "I am glad to have met you, Mrs. Smith." He offered his hand to Bill. "Keep up the good work, Senator. I think we would all like to see changes."

"What on earth was that about?" Nana asked as Captain Fowler walked away.

"I think it was about speaking ill of the dead," Bill replied.

Knox, Pennsylvania
Joe Bayliss

Joe's patience, never his strongest suit, gave out when he stepped off the train at Knox and was informed that he could not take a train to Royston.

"Why not?" he growled. "The B&O in Washington told me this was the route, so why can't I go?"

The ticket clerk, alarmed by Joe's fierce glare, took a step back from the window. "You can go as far as Loggers Run," he said, "but there ain't no tracks after that. You'd think they'd know that in Washington."

Joe tried not to growl again. "Well, they don't," he said.

"You can go by rail to Loggers Run," the clerk said, "but then you'll have to walk."

"How far?"

"About a mile, I would say."

"Okay, sell me a ticket to Loggers Run."

The clerk scratched his head. "There ain't no train today."

"Tomorrow?"

The clerk shook his head. "Wednesday is the soonest. Only comes every three days. Not much call to go there since the flood, what with the mill being closed and most of the people gone."

"I can't wait until Wednesday. What am I supposed to do here until Wednesday?"

The clerk shrugged. "We have a hotel, and we have moving pictures showing at the Grand Theater. A man can spend a few days here without being bored." He cocked his head to one side and reassessed Joe's face. "Maybe not you," he said. "Maybe you won't find much to do. We're quiet people."

"What about a livery stable? I'll rent a horse and buggy."

The clerk pursed his lips. "Not sure about getting a buggy down that road. They're still picking up the pieces, you know." He shook his head and sucked his teeth. "Terrible business. The fellow killed himself, or so they say."

"People say all kinds of things," Joe said. "Doesn't mean you have to repeat them. Point me to the livery stable. I'll get a horse."

An hour later, with the sun riding high in a cloudless sky, Joe was riding an uncooperative brown gelding on a narrow trail that threaded its way through forested hills in a generally northward direction. He sat deep in the saddle and exercised considerable patience in letting the gelding discover who exactly was going to be in control. He'd never seen the point of treating an animal harshly just because it had never been taught the right way to do things. With the sun warming his shoulders and birds warbling and cheeping from every tree, he was content for the moment to allow the gelding its head, so long as it continued to plod along the trail in the right direction.

At least the horse didn't startle or buck at every creature that disturbed the undergrowth around them. As for the creatures themselves, well, their brains seemed to have abandoned them with the arrival of spring and the start of the mating season. Creatures that should have been hiding in the tall grass as he passed flung themselves carelessly across his path. Two squirrels blocked his way, chittering angrily at each other. Males, he thought, fighting over some girl squirrel, who was no doubt perched in a tree and looking down in satisfaction at the trouble she had created.

Making fools of themselves, he thought. *That's what we men do in spring. That's probably what I'm doing, and I can no more stop myself than the two squirrels rolling and scratching each other on the dusty trail.*

He detoured around the aggressive suitors and encouraged the gelding into a lazy canter. He didn't have all day to wander through the woods and contemplate the foolishness of chasing after Kate Royston. A man like Jacob Astor could marry a girl half his age and be applauded by society, but there was surely something pathetic about Joe's desire to take care of Kate. Even now he could not admit, even to himself, what he really wanted. He settled for telling himself that he only intended to make sure she was safe. He knew how much money she'd received for the pearl brooch, and he knew what the train journey had cost him. She was three days ahead of him, so by now she would be penniless again. She was going to need someone to take care of her and see her back to New York, where she would be safe with Eva Trentham. Despite her bitter remarks, he knew Eva would take her back. So perhaps he could help her reach New York, and if not New York, maybe Michigan … maybe.

The gelding slowed to a halt as the path emerged from the forest onto a promontory overlooking a deep valley and a ruined town. Joe sucked in his breath. The devastation was astounding. He'd seen floods before, resulting from ice jams on the St. Marys River, but the damage they caused was gentle compared to what had happened to the town of Royston. Here the hand of God had been harsh and violent, and had smashed the community into matchsticks.

He looked away from the town. The report Myra Grunwald had found spoke of the Royston mansion being situated above the town and away from the flood damage. He could easily see where the dam had once been, not just because of the tumbled remnants of cement but because there was only one place where a narrow gap between the hills offered the perfect place to build a dam.

He turned back to the trail and was pleased to see that it did not lead downhill, but instead, it wended its way along a ridge, following a path that would take him above the ruined dam. He caught a glimpse of a brick building some way ahead and encouraged the gelding into a lumpy canter. Kate's house had burned, but apparently, some buildings remained.

The path brought him to a solid redbrick church with a squat tower and clear glass windows. Unlike the devastation down below in the valley, this building appeared undamaged. He moved on past the church and realized at once that he was on a path that had once followed the shore of the lake that had been created by building the dam. A stand of weeping willows lowered their budding branches hopefully to the ground, but they would not be trailing them in the water this year. The water had retreated back into the original valley, leaving behind a wasteland of mud traversed by a meandering creek.

He could see the remains of a house on the far side of the dried-up lake. So this was the Royston mansion. He thought it had once been quite splendid, and even in its burned and ruined condition, it showed signs of the Italianate style currently favored by the wealthy. It had been built in the same red brick as the church, and although its bricks were scorched and the roof had collapsed, he could still discern a fanciful tower and even some intricate fretwork around

336

what had once been the front porch.

Was it habitable? he wondered. Was Kate somewhere inside, among the ruins of what had once been her life? He urged the horse forward. If she was not in the house, he would have to turn back and go down into the ruined town. He thought she was probably unsafe in either place. If her father had been blamed for the devastation Joe had witnessed, she could not be safe among the people who had blamed him.

He saw a small graveyard set midway between the house and the church and bounded by wrought-iron railings. He caught a flash of color and movement among the white headstones. He knew her immediately, in the dark coat she had worn when he had first met her on board the *Carpathia*. It was not the color of the coat that had caught his attention but the flowers she was arranging on a mound of spring grass—a grave that bore no headstone. Her head was down, focusing on the flowers. Daffodils, he thought. Where had she found daffodils?

He dismounted, hitched the gelding to the railing, and approached her slowly, allowing his boots to crunch against the gravel path so that she would not be startled when his shadow fell across her.

She kept her head down. She would not look at him.

CHAPTER TWENTY-THREE

Kate Royston

Kate kept her head down. If she did not look up, she could hold on to a moment of hope. A few minutes ago, she had caught a glimpse of a man on horseback threading his way through the trees toward the church. Although her heart beat a little faster in wild and unreasonable expectation, she told herself it was not him. The visitor was surely someone who had ridden out from town to see the Reverend Mr. Dayton. The road up onto Royston Heights was not yet sufficiently clear of debris for an automobile or a pony and trap. To reach the church, it was necessary to either walk or ride one of the remaining horses. Logic told her that the new arrival was probably Cecil Huygen the banker or Josiah Cartwright, who had been foreman at the mill, or maybe some other man from town who had come to visit the grave of Philip Royston and mutter his own apology.

Her hands shook as she knelt beside the grassy mound to arrange the daffodils. So long as she did not look up, she could still keep a flicker of hope alive. She no longer clung to her self-righteous indignation that Danny McSorley had saved his own life by finding a place in a lifeboat. Now that she was away from Washington and the heated rhetoric of the senators and the witnesses, she had managed to put Danny's actions into some kind of perspective. She wished she had asked him what had happened instead of walking scornfully away. No, not walking, running. She was still running.

This was foolish. She could not ignore the visitor forever. His shadow fell across her, and she raised her eyes a little and studied his well-worn boots. For one brief moment, she tried to keep hold of the idea that these were Danny's boots. He had somehow seen through the defensive wall she had built around her heart, and he had come to forgive her for doubting him. At last she looked up.

Her heart had no idea what to do. It plummeted and swooped and hammered against her ribs in shock. The daffodils fell from her hands and spread a carpet of yellow across the grave. Her shock seemed to be mirrored by the stunned expression on Joe's face. Was he surprised to see her? No, that was not possible. Surely he had come here to find her. What other business could have brought him to Royston?

"Is this your father's resting place?"

She hardly understood the question. His gravelly voice had transported her back to the rain-soaked deck of the *Carpathia* and her first sight of the tall, craggy man with dangerous gray eyes. What was he doing here? Had she been recalled to Washington? No, she could not go back there to the endless questioning that reduced the horror of the sinking to mere recitation of facts. She could not go back to the Willard, and she would not go back to Eva Trentham.

"Miss Kate?"

He was expecting an answer.

"Yes, this is my father's grave. We buried him quietly without a headstone. The Reverend Mr. Dayton thought it would be safer ... thought I would be safer ... if we did not draw attention to his resting place. My mother is buried just a short distance away. I left here immediately after the burial."

Joe frowned. "Are you safe here?"

Kate stood up, leaving the daffodils scattered where they had fallen. "Yes, I'm safe. There was an investigation, and it turns out that the engineer my father hired—"

"Petrov," Joe said.

Kate stared at him in amazement. "You know about him?"

"Myra Grunwald told us your story."

"Well," Kate said, "Petrov lied. He was the one who changed the plans for the dam. He was to blame, not my father."

She looked down at the grave. She could feel nothing now for her father except a distant sadness. He, too, had been a runner. She was his daughter in every way, running instead of waiting. If he had waited, he would have been present to see Petrov taken to jail. If she had waited, she would have been here to help him rebuild the house and the mill, and she would not have been on board the *Carpathia* on the night of April 14, when Harold Cottam had received the *Titanic*'s message.

She considered the tall figure of Sheriff Bayliss. She would never have met him or seen the danger in his eyes turn to a new questioning sadness. She leaned down and picked up one of the daffodils. "I found them growing around what is left of my house," she said. "My mother planted them, and they came back every year. They're still coming back, although now there's no one to enjoy them."

"What will you do?" Joe asked.

"Well," Kate said, "I was absolutely penniless when you found me on board the *Carpathia*, and that is no longer the case. Back then I had some wild idea of leaving the ship at Gibraltar and making my way across Europe to England."

Joe raised his eyebrows, and Kate found a sudden ability to laugh at her former self. "Ridiculous, I know. Eva Trentham explained quite clearly what kind of trouble I would be in if I tried that on my own."

"Why England?" Joe asked.

"My mother's family is there. I had no welcome from my father's family, so I thought I would try my luck with them. It was an absurd idea. I should have stayed here, although I would have missed a great adventure. I would never have met you, Sheriff, or Mrs. Trentham, or Wolfie, or …" She fell silent. There was no point in saying his name.

Joe looked past her at the ruined house, only half-hidden behind a screen of budding trees. "Are you going to rebuild it?"

Kate struggled to find an answer for him. Did she really want to rebuild the mansion? Did she want to stay in Royston and see the restoration of the pulp mill and the return of the sulfurous odor that was the perfume of success for Royston?

"My father had a safety-deposit box at the bank," she said. "It survived the flood and the fire."

Joe nodded. "That's what they're designed to do."

"Mr. Huygen, the banker, is an honest man," Kate said. "He stood his ground and would not allow anyone access to the contents, even when the workers from the mill threatened his life. Of course, when they found out that the dam collapse was not my father's fault, everything changed. They were looking for me, Sheriff. For months now, Mr. Huygen and Mr. Dietrich the lawyer have been looking for me. They finally traced me to Pittsburgh, but I had already left by the time they wrote to my great-aunt Suzanna, not that she would have helped them."

"Why not?"

"Because if I could not be found, she would be my father's heir. You would have to meet Suzanna Royston in person to understand how awful that would be."

"And so you will stay here?" Joe asked.

The answer came surprisingly easily. Her head had been spinning for the two days since Cecil Huygen had told her about the money, but now she knew. "No, I can't stay here."

"What about the mill?"

"Mr. Dietrich says I can deed the mill over to the town."

"So you've already talked about leaving?"

Kate nodded. "Yes, I have."

"Will you go to England, as you originally planned?"

A little bubble of amusement rose in Kate's throat. "Well, I won't sign on as a governess in order to get there. I am not cut out to be a governess. Maybe I'll just travel around until I find a place I like or until my money runs out."

She regretted the words as soon as they had left her mouth. "Travel around until I find a place I like" was just another way of saying that she would run.

Joe regarded her curiously. "Have you thought of Michigan?" he said.

Michigan! The thought had never crossed her mind. What did she even know about Michigan? She imagined pine trees and snow and a great gray lake that stretched across the horizon. Obviously, Joe loved the place, but why would he imagine that she would find it worth visiting? Surely she had seen enough of cold gray water.

She shook her head. "I was thinking of somewhere a little more exotic."

A shadow fell across Joe's face. "Of course you were. It was a foolish idea."

She heard such regret in his voice that she wondered if she had said something truly offensive. Of course he was proud of his home state and his position as sheriff of Chippewa County, but he surely didn't think that it was a place where someone like Kate could ever settle down to a life of … of what? What was he really asking?

No, surely not. He was old enough to be her father.

Joe reached down and picked up a daffodil. For a long moment, he stared into its sunny yellow center. He lifted his head and smiled at her. "Have you thought of Newfoundland?"

She could not stop the rush of blood to her cheeks or the tremble in her voice. "All the time," she whispered. "I think of it all the time."

Joe gestured to the brown horse, who had his head down and was happily grazing on the new grass along the fence line. "He's a sturdy animal," Joe said, "and you don't weigh more than a bag of feathers. We'll ride out together, and I'll set you on your road, now that you know where you're going."

"I'm not sure."

Joe shook his head. "Yes, you are."

"But he never said anything."

Joe grinned, and the shadow of sadness retreated from his eyes. "He said plenty. You weren't listening."

"But he's gone," Kate said. "He's in Newfoundland by now. I don't know how I'd get there."

"It's easy," Joe said. "Think of how far you've already come. We'll ride back to Knox and take the train to New York. From New York you can take a packet steamer to St. John's." The shadow returned briefly to his eyes. "You'll have to make that voyage on your own."

"But he won't know I'm coming," Kate said.

Joe smiled and shrugged his shoulders as though he had just released a heavy burden. "He's a Marconi operator at the world's most important relay station. I don't think we'll have any trouble sending him a message."

May 27, 1912
The Home of Senator William Alden Smith
Washington, DC
Senator William Alden Smith

Nana walked quietly into Bill's study and laid a hand on his shoulder. "It's late, Bill. You have to come to bed."

Bill gestured at his wastebasket, stuffed with crumpled papers—the innumerable false starts he had made on his speech for tomorrow.

He rested his head in his hands. "I don't know how to say it," he groaned. "I don't know how to do justice to the survivors. I've failed, Nana."

"No, you haven't."

"I thought I could bring it all down to questions and answers, but I can't." He swept his hand across the desk, knocking the scattered papers to the floor. "It's too big, too much—a thousand individual tragedies."

Nana bent down and picked up a sheet of paper. She studied it for a moment. "Are these the new laws you're recommending?"

Bill nodded. "That's the easy part. It's obvious what has to be done in the future."

Nana moved into the pool of light cast by a gilded lampstand. "'New regulations to be imposed on passenger vessels wishing to use American ports,'" she read. "'Ships should slow down on entering areas known to have drifting ice and should post extra lookouts. Navigational messages should be brought promptly to the bridge and disseminated as required. There should be enough lifeboats for all on board.'"

She looked up from the paper. "This is good, Bill. This is what needs to be done. When I saw those lifeboats on the deck of the *Olympic*, I was horrified. So few boats for so many people, and Captain Fowler said that even those few were more than was required by law."

Bill lifted his head from his hands. "It will apply to all ships that want to use American ports. We can't fix the whole world, but we can make things safer for people coming to America."

"Have you written anything else?"

He handed her another sheet of paper. "These are just regulations. I wish it hadn't taken a tragedy like the loss of the *Titanic* to make us realize what we have to do."

Nana took the paper and continued to read aloud. "'All ships equipped with wireless sets should maintain communications at all times of the day and night. Rockets should only be fired by ships at sea as distress signals and not for any other purposes.'"

She set the paper back on his desk. "If you can push this law through, you will save thousands of lives. Nothing like the *Titanic* will ever happen again."

Bill shook his head. "It won't be enough. I've tied up the Senate for weeks. I've alienated the British, and I've turned a tragedy into a circus. And at the end of all that, what have I really achieved? I am expected to point the finger of blame at someone."

"What about Captain Lord on the *Californian*? Surely he can be blamed."

"Oh, yes," Bill said. "I have that piece already written, and you're quite correct, my dear. I will draw attention to his lies. He contradicts himself at almost every turn. I have no doubt that he was within easy reach of the *Titanic* and he knew she was there. I can't know why he failed to act. He was either drunk or a coward—I can think of no other explanation—but his fate will have to be determined by the British. I will say what I think, but they will have to act upon it. Whatever else he did, however cowardly his behavior, he did not cause the *Titanic* to sink."

"Then who did?" Nana asked. "What about Ismay and the way he saved himself?"

"That's not a crime."

"He gave instructions to the captain. He wanted to achieve a speed record. He wanted the Blue Riband."

"Did he?"

Nana sighed and shook her head. "I don't know, Bill."

"You go up to bed," Bill said. "I'm going to place a phone call."

"Don't be long."

"I won't."

Bill lifted the receiver, cranked the handle, and instructed the operator to connect him with Bruce Ismay at the Willard Hotel. As he sat and listened to the unfathomable clicks and buzzes of the telephone system, he added an addendum to his list of new regulations. On the night of the sinking, a dozen or so ships had been sending messages back and forth across the ocean in a chaotic chorus with no assessment of what was urgent, what was private, or even what was frivolous. The ice warnings for the *Titanic* and even the SOS from the ship had been sandwiched in between messages of congratulations, greetings of relatives, and messages from one businessman to another. Things would have to change. Priorities would have to be established. No ship should ever have to sink because a wealthy socialite was telegraphing instructions to her servants.

"Ismay here. What can I do for you, Senator?"

The crackling had reduced to a background murmur, and Ismay's voice was clear. Bill would like to have done this in person, but his time had expired. He would have to read what he could into Ismay's tone without seeing his face.

"I have to ask you one more time, Mr. Ismay. Did you have any talk with the captain with reference to the speed of the ship?"

"Never, sir."

"Did you at any time urge the captain to greater speed?"

"No, I did not."

"Do you know of anyone who urged him to greater speed than he was making when the ship was making seventy revolutions?"

"No, Senator. It is really impossible to imagine such a thing on board ship."

Bill found himself nodding, although he knew Ismay could not see him. He sighed. Ismay would surely hear him sighing. For the very first time, he used Ismay's title. "Sir Bruce, I am sure you are aware that I was a friend of Captain Smith. I sailed with him several times."

"As did I," said Ismay. "He was a fine fellow."

"And brave," Bill said.

Now it was Ismay's turn to sigh. "Yes, Senator. He was a brave man."

Bill allowed a moment of silence to pass as he remembered the jovial captain, with his neat white beard. Finally he spoke. "Sir Bruce, what can you say as to your treatment at the hands of the committee?"

"I have no fault to find," Ismay said. "Naturally, I was disappointed in not being allowed to go home, but I feel quite satisfied you have some very good reason in your own mind for keeping me here."

"Would you now agree that it was the wisest thing to do?"

Ismay's voice was firm. "I think that under the circumstances, it was."

"Thank you, Sir Bruce. You are free to go home. I believe the British tribunal is waiting to hear from you."

"I'm afraid they are."

"Good night, Sir Bruce."

"Good night, Senator."

Bill set down the telephone receiver and shuffled through the papers on his desk until he found what he needed. He spread the papers out and read them in chronological order. He began to write.

May 28, 1912
The Senate Chamber
Washington, DC
Senator William Alden Smith

Bill rose to his feet and surveyed the chamber. Weeks of interrogation, sleepless nights, and tears cried in secret had brought him to this moment. He set his notes on the podium. This first part was the easiest. For this, he had the words.

"Mr. President, my associates and myself return the commission handed to us on the eighteenth day of April last, directing an immediate inquiry into the causes leading up to the destruction of the steamship *Titanic*, with its attendant and unparalleled loss of life, so shocking to the people of the world. Mindful of the responsibility of our office, we desire the Senate to know that in the execution of its command, we have been guided solely by the public interest and a desire to meet the expectations of our associates without bias, prejudice, sensationalism, or slander of the living or dead. To this end, we immediately determined that the testimony of British officers and crew and English passengers temporarily in the United States should be first obtained."

He caught sight of the British ambassador, seated in the spectator gallery. His disapproval no longer mattered. Ismay and the White Star witnesses were already on their way home.

As he continued speaking, he was aware of every eye on him, every muttered word, and every audible gasp of surprise. He took his time and told his story. He drew from the testimony of every person, rich and poor, who had come before him and his committee. The longer he spoke, the more details he gave, the quieter the chamber became. They were waiting with bated breath for an answer to the question that had consumed their thoughts for weeks. Who was at fault? Who would he blame?

"I think," Bill said at last, "that the presence of Mr. Ismay stimulated the ship to greater speed than it would have made under ordinary conditions." He paused and looked around. "But," he continued, "I cannot fairly ascribe to him any instructions to that effect."

He was certain that he heard a collective sigh of disappointment. For weeks now, the newspapers had vilified the sullen, haughty Englishman. They wanted him to be at fault. They wanted to see him suffer. *But he will suffer*, Bill thought. *Whatever I say here will make no difference to the way history will treat Sir Bruce Ismay.* His crime did not lie in urging the *Titanic* to greater speed. His crime lay in saving himself while others died.

Bill moved on. *Might as well say it now and be done with it.* "Captain Smith knew the sea, and yet overconfidence seems to have dulled his faculties. With the atmosphere literally charged with warning signals, the stokers in the engine room fed their fires with fresh fuel, registering in that dangerous place her fastest speed. And when disaster struck, there is evidence to show that no general alarm was given, no ship's officers formally assembled, no orderly routine was attempted, or organized system of safety begun. We have to conclude that Captain Smith's indifference to danger was one of the direct and contributing causes of this unnecessary tragedy, while his own willingness to die was the expiating evidence of his fitness to live."

He looked up. The deed was done. Despite everything the witnesses had told him, and despite every accusatory newspaper article on both sides of the Atlantic, he had not given them a living criminal—only a dead captain who had gone down with his ship.

He reached into his pocket and brought out a small bundle of Marconigrams. He spread them on the desk in front of him. He looked up and spoke slowly, his eyes roving around the chamber, looking for the moment when the spectators would abandon their need for a scapegoat and truly understand the unspeakable hubris that had led the builders to claim that their ship was unsinkable and they had no need of lifeboats.

"In our imagination," he said, "we see again the proud ship, its decks swarming with musicians, teachers, artists, and authors, soldiers and sailors, and men of large affairs—brave men and noble women of every land. We see the lowly and unpretentious turning their backs upon the Old World and looking hopefully to the New. At the very moment of their greatest joy, the ship suddenly reels, mutilated and groaning. With splendid courage, the musicians fill the last moments with sympathetic melody. The ship wearily gives up the unequal battle."

He picked up the first Marconigram and read aloud. "'*Titanic* to all ships. Sinking head down. Come as soon as possible.'"

He set the paper down and looked around the room again. Were they listening? Did they really understand?

He spoke softly into the smothering silence. "Only a vestige now remains of the men and women that but a moment before quickened her decks with human hopes and passions, sorrows and joys."

He picked up the next Marconigram. "'*Titanic* to all ships, we are putting the women off in boats.'"

He read on, picking up the papers and setting them down again reverently, as though they were precious artifacts.

"'*Baltic* to *Titanic*, we are rushing to you.'

"'*Olympic* to *Titanic*. Am lighting up all possible boilers as fast as we can.'"

He paused, hoping that the spectators could now see what he could see. He wanted them to be with him on the deck of the *Titanic*, struggling to believe the great ship would truly sink. He wanted them to imagine the cries for help crackling and sparking through the radio rooms of so many ships, all so near and yet so far.

```
    "'Titanic   to   all   ships.   Engine   room   getting
flooded.'
    "'Baltic   to   Caronia.   Please   tell   Titanic   we   are
making towards her.'
    "'Titanic   to   all   ships.   We   are   about   all   down.
Sinking.'
    "'Cape   Race   to   Virginian.   We   have   not   heard   from
Titanic. His power may be gone.'
    "'Carpathia   to   Titanic.   If   you   are   there,   we   are
firing rockets.'
    "'Olympic   to   Virginian.   Keeping   strict   watch   but
```

hear nothing from MGY Titanic.'

   "'Ypiranga to all ships. Have not heard Titanic since 11:50 p.m.'

   "'La Provence to Celtic. Nobody has heard the Titanic for about two hours.'"

CHAPTER TWENTY-FOUR

Eva Trenthams's Mansion
New York City
Kate Royston

The bedroom window was open to admit the warm breeze of mid-summer. Sunlight filtered through the fluttering curtains and cast a shifting shadow across Kate's trousseau laid out on the bed for Eva's inspection. Six weeks had passed since Joe Bayliss had escorted Kate back to Eva's house in New York and helped her to send a message to Danny McSorley at Cape Race.

In the weeks that followed Kate and Danny had exchanged long and increasingly romantic letters leading eventually to the conclusion that they wanted to spend the rest of their lives together. Kate was still not sure which of them had first decided that they should marry because their letters, each with a stammering, hesitant suggestion of marriage, had crossed in the post. None of that mattered now because the final result was that by this time tomorrow Kate would be Mrs. McSorley.

Danny would soon be arriving on a packet steamer from St. John's and tomorrow there would be a wedding. Eva's servants had decorated the reception rooms with summer blossoms and white ribbons, and the parlor maids were twittering in anticipation as they plied their feather dusters. Eva's cook was at work in the kitchen making cakes and pastries for the guests and Eva's butler was making sure that the silver serving pieces were polished to a mirror shine. Senator and Mrs. Smith would be the guests of honor along with prominent members of New York society. Joe Bayliss had sent his apologies in a brief note mailed from Sault Ste. Marie.

Everything was ready for the big day including the trousseau Eva had insisted on ordering. Kate and Danny would not be taking a honeymoon and would go straight to Cape Race but Eva insisted that the bride should have a trousseau. Now, Kate watched in amusement as Eva stomped around the room inspecting her purchases and leaning heavily on a cane. Bridie followed behind ready to catch the old lady if she stumbled. Eva's face was a mask of disapproval as she studied each garment. She frowned at the heavy wool jackets, sturdy shoes and small practical hats. She gestured toward a garment that seemed to meet with her most extreme disapproval.

"What is that?"

Kate picked up the offending item and held it out to display its merits. "It's called a divided skirt."

"And why, in the name of all that's holy, would you want a divided skirt?"

Kate held the skirt at her waist and demonstrated its benefits. "In most circumstances it would look like a walking skirt," Kate said, "but it's divided in the center like a man's trouser. If the wind blows, as I understand will be the case, it will not blow up. Should I wish to climb a rock, or ride a bicycle..."

"Ride a bicycle!" Eva exclaimed. "Climb a rock! Why ever would you want to do such a thing? When I think of all the opportunities you could have in European society I could just ..."

Bridie caught Eva's arm as Eva made wild gestures with her cane. "Shush now," she said. "Miss Kate has made her choice and she'll not be changing her mind just because you don't like her clothes. As for me, I must say the divided skirt seems a sensible thing."

"And better than bloomers," Kate added.

She smiled as she watched Eva's expression soften. "Bloomers," Eva declared, "are designed to make women look ridiculous." She studied the divided skirt again. "I suppose it is a sensible solution" she admitted, "for the life you are going to lead."

She moved to the other side of the bed where Kate had laid out her new lingerie designed by Lucy Duff-Gordon at Eva's insistence. Kate allowed her hand to trail across the soft silks and fine lace. She looked at Eva. "Well," she asked, "what do you think of these?"

"Nothing there will keep you warm on a cold night," Bridie said. "I'm hoping you've some woolies tucked away somewhere in your trunk."

"She won't need woolies," Eva declared. "She'll have her man to keep her warm."

Kate felt a flush rising in her cheeks at the thought of being kept warm by Danny McSorley. She had never kissed him, never even felt his hand at her waist and now Eva was talking about him keeping her warm in bed.

Eva leaned down and picked up a wispy silk garment trimmed with fine Brussels lace. "This," Eva declared, holding it out to admire its brevity, "will ensure she's warm at night."

The words were out of Kate's mouth before she could stop herself. "I don't see how…. how…" She stuttered into silence as Eva and Bridie stared at her.

"What don't you see?" Eva asked.

Kate hung her head, suddenly fearful of what she might hear. "I don't understand about…"

"About what?" Eva asked, and her voice was not unkind.

"The lingerie," Kate mumbled, "the keeping warm…. the … er … the wedding night."

"Oh glory be! Bridie exclaimed, "The girl doesn't know. She really doesn't know."

Eva turned away from Kate and addressed herself to Bridie. "That's how it is with well brought up young ladies," she said. "I know it's absurd but society insists that young ladies such as Kate are kept in ignorance so they can be presented as terrified virgins on their wedding night. I suppose that Kate's mother intended to explain the most basic facts on the night before the wedding, but of course Kate's mother is no longer with us to fulfill that duty." She turned back to Kate. "Perhaps it's for the best. Your mother would no doubt have told you that you were going to experience something dreadful that men do to women, and she would have encouraged you to just close your eyes and it would soon be over."

Kate felt a rush of fear. "What do you mean? What's going to happen to me?"

"Well, saints preserve us," Bride declared, "have you never seen two dogs going about their business, horses, even frogs? Do you know nothing of baby making? Have you never wondered?"

Eva sat down on the bed and pushed aside the wispy petticoats, drawers and nightgowns. She waved a dismissive hand at Bridie. "Leave us alone, woman!, I'm going to tell this girl what she needs to know."

Bridie frowned in disapproval. "Do you think you should do that? I'm sure that neither one of us knows what a fine young lady would expect to hear from her mother."

"I should hope not," Eva said. "I'm sure that any number of marriages have been ruined by mothers telling their daughters what to expect and filling them with fear. As for me, I had brothers and sisters to tell me what was what and no one to curl their lip and say that I wouldn't enjoy it. So be off with you Bridie and leave Kate to me."

"Don't tell her too much all at once," Bridie warned. "If the girl knows nothing, it's all going to be a shock."

"Better than a nasty surprise," Eva said. She turned to Kate with a smile lighting up her face. "Sit down, Kate, and let me tell you what's going to happen. It's not right that a girl like you should be kept in ignorance. I should have realized when you first told me you were going to jump ship in Gibraltar that you had no real idea of what goes on between a man and a woman. I'm sure Danny will be kind, but it will be better if you know what to expect and if you are not afraid. There's nothing to be afraid of."

A half hour later Eva stomped out of the bedroom leaving Kate alone with her tangled thoughts. She stared down at the pile of silken undergarments, minuscule shifts, ribbon accented drawers, fine silk stockings, and a new garment that Lucy Duff Gordon called a brassiere. She touched them tentatively. According to Eva these garments were intended for only one person. They were not for wearing, they were for removing and she would not be the person doing the removing. Her cheeks grew warm at the very idea of Danny seeing her this way. Her hand trembled as she allowed the garments to slither though her fingers. She wondered if Danny would know what to do once they were alone and she presented herself to him dressed only in these scandalous wisps of silk. Joe Bayliss would know what to do she thought irrationally. She dismissed the thought immediately. Even if Joe would know what to do, she didn't think she would want him to do it. She wasn't sure that she wanted anyone to do it.

Her mood veered from fear to anger at her mother for keeping her in ignorance and anger at herself for never wondering. How could she have been so stupid? She thought of all the babies she'd seen in her lifetime. Why had she never wondered exactly how they were made? Her mother had told her that babies came after marriage and that was all she needed to know. Her father had told her nothing. She finally understood Eva's scorn at hearing that Kate planned to leave the Carpathia at Gibraltar and make her way alone across Europe. She must have sounded like an ignorant fool. For all her education she did not have the knowledge available to any scullery maid or farm worker. She thought of all the married men she had met. The Revered Mr. Dayton, Cecil Huygen the banker, Josiah Cartwright from the mill, Senator Smith, Sir Bruce Ismay. Did they all behave this way?

She tried to reassure herself with Eva's promise that the wedding night would be fun but in her current state of panic she could not see how that would be possible. Eva's eyes had been alight with resurrected memories and a flush had come to her pale withered cheeks. "Fun," she said, "great fun. Just wait and see. There'll be a little pain at first but it will be worth it and he's a fine strapping young man and no doubt well-endowed which is something you'll learn to appreciate. Don't look so afraid. With the right man at the right time there's nothing better."

Kate's fevered thoughts were interrupted by a flurry of sound from downstairs followed by a volley of loud enthusiastic barking. Wolfie? Danny was here already and he'd brought Wolfie with him. She tiptoed to the top of the stairs and looked down into the entrance hall. She stood for a moment studying her bridegroom. She had forgotten how very handsome he was with his curling blond hair and broad shoulders. He had a flower in his buttonhole and a small bouquet of violets in his hand. His eyes were on the butler who was indicating that Danny should go ahead into the parlor but that Wolfie should... Before the butler could come to a firm conclusion as to where Wolfie belonged, Wolfie raised his head and looked directly at Kate.

Danny followed the dog's gaze and saw Kate at the top of the stairs. She stared into his eyes. She had forgotten how blue and how bright they were. Danny leaned down to Wolfie and unclipped his leash. He offered Wolfie the bouquet of violets and Wolfie took them carefully from his open palm. Kate grinned thinking of Danny spending hours teaching Wolfie a new trick. Wolfie, with the bouquet in his mouth, bounded up the stairs and met her as she descended. She took the bouquet from him, ignoring the fact that the decorative doily wrapped around the stems was damp with dog slobber. Keeping her eyes fixed on Danny, she descended the last few steps. She wished that Eva had not explained what was going to happen after the wedding. She wished that she was not so terrified.

She reached the bottom step and hesitated. Danny smiled at her the way he had smiled the first time she met him on the Carpathia. He took a step forward and held out his arms. As she had done so many times before, Kate threw caution to the winds and flung herself forward. Danny caught her and gathered her into his arms. She lifted her head for his kiss. She dropped the bouquet of violets and wound her arms around his neck. As she responded to the warmth of his lips, her fear vanished. She could hardly wait for what would happen next.

She was only dimly aware of Wolfie's contented growl as he settled down to eat the bouquet.

☐

EPILOGUE

Cape Race, Newfoundland
Kate Royston McSorley
September 1912

Kate stood on the rocky headland with Wolfie waiting patiently at her side. Together they stared out at the vast reaches of the Atlantic Ocean. The mist that so often shrouded the peninsula had been burned away by bright autumn sunlight. The lighthouse was dazzling white against a background of clear blue sky. A pod of whales breached the surface of the shimmering ocean, and a flock of puffins passed noisily overhead.

Kate gazed in wonder at her new home. There was nothing of Pennsylvania in this remote place. Few trees managed to obtain a foothold in the rocky soil, and no farmers plowed the land. The most bountiful harvest lay beyond the horizon, where Newfoundland men fished for cod. A very different harvest was gathered in the quadrangle of sturdy clapboard buildings that contained the Cape Race relay station, where messages from ships were snatched from the air in bursts of Morse code.

Kate glanced up at the tall, skeletal radio towers. Of course, it was impossible to see the radio signals flashing out across the ocean, but she painted them in her imagination as ever widening circles. She imagined the words they carried, important and unimportant, but no longer chaotic. Senator Smith had succeeded in taming the previous wild piracy. Priorities had been established. A small part of the world had been made safer.

On the other side of the Atlantic, the British had conducted their own inquiry into the loss of the great, unsinkable *Titanic*. Once again the surviving officers and crew had been forced to relive the tragedy and reexamine their own actions. Captain Lord had been relieved of his command. Captain Rostron had been commended for his actions. And Captain Smith had been given the blame.

For Kate, so far away and engrossed in a life she could never have imagined for herself, with a man she loved more and more each day, the results of the inquiry no longer mattered. The last dead body had been plucked from the ocean in July and taken for burial in Halifax. The reporters had returned their attention to presidential politics. Madeleine Astor had given birth to a son. Rumors of war rumbled on the horizon, but Washington and London were both very far away.

Sometimes her thoughts strayed, and she remembered a gray-eyed man who had traveled a long way to find her. She knew what he had wanted to say, and she did not regret that she had stopped him. She didn't belong in Michigan any more than she belonged in the rebuilt town of Royston. Her place was here, at the windswept edge of the world.

Wolfie turned his head and looked toward the open door of the relay station. Kate followed his brown-eyed gaze and saw Danny, her husband, coming toward her with an eager expression on his face.

She ran to meet him. "Is it the *Carpathia?*" she asked breathlessly.

"It is," Danny said. "And it's Cottam himself."

Kate glanced back at the great sweep of the horizon. The *Carpathia* was out there, passing the last headland before she headed out into the empty Atlantic.

Inside the cramped shed, Danny ushered her into a seat and handed her the headphones. "You can do it," he said. "I know you can. He's taking it slow just for you."

Kate clamped the headphones on her head and listened anxiously. She had been studying Morse code for weeks. She could do this. She picked up a pencil and pulled the paper pad toward her. She listened and smiled and began to write.

CARPATHIA TO CAPE RACE. GLAD TO KNOW YOU ARE KEEPING US SAFE. CONGRATULATIONS TO YOUR HUSBAND, AND BEST WISHES TO THE BRIDE. COTTAM, CARPATHIA.

Kate rested her hand lightly on the Morse key and transmitted her reply.

CAPE RACE TO COTTAM, CARPATHIA. MANY THANKS. SAFE VOYAGE. KATE MCSORLEY, CAPE RACE.

The End

Read on for author's notes.

The Girl on the Carpathia is a work of fiction based on facts. The U.S. Senate hearings lasted from April 19 to May 25, 1912. Because several of the witnesses were recalled to give additional evidence, and much of the evidence was repetitive, I have taken some of the testimony out of its correct order, and also used some of the testimony in conversations to convey the truth and avoid tedium. Readers may be familiar with some of the names I have included in *The Girl on the Carpathia*. My cast of characters contains many people who truly existed and were involved in the Titanic sinking and its aftermath. Only a few of my characters are fictional. You may be surprised.

FICTIONAL CHARACTERS
Mr. and Mrs. van Buren
Bridie Conley
The Reverend Mr. Dayton
Captain Gregory Fowler
Myra Grunwald
Richard LaSalle
Kitty and Maeve McCaffrey
Danny McSorley
Kate Royston
Eva Trentham
Wolfie the otterhound

REAL PEOPLE

On the Californian
Ernest Gill
Captain Stanley Lord
James McGregor

On the Carpathia
Radio Officer Harold Cottam
Carlos Hurd
Dr. Arpad Lengyel
Captain Arthur Rostron

Titanic Passengers
Major Archibald Butt
Lucy Christiana, Lady Duff-Gordon
Sir Cosmo Duff-Gordon
Archibald Gracie IV
Sir Bruce Ismay
Lucy Noël Martha Leslie, Countess of Rothes
Arthur Peuchen
Emily Ryerson
Charles Stengel
John "Jack" Thayer III
Marian Thayer

Titanic Officers and Crew
Fourth Officer Joseph Boxhall
Radio Officer Harold Bride
Frederick Clench
Alfred Crawford
Frank Evans
Frederick Fleet
Second Officer Charles Lightholler
Fifth Officer Harold Lowe
Third Officer Herbert Pitman

In the Senate Hearings
Sheriff Joe Bayliss
Senator Jonathan Bourne
Senator Theodore Burton
Senator Duncan Fletcher
Charles Hilles
William McKinstry
Senator Francis Newlands
Senator George Perkins
Daniel Ransdell
Senator Furnifold Simmons
Nancy "Nana" Smith
Senator William Alden Smith
President William Taft

On the Olympic
Fred Barrett
Captain Haddock

HAROLD COTTAM
Cottam was modest about his role in the disaster and, outside of a few interviews, rarely spoke of it to friends and family, preferring privacy. He turned down an offer to play himself in the 1958 film *A Night to Remember*. He continued to work as a shipboard wireless operator on various ships until 1922, when he married Elsie Jean Shepperson and took a job as a sales representative of the Mini Max Fire Extinguisher company. He died in 1984

FREDERICK FLEET, the *Titanic*'s lookout, faced severe criticism from his crew mates for revealing the lack of binoculars. After his retirement he sold newspapers on the street corners of Southampton. On January 10, 1965, at seventy-six years of age, he committed suicide by hanging himself.

J. BRUCE ISMAY returned to England to testify at the British Titanic Inquiry, where he was severely criticized by the British press for not "going down with the ship." He was forced to give up his chairmanship of the White Star Line and retired to live in Ireland. He was seldom seen in public again, and died on October 17, 1937 following the amputation of his leg.

CHARLES H. LIGHTOLLER, survived three shipwrecks, a fire at sea, and being stranded on a desert island. He served his country with distinction in World War I, but he was always tainted by his association with the Titanic Inquiry and was never given his own command by the White Star Line. In World War II he sailed his personal yacht to Dunkirk and, despite heavy bombing of his unarmed craft, brought home 130 men. He died on December 8, 1952.

CAPTAIN STANLEY LORD was denounced by both the American and British Tribunals and was forced to resign from the Leyland Line. He spent the next fourteen years as a commander for the Nitrate Producers Steam Ship Company and the rest of his life maintaining his innocence. He died on January 25, 1962 at the age of eighty-four.

J. P. MORGAN remained in seclusion in his French chateau throughout the period of the investigation. The Titanic inquiry led directly to a House inquiry into the power held by the nation's leading corporations. Morgan was called as a witness at this hearing and was severely criticized for his use of his financial power. His personal physician attributed the strain of these hearings as a cause of Morgan's death in March of 1913. He was seventy-six years old and worth $100 million.

CAPTAIN ARTHUR ROSTRON was presented with a silver cup and gold medal for his efforts the night *Titanic* sank. In October 2015 the cup was sold at auction for $200,000. Captain Rostron was also awarded the Congressional Gold Medal, the Thanks of Congress, the American Cross of Honor, and a medal from the Liverpool Shipwreck and Humane Society. He served in World War I and died in 1940 at the age of seventy-six.

WILLIAM ALDEN SMITH won reelection to the Senate in 1912. As a result of the Titanic Inquiry, Smith authored a bill regulating the number of lifeboats to be carried by passenger vessels, the hours to be worked by wireless operators, and the discharging of rockets as distress signals. Smith became a ranking member of the Foreign Relations Committee and a vigorous opponent of America's entry into World War I. Although he intended to run for the presidency in 1916, his hopes were dashed when Henry Ford won Michigan's nomination. He died in 1932 at the age of seventy-three.
☐

COMPENSATION

In October 1912, the Oceanic Steam Navigation Company (more commonly known as the White Star Line) filed a petition in the Southern District of New York to limit its liability against any claims for loss of life, property, or injury. In this petition, the White Star

Line claimed that the collision was due to an "inevitable accident." Over several days in June and July 1915, testimony continued. Negotiations carried on outside of court led to a tentative settlement with nearly all of the claimants in December 1915. The settlement was for a total of $664,000 to be divided among the claimants. "In the Matter of the Petition of the Oceanic Steam Navigation Company, Limited, for Limitation of its Liability as owner of the steamship TITANIC" (A55-279) is a part of the National Archives holdings in New York City.

CAPE RACE MARINE RADIO STATION went off the air in 1965. After 61 years of continuous operation it had been made obsolete by modern equipment at St. John's and St. Lawrence. A replica station has been constructed and is open to the public.

THE INTERNATIONAL ICE PATROL was established in 1914 by the agreement of 16 nations with shipping interests in the North Atlantic Ocean as a direct result of the *Titanic* disaster. The patrol locates icebergs in the North Atlantic, follows and predicts their drift, and issues warnings to ships in the vicinity. Reconnaissance is conducted by the U.S. Coast Guard, using planes equipped with radar that can detect icebergs in all but the roughest sea conditions. The Coast Guard exchanges information with the Canadian Ice Services and also receives reports from passing ships. During the patrol season, which normally extends from March through August, the Coast Guard broadcasts twice daily by Inmarsat satellite and by high-frequency radio facsimile, issuing reports on the locations of all known sea ice and icebergs. Approximately 1,000 icebergs are tracked each year.

Find additional author information at
www.eileenenwrighthodgetts.com